THE
SHAKING

THE SHAKING

OLIVIA CALLAHAN SUSPENSE

KERRY PERESTA

"Sometimes your medicine bottle has on it,
'Shake well before using.' That is what God
has to do with some of his people. He has to
shake them well before they are ever usable."

— Vince Havner

Contents

Praise for The Shaking

"In *The Shaking,* the latest Olivia Callahan Suspense Novel, P.I. Olivia juggles an insurance fraud case, a background investigation into a woman who is not whom she seems, and other cases while struggling with her own internal demons, a relationship teetering on the edge with her fiancé, and broken friendships that need mending. Full of twists and turns that will keep readers guessing, and just when you think Kerry Peresta is wrapping up Olivia's cases with a neat bow, another ball drops."—Brian Thiem, author of The Mudflats Murder Club Series

"Kerry Peresta's Olivia Callahan series keeps getting better and better. Starting off with a bang, *The Shaking* doesn't let go until the nail-biting final pages. With its complex characters and ripped-from-the-headlines plotting, *The Shaking* will keep readers up late into the night!"—K.L. Murphy, Award-nominated author of *The Great Forgotten* (November 2025) and the Detective Callie Forde Mysteries

"Olivia Callahan has a lot going on—PTSD is causing seizures that terrify her family, her fiancée is giving her an ultimatum, and her demons have caught up to her. When her fiancée's investigation intersects her own, the separate cases tangle in a web of corruption. How it all shakes out will change her life forever. A riveting, page-turner you won't want to miss."—Lisa Black, *NYT* bestselling author of the Gardiner & Renner series

"With its cast of intriguing characters, *The Shaking* grabbed me from the first chapter and didn't let go until well after the last page. Peresta is a mastermind when it comes to fast-paced, high-stakes plotlines; a maze which we happily journey through, loving every twist and turn. Some will make it through. Others won't. The final book in the Olivia Callahan Series, *The Shaking* gives these multilayered heroes the send-off they deserve. Peresta's books just get better and better."—Susan Crawford, author of the international bestseller, *The Pocket Wife*

"Never count Olivia Callahan out. *The Shaking* gets personal as Olivia chases her demons only to find even more sinister figures looming. With Peresta's trademark clever plotting, and a heroine you can't help but love, *The Shaking* is the best yet."—James L'Etoile, award-winning author of The Nathan Parker series and the Emily Hunter series

"The gang's back for Book 5 of the Olivia Callahan Suspense series. Feisty heroine Olivia Callahan is far from perfect, and she knows it. As she struggles to learn and grow, things are imploding at her PI business. She's ready for an assist, and her friends—especially the level-headed Sargeant Hunter Faraday and her amazing dog, Marlowe—are more than up for the job. Seemingly unrelated storylines come together flawlessly. But when you think it's over, don't catch your breath! Peresta drops another bomb. A solid page-turner that will keep you up at night."—Cindy Goyette, award-winning author of The Probation Case Files Mystery series and The Wiggle Butt Manor Mysteries

"Kerry Peresta's newest thriller, *The Shaking,* plunges readers into Olivia Callahan's relentless pursuit to uncover a killer. Fast-paced, every twist and turn methodically heightens the suspense and deepens the intrigue. Her vivid characters and sharp storytelling propel the plot toward a gripping and satisfying conclusion. One that will stay with you for a long while."—Suzanne Baginskie, author of the FBI Affairs Series

Chapter One

Sherry yanked her cell off her desk and pressed in Olivia's number for the third time. Voicemail again. "What the heck," she muttered, glancing at the time. "She's always here early." The new administrative hire, Jason, gave her a puzzled look. "Olivia should be here by now," she explained, rising from her desk. "I'm going to run down to her house and check on her."

She jogged to her car and sped down the half-mile lane to Olivia's house and parked in the driveway. "Olivia! Are you here?"

Nothing but the chirping of birds and sounds of leaves rustling in the breeze. "Olivia!" She approached the front door and knocked. "Are you in there?"

Silence.

Her eyes scanned the two-story farmhouse, the wide front porch, its wooden planks painted a crisp white, the tidy yard surrounded by a picket fence. Birds populated the feeders, as usual. The trees and bushes in the yard had sprouted new, pale green, spring leaves. Nothing seemed out of place, but her boss wouldn't arrive this late without letting her know why. Something was wrong. Olivia's ginger tomcat regarded her suspiciously through the glass from his perch at the front window. She tried the cell number again. Voicemail. Shuffling noises erupted from the backyard. She sprinted from the porch to the side of the house.

Olivia's dog loped toward her, tongue lolling, his forehead furrowed like her own. What the heck was he doing outside the fence?

The rangy German Shepherd-Lab mix whined. "Something wrong, boy?"

Scratching Marlowe's head, she mentally retraced Olivia's morning routine: feed animals, eat breakfast, walk out the kitchen's back entrance, and through the breezeway to the garage's side door. Put Marlowe in the back seat. Drive to the office. Arrive by eight a.m. Every. Single. Day. If diverted from her usual timetable, she would've let them know.

Marlowe turned his nose to the garage and barked twice.

Her heart stopped cold. "Oh, no."

Sherry shot through the yard to the breezeway and followed it to the garage's side door. Her arms trembling, she jerked it open, stumbled over the threshold, and practically face-planted on the concrete floor. Marlowe cleared her with one, huge leap, and raced to his owner's Land Rover. A slight beeping reached her ears, and shadows flickered across the walls. Letting her eyes adjust, she located the source of the beeps. "Why is the back door of her car open?" she whispered, rising from the floor. She found a light switch and flicked it on. The smell of vintage wood and decades of gas fumes and motor oil and rusting tools curled up her nose.

"Anyone in here?"

Marlowe whined.

"Olivia!"

The beeping continued. With a sigh, she walked across the space to close the door before the battery drained completely.

On the way, she pressed the garage door opener. The old, wooden doors creaked their way up the metal sliders, allowing daylight inside. Marlowe's barks ricocheted off the ceiling, the walls, the floor. A prickle of fear crept along her spine. Rounding the vehicle, she approached the driver's side. As her fingers touched the door handle to close the door, she realized Olivia's prone body lay five inches from her feet. She gasped.

Olivia's auburn hair fanned out on the concrete. Her purse and backpack lay on the floor beside her. Marlowe's leash had been rolled into a tidy circle and put in the back seat. Sherry swallowed the lump in her throat, squatted, and touched her pale neck. "There's a pulse," she told Marlowe, dropping her head. "Thank God," she whispered, tugging out her cell to call nine-one-one. Marlowe smothered Olivia's cheeks with frantic, wet licks, until he finally sank to the floor beside her motionless body.

Chapter Two

Olivia Callahan

My mind flung itself in determined circles, like the cotton candy machines which had mesmerized me as a child. A whirling dervish, spinning sugar into strands of pink deliciousness. A rising tide of pain from a monster headache overtook the lovely vision as I struggled to consciousness. I tested my arms, flexed my hands. *Sheets. I'm feeling sheets.* I shifted my body. Confusion closed my throat just before the bolt of fear hit me square in the chest.

Where the hell was I?

A light came on. I blinked. Steps pattered toward me. The mixed smells of air freshener, ammonia, and antiseptic reached my nose. *Ohmigosh. I'm in a freaking hospital.* My mind flew back seven years to Mercy Hospital in Richmond. The long recovery from an assault resulting in a traumatic brain injury, amnesia, and five weeks in the hospital. The incessant interrogations from the investigator assigned to my case. I'd returned home without a single memory of my house, my mother, or my two daughters. In a wry moment of self-congratulation, I whispered a prayer of thanks that I hadn't lost my memory this time.

Someone plopped an extra pillow behind my head. I opened my eyes. The wall of pain receded a little. I stared at the IV in my arm.

"Hi there, Olivia. Can you understand me?" I focused my gaze on the business-like nurse holding a tablet and making notes.

My response sounded garbled. I tested my arm movement with a smile growing wider by the second. I could move! The last time I regained consciousness in a hospital at this stage, I couldn't move, speak, or remember a thing. I burbled out something more intelligible.

"Good job. How much do you remember?" The nurse smiled, pecked at her tablet, and waited on my response.

Any attempt at coordinating movement felt eerily like the Tin Man rising from the yellow brick road and clanking himself together. "Not much." I looked at my arm, then at her, which translated: *take the damn needle out of my arm.*

She glanced at the IV drip. "The doc will probably take you off the drip today. I'm Lucia. You had a seizure caused by a small brain bleed. Your colleague found you in your garage, lying on the floor. You had tried to go to work, but didn't make it. "Did you experience any indication beforehand? Often, there's an aura, or a part of your body twitching, or a horrible headache?"

"How long have I been here?"

Lucia grinned. "Three days. And, your words are already back! It's Wednesday afternoon."

I gaped. "Phone?"

She rummaged in the drawer. "We kept it charged. I'm warning you, though; it takes a minute for speech to come all the way back. And, we need to test your mobility."

The door swung open. My mother and daughters walked in. "Mom!" Lilly yelled, diving for the bed. I laughed and snuggled my youngest child.

"I'm okay. Just a speed bump."

Mom sat in a guest chair. "A 'speed bump,'" she repeated, shaking her head. "We've been here since Monday night, and you've been unconscious until now. I doubt it's a 'speed bump.'"

"Are you sure you're okay, Mom?" my younger daughter, Lilly, asked. Serena, her older sister by two years, bit her lower lip.

A wraith of a man in a white jacket slipped inside. Silver, wispy hair, slight build, lips curved in a perpetual sneer. He took a quick look at his tablet, made a few swipes, then looked at me. "Let's get you out of bed." He laid the tablet on my nightstand and extended his hands. I blinked in confusion. Oh. He wanted me to stand up. I sighed. *Please God, let this go well for my family's sake. I can't put them through another five-week recovery.*

I gripped his hands, slid my legs over the side of the bed, and put my feet on the floor as he steadied me. Slight dizziness, a bit of weakness, but decent balance. "I'm fine," I announced.

Assured I wouldn't lose my balance and crack my head on the floor, he let go of my hands and regarded me somberly. "You've had a focal seizure, a common occurrence after traumatic brain injuries. However, you've gone years without a major incident like this one. Have you experienced an unusual amount of stress, or a big life change?"

I laughed.

His sparse gray eyebrows pulled together. "Am I being funny?"

"Have you read my book, by chance?"

"What book?"

"I have a book out, *Mercy's Miracle*." I pointed at his tablet. "The initial TBI inspired a lot of attention, so I wrote a book about it. Anyway, my whole life is stress." I made an attempt at shrugging, but lost my fragile balance and stumbled against the bed instead.

My mother closed her eyes. Lilly chewed on her thumbnail.

Seconds of silence ticked by.

The doctor cleared his throat. "The EEG showed erratic electrical activity, even well after the event. My recommendation is to stay another day or two. We should do more tests and discuss lifestyle changes."

I said nothing, but no way would I stay another day or two. Watchdog Investigations had exploded with new business, and seizure or not, I needed to get back to the office. "What are the normal aftereffects?"

He stuck his tablet under his arm. "You'll need to contact my office if you notice unusual movements or spasms, brain fog, slurring your words, or a desire to sleep more than usual."

"None of that is going to happen," I declared. If he expected me to sit around and become a vegetable, I needed to change doctors.

"Mom," Lilly cautioned. "You need to be careful."

I grunted. "When have I ever been careful?"

Serena stood. "Don't *say* that. You need to make some changes."

I'd felt woozy on the way to the car the morning of the seizure, but I'd blamed it on three glasses of wine the night before. I'd had my hand on the driver's side back door of the car, ready to let Marlowe jump inside and ride with me to the office as usual. My vision suddenly blurred; one dog had turned into three. I must've fainted then, because I couldn't remember anything else until Lucia woke me this morning.

I stared at the miniature, irritable doc whose nameplate said 'Neurologist, Sylvester Stein, MD'. "I'm remembering. I started getting in my car to drive to work when my vision deteriorated. I felt dizzy and couldn't focus. I-I think I had a headache, too, but I live with headaches, those are nothing new. Next thing I'm aware of is...this room. Lucia looking down at me."

Serena let out a little huff of impatience. "Tell him, Mom."

I squinted. "Tell him what?"

"He asked if you had a big life change. You didn't use to drink like you do now. What if drinking caused the seizure?" Tears leaked down her cheeks. "You have to be careful, Mom. You can't act like *normal people*. The assault changed your life forever." I watched my mother put her arm around Serena.

Dr. Stein's lips pursed in disapproval. "Stress plus an excess of alcohol can definitely trigger seizures in brain injury patients. How often do you drink?"

I slid my socked toe across the floor. "Too much."

"*Every night*, Mom. Like, half a bottle or more." She wiped away urgent, anxious tears.

My heart broke in two.

Dr. Stein started typing on his tablet. "If you want to control the seizures, you should adjust your lifestyle."

I let out a long, dramatic sigh.

My mother—the indomitable Sophie Pellegra-Sturgis—the woman who had supported me through all my adventures and spoon-fed me her faith, hope, and strength—stood to her full height. Her expression held that certain, laser-focused fury common to mothers who have been through hell and back. I snapped to attention.

"Olivia. Rosemary. Callahan. You mean to tell me you are going to make us hold our collective breaths and wait until you have another seizure or two? Or three? When can you *stop drinking* and be done with it? Please tell me you understand there's *one* choice, here."

Dr. Stein nodded a curt farewell to our tight-knit little group, muttered a few words to the nurse, and strode from the room.

I marched defiantly back and forth across the floor, swinging my arms, swiveling my head. "See? I'm fine."

"If you're determined to leave, you'll need to sign an AMA form, which indicates you are leaving against medical advice." Lucia cast a doubtful glance at Mom and my daughters.

"Great. Get me the form." Fuzziness still claimed my thoughts, but I ignored it. "See there, girls? Mom's going home."

Chapter Three

Sergeant Hunter Faraday

The minute he learned of Olivia's release date, he'd moved his appointments, put his best criminal investigator in charge, and begun the two-hour drive to Maryland. He'd taken for granted his lieutenant would understand, but as he listened to the irritated voice coming through the Bluetooth connection of his Jeep, he realized taking *anything* for granted was just plain stupid.

"Faraday, you've used all your medical leave and then some. I know you have this long-distance relationship going on, but it can't interfere with your work again. Do you understand?"

Approaching an intersection, he downshifted. "Got it."

"I know it's tough, Sergeant. We've had an increase in these damn political protests all over the city, and your team is spread thin. I need you here, though, not running from Richmond to Maryland to see your fiancée. You told me she was moving. Why hasn't she moved yet?"

"I'm working on it." He agreed with Lieutenant Nicholson. They'd been engaged an entire year, for God's sake. She needed to make a decision. "This is an emergency, and I—"

Trying to continue the conversation with half his brain, he watched a woman stumble into the path of an oncoming car at a four-way stop. He blinked. What was she doing? The poor woman had become a literal deer in the headlights. Horns honked. A car screeched to a stop. The driver powered down his window and yelled at her. "I have a situation, Lieutenant. I'll do my best to limit these trips."

"What kind of situation? You don't have jurisdiction in—"

He ended the call and parked his four-door Jeep Rubicon on the sidewalk. The woman stared at him blankly from the middle of the intersection. He recognized the slack expression and disorientation indicative of stroke, dementia, or any number of brain misfires. Hunter jerked out his badge and flashed it to each of the waiting drivers. "Richmond PD! Let me get this woman to safety."

She allowed him to propel her to his Jeep. "What's your name?" he asked, scrolling for the number of local PD in the area. After he seat belted the woman into the passenger seat, he signaled the other drivers to move on. The small town of Locust Grove, Virginia, had a decent-sized police department. He called and explained the situation.

"Huh," the voice at the call desk said. "We've been looking for her. Who you've got there is Mayor Stricklin's wife. She's fond of wandering off."

He frowned. "From where? Is she institutionalized?"

"From her house. Our mayor works remotely so he can keep an eye on her. We'll get a cruiser out there. What's your location? I've got them on the line."

"Hold on," he said, putting his phone on mute. He turned toward her. "What's your name?"

"Matty."

"Are you the mayor's wife?"

She twisted her fingers together in her lap and nodded, staring at the floorboards. "Don't make me go back there," she whispered. "He'll be mad."

Great. This is all I need. Should I call social services?

He made a quick decision and returned to the call he'd put on hold. "Tell your patrol officer I'm in a black, four-door Jeep Rubicon, parked on the shoulder. I'll wait." After he'd gotten Matty on her way home, he left a voicemail with the facility local PD suggested, and requested an appointment.

An hour later, he sat in a hotel room off I-95 waiting on DoorDash to bring him a burger. The facility had responded to his voicemail, and yes, they had a morning appointment open. Rubbing his eyes wearily, he figured he'd better let Olivia know he wouldn't be making it to Maryland this evening. She answered on the first ring. "Hey! You don't need to come. Your lieutenant is going to kill you if you don't stop coming to see me every five minutes. I'm fine."

He chuckled. "I doubt you're fine, babe. Regardless, I'm going to make sure my future wife is taking care of herself. I'll help out with whatever you need, as long as it keeps you in bed or on the couch. The doc told you to *rest,* which seems unlikely unless someone holds a gun to your head."

She laughed. "I've already slept a total of five days. I'll try to rest another few days, but it'll be hard. What's taking you so long, anyway? Did you have car trouble?"

"I'll see you around noon. Please. Wait a few more days before you go into the office."

"No promises. Why aren't you driving straight through?"

"I ran into an issue."

Two beats of silence. "Who did you rescue *this* time?"

He stroked his chin, wondering how the latest seizure had affected her brain. The research he'd done on post-TBI recovery studies indicated difficulty identifying significant functional impairments. Her cavalier approach to recovering from the seizure concerned him, and no matter how his lieutenant felt about his absence, he needed to babysit her a few days for his own peace of mind. He wrote off her sarcastic response to a lack of impulse control, a common side effect of TBI recovery.

"A woman wandering around in the middle of a four-way stop. She needed help, and I gave it."

"Did you find out who she belonged to?"

"I did, but she seemed conflicted about it. A patrol cop took her home. Says he does it all the time, like she's the town's project."

"That doesn't sound good."

"Yeah. Something's not right. I'm trying to figure it out."

"You're a sucker for the downtrodden, you know."

Hunter felt a prick of resentment. He reminded himself to be patient. "An officer of the law is sworn to help. It's my job."

"I understand." After a pause, she said, "I love you."

He smiled. "I love you, too. When are you going to marry me?"

"Soon."

"Okay."

He yawned. "I'm beat. Tomorrow, I have an appointment with Woodlawn Acres, an adjunct facility of their family services here. Her husband threw a fit, but he's agreed to bring Matty and meet me there. I sure hope he's not the clueless dumbass I think he is. Maybe I can facilitate an intervention. She needs an advocate." Knuckles pelted his hotel room door. "Hey. My dinner's here. I'm going to eat and hit the sack. The appointment's at nine. Stay home and rest. I'll let you know when I'm on the road."

"Okay. Be safe."

"Always. Sleep well. See you tomorrow."

Hunter strode to the door to get his dinner, muttering in frustration. The stick-of-dynamite woman he'd decided to marry would be hard to keep down.

The next morning, per usual, he jerked awake at 5:30 a.m. and groped for his weapon underneath his pillow. After sliding his fingers along the cold, hard metal, he relaxed. Three sharp knocks banged on his door. He frowned, tugged on his boxers and a T-shirt, grabbed his weapon, and cracked the door. No one there. He looked left, right, down. A nine-by-twelve manila envelope lay on the carpeted corridor in front of his door. He scooped it into his hand and closed the door.

The photos he pulled from the envelope were grainy, but he recognized Matty. "What the hell is this?" He took photos of the pictures in the envelope and saved them to his phone. He'd give the envelope to social services.

* * *

Fifteen minutes before nine o'clock, he arrived for the appointment. The young woman at the front desk smiled in welcome, but the smile faded at the sight of the badge on his belt.

"Good morning, uhh…"

"Sergeant Faraday. Richmond PD."

"What can we do for you today, Sergeant?"

"I have a joint appointment with Mr. and Mrs. Stricklin."

Her pretty face wrinkled in confusion. "Matty and Dink?"

"Dink?"

She laughed. "The mayor. He's her husband. His real name is Thomas. Larissa will come get you when she's ready. Coffee's over against the wall." She pointed.

He passed on the coffee since he'd already had his fill at the motel. The door opened five minutes later, and Matty and her husband walked in. Cosmetics and a nice dress had transformed everything but her soft, vacant eyes.

Matty smiled in recognition, sat in one of the chairs placed along the wall, then looked away. Her husband wore a short-sleeve, light blue shirt, and granddad jeans. Instead of offering his hand for a shake, he sat stiffly beside his wife and folded his arms.

"What're you doin' in these parts, Sergeant Faraday?"

"Making sure your wife doesn't get hit by a car. How about you?"

Thomas "Dink" Stricklin chose not to respond.

Tense minutes passed.

Hunter's thoughts alternated between cursing his own stupidity at becoming involved, and humble pride at helping out a fellow human—the cop pendulum which never stopped swinging.

A different door opened, exposing the long, dark hallway behind it. "Hi, everyone. Come on back." She stuck out her hand. "Sergeant Faraday, I'm Larissa Ivanov." Her voice held a slight European accent. He took in her flowing skirt and sensible shoes as they shook hands.

He followed her into the corridor. Matty and Dink fell in behind. He heard Dink muttering to his wife. She remained quiet. Chairs had been arranged in a loose semi-circle in front of Larissa's desk. Matty sat in one, and kept checking and rechecking the interior of her purse, as if fearing someone had removed something from it. With a sigh, he moved his calm gaze to Dink. The man sniffed every few seconds, and looked away when Hunter studied him. His nose glowed bright red, like Rudolph's. Cokehead? Meth? Maybe he should give the guy a break and stop thinking like a cop. It could be as simple as a pollen allergy.

Larissa opened a file, placed her elbows on her desk, and steepled her fingers. "So. Here we are again."

Hunter's eyebrows lifted in surprise. Again?

"I'm doin' my best," Dink muttered.

"It's not his fault," Matty said, with a nervous glance at Hunter.

The counselor remained silent a couple of heartbeats. "Tell me what happened, Matty."

Dink glared at his wife. "She can't remember a damn thing, so we can't trust what she says." Hunter watched her shrivel in her chair.

"Let her talk," Hunter said.

"Stay outta this! Why are you here, anyway?"

"*Someone* needs to speak for her. She could've been killed, Mr. Stricklin."

Larissa tilted her head at Dink. "He's right. It's time to think about a facility."

Matty frowned. "I get lost." She opened her purse again, counted the items within, and closed it.

Dink gave Larissa an odd look which Hunter couldn't identify, then twisted toward his wife with a scowl. His hand flexed in irritation, as if preparing to snatch his wife's purse so she'd stop fiddling with it. Hunter's opinion of him dropped from a five to a three.

Larissa studied the open file on her desk. "For now, let's adjust her meds. Would you be open to making an appointment for a second opinion?"

Dink jammed his arms across his chest. "What the hell do you mean? She has a diagnosis."

A shadow crossed her face. "It doesn't hurt to get a second opinion, Dink."

He looked at her, loathing in his eyes. After a few seconds, he rose and walked out.

Larissa placed her elbows on the desk and steepled her fingers. "Sorry about that, Sergeant. How did you come to be involved with Matty?"

"When I watch a confused woman wander into a four-way stop with no idea what she's doing, I park my car and help." He lifted a shoulder. "I did what anyone would do."

"Not everyone. Your assistance is appreciated." She shifted her attention to Matty. "How are you?"

She glanced at the door. "Is it okay if I go to the bathroom?"

"Of course you can go to the bathroom."

She left.

"Does she need help finding the ladies' room?" Hunter asked.

"She's been here often. It's fine. As you might have guessed, she struggles with Alzheimer's. The latest incident compels me to insist he find a different neurologist or a facility." Larissa studied her fingernails. "Her husband's had trouble accepting the reality, and is convinced he can take care of her. When he has a problem, he brings her in." She chuckled. "I hope I'm doing some good."

"It seems to me her biggest problem starts with 'D.'"

"What am I supposed to do? He's in charge of the whole town. If he won't admit her, I can't force him to."

They scrutinized each other for a few awkward seconds.

Hunter pulled the envelope containing photos out of his jacket and handed it over. She flipped through them, color blooming on her neck like a bad rash. "Where did you get these?"

"Someone left them in the hall outside my door this morning at the hotel. Whose house is it?"

"It looks like one of her neighbors." Uncertainty flitted across her face. "It's her neighborhood." She stopped talking, pursed her lips, and slapped the file shut. "I'm sure there's a reasonable explanation. Matty loves to talk to people. Kids have been known to make fun of her. Maybe it's a sick prank."

Hunter narrowed his eyes. "I disagree. Someone *wanted* me to see them. This is a concerned citizen seeking help from an outside source. It's obvious."

She rose from her chair as Matty returned. "Thank you so much for your help. I'll see to getting her home."

"I'll take her home," Hunter said, quickly. "You'll look into those photos, though, right?"

"I reassure you, Sergeant. She's safe in Locust Grove." She opened one of her desk drawers, tossed the envelope inside, and closed the drawer. After scrawling Matty's home address on a Post-it, she handed it to him.

As he escorted Matty out of the building, he realized two things. One, Dink had abandoned his mentally ill wife. At the very least, he figured Dink might be throwing his little temper tantrum out in the lobby to calm down and wait on his wife, but he hadn't. He'd left. Two, from the way Larissa had popped the envelope in a drawer, he doubted she'd look into the cry for help from someone bothered enough to take notice.

He glanced at his passenger with regret. He couldn't take the time to go down this rabbit hole any further.

Right now, his priority would take him to Glyndon, Maryland, and his future bride, who needed him. He had no choice but to return Matty to Dink.

"Do you know where you are?" he asked, gently.

She looked out the window, her fingers playing with the door handle. "With you. A nice man."

"What's my name?"

"Sergeant."

He smiled. "Be careful with the door handle. I don't want you to fall out." She jerked her hand away like a child caught playing with matches.

"Do you want to go home? Can you tell me how to get there?" he asked, as a mental exercise.

She shook her head, then opened her purse and retrieved a worn piece of paper. "This is the address." Her brow wrinkled. "Is it Friday?"

"Yep."

A satisfied smile washed across her lined face. "I have to get the package today."

She looked out the window at a row of brick buildings on a tidy street and the puffy clouds in a bright, blue sky. "I have to wait until dark," she whispered, her eyes slicing toward him.

Like hell, Hunter thought, thinking about the photos. He'd confront whoever answered the door if she could point out the address where the "package" originated.

"Read me the address." He entered it into his GPS. Even before she told him, he predicted a match with the photos, and what do you know, the addresses matched. After a U-turn, he sped through the heart of Locust Grove to a placid community of two-story, redbrick homes sitting on large, manicured lots. He stopped at a tall set of wrought-iron gates. As he prepared to press the buzzer, the gates opened.

Cool. No code buzz-in. He'd take it.

"There. Where I go," Matty said, pointing. "Dr. Franken. He's nice."

"You go every Friday?"

She bounced in her seat. "Once, I got an ice cream bar."

Hunter felt his face heat with anger. He'd lost relatives and friends to this disease, and he knew firsthand how easily they could be manipulated. He parked on the curb in front of the house. She tried to get out of the car.

"Wait," Hunter told her. "I'll see if anyone's home."

"See if he has the package ready." She stuck a finger in her mouth. "It's early, though."

He patted her arm. "Be right back."

After a few punches on the doorbell, he guessed the occupants were out. But he'd verified the photos on his phone had been taken at this front door, and a drop-off occurred each Friday after working hours, according to Matty. He'd hand off the information to someone in charge.

Jogging back down the driveway to his Jeep, he buckled in and started the car. "How do you get here on Fridays, Matty?"

"Forty-four-thirty-two Belmont. Forty-four-thirty-two," she recited. "My house."

Okay. Her home address. At least her husband had made her memorize it. As he pulled to the curb in front of her house, he added the information to the growing file in his head. *Four blocks away.* Her husband made her collect a package every Friday in the same neighborhood as their home, and she had to walk four blocks. He rubbed his chin. *What was in the package?* No wonder he wouldn't admit her to a facility. Sounded like Dink had something going on the side, and the perfect mule. He ran his hand through his hair, glancing at Matty. Would she be safe if he took her home? In a mic drop moment, he pivoted.

"How would you like to stay at Woodlawn a few days? With Larissa?"

She grinned. "Larissa is my friend. I like her."

Hunter thought about it. Dink would never let her go of her own free will, but if Matty admitted herself, at least she'd be safe while he tried to figure out a way to help her.

"If you want to stay with Larissa a few days, I'll take you to Woodlawn."

Matty opened her purse, rifled through the interior, then closed it, a satisfied look on her face. "I want to go."

"Are you sure? I can take you home, or I can take you back."

She cast him a stern look. "I know what I want. I want to see Larissa."

Good enough for me, he thought, smiling. He pulled away from the curb and exited the gated community.

Chapter Four

Olivia

I'd had enough of wandering around my house bored out of mind. My bad mood had blossomed into a headache and cold sweats, and I'd had so much coffee my nerve endings crackled and sparked like downed electrical cables. Though I didn't want to admit it, the wine *had* contributed to my latest health setback. The last four days of white-knuckling it through not drinking had knocked me on my ass.

Not good.

Serena, Lilly, and Mom had caravanned back to their respective responsibilities in Richmond and D.C., and Hunter would arrive any minute. My phone chimed with a text. *I'm ten minutes out. See you soon!*

Another text appeared, this time from Sherry. *What do you want to do about the Collins situation?*

I walked outside to my front porch to wait for Hunter. As I watched for his Jeep, I called her.

"Are you coming back to work soon? Jason and I are swamped."

"I want to, but I'm not supposed to."

She huffed in exasperation. "I got Jason certified as a process server, so he can take the small stuff off our plates, but the cases keep coming in. It's a lot of work to handle alone, and I can't use Jason without a PI license. I'm sure he can do simple surveillance with his cop experience, but I don't want the firm to get in trouble."

"I can't believe how much business we have, now." I thought about how far we'd come in the past couple of years. We couldn't wait to get Jason on the street and hire someone else for the phones and day-to-day stuff. "You're going to have to schedule the new business meetings further out. Or refer them, maybe? Don't kill yourself trying to take care of everything."

"Please. Tell me you're *getting back to normal.*"

"Almost." I sighed. "The brain fog is clearing. It's killing me not to be in the office. But Hunter, my mom, my girls, and even my neuro insisted on three more days."

"Okay. So." She took in a breath, released it. "Tell me what direction we should take with Collins."

I rubbed my forehead. Sherry's friend, Collins Browning, had been asking us to do background and surveillance on a woman he met online. He'd fallen hard for this woman, she'd asked him for a favor, and he suspected a scam. "Can he pay?"

"He says he can."

"What's our exposure?"

"I'm thinking two grand."

"Okay. Work him in. Next?"

I heard shuffling of papers and visualized her at her desk in the corner of Watchdog Investigations' lobby, bookended by faux plants and a pair of minimalist bookcases. She'd made the corner her own, including matching brown, leather barrel chairs in front of her desk.

"This next one is Alex Barnes of Barnes Imports. It came in late yesterday."

"Yeah? Tell me."

"Insurance dispute involving a vehicle collision. He uses his employees to take fresh arrivals out on the road and go through a routine checklist. Someone ran into one of his super-duper expensive car-babies, a Lotus Emira. It's totaled. Both insurance companies are throwing a fit. I haven't seen the accident report, but he insists his employee is not at fault. Have we restaged an accident scene before? Seems like we have."

"Tom did one for us, remember? About three years ago."

"Aw. I miss Tom."

"Me, too. Every day."

We shared a moment of silence for our dear departed mentor and the inspiration behind Watchdog Investigations. The framed photo of his headshot hung in a place of honor in our lobby. We had grown fond of touching it for good luck.

"Why don't we check and see how specific the police reports are and go from there? Is the guy a…"

"An asshole?" she finished. "I don't think so. He seemed nice to me."

"*Not* what I was going to say," I told her, grinning. "I'm wondering about his reputation."

"A background check disclosed three speeding tickets and a DWI. His socials are mainly marketing for his exotic cars. Some posts include his mom."

"Okay. 'Close with mom' is good. Have you checked his financials?"

"I called and asked if he could cover a check for twenty thousand, and the teller laughed at my question. I got the impression Alex Barnes is loaded. We should ask for a huge retainer. Ginormous."

"Let's have a look at the accident report before we sign him."

"I'll go to Central Records tomorrow and grab it."

A vehicle muscled its way down my twisty, half-mile lane. I smiled. The roar of the Jeep's overlarge, all-terrain tires had been seared into my memory. "Hunter's here. Gotta go."

"Wait! There's another pending case I need to talk to you about."

"How about I get him settled, then we'll both come to the office. Maybe thirty minutes?"

"Okay."

I walked down the front porch steps with a smile. Hunter bounced from his vehicle, grabbed a duffle bag, and strode to the white gate opening into my front yard. I glanced at my emerald engagement ring, glinting shades of green in the morning sun. I loved the ring he'd chosen for me.

He dropped his duffle and lifted me a foot off the ground. "How are you, gorgeous?"

"I'm good," I said, looking into the eyes dark with concern, loving him for caring so much. "Almost one hundred percent."

He placed me on the ground and grabbed his duffle. "Am I stayin' in the house or the office? I'm surprised you're home. I almost stopped at the office."

"I've been trying to *rest,*" I grunted in disgust. "This is the fifth day of doing nothing, and I thought we'd go into the office this afternoon and talk about where you can take up the slack while you're here. You can stay wherever you want, babe. The guest bedroom at the office is open, or you can stay here."

"I'll stay in the office guest room. I don't want you to feel tempted to overdo it, and if I stay in your house, I won't be able to keep my hands to myself." He grinned. "I'm serious. I want you to *rest,* no matter how much I'd like to, uh…"

"You're sweet. I understand. And, I repeat: you did *not* have to come. I'm fine, and all this 'resting' is making me crazy." An anxious feeling flashed across my soul. Sweat broke out on my forehead. Suddenly, I felt clammy. I knew I wasn't quite myself yet, and also…I longed for a glass of wine. Or two.

Marlowe's claws skittered across my hardwood floors. He nosed the front screen door open, dashed out, and danced around us, his tail wagging so hard it shook his whole body. Hunter bent to hug him. "I've missed this dog." He looked at me. "I've even missed your stuck-up cat, Riot. When are you moving?"

Did we have to have that conversation right now? "Let me fix you some lunch, then we'll go to the office."

He gave me a look. I averted my eyes and walked toward the kitchen.

As he munched on the sandwich, I sat across from him at the kitchen table, cataloguing my symptoms silently. I felt like I'd been time-capsuled back to the months following my assault seven years ago. Headaches, fatigue, brain fog, and lack of coordination. Familiar. Troubling. This seizure hadn't been a huge deal, but I needed to be proactive in preventing more of them.

"What're you thinking about over there?" Hunter smiled at me through a milk moustache.

"I'm thinking about how much I miss wine."

His forehead furrowed. "Why?"

"My family and neuro jumped all over me. A TBI survivor is susceptible to seizures, and wine is a trigger. I'm so depressed."

"I see," he said, wiping his mouth with a napkin, carrying the plate to the sink. "Is there an acceptable minimum?"

I shrugged. "It scared my girls. I don't want it to happen again."

He nodded. Walked back to the kitchen table. "Of course you don't."

"The neuro asked if I had a drinking problem.".

Hunter's jaw flexed. "Do you?"

"Didn't think so. But our Wine & Whine group is dedicated to drinking great wine and it feels so…so *empty* thinking I can't get a little loose and enjoy our crazy discussions. Maybe I started enjoying it too much?" I cast a searching look at him, needing reassurance that I wasn't a drunk.

He put his hand on my shoulder, an indulgent expression on his face. "You ever think life might be *better* without the booze?"

I ran my fingers through my hair in frustration. The comment did not help like…even a little bit. "I have to shower. I'll be back down in twenty, okay? Then we can go. I won't stay long, promise."

* * *

Marlowe ran ahead of us and sat on the front stoop of Watchdog Investigations. When I opened the door, he took a hard right and raced through the break room into my office to the dog bed beside my desk. Sherry beamed. "Welcome back!"

"Thanks. I figured I can handle a couple of hours."

Hunter walked over to Sherry's desk, who gave him a hug. "How's my favorite detective?"

"Sergeant," he amended.

"You'll always be 'Olivia's detective' to me." She flashed Olivia a teasing grin. "Remember those days? You'd get so mad at us. 'He's not *my* detective' you'd say." She laughed. "We all knew better. It just took you an infuriating six years to figure it out."

"Very funny," I said. For Jason's benefit, I added, "Hunter's the head of the Richmond Criminal Investigations Unit, now."

I dragged Hunter over to the reception desk. "Jason Vargas, meet my fiancée."

He stood, extended his hand. "I've heard good things. Great to meet you, Sergeant Faraday."

"Same. Call me Hunter."

The awkwardness grew as I watched them study each other, fumbling at conversation. It felt like two alpha dogs staking out their respective territories. I tried to view Jason through Hunter's lens: mid-thirties, a mop of thick, blonde hair, in great shape, an ex-cop's inquisitive manner. In an *administrative* role. I knew Hunter well enough to realize he'd go straight to "why."

"Jason's made a decision to leave the police force after two years. He's training to be a PI."

Hunter scanned him head to toe. "Didn't like the restrictions?"

Jason smiled. "Already figured me out, huh?"

"Over twenty years on the force. Fifteen of them as a detective." He cocked his head, studying Jason. "Fresh tats, stud in one ear, overkill on the casual wear..."

Jason scrolled his chair out from under his desk and stuck out his legs. "What? You don't like my Birkie's?"

Hunter laughed. And, just like that, the awkwardness vanished and the cop-bonding began.

Sherry and I looked at each other. I tilted my head toward my office. She rose from her desk. The guys didn't even realize we'd left the room.

It felt great to be back, if only for an hour or two.

Chapter Five

Olivia

We positioned ourselves in our typical conversation spots. Glancing at my desk against the back wall, I noticed an impressive stack of file folders awaiting my attention. "Man. It feels so good to be in my space."

Sherry's dark brows knit together. "Are you sure you're ready? I mean, I'm glad you're here, but I don't want to throw you into some kind of event—"

I frowned. "Would you *stop!* I'm fine. Promise. Fill me in on what's happening. How long have I been gone?"

"I found you on Monday morning. It's Friday."

I cocked my head at the huge pile on my desk. "I doubt if I should dig into those, yet. How's Jason's training going?"

"He's still taking online classes. Since he already had his concealed carry, he'll be good to go when he gets his license."

"Okay. Maybe we can fudge on that a little. Once he passes the exam, let's assign him a few cases. I mean, who will know? We can give him easy stuff. Tell me more about the Barnes Imports request."

She sucked in a breath. "*That* guy is a trip. He's definitely your type."

I grabbed a lock of my hair and twirled it around my index finger. "What's my type?"

"Classy. I'm more the 'girl next door', but you can pull off an evening gown and pass for one of the elites. You've even got the cheekbones for it."

"Are you giving me a compliment or a slam?"

She laughed. "You know what I mean. You'd look much better behind the wheel of a Maserati than I would."

"Everybody looks good behind the wheel of a Maserati."

"Agree to disagree," she said. "The potential client owns a luxury vehicle repair-slash-showroom type of place. It's in a warehouse down by Baltimore's Inner Harbor. Here's the expanded story: some random guy ran into one of their high-end vehicles. Worth, like, one-point-five-mil or something. Alex Barnes, the owner, had taken possession of a new vehicle, and one of the salespeople had been test-driving it to make sure all the bells and whistles worked. There's a disagreement about who caused the accident, and his vehicle is totaled. The other driver is throwing a fit, and so is his insurance company, because the payout is going to be huge. The driver of the other car says he got hurt, and Barnes is contesting this information. So, long story short, the import company has deep pockets, and the guilty driver of the other car is looking for a payday. Alex wants fresh eyes on the accident report and surveillance of the other driver."

"Alex *Barnes*," I repeated, tapping my chin with my index finger. I glanced at the bowl full of Barnes mini-candy bars on the coffee table. "Should I ask?"

"You should, and the answer is yes. Barnes confectionery empire: Chocko Bars, Barney Bars, Chocko Pieces, all of them. He *is* related, like, three generations removed or something." She tilted her head at the bowl. "He came bearing gifts."

"Huh."

"Is that all you can say? Wow. I saw literal *dollar signs* walking in the door." Sherry made little walking motions with her fingers.

I laughed. "You're so materialistic."

"Have you checked our bank account? It's not cheap to do this for a living."

"I have investments. We can always tap into those. But you don't see any red flags, right? Sounds like you've dug into him."

"None."

"Schedule him, then. Give it a few days, so Hunter won't nag me about resting." I smiled. "The three of us. Let's meet at one of the nice restaurants downtown, close to his warehouse. I'd like to get a look at it."

"I'll arrange it." She flipped open a different file she'd brought. "Here's Collins's signed contract. Do you want to do the dating site discovery, or should I?"

I made a face. "Please. You do it. The thought of sifting through dating profiles would trigger a seizure, for sure."

Her jaw dropped. "Don't you dare make a joke about seizures. If I hadn't found you when I did, who knows what would've happened?"

"Sorry. But I *don't* want to do a dumpster dive into dating sites. Maybe give it to Jason. Anything else?" I stared at the remaining file in her lap. Unopened. A mystery. Her fingers trailed back and forth across the file; her lips pursed, as if unwilling to discuss.

I pointed at it. "Next?"

After a few seconds, she blurted, "Callie."

I blinked. Callie? My next-door neighbor and best friend? She hadn't said anything to me about needing our help. My head started to pound…my signal to leave soon. Marlowe lifted his noble, tapered head and looked at me, his ears perked. The dog had a sixth sense or something. I put my palm against my forehead, closing my eyes. "Why didn't she approach me about this?"

"She couldn't," she admitted, with an apologetic look. "She has a problem with how you've been…uhh…."

"Been what?

"It's the drinking," she whispered. "I didn't want to say anything."

My mind spun with excuses, but I came up with nothing.

"I have to admit, honey, Callie has a point. You've got a short fuse and a hangover most mornings." She averted her eyes. "Sorry. I know this isn't a good time to tell you."

My hands clenched. My pulse hammered at my temples. Great. The perfect storm for a seizure. I told myself to calm down.

"What's the ask," I managed.

"Her ex, Graham, is getting released from the Maryland Corrections

Center to an approved housing situation in two weeks. She wants surveillance and a check of his financials. He's become a real hard-ass in prison, and she's nervous about his visitation rights with Amy."

I frowned. I couldn't believe Callie hadn't come to me first.

A knock on my door made me jump. "Come in," I snapped.

Sherry rose from her chair, holding the file to her chest. "I'll take Callie's case."

I lunged for the file and yanked it from her grip. "Like hell you will. This is mine, whether she likes it or not."

Hunter stuck his head inside the door. "Jason and I ran out of things to talk about. It's getting late. You ready for a break?"

"I am," I said tersely, and stalked outside, Marlowe at my heels.

Behind me, I heard Hunter saying his goodbyes to Sherry. I got in his Jeep, slammed the door, and stared at the file in my lap.

He arched his eyebrows at the file as he drove us back to my house. "Homework?"

I nodded. Marlowe pushed his nose into my shoulder from the back seat. I kissed him on top of his head.

Chapter Six

Hunter

"What's with the attitude? You and Sherry have a difficult conversation?" He navigated the curves in the lane to my house, trying to keep his Jeep from getting scratched by low-hanging branches. He downshifted and stomped on the brakes as a young doe stepped out of the trees, then leaped away.

Olivia frowned. "Somewhat."

"The file have something to do with it?"

"I have to review it."

Hunter nodded, pulled in front of the garage, and parked the Jeep. He followed Olivia into her cozy farmhouse. Marlowe swept past them and raced through the house in search of his tomcat buddy, Riot. She put the file on her kitchen table and grabbed a bottle of water out of the fridge. "I don't want to talk about it."

After a pause, he said. "You don't need the stress, babe. You'll do what you want, but I'm here as the voice of caution. Can't it wait?" He sighed. "I forgot to drop my stuff in the office guest room. I'll be back."

Olivia smiled. "Sorry I'm so irritated. Go. I'll be fine."

"Okay. If you're sure you'll try to rest. Don't go anywhere," he joked.

Olivia walked upstairs to a desk she'd placed at the end of the hall. Hunter heard her turn on the lamp, a signal she'd be engrossed in the contents of the file as he drove back to their office and drilled Sherry about what was really going on.

Ten minutes later, his duffle and backpack stashed in the guestroom, he strolled into the lobby, hands in pockets. "Got a minute?"

Sherry continued typing. "Sure."

His cell buzzed. "Let me take this, and I'll be right back." He walked out the front door and sat on the steps of their small porch.

"Sergeant Faraday, this is Larissa from the rehab facility."

He winced. *Matty.* He hadn't thought about her since he'd dropped her off at Woodlawn. "Yes?"

"She put you down as her emergency contact."

"What happened?"

"She wants to go home. Throwing quite the fit about it. We can't keep them if they don't want to be here. She admitted herself of her own free will, and a lot of our patients experience a remorse period before they start getting better, but this is a unique situation. I know you're concerned about her safety. Maybe you can talk to her?"

"Put her on."

He heard steps walk away. Voices in the background. The shove of drawers closing. The squeal of a door opening. Then, the tentative sound of Matty's voice. "Sergeant Faraday?"

"Hello, Matty. How are you?"

"I can't stay here."

He'd expected pushback. "It's temporary. And, you do need help managing your medications. It's just a few days. You didn't want to go home, remember?"

"They're trying to put me on *more medication.*"

Hunter felt the furrow between his brows deepen. More meds? Why? She needed weaning *off* some of the meds.

Her voice dropped to a whisper. "I held them in my mouth until the nurse went away. The patients here tell me they have to take lots of pills."

Matty's voice held a hint of fear. Paranoia symptoms? Or fact? "Put Larissa back on the line."

"Don't tell her what I said. She'll tell Dink."

"Okay. We'll figure this out. I won't say anything about what you told me."

"They took my phone."

"They do that with everyone."

Silence.

"Has Dink been there?" Hunter asked.

"I don't know."

He listened to the background sounds. In retrospect, it *did* seem quiet for a rehab facility. In his experience, rehabs vibrated with a kind of drug-deprived, erratic energy. Loud voices, belligerent conversations, or high, tittering laughter. This rehab sounded more like a nursing home.

The slap of footsteps reached his ears. "Here's Larissa," Matty said.

"I'm here, Sergeant."

"I'm wondering why she'd contact me so soon."

"I'm not sure. She seems comfortable."

Hunter frowned. "Have you had a physician check her meds yet? Her dangerous dosage is why I thought she'd be safer with you."

"Oh. I thought it was her decision to come."

Oops. "I asked the question, and she said yes. She didn't want to go home."

"We haven't been able to get her scheduled with the on-site physician, yet. We have what she brought with her, but before we take her off anything, we need to know her medical history," said Larissa.

Hunter groaned. Dink seemed to have bribed the whole town into buying his story about caring for his wife. Dink would be the one to ask about her medical history, not him. Had he made the wrong judgment call in taking her back to Woodlawn? "I think I settled her down. Please don't release her, yet. Obviously, I can't speak to her medical history."

"Of course. We'll keep her as long as she's willing, but if she becomes confrontational, we have to release her to her husband."

"I understand. Thank you."

As he ended the call, he wondered if he should go ahead and shoot himself now. Why did he do stuff like this? If his lieutenant caught wind of it, he'd be out the door.

He walked into Watchdog's lobby and stood in front of Sherry's desk.

Sherry smiled, extending an arm toward one of her guest chairs. "Sit. What's on your mind, Sergeant?"

He settled himself in the chair. "Olivia is wound so tight I can't even talk to her. Did anything happen out of the ordinary before she had the seizure?"

She crossed her legs and looked out the window beside her desk, thinking. "We've gotten *so* busy. I mean, it's a good problem, but I'm sure Olivia's felt more pressure than usual."

"Any news about our old friend, Olivia's ex, Monty?"

"He's leaving her alone. And he better not start his crap again, or he may never get out of prison. Where is she, anyway?"

"She's studying a case file. I got the feeling she wanted to be alone." Hunter stroked his chin. "I've heard a rumor about too much drinking?"

"So, you know, then?"

"I really don't," admitted Hunter.

Folding her arms, she met his gaze with a quiet, knowing look. "When you think about it, Olivia's been hustled so many times by people she thought were decent, I'd be wanting to check out, too. Think about it, Hunter. In our wild goose chase through Florida looking for Hannah, she worked her butt off. So did I, actually, and you, as well." She touched her tight, short, curls. "And, what did she get in return?" A shadow crossed her face. "Betrayal of the worst kind. It about killed her."

Hunter leaned in, put his elbows on his knees, and tented his fingers. Chasing all over Florida after Hannah had about killed him, too. He could only imagine what it had done to Olivia, and she wasn't a woman to share her feelings when going through a rough patch.

Sherry continued. "To be honest, I think she's suffering with PTSD. Today, I had to tell her about an investigation Callie wanted us to take on, and Callie approached me, asking to keep her out of it. *Another* betrayal. Olivia got mad and snatched the file, which is probably what she's studying."

"And Callie didn't come to Olivia because…"

She sighed. "It's the booze. I'm not sure how much she's drinking, but it's getting harder to talk to her without an argument." Processing his stunned expression, she added, "I'm sure she'll pull out of it."

"I've noticed it, too," he said. "She's become sarcastic, almost cynical." He laced his fingers, studied his hands a few seconds, and lifted his head. "Do you think the drinking caused the seizure?"

"According to her neurologist, it's a large contributing factor. Olivia needs to stop drinking, and you know how much she loves her wine."

"On top of everything else, her stepdad's diagnosis is on her mind," Hunter added.

She tapped her chin. "Good grief. I'd forgotten. How's he doing?"

"He's in a wheelchair, now."

Sherry's eyes puddled with tears. "First Tom, now Gray." She jabbed her index finger in his direction. "You'd better stay healthy. You're the last man standing."

"Plannin' to."

They indulged in a comfortable silence. Hunter straightened in his chair. "I better get back." He rubbed his hand across the stubble on his jaw. "I appreciate the insight. For the record, she tells me she's not drinking."

Sherry grabbed her purse, slung it on her shoulder, and tidied her desktop. "Well, she's had a lot of people tell her she should stop tempting fate. Maybe it's sinking in."

He shrugged. "All I know is what she told me."

"Don't get me wrong, if I'd been the one dealing with Monty's threats, the disaster in Florida, the neighbor from hell, and her stepdad's diagnosis last year? I'd be drowning in wine, too. But there's a time to get a handle on it."

"Keep this between us, okay?"

"Will do." She approached him and put her hand on his shoulder. "She'll be okay, Hunter. It takes her a minute after she has these episodes."

He winced. "There've been others?"

"Tiny ones, which were caught in time. Remember coffee? Her best friend? She's back to herself in half an hour or so. Okay, I'm off to the library to anonymously research dating websites."

He accompanied her to the parking lot. "Work or personal?"

She laughed. "It's for an investigation. Take care, now. Do you need a key?"

"Already have one."

"Okay, then. See you later."

As Hunter got into his Jeep to return to Olivia's house, Jason turned into the lot and parked beside him.

Rolling his eyes, Jason got out of his car and walked around to the driver's side. "Hey, man. How's it going? I just experienced my first official process serving assignments. A restraining order, a summons, and an eviction notice. Wow. Talk about people hating your guts."

"Not a pleasant task, for sure."

"Are you here to help out while your lovely fiancée recuperates?" His head swiveled as he looked for her car. "Where is she?"

"Home. I'm headed that way."

Jason pointed. "Isn't that her car? She's taking off down the highway."

Hunter cursed, started the Jeep, and squealed out of the parking lot after her.

Chapter Seven

Olivia

I pulled into the non-profit where Callie volunteered her time, feeling the chip on my shoulder growing heavier by the minute. Judging by the number of faces looking out windows, the angry squeal of my tires had drawn attention.

Glancing at the file in the passenger seat, I fumed. Why did she approach my colleague instead of me, her *best friend?* Sure, I knew my drinking had caused significant bad moods, but still. She could've at least given me a chance, or a heads-up.

I hopped from the Land Rover, slammed the door, and covered the distance to the front door in three strides. My palms had become sticky with sweat, and I couldn't get a good grip on the doorknob. I tried again, looking at her through the big, plate-glass window. Callie's eyes grew big and round when she saw me. I watched her race to the door and swing it open. "Is everything okay?"

I blinked. How could she think I'd come to ask for *her help?* Anger twisted through my stomach. "Everything is *not* okay. We need to talk."

Callie looked behind her at the kids sitting in kid-sized chairs at a kid-sized long table with baskets of crayons and markers in the middle. "Now? Kind of busy here," she whispered.

"Now."

"Wait a sec." Callie disappeared into a back room and returned with a woman in tow, who glanced at me, then took a seat with the children. "Okay," she said, joining me outside.

I pointed to a bench in the quaint, landscaped space surrounding the building. "Let's sit over there. I need to know what's going on with you."

On the short walk, I tried to manage my emotions and breathe. If I gave a damn, this behavior would be considered extreme by my neuro. Heck, by anybody. I pushed the thought away. I needed to know. Period.

"What is it?" Callie asked, her expression a mixture of irritation and concern.

"How long have we been friends, Cal?"

Her forehead wrinkled. "I don't know…twenty-five or thirty years?"

"How many times have you *not* been able to depend on our friendship? Or depend on *me?*"

Awareness fluttered across her features. She stared at her perfect nails. Lime green with white tips, accented by a tiny lemon. "This is about the request to surveil Graham, isn't it?"

"You think?" I jammed my arms across my chest. "What the heck, Cal? Why didn't you come to me?"

Her cheeks flushed bright pink. "What did you expect? Look how you're acting right now! It's so inappropriate to show up like this and demand we talk. I get tired of dealing with the "Freakout Olivia.""

"Freakout Olivia…?" I echoed, with a puzzled frown.

"I wanted to give you guys the business, but I can't talk to you anymore. You're either hungover and mad, or sober and mad…because you're sober."

"What?" My jaw dropped. She'd never talked to me like this, not once in all these years. It felt like a slap in the face. "I'm *not.*"

"I don't want to argue, and I'm not into a…what's it called? An interception?"

"Intervention."

"Right. Whatever. You've become a different version of the Olivia I used to know."

I stiffened. "So. When have I 'freaked out' on you?

She chuckled. "Besides now? Many times, and another thing, you are in *complete* denial about it. You won't listen to a word I say." She studied her hands in her lap. "Sherry was supposed to handle the case quietly. I guess she changed her mind."

"Guess so." My self-righteous attitude deflated like air escaping a balloon. The awkwardness grew. One of us needed to say something.

"Get on with it," said Sherry.

"With what?"

"Unloading. Go for it." She lifted her chin and winced, as if preparing to take a blow.

The fuzziness in my brain sputtered to life. I felt dizzy, but held on, hoping it would pass. I'd become expert at masking two kinds of hangovers: one from alcohol, and one from brain injury deficits. I couldn't make excuses, anymore, I had to accept the truth. Even my best friend can't stand to be around me. My thoughts spiraled to Hunter. Did he feel the same?

Accepting the truth is hard.

I calibrated my tone. "I grabbed your client file from Sherry. It upset me to think—"

"Think what?" she shot back. "That I'd dare transgress your feelings? That for once, I'd put my needs above yours?"

I drew back in shock. "This has to do with Graham, Cal. His release could trickle down to Monty, which would trickle down to my girls and me. I don't want to be blindsided by him, ever again. It felt like..." I took slow breaths, trying to get a handle on the emotions pinging through me. "It felt like *abandonment.* After all we've been to each other, I thought you'd give me the benefit of the doubt, even if I'm not myself at times."

"Yeah, and the way you've been treating me feels the same. So, we're even." She glanced at the building. "I need to get back in there. They depend on me."

"And I don't?"

She rose from the bench, a slight groan puffing from her mouth. "I'll take my business somewhere else, okay? If you can't see what's happening with you..." She closed her eyes briefly. "I'm so over this."

I watched her walk away. Taking her business elsewhere would not solve anything. An overwhelming, familiar heaviness washed over me. These days, it felt more normal to be disgruntled than content or happy. Heeding my neurologist's warnings, I took a quick survey of my physical symptoms. Jaw clenched, tight knot of stress in my belly, racing heart, cold extremities. *All warning signs.* I looked at the blue of the sky and silently asked God for help. Whatever had been happening, I needed to figure out how to stop it.

A car pulled in and parked. I heard the slam of a door and quick footsteps on pavement.

"Olivia, *what* are you doing?" Hunter asked as he walked in my direction.

I grimaced. Once again, I'd chosen emotional frenzy over common sense, and of course, he'd be concerned. "Sitting here counting my blessings," I deadpanned. "How did you know where to find me?"

He dropped onto the bench Callie had recently vacated. "You are *not* okay."

"I know," I whispered, putting my palm on his thigh.

"Sherry told me where you might be, and I saw your car. What's going on?"

"Callie volunteers here. I needed to talk to her."

I watched his mind work, the puzzle pieces slotting.

He nodded, slowly. "You're here to confront her?"

"Wouldn't you?"

"I wouldn't drop in unannounced and go ballistic, which is what I assume happened."

I frowned. "It's different with you."

"Is it?"

"For God's sake, it concerns Graham! Anything Callie's ex gets involved in leads to my own ex, so yeah. I'm not happy about it. As you may remember, Monty isn't exactly *sane* where I'm concerned," I insisted, my voice shrill.

"I understand, but remember, Monty's not allowed anywhere near you. He even stated he'd stopped making your life miserable in a letter. So, if anything happens, you have a backup. You don't have to worry."

Anxious tears leaked down my cheeks. "You know Graham could facilitate a new plan of attack. Callie didn't even think about that. She should've let me *know.*"

Hunter put a hand on my cheek and turned my face to his. "The investigation request is about *Callie*. Not you."

The simple statement of fact clicked like a key unlocking a compartment. When had everything started revolving around *me?* Callie had good reason to be concerned about Graham getting out, given his past actions over custodial issues with their daughter, Amy. My shoulders sagged. "I'll apologize."

"You might want to give her some time."

I jumped from the bench. "No! I need to get it resolved."

Hunter grabbed my arm and held on. "Not now. Trust me."

I dropped onto the bench. "Why?"

"Think about Callie. It took her a long time to get to this place. Under normal circumstances, she'd never act like this."

I hung my head. "She called me 'Freakout Olivia.'"

Hunter looked away to hide a smile.

I frowned. "What are you thinking?"

"I think it's a nice way of putting it."

"Wow. Thanks."

He stared at the ground a few seconds. "Let's go back to your house. I'll be right behind you."

Chapter Eight

Sherry Lattimore

Pinching the bridge of her nose, she focused on another dating site. "Crap!" she hissed under her breath. "When do these people even work? Don't they have jobs?" She leaned back in her chair and surveyed the quiet library, thankful for a respite from the noisy children's story hour and adult presentation series. Didn't libraries used to be quiet? The research had been mind-boggling. Hooking up had ratcheted to levels she couldn't even believe, and both men and women exposed so much flesh she'd laughed out loud. Logging off, she muttered, "Who wants to see that?" Jason would be a much better candidate for this work. The 'Bella' in question had made profiles on at least four dating sites under similar names, which did not bode well. She stuffed the file, notes, and pen into her backpack to drop on Jason's desk. Dating after age forty was overrated, she decided. With a smile at the thought of courteous, predictable Duncan, whom she'd met in a coffee shop, she whispered, "Thank God for you, Duncan."

Stretching and stifling a yawn, she slung her backpack over her shoulder, and drove to the office.

Jason walked in from the break room as she entered. "Hi. All quiet, here. How's it going?"

"Terrible." She fished out the file and walked over to his desk.

He put his fresh mug of coffee on a coaster, and sat at his desk. Sherry slapped the file down.

"How long have you been working here?" she asked.

"Ten months, give or take."

"How'd you like to take on your first investigation?"

He beamed. "I hope you're serious."

"You spent two years on the force. I think this'll be easy for you."

"What do you need?"

"Have you ever done any dating online?"

He scratched his head. "Some. Never had anything work out, though."

She grunted. "I spent three hours researching a client's new girlfriend. She's on four dating sites."

Jason laughed. "Are they not exclusive?"

"Supposed to be."

Jason rolled his eyes. "He's getting played."

"Okay. You're hired. We need evidence of that. Surveil her online, and if possible, offline. Let me know what you discover."

"Got it. Want me to start now?"

She tapped the file she'd put on his desk with her index finger. "This is what I have so far. Let me know if you need help." She eyeballed him. "Don't go all cowboy on me until you have your PI license in your pocket."

Sherry walked across the lobby to her desk, feeling pounds lighter, and opened her laptop.

Ten minutes later, a scowling Olivia exploded into the lobby and strode into her office, slamming the door behind her. Hunter strolled inside two minutes later casting them a bemused glance.

"Is everything all right?" Sherry mouthed, with a stunned expression.

He stuck his hands in his pockets. "I tried to get her to go home, but she wanted to come in for a minute."

Jason grinned. "Workplace drama. Always fun."

"*Not* the right time," Sherry warned.

He returned his attention to his laptop.

"She needs to work some things out in her head," Hunter said. "I'll wait back here if you guys don't need me." They didn't, and he walked down the narrow hallway through the break room, past her office to the guest room.

Marlowe followed.

Sherry chewed her lip and stared down the hallway toward Olivia's office.

"Yes. You should. Go talk to her," Jason said.

With a curt nod, she massaged her dark-brown, tight curls into place, straightened her shoulders, and started down the hall. She paused in front of the door. "Can I come in?"

She heard a muted grunt of acknowledgment.

Heading straight to the cozy cuddle of four upholstered armchairs around the coffee table, she dropped into her normal spot. "Dark in here," she said, switching on a table lamp.

The light accentuated Olivia's deep undereye circles, the slight tremble of her hands, and pale complexion. She joined Sherry in the center huddle.

"It's darker in my head."

"Looks that way."

She flung her arms into the air. "I'm having a bad day. It'll pass. What do you *want* from me?"

Considering the next words with care, she responded. "What we all want, honey. For you to be okay."

Olivia rubbed her face. "Is it true? Do I have a drinking problem?"

"We all have spurts of drinking too much, I think. Life can be tough." Feeling the fragility of the moment, she prayed for the right words.

"Look at this." Olivia held out a shaky arm. "It happens if I don't have my normal after-work wine."

"How long has it been since you've had a drink?"

"Six days." Wincing, she corrected herself. "I had half a bottle in the house, so I did drink that, but only half a glass at a time."

"Then, yeah, I'd say you have a problem. Tremors are common when trying to drink less."

Olivia stared at the floor. "I'm scared."

A gush of compassion flooded Sherry's chest. She reached out to her friend and squeezed her arm. "I've never known a woman who's overcome as much as you have. You can beat this."

"I have to," Olivia whispered.

A shiver ran along her arms. Why did she feel a sense of déjà vu? Adjusting her position in her chair, a thought stuck. Could excessive alcohol use cause regression in TBI patients? Would the latest seizure compromise her ability to make good decisions? Would Olivia's ability to lead the firm become compromised? What if it's thrown her back to her pre-TBI personality? She needed to research post-TBI behaviors before spiraling. *Positive. Be positive. Say something positive.*

"You're fresh from a health setback. It takes time to recover."

Olivia rubbed her face and nodded. After a few seconds, she lifted her head and forced a smile. "Shall we talk about work?"

An hour later, Jason rapped his knuckles on the door. "Ladies. I'm leaving now. Do you need anything?"

"Please come in," Olivia called.

"Everything okay out there?" Sherry asked.

"I've dug into Collins's lady friend." He wrinkled his nose. "Something doesn't smell right. Tonight, I'll stake out the gym where this chick works."

"Keep track of your hours," Olivia reminded him.

"Will do. See you tomorrow."

Olivia lifted her chin, gathered her purse and backpack, and glanced at Sherry in appreciation. "You're such a good friend. Thanks for your encouragement." She smiled at her dog. "Let's get Hunter and go home, Marlowe."

Sherry folded her arms and walked into the lobby. Had she said the right things? If she were honest with herself, Olivia's current mindset could affect the future of the firm, their friendship, and her job. She brightened at Duncan's face on the ID of her cell, and answered his call. "Hey. We still on for tonight?"

Chapter Nine

Olivia

I knocked on the guest room door.

"Yeah?" His voice sounded groggy.

I smiled. "I'm going home, now. Drive on down to my house, and I'll fix us dinner. I have to run an errand first. You have a key. I love you."

He opened the door, pushing his hair out of his eyes and yawning. "I guess yesterday wore me out."

I arched an eyebrow. "I'd imagine so. What's her name? Matty?"

He nodded.

Olivia chuckled. "If memory serves, your rescues—including me—tend to get complicated."

He scrutinized me. "You're sounding better."

"I am, aren't I?" I pulled him down to my height and kissed him. "I'll be there in twenty, okay?"

With a furtive glance at Hunter's car rumbling down my lane, I resumed the task at hand. The wine habit had dug in deeper than I thought, and of course, I believed what everyone had said…however, one or two glasses of wine wasn't a problem, it was a release from the world for a bit. *That's all.* And, I needed to wind down. I needed the weight I carried to lift. Relocating to Richmond would be a huge change, and with everything else going on, I couldn't even think straight. A glass of wine would restore me to sanity.

I frowned.

Maybe it's the thought of relocating that's driving me crazy…should I move? Uproot myself from the place I'd raised my kids? I pressed my fingers against my temples, and made a decision.

"Six days is long enough," I reassured myself as I got in my Land Rover and pulled out onto the highway. No one expected me to forsake wine for good, did they? Impossible.

An hour later, I sat in a stupor in my car in the parking lot wondering what happened. I hadn't even waited, I'd bought a wine opener on the spot, opened the wine in the car and drunk from the bottle. I stared at its contents. About half a bottle left. "Hunter's going to kill me," I told my car, patting the dash with affection.

I pressed the "start" button. Nothing. Pressed it again, and listened to "click-click-click" several times until I realized my car would not start. I exhaled noisily. So much for drinking under the radar. I pressed Hunter's number and attempted an explanation, and he told me he was on the way. I scanned my immediate situation in the front seat of my Rover…wine opener, crumpled paper sack, crumbs stuck in the seat seams from the snack I'd bought to go with the wine. I gathered the trash, stumbled from the car, and tossed it in the store's bin, then returned. Did I have breath mints? Gum? Anything? I shoved the almost-empty wine bottle underneath the passenger seat.

Five minutes later, his Jeep roared into the parking lot. I watched him take in my "errand," which bore a huge LIQUOR STORE sign out front. The expression Hunter wore as he got out of his car made me nervous. He opened the driver's side door. "I tried to call."

"I was busy." I giggled, looking at the store. "Some habits are hard to break."

His eyes grazed my face. Maybe I shouldn't talk. My breath would shower him with proof I'd ingested a crap-ton of wine. I cursed my weakness.

"Get out," he said.

I frowned. "What?"

"We'll get your car tomorrow. You're damn lucky it's me and not a cop with a breathalyzer."

I spread my arms. "I haven't even been inside." Not a lie. I got it from the drive-through. I gave myself a mental pat on the back.

"I want to know how much you've had to drink."

As I shoved out my lower lip like a rebellious teenager, he looked underneath my seat, and in the back. Then, he stalked around to the other side and did the same, pulling out the bottle and showing it to me.

I sighed.

"Give me the keys."

"It won't start." I slid from the seat and stood beside him with a bit of a wobble.

He reached inside for the hood release. Fiddled around with the battery, tried again to start the car, and it whooshed to life.

I whooped. "A miracle!"

"More like a loose wire. We'll get it looked at tomorrow." He held my elbow and propelled me to his Jeep.

I stumbled on the running board steps. Hunter hoisted me into the seat, then moved the Land Rover, retrieved my things from the car, and brought the wine with him. "Still want this?"

I nodded.

The tense silence on the short drive home emphasized my guilt. I hadn't wanted him to see me in this condition. What had I been thinking? "I've had so much going on…" I said, painfully executing a limp excuse.

"I know."

"The last several months have been hard."

He nodded. "For me, as well."

I frowned. "I'm all alone, now. Hannah's gone. Callie doesn't want to be around me. Sherry has a boyfriend, I don't see her as often, and…"

"I understand."

I burst into tears. "I don't know how I could drink so much at once."

He reached over and patted my shoulder, but it felt forced instead of affectionate. "It's good it's out in the open, babe."

I sniffed.

"You need help to dry out. I know somewhere." His jaw clenched. He shifted into third gear.

My back stiffened. "I need to work."

My body jerked with his hard shift into fourth gear. His irritation became apparent with the jab of his foot on the clutch, his white knuckles on the gearshift.

I lowered my window and straightened in my seat. The large infusion of wine had settled into a monster headache and I hadn't eaten in a while. "I need food."

"Since you didn't return home right away, I started dinner. It's in the oven." He gave me a look. "You're welcome."

"Thank you." I reached for his hand. He didn't respond.

After dinner, I fixed tea and served it on my front porch, fighting the sluggishness of coming off too much booze in a short amount of time. We watched the stars and drank the hot tea and attempted superfluous conversation until I thought I'd go mad. In desperation, I blurted, "I know I screwed up. I'm sorry, okay? It won't happen again."

Hunter studied the floor, deep in thought. His jaw flexed, a movement I recognized as tension. He'd chosen to sit across from me instead of beside me on the loveseat. I glanced at my beautiful engagement ring and braced myself.

"Let's make a deal," he said.

I laughed. "What kind of deal?"

"You could use help with this, don't you think?"

My mouth dropped open in amazement. How could he suggest such a thing? "No. I do not need help."

"I've talked to Sherry about it. She thinks it's a good idea."

"What's a good idea?"

"A short stint in a rehab."

My emotions had wrinkled into pruny versions of themselves. I could only nod. Or, drink more wine, which, sadly, wasn't an option until he left. "Is this your idea of an intervention?"

He rose from his seat and looked out into my yard. A full moon graced the night. New spring leaves rippled in the breeze. Fireflies blinked in erratic, tiny bursts, and a raccoon crept across the grass, followed by kits about half its size. He turned around and leaned against the banister, crossing his arms. I took in his handsome face, more weathered than when we first met, but every bit as youthful. The oxford-blue shirt he wore looked tired, and his khakis no longer held their knife-sharp crease. For the first time since our engagement, I wondered if our relationship would make it to the altar.

Not quite looking at me, he continued our conversation. "In case you haven't recognized it, this is an ultimatum."

I felt blood leave my fingertips.

"I've thought long and hard about our relationship. Leaving Richmond isn't an option for me. If I left my jurisdiction, I'd have to start over as a patrol cop, which I'm unwilling to do. I have ten years left until full retirement benefits, and then we can do whatever. But for now, my life is in Richmond. I want you with me. We've talked about this. You can move your firm, or open a new office, whatever you decide. Sherry's more than capable of managing the business, here. But, if you're not willing to let go of the wine habit, I mean, maybe we should call it what it is? A dependency? Whether you agree or not, it's become a big problem. Both Sherry and I feel you need professional help. Unless it's addressed, I don't see a way forward."

"It's not an *addiction!* For God's sake, it's a few months of overreach. I'm fine."

Hunter sat beside me, putting his arm around my shoulders. "I love you. But do you have any idea how hard this has been for me? Driving to Glyndon every two seconds? Monty's constant threats, the complicated situations you get yourself into? Aannnddd..." he let the word hang. "Now, we have a drinking problem. Please." He took my cold hands in his warmer ones. "Consider moving. Your mother's there, and she's going to lose Gray soon. She'll need you. One of your daughters works in DC and loves it, and the other is about to graduate from Richmond University. My guess is she will settle in the area, too. What's holding you here except torturous memories and Watchdog Investigations?"

Doubt seeped into my heart. How could I leave my beloved farmhouse? All I'd built, here? All the struggles I'd survived? I'd worked hard to restore every single memory of raising the girls and trying to maintain a marriage after recovering from the brain injury. I stared at my engagement ring and thought about Monty. Our marriage had been a farce from the beginning, unlike this relationship, which had every indication of a solid, pure love for each other. I had no idea what to say. Since he'd made it an "ultimatum," I needed to weigh the options with care. A move would uproot me in ways I couldn't foresee, a shaking of every familiar foundation. But, hadn't those foundations been crumbling for years? Callie had made her intentions clear, and I missed her. My ongoing issues had worn out even my closest friends. They'd cracked under the pressure and walked away. Even though we were colleagues, Sherry had sided with Hunter and Callie in their quest to rehabilitate me, so I didn't think she'd feel like talking with me about personal decisions.

Suddenly cold, I withdrew my hands from Hunter's and rubbed my arms.

In an uncomfortable moment of revelation, I understood. Like my farmhouse after the terrible fire three years ago, a renovation must take place in my life. A tearing out in order to build something stronger and better. Hunter's bluntness forced me to look at myself with brutal clarity—a selfish, unwise woman who insisted on putting herself first under the guise of independence, pickling herself with copious amounts of wine to soften the dark underbelly of everything she'd been through. I'd chased my people away with bad moods and depression, and now...I had nothing. No one. Even my family had distanced themselves. To imagine not even having *wine* to lean on was scary.

I snapped back to Hunter

He gave me a puzzled look. "What are you thinking?"

"I'm thinking you need to go back to the office guest room, and I need to dissect what you're telling me. This is a lot."

He pulled me to his chest and hugged me, hard. "I'll see you tomorrow." I watched him stride to his Jeep. He got in and drove off.

No "I love you," no long, sexy kiss leading to the bedroom, no "we'll be okay."

That's what bothered me the most. Would we?

Chapter Ten

Olivia

The minute Hunter's taillights disappeared down the lane, I made a mad dash for the wine bottle. I got a wine glass out of the cupboard and started to pour. My head pounded. My stomach constricted. I stared at the bottle in my hand, poised over the wine glass…and moved to the sink, instead. The gurgle of the rest of the wine going down the drain made me sad, but I couldn't put it off any longer. This had to stop.

I'd sunk lower than low. The lowest. I grabbed my phone to call Mom, and when she answered, I started crying. I poured out the sad saga piece by bitter piece until I felt empty. The anger and shame I felt at what I'd let happen had become a hard stone in my chest, and instead of using the tired phrase, "It's going to be all right," Mom interrupted my sad tirade with prayer. She prayed I'd be free of the drinking habit which had burrowed itself inside me and that I wouldn't condemn myself for being human. She prayed the relationships I'd damaged would be restored. Her prayers hit home, and during the final few minutes before her prayer ended, my hot, angry tears felt like a cleansing flood.

Afterward, I slept through the night for the first time in months.

* * *

The minute my eyes popped open the following morning, I knew what I had to do. Call it a miracle, call it a revelation; call it whatever you want, but I *knew* my path had been clarified by Mom's prayers. I tossed off the comforter and bounded from the bed, thrusting a victory fist into the air. Let the renovations begin.

Ignoring the monster headache and sick feeling in my stomach, I rushed through getting ready, ran downstairs to eat a bite of breakfast and feed my animals, then called Hunter. His phone rang and rang. No answer. I tried again. No answer. I felt sweat pop out on my forehead. "I won't let this happen," I muttered, trying again.

"Good morning," he said.

My body sagged in relief. "I can't lose you."

He laughed.

"I'm not wild about losing you, either."

"I can change."

"I know you can. But do you *want* to?"

"Yes. *Yes.* I want to," I insisted.

"Should I see when the next opening is?"

"Yes. Make the call. I'll do it. I can do anything for a week."

After a pause, he responded. "You might want to be flexible about the time."

I resisted an angry retort. "You said a week."

"If you do the work, if you're motivated, a week can make a difference. It's learning to take a day at a time. There's homework with this program. It's intense. You might need to stay longer than a week."

"Ok." I thought about how to juggle work and rehab. I could work remotely. It would be fine. "Do you think they'd let me have a laptop?"

"No phone. No laptop. You're incognito and off the grid and expected to focus on the program."

I winced. Work would have to wait. "Ok. Give me a few days to sort things out."

"Let me find out availability. Then, you'll have to make the call. It would be best if they feel you've made this decision on your own, and I don't want to complicate the situation with Matty. They've seen enough of me on her behalf." He chuckled.

I took out my phone, calculated the workload and Sherry's willingness, and gave him potential dates. I still thought I could manage the drinking on my own, but I wanted to convince him I'd let go of *anything* that hindered our relationship. As a peace offering, I told him I'd bring him the pumpkin-cream cheese muffins he loved into the office this morning.

An hour later, I walked into the office, holding the box of muffins. Jason sat at his desk, and Sherry waved from her corner office. I gave her a half-hearted smile, but didn't return the wave. It rankled that she'd talked to my fiancée behind my back about rehab. As if she'd heard my thoughts, she asked, "Can we talk?"

"Sure," I said, tersely. "Give me half an hour."

I walked into my office, dropped off my purse and laptop, and approached the guest room door. As my knuckles hit the door, it opened. There he stood, smiling from ear to ear and smelling of soap and the light cologne I loved. "Where's my muffin?"

I pointed. "They're in the break room, but I have a better idea."

Nudging him back into the bedroom and shutting us in, I wrapped my arms around him and pressed my lips against his. I apologized, told him I understood about his work, and yes, unfair of me to think he'd give up a career to move to Maryland. He responded by pulling me onto the bed and holding me hostage. I laughed, breathing him in. Loving him. After that, the longing of wanting him hit me so hard I lost my breath, and we both forgot about everything but our urgent, physical need for each other.

Thirty minutes later, I walked into the bathroom to freshen up as he lay on the bed, his head on a pillow, fingers laced behind his head. "You. Are Breathtaking. *Please* give moving your full attention. I don't want to be away from you."

Peeking out at him from the small bathroom, I smiled. "It's not that easy."

"Sure, it is," he said, grabbing his boxers from the floor and stepping into them.

"If Mom can move from West Palm Beach to Richmond for Gray, I guess I can take a stab at it, too." *Did I really just say that?*

He walked into the bathroom and stood behind me, kissing my neck, and running his palms down the length of my arms. "We can get married here, then move. How's that for a compromise?"

I smiled. "Maybe." I stepped around him. "Work is waiting," I stated with a determination I didn't feel. In his paisley boxers, he looked…well, he looked good enough that I did *not* want to leave the bedroom.

He let his arms drop to his sides. "Okay. What do you have for me? I have today, then I need to head back." He scrutinized me. "Are you dizzy? Sleepy? Slurring words? Remember what the doc told you."

"I'm fine. Maybe you can ride with Jason if he's surveilling tonight? Give him some tips?"

"I'll be glad to keep him company, but he's got two years on the force. He knows how to surveil. Catch me at lunch, okay?"

"I will." I left the guest bedroom and walked into my office, where Marlowe and Sherry looked at me expectantly.

"Hey," she said, her voice bright. "I'm ready to meet whenever you are. How are you feeling?"

"Much better, thanks." I felt my cheeks get warm as I thought about the little romp in the bedroom, the *real* reason I felt better. "Come on in."

We walked into my office and sat in the armchairs. After an awkward pause, I cleared my throat. "Before you get started, I…I want to apologize for checking out the last few months. Well, year, actually." I took a deep breath. "I'm working on it."

She nodded and studied my expression as if searching for clues. "Good to hear."

"My life took a turn yesterday," I told her.

"For the better, I hope."

The folded arms across her chest felt like an impenetrable wall. Her jab hurt.

"I'm checking in to the rehab Hunter suggested. They have an opening next week."

She didn't respond.

"I've been treating everyone terrible; you included. I hope you can forgive me."

We didn't speak for several seconds. Sherry slid her hand across the envelope she'd brought with her.

"I'll have to reassess what I came in here to say, I guess."

"Which was…?"

She handed me the envelope.

I read the letter. My mouth dropped. Tears stung my eyes. "You're leaving?" I whispered.

"Since you're going to rehab, I'll reconsider."

"I had no idea you'd become so frustrated."

Staring at the patterned carpet beneath our feet, she muttered, "And that's the problem, isn't it? You can't see what you're causing. Resigning seemed a better option than ending the friendship. Hunter did mention rehab, but I didn't think you'd go."

"I am. This is going to get better."

After a slight pause, her shoulders relaxed. "Guess we're stuck with each other, then."

I shook the letter at her. "I'm throwing this away." I crumpled it into a ball and tossed it in my trash can. "Before we turn to business, I want to ask you to consider something,"

She straightened. Her eyes narrowed in suspicion.

"Do you think you could manage on your own, here? With Jason, if he stays?"

"What does that mean, 'if he stays'?"

"After he's a full-fledged PI, has he indicated he'll be staying with us?"

"He's not indicated anything *else*. What are you getting at?" Her cheeks popped with a smile. "Wait. You're moving?"

I let out a long exhale. There. I'd done it. I'd said it out loud. "I *am* moving. There'll be things to sort out, but one possibility is opening a second Watchdog Investigations location in Richmond."

Sherry blinked. "Good grief. I didn't see that coming. I thought I'd have to go work for someone else after…"

"Would you be open to taking over this location?"

She bit her lips a few seconds, studying the wall, slowly nodding. "The thought of it makes me nervous, but it's a good nervous." She threw out her arms, a typical response to her personal brand of jubilation. "Watchdog One and Watchdog Two. I love it! Maybe we can franchise."

Hope blossomed in my chest like a sunrise. Then, the *Fait accompli* which sealed the plan.

"What about your house? Are you going to rent it? Sell it?" She blushed. "Duncan and I are getting serious."

"You're kidding," I said, astonished. Selling my house had been too sad to think about, but the thought of my friend and trusted colleague living in my house would soften the blow. "I'd *love* someone I know living there. Someone who would take good care of it."

"Who would always have the guestroom ready…"

"And would welcome Marlowe and Riot as guests…"

"Who would take care of the big boss when she came to town to check on Watchdog One…"

"Ohmigosh," I breathed, overcome with emotion. "This sounds right, doesn't it?"

She jumped from her chair and stuck out her hands. We performed a ditzy, middle-aged-woman, happy dance right then and there.

Jason poked his head in the door. "It sounds like a damn stampede in here. What are you two doing?"

"Celebrating the future," I huffed, panting as we pounded on, circling and circling until we both fell exhausted into the chairs.

Hunter popped in with a wary glance at Jason. "What's going on?"

"Some kind of celebration," he said, shrugging. Closing the door, they left.

We exchanged grins. For now, opening a second location in Richmond would remain our little secret.

Chapter Eleven

Hunter

"What do you think they were celebrating?" Jason asked, as he and Hunter walked back into the lobby.

"You'll have to ask them," he said. "Olivia wants me to assist with the case you've been assigned. Where are you with it?"

He poked his laptop and stared at it a few seconds. "Wait. Let me get these taken care of." His hands blurred on the keyboard. "I can't believe all the business coming in. No wonder they want to put me to work in the field."

"How's the private investigation course going?"

"It's done. A piece of cake. After working patrol for two years, it felt like a refresher. The state exam is the next step. After I pass, I think they want to find another admin and add me to the team."

He rolled his chair back, leaned down, and pulled out the Browning file. "Take a look."

Flipping through the information, Hunter laughed. "She's juggling four different men?"

Jason grunted. "Tell me about it. And to complicate things, Collins is a close friend of Sherry's. She's worried about his feelings." He grunted. "So. I went to the gym where she's supposed to be employed, and guess what?"

"No one's heard of her," Hunter quipped.

"Exactly. The woman is a total fraud."

"I'd be more worried about his bank account. Did you crack this woman's financials?"

"LexisNexis had minimal assets, no liens, no judgments, or bankruptcies. No residential ownership that I could find under her name. I'm positive it's not her real name. I couldn't find a place of employment, either, nor much of a history." He rolled his chair closer to his desk, and opened multiple dating sites. "There she is."

Hunter studied the pictures on the sites. Different looks and poses for each site. Each profile had been tweaked to match the demographic of the site. "Interesting. She's fishing for different fish. Why?"

Jason let out a long breath. "Strange. Also, her socials are boring as hell. Pictures. Quotes. That's it."

They stared at the laptop, and arrived at a mutual possibility. "Could she be a UC? Maybe we should be looking into Browning instead of the girlfriend," Jason said.

Sherry walked into the lobby with a bottle of water in her hand. "Yikes. You two look serious. What is it?"

Jason motioned her over, pointed at his laptop. "You already looked into this, but Hunter and I think she might be a UC. Undercover cop."

"You have got to be kidding."

"How much do you know about your client?"

She chugged the water, then delicately wiped her mouth. "He and I used to date; it didn't work out, and now we're friends. We're taking his case as a favor."

"Did you do any background?"

She shook her head. "On Collins? Why? You think he hired us under false pretenses?"

"What better way to find out if she's a cop?"

Sherry scratched her cheek, thinking. "But, why would he care? That'd be a good thing, wouldn't it?"

Hunter and Jason glanced at each other and remained quiet.

"Ohhhh. You think he's into something, um…"

"Illegal," Jason finished for her. "You said she asked him for money?"

"I assumed money, but it could've been something else."

Hunter studied Jason's screen again. "She's wearing wigs. And look." He pointed. "In this one, she's wearing glasses. All the profiles have different vibes. She's a UC." Pulling out his reading glasses, he took a closer look. "Holy crap! I know her."

Olivia walked in. "Know who?"

Sherry pointed to the laptop screen. "Collins Browning? The case I gave to Jason? They think his girlfriend's an undercover cop. And, Hunter knows her."

"Let me guess." She rolled her eyes.

Hunter laughed. "Yeah. It's Shiloh."

The next thirty minutes, the three of them tossed around possible scenarios, a discussion backdropped by Olivia's obvious irritation. Glancing at his fiancée, his mind flashed back to Shiloh McPherson, an undercover cop based in Savannah who managed to snag him on a rebound every time he and Olivia parted company. He hadn't seen her since their stilted conversation about his engagement to Olivia a year ago.

"I've known the guy for twenty years. None of this sounds right," Sherry said.

Hunter offered a knowing grin. "I've been a cop a long time, and I *still* have trouble believing certain people are capable of doing what they do. I don't always see it coming."

"Which is one of the reasons I left the force," Jason said. "The darker side. It got to me."

Olivia laughed. "Oh. And you think private investigation is all roses and sunshine?"

"No, but…there *are* moments. A client's gratitude. The twist is when we find out something good instead of bad. I don't have to read people their rights anymore or roll crime scene tape. I don't have to pretend a mangled, bloody corpse is no big deal." He blew out a long exhale, closing his eyes. "I don't have to testify at a victim's trial or wear a vest and bodycam. So yeah. There's a *lot* more roses and sunshine here than on the street."

Hunter put his hand on the younger man's shoulder in solidarity.

Marlowe barked. His claws scrabbled across the floor as he rushed to the front door. Sherry looked out the window and gasped. "It's Collins. What do I do?"

Olivia got nose-to-nose. "Focus. You're his good buddy, remember? He wants a status report, I imagine. Do you want me to join?"

Jason sprang from his chair. "I've got the file right here." He looked out the window at the car parking. "Wow. You didn't tell us he drives a Maserati."

He handed over the file.

Sherry scanned the reports, wincing at the sound of a car door closing, footsteps scooting across the parking lot.

"He's done well for himself…" Her cheeks flared pink. "Holy moly." She clapped her hand across her mouth. "Doesn't Barnes Imports handle those kinds of cars? Do you think…" The question hung in the air, unanswered.

Hunter laughed. "Ladies, let's not get ahead of ourselves. We've got some work to do before we assume anything. Let's see what he wants, and I think it'd be good to proceed with a nice sit-down in Olivia's office. Offer him coffee. Make it casual."

Olivia nodded. "Agree."

Marlowe's tail thumped the floor.

"He's been here a few times. He loves Marlowe," Sherry explained.

A knock rapped on the door. Marlowe stood. The door opened. Collins leaned inside. "Anybody home?"

"Come on in."

Marlowe rushed him. He laughed, and bent to pet him. "My apologies for dropping in unannounced."

"No problem," Olivia told him. "It's a good time."

He walked inside, tucking his aviators in his shirt pocket. "Since I was this close, I thought I'd get an update."

"Do you want coffee or anything? Water?" Jason asked.

"Coffee would be great, thanks."

"Love the car," Sherry said. "Did I know you had one of those?"

"I've had three of them over the past five years." He grinned.

As Olivia, Collins, and Sherry walked into Olivia's office, Hunter overheard him say, "I have a friend down by the Inner Harbor. He owns Barnes

Imports."

Chapter Twelve

Olivia

As usual, Sherry and I sat in the two corner chairs separated by an end table, and put the client across from us in his own space with his own end table and lighting, the large coffee table within arm's reach if needed. No overhead lighting in this room, as we'd thought it best to stick with indirect to create a warm space. All details we'd discussed at length, with the intent of maximizing a sense of confidentiality, spatial comfort, and the blurring of professional and personal boundaries. Our clients felt safe in this space, but also dropped their guard and spilled their deepest, darkest secrets.

Marlowe gave a contented sigh from his spot beside the desk in his dog bed.

Collins flicked on his end table lamp and crossed his legs. Twisting around, he located Marlowe beside my desk located against the wall behind us. "Is he the 'watchdog' in Watchdog Investigations?"

I nodded. "We got him at the Humane Society, but he must've been a police dog or something. He's so well-trained. We've been scratching our heads over why anyone would give him away."

"What are you into, now?" Sherry asked. "Sounded like you had a lot going on last time we talked."

He laughed. "An understatement."

I gave her a look. *He didn't tell us what he does for a living. Again.*

"Have you discovered anything yet? About Bella Franco?"

"We have," Sherry said. "Before we discuss, you mentioned she'd requested something. What did she request?"

The large, round clock on the wall ticked off long seconds as he tried to formulate a response.

He stared at the floor. "I…I'm in a weird place."

"Personal weird or business weird?"

"Both." He took a deep breath and blew it out, as if regretting what he was about to tell us. "Please understand. Bella is a wonderful person. Thoughtful. Generous. So, it felt like a brick to the head when she asked if I'd consider joining a male escort agency."

I laughed. "Are you serious?"

He nodded, spreading his hands and widening his eyes.

"Must be the car," Sherry said. "Hot guy, hot car…could it be a joke?"

He shook his head. "She's pressuring me, now. Says we can make a killing, and I'm the perfect package."

Sherry howled. "No pun intended."

Trying to resist grinning, I gave her the side-eye to get her back on track. Yes, Collins had been a friend of hers, but as a client…I wanted to keep it professional. "I can see why this is troubling for you."

"I like this woman. A lot. But, something's off, and when she started talking about this, I didn't know what to say."

"How did you respond?" Sherry asked.

"I told her I'd think about it." He chuckled. "Stupid, I know. But now, she's offering a lot of money."

"With a buy-in, of course." Sherry folded her arms. "Why can't you tell her no? I mean, seems easy enough."

He sucked in his cheeks. "I want to see what plays out, I guess."

"Have you ever been involved in an escort service before?" I asked.

"God. No."

Sherry's expression told me she believed him. However, professional relationships with personal friends had a way of hijacking objectivity, and I didn't quite trust Collins, yet.

Sherry flipped open the file in her lap, and started reading. Aliases. Personal descriptions. Number of log-ins. Title of each dating site and parameters. Conversations, more. By the time she finished, Alex rose from his chair, his jaw flexing; the lines on his forehead deepening. "She's trolling for recruits. It's a con."

Sherry's lower lip popped out. "Aw. You couldn't have known. People who do this are pros."

The slightest of smiles touched my lips. He had no idea the person "trolling him" happened to be one of Savannah's finest criminal investigators.

"I'm sorry it turned out this way. We can keep digging or…"

He shook his head. "No. Send your invoice with the report. You've told me what I need to know." Collin rose, gave Sherry a side-hug and swiped at his face. "Thanks." He left. We heard the roar of the Maserati leaving the parking lot.

Jason's curious gaze followed us as we filed into the lobby. Sherry sat at her desk, tapping her fingers and looking sad. I sat in one of her guest chairs and swiveled.

"Clients won't always be happy with the results. We did the work. Case closed. On to the next one. Do we have a lunch date with Barnes Exotics, yet?"

"Yeah, it's in your email. Tomorrow at noon. Cheesecake Factory. It can't be a coincidence that Collins purchased three Maseratis there." She tapped her chin. "Collins used to be a car wholesaler, so he knows the industry. Which, in my seedy little mind, tells me a working relationship with Alex Barnes isn't a stretch."

"It's over. Billable. Done."

"Another thing." Ignoring my gentle nudge to move on, she lifted her index finger and locked onto my face with those startling, topaz eyes of hers. "His *reaction*. I mean, he got all sad about Bella and everything, but when he walked out, he was smiling."

Hunter, who had been listening quietly, made a karate chop with his hand. "Ladies. Do *not* assume. You'll find out more at the lunch. Do you want me to go?"

I shook my head. "Thanks, but Alex might be more forthcoming with two women. We've already talked about it." I grinned. "Remember all your nagging about trading in my Land Rover?"

"Yeah, but…" He frowned.

"Don't you think I'd look good in a new Porsche?"

Jason, listening with rapt attention from his desk, smiled. "Yes. Porsche. I can see it."

Sherry laughed. "Works for me."

I lifted a shoulder. "I turn myself into an interested customer, there's no way he won't show me his inventory. I want to see his showroom, and the accident site."

Sherry shivered with excitement. "I can't wait. I love high-end cars."

Hunter eyed me. "You're supposed to be *reducing* stress. I can go in your place. In fact, I strongly recommend it." He crossed his arms.

I threw him a pouty face. "This isn't stressful. This is *fun.*"

"Good luck trying to keep her away from work, bro," Jason said.

Hunter groaned. "You'd think after all that's happened, you'd take some time to regroup."

"Right," I said. "Let's talk about how you run into the middle of a four-way stop to rescue someone you don't even know, and stay in town to make sure she's taken care of. What do you call that?"

"I call it my job to serve and protect," he shot back.

"Exactly what this is. My *job.*"

Our stalemate staked itself to the floor.

Sherry and Jason glanced at each other. I didn't know why I'd gotten so irritated, but here we were.

Tense, silent seconds passed. He threw up his hands in surrender. "You *know* me. I'm not going to let some poor woman get run over at a four-way stop! She needed help. You should be grateful I'm that guy! I'm *here* because I'm that kind of guy. If you don't accept me for who I am by now, something's wrong. I came to give you a break, but go ahead, work yourself into another health crisis. I don't want to be around to watch."

I struggled to keep my lips pressed together before saying something I'd regret.

He let out a tired breath. "Since you don't seem to need or want me here, I guess I'll head back. I can stop in at Woodlawn on the way."

He disappeared down the hall without another word.

Sherry gave me a piercing look. "Are you going to let this happen again?"

I gave my unreasonable fury full vent. "Let *what* happen? He has his job, and I have mine. I don't have time to rest. I'm fine, and he should've stayed home." Spinning around, I stalked to my office and slammed the door. Marlowe lifted his head and gave me a questioning look. "Shut up," I told him.

Chapter Thirteen

Olivia

I woke to the pummeling of Riot's paws on my bedroom door. "I'm awake, Riot," I told him, throwing the comforter aside. "Whoa." I grabbed the headboard for balance and blinked. The walls, the window, the ceiling became a whirling montage. A weird weight in my head pushed me back onto the pillows. After waiting a bit, I eased carefully into a seated position, closing my eyes. Pound, pound, pound, continued my determined, hungry cat. "I'm coming," I said, resisting the tidal wave of pressure. *Vertigo.* A side effect of a seizure. "Dammit," I muttered. When would this TBI journey stop affecting my life? I heard Hunter's voice in my head: *There's no reason for me to be here.* "Oh, babe, I'm sorry," I whispered into the lonely air of my bedroom, realizing I did, in fact, still need help.

Ten minutes later, the world stopped spinning. I grabbed the bottle of water I kept on my nightstand and guzzled it, then tried to stand up an inch at a time, my legs like sticks of butter on the edge of melting. Taking a few steps, I reached out to the dresser for support. Better. The staircase was next. Breathing deep, I made it down the stairs. Success. See? Fine. I'm fine.

I fed Riot, then walked carefully into the bathroom and turned on the shower. "Thank you, God," I whispered upon successful completion of the shower without falling on my ass. I reached for a towel, convinced the episode had breathed its final breath.

You should rest today, God nudged.

However.

The importance of our lunch date with Inner Harbor Exotic-car guy could not be understated. Or rescheduled. My eyebrows jerked together. Hunter! Had he already left?

I grabbed my phone and called, my pulse racing. What had I done?

"Morning," he responded, stiffly.

"I'm sorry about yesterday." Biting a fingernail, I squeezed my eyes shut.

His sigh lingered, weighted with exhaustion.

"Me, too. I guess I'm irritated in two directions: getting you to rest and recover, and wondering if Matty's okay."

I shoved a celebratory fist in the air. We were fine. It was okay. "Where are you?"

"About to get on the highway."

"Don't leave!"

"Too late. It's obvious you don't want my help or suggestions. But, listen to me, for once. Rest. Do it for yourself if you won't do it for me."

A little zing of guilt pierced my soul. "I'll try. But there's so much going on..."

He groaned. "There's *always* going to be a lot going on. You're so damn hard-headed. But you have a choice, here. Your health, or...what? Another episode? Think about it. I love you." He ended the call.

I stared at the phone, willing him to call back. When he didn't, I shoved the phone into my pocket. He was right. My head *was* hard, and getting harder, judging by the intensity of the vertigo. Did I want to get worse? No. I'd rest after the client lunch. Right now, I needed to get dressed. I checked in with Sherry, made sure we were still on track to meet with Barnes Imports. I walked into my closet to pick out something to wear and grabbed a red, silky top and a black skirt. A lunch date with a prestigious business owner such as Alex Barnes demanded more than my usual casual wear. And who knows? Maybe I *could* trade in my Land Rover for a Porsche.

An hour later, I pulled into a public parking lot within walking distance of the restaurant. I teetered down the sidewalk into Baltimore's celebrated

Inner Harbor district on three-and-a-half-inch black heels I hadn't worn in a year. I'd even beach-waved my hair. As I strutted down the sidewalk getting used to wearing heels again, the locket Serena and Lilly had gotten me two Christmases ago bounced gently on my chest. I opened it and looked at the tiny photo of my beautiful girls. While doing so, I walked straight into a rock-hard male chest. I toppled backward, and the world swayed more than usual with the leftover effects of vertigo. His arms shot out to help me balance, thank goodness, or I would've landed on the sidewalk in a distinctly non-graceful splaying of limbs.

When he thought I could stand on my own, he let go. His shaved, shiny head and well-styled beard made me think of every hot, bald actor I'd lusted over in movies. Jason Statham, for instance. I stared at him until I felt my cheeks grow hot, then backed away. "I am *so sorry.* Not an excuse, but I was looking at a picture of my daughters. Are you okay?"

He swiped at a lipstick stain in the middle of his shirt.

I gasped. "I'll have it cleaned."

He waved his hands. "No, no. It's fine." We both started walking in the same direction. He smiled. "Where are you headed?"

"Cheesecake Factory. You?"

"Same."

He put his hands in his pockets and cocked his head. "Your name wouldn't be Olivia, would it?"

I laughed. "Yours wouldn't be Alex, would it?"

We shook hands and walked the next block together, chatting about superfluous topics common to people who don't know each other, but hope to make a good first impression. Between ramming him like a bulldozer and trying to control my lingering dizziness, any hope of earning his favor had become a distant fantasy. Maybe I could redeem myself during lunch.

The hostess showed us to our table. Sherry looked gorgeous, as usual; the brilliant, spring green of her blouse accenting her coffee-with-cream complexion and Meg-Ryan-cute face. After the exchange of mutual greetings and our crashing into each other story, we ordered lunch, put our napkins in our laps, and stared politely at one another. Sherry and I sat together on one side of the booth, and he sat on the other. Voices burbled in the background, and servers raced through the space balancing large trays of food. Our booth sat beside a large, plate-glass window framing a panoramic view of Baltimore's Inner Harbor. Paddle boats bobbed in the marina. A replica of a pirate ship boarded tourists, each kid brandishing a plastic sword.

He cleared his throat. "I'm not sure why we needed to meet. Insurance fraud isn't that complicated, right?"

Sherry and I glanced at each other.

"We need clarity on the scope of the case, which is why we wanted to meet before we agreed to move forward," I told him.

"I would've come to you."

"I hoped you would walk us through your place of business and show us where and how the accident happened. Also, there's an ulterior motive."

He grinned. "Isn't there always?"

"It's a *good* ulterior motive." I smiled. "I'm ready to upgrade."

"Okay."

I told him the make and model of my trade.

"Land Rovers make great kid cars, you know. Empty nesters are always looking for something substantial for their college-age kids."

Sherry chuckled. "A Land Rover? I felt lucky to get my parents' old Toyota."

His smile crinkled the corners of his eyes. "My clientele is extremely discerning."

"We've heard," I said.

"You've heard of my business? Huh. We try to keep it quiet. Must be word-of-mouth."

He stroked his beard for a few seconds. "As you know, I want to investigate the person who rammed his vehicle into a Lotus Emira being tested by my driver. Driver of the other car says his injuries will affect him for life. I need hard corroboration of this, or proof we can rebut, before my attorney and I go into mediation. We're hoping to settle, but I'd like some specifics I can pull out if there's pushback. You'll see from the accident report we weren't at fault. Of course, he'll provide a medical report at the mediation table, but I'd like your firm to watch him the next few days. If he has major injuries, he won't be doing any hard, physical work, and if he is, I want a record. My employee will testify to his innocence. And I quote, 'The car came out of nowhere' and crashed into me on the driver's side'. Insurance fraud is rampant in the exotics market." He scratched his cheek. "My gut is the other driver anticipates a huge settlement."

I drummed my fingers on the table, thinking. "Why us, Alex?"

"You were recommended."

"Who, if I may ask?"

"One of your clients. Collins Browning, who also happens to be one of my customers."

Okay, I thought. That tracks. "I hope you don't mind our questions. Exotic cars are unknown territory for us."

He laughed. "An interrogation before I even sign the contract?"

"Don't think of it as an interrogation. Think of it as an investment in your reputation."

His eyebrows rose. "Oh. Clients of Watchdog Investigations are top-tier, huh?"

"Strongly vetted."

"Okay," he said. "Ask away."

Over the next hour, he plunged us into the high-stakes world of exotics. Alex explained the importance of skilled, delicate maintenance with this vehicle niche, and how his business provided an excellent selection of high-end vehicles as well as expert servicing. We learned the Barnes family had long collected vintage and exotic automobiles, and he'd inherited the family's love of fine cars. He guarded his clients' privacy and purchases. Rampant theft, insurance fraud even more rampant, and Alex needed to verify his damaged vehicle hadn't been a planned collision. Multi-million-dollar vehicles required specialized coverage, and scams abounded. Alex had half his financing in the vehicles on the floor, and the other half in the service and repair business. One fed the other. Alex imported everything from McLarens to Ferraris, Porsches. Lamborghinis or Maseratis.

After lunch, we walked two blocks to his showroom.

When we entered, my jaw dropped. I'd never been in the presence of such magnificent vehicles, and I thought about the Jay Leno documentary I'd watched a few months ago. Barnes Imports made Jay's collection look like Matchbox cars. Red velvet ropes supported by stainless steel posts surrounded the exquisite vehicles sitting like pieces of art on a shiny, white floor. Subtle fluorescent lighting illuminated the showroom. Black leather benches had been placed in strategic viewing areas. As we threaded through the roped-off displays of every sports car imaginable, he told us the stars of his showroom included the rare Lamborghini Siam Roadster at five million a pop, and the coveted Mercedes AMG One, which had a similar price tag. Some of his vehicles were not allowed on the road in the United States, he explained. Too powerful, too fast. I thought Sherry would faint.

"You're really into this, aren't you?" I laughed.

"I dated a guy who drove a Maserati Grecale GT. Which seems like scraping the bottom of the barrel after seeing Alex's inventory. It lit a fire in me, though. I fell in love with exotics." She spread her arms and whirled in a circle. "I'm in car heaven."

"It's not unknown territory anymore, is it?" Alex smiled at Sherry's rapt expression.

"Do you mind sharing the total value of the inventory you have on hand here?" I asked.

He let his gaze bounce around the showroom and rise to the second floor. "Two hundred fifty million, give or take."

I shook my head. "I'm embarrassed I even asked about trading in my Rover."

He shrugged. "I can put you in touch with a wholesaler. You'll get a better deal. I thought maybe you had a rich boyfriend." He grinned.

"Not *that* rich."

"We have several royals as clients. They come from Germany, Russia, the United Kingdom…but by far, the United States is the biggest purchaser of exotics in the lower price range. Europeans are some of our best customers for the rarer vehicles. It started out as a hobby, and now…I don't know." He shook his head. "Sometimes I wonder why I do this. Our security alone costs a fortune."

Sherry and I looked at each other. A hobby? Oh. We kept forgetting his confectionery empire roots. As it turned out, Alex was one of many grandchildren and great-grandchildren strung across the country and Europe.

"Are you sure about hiring Watchdog Investigations? We're certainly not in your league." Trying to shake off double vision when I looked at him, I waited on his response.

"I need someone good, not someone who rips me off because of what I do. I don't need notoriety, I need diligence. Collins gave you an excellent reference."

I glanced at my colleague. Collins recommended us before we even began working on his own investigation? It didn't make sense.

A text vibrated from my purse. I pulled out my phone. Hunter texted: *Remember to rest. Lay down this afternoon.* I dropped the phone back into my purse.

"Walk us through what you've been told about the collision, Alex," Sherry said.

He strode toward the service area, and we followed. The men working on repairs all had on pristine, navy coveralls emblazoned with the business name. The spotless floor highlighted custom niches for every tool imaginable.

"I have security cameras all over the place, and when we close for the night, a private security detail takes over. We have five full-time guards now, all impeccable."

"At what?"

"They can take out a threat from 2500 feet. They're ex-cops or former military."

"Wow."

"In addition, we own guard dogs. Rottweilers. Dobermans. Trained to rip out a throat on command." We followed him as he walked. "We have electric fencing all the way around. When we open the gate to test drive a fresh vehicle, we are outside the property for a very short amount of time."

Sherry and I added more scribbling to our notebooks. "How short?"

"Twenty minutes, maybe. It's a simple checklist. These cars are immaculate, but we double-check certain things."

My eyebrows drew together. "I'm getting the definite vibe you think someone planned this."

"Your vibe would be correct."

"Why not leave it with the cops?"

"They're polite and they try, but they don't have the resources to help me build a case. The airbag deployed and almost knocked out my driver. He couldn't remember details." He started to say more, but stopped.

"What?" I prodded. "We need to know everything, Alex."

He smiled. "Just take a look at the police report, and go from there."

"Okay," I said, thinking the complex world of exotic cars had turned a simple fraud investigation on its head, and we might regret taking his case. Hunter would have a freaking fit if we took this on.

"So. Do we have a deal? Have I answered your questions adequately?" Alex asked.

Ignoring the warning flags, I turned to my faithful associate. "You brought a contract, right?"

She handed it over as I dug in my purse for a pen and gave it to Alex.

Alex looked around for a surface, and finding none close by, gingerly signed the contract on the hood of a 2024 McLaren 750S Coupe.

As we walked back to our cars, Sherry and I said little, both of us stuck in the wonderland of million-dollar cars and European royals. It had felt like walking through a dream, but I'd become distinctly aware of shenanigans underfoot. A sudden glance over his shoulder, a slight avoidance of meeting my eyes.

"If Hunter calls, let's not tell him about this case. Okay?"

Sherry slid into the passenger seat with a cut-the-crap expression. "I'll agree if you lay down for a while this afternoon. Without looking at your phone or answering emails."

"I will. Promise," I said, lifting girl scout salute fingers.

Chapter Fourteen

Hunter

It took forty-five minutes to get from Olivia's house to Woodlawn Acres. The receptionist remembered him. She spoke into the phone, her eyes flitting across his face every so often. Yes, she had a few minutes, and yes, he could come on back to her office. Did he remember how to get there?

"Yep," Hunter told her, walking toward the hallway.

Larissa stepped out into the hall. "Sergeant Faraday." She stuck out her hand. "Nice to see you again. Come in."

He folded his lanky frame into one of her guest chairs. She sat beside him rather than behind her desk. "What's on your mind?"

"Couple of things. One, how is Matty? Have you looked into what we talked about?"

"You mean the photos?" With a chuckle, she continued. "We decided it had to be some of our bored high school kids messing around. They saw you rescue Matty and decided to have some fun," She flipped her hair over her shoulder. "I've given her husband my recommendations." She made a fuss of smoothing her skirt. "We've done all we can, Sergeant."

"Thought she was a 'danger to herself and others'," he said. One of the programs outlined in a brochure on the end table looked perfect for Olivia. He put it in his pocket.

She sighed. "All we can do is recommend."

Hunter thought about what Matty had told him. *Dink's so happy when*

I bring him the package. Had the neighbors locked arms in a misguided attempt to take care of their 'project'? The thought made his blood run cold. Larissa should have insisted he explore qualified Alzheimer's facilities for placement, yet she'd done nothing. He frowned. Discussing Matty's situation with him transgressed ethical boundaries, as well. He made a mental note to check into Larissa's background.

Lest Matty's husband unleash holy hell on him, he gave careful thought to his next words. "She told me he sends her on errands. These errands make him proud of her."

Larissa beamed. "Sounds like a great approach."

"Except the errands are four blocks from her house and a stone's throw from the front gate of the community, which is why she gets lost and stumbles into intersections."

Her hand rose to her chest. "Oh, my. I would agree, but…" Her gaze darted around her office. "Are you sure, because she often thinks things happen when they don't. We've talked through these incidents. Matty becomes belligerent to the point of being out of control. Dink has to medicate her to get her to calm down."

I bet, Hunter thought. Is Larissa part of whatever is going on? Did Dink have the whole damn town convinced of his sainthood? Did everyone believe he had Matty's best interests at heart? As mayor, he could wield a heavy sword. Had he hamstrung his constituents?

He focused on Larissa's twisting fingers and jiggling leg.

A nervous laugh bubbled out. "I can't imagine why you're so concerned about this. We've been taking good care of Matty for a while." She frowned. "It's what good neighbors do."

Hunter resisted rolling his eyes. "What's Dink got on you, Larissa?"

A flush climbed her neck and spread itself across her cheeks. "I think you need to leave, now."

He pushed himself out of the chair with an easy grace. "You're a *rehab.* Why does Dink drag Matty in here to talk to you?" He scanned the walls in her office. "Where are your diplomas? Certificates? Are you licensed?"

Her mouth a tight line, she rose from her chair, marched around her desk, and grabbed her landline. "Tiffany? Get Security in here. Sergeant Faraday needs an escort." She banged the receiver down.

The confirmation of his suspicions rang bells all the way down to his toes. "I'll see myself out. You've been so helpful."

Larissa glared.

Hunter walked outside. Clouds darkened the horizon. Rain on the way. He punched the start button of his Jeep.

Okay, fine. He'd burned his bridges with Larissa. Next stop, Locust Grove PD.

The tidy, two-story police station rested between a Food Lion and a Ford dealership. Designated as a "historic building," the aging, brick structure didn't go with the rest of the street, which had left the 1830s behind a long time ago. He sensed the dainty touch of a "save our town's history" committee that demanded the Locust Grove PD building remain a testament to the past, but hadn't been able to get the zoning laws changed on either side of the building. Two narrow windows flanked a glassed, double door emblazoned with matching LGPD shields. An original transom window above the door displayed the street address with Ace Hardware stick-on numbers. Black on a gold background and slanted, like they were trying to run away.

As he stood on a stone stoop in front of the doors, his phone buzzed. Olivia had texted a happy face and a GIF which said "Don't worry. Be happy." He slid the phone back into his pocket, pushed open the door, flashed his badge, and asked to see whatever investigator happened to be available.

The admin behind the desk told him the Police Chief Watters's retirement party would be the best bet to find someone, and it happened to be in Matty's neighborhood. Hunter couldn't believe his luck. "Thanks," he said, thinking if a desk admin had told someone where half the cops in the district were on a weekday in any other decent-sized jurisdiction, they'd be fired on the spot. He chuckled, shook his head, muttering, "Small towns." He pushed the doors open and left.

Ten minutes later, he entered the wrought-iron gates, drove past Matty's house, and through the pristine neighborhood. Blaring music pointed him to the celebration. He parked and sat in the Jeep a minute. Out of the corner of his eye, he watched Matty recognize him and start in his direction.

"You came!" she yelled, her arms waving in the air.

He got out of the car. With a wary glance at the surroundings, he locked it. "Hey, Matty." She'd been let loose unsupervised. Again.

"I told Dink and Chief Watters you were coming, but they said you weren't."

"Point them out, Matty."

Taking his hand, she led him to the backyard. "Look who I found!"

Dink's head whipped around. He paled as if he'd seen a ghost. He stopped tending the grill, plopped his drink on a table, and strode toward them.

"See? I told you he'd come."

He reached out and patted her shoulder. "Why don't you go get the Sergeant something to drink?"

She ran off.

Dink gave him a hard stare. "What. The. HELL. Are you doing here?"

"Cop courtesy. You know, it always pays to have a friend in other jurisdictions. I hear your Chief of Police is retiring."

Dink remained quiet.

Hunter recognized the man approaching as the one in the photos who gave Matty her "delivery" to take back to her husband.

"Hey, Mayor, we got a Corn Hole game goin' over here. You coming?" He gave Hunter a look, waiting for an introduction.

It did not come.

"Give me a minute. I'll be there," Dink said.

Matty skipped across the lawn with a drink sloshing over the rim and stuck it out. "Here. Lemonade."

Hunter smiled. "Thank you, Matty."

She meandered away, a nonsensical song on her lips.

Dink glared. "What do you want?"

"I want to make sure your wife gets the care she needs."

"This is none of your business!" Dink's face reddened. A vein stood out at his temple.

An older man approached. "Mayor? Everything okay, here?"

Hunter looked at him. "Is this your party?"

He smiled. "Retiring after thirty years of service on the force." He stuck out his hand. Hunter shook it. "Chief Watters."

"Sergeant Hunter Faraday, Richmond PD."

The Chief's eyes widened. "Mighty nice to meet you. Did someone invite you to my party?"

Dink's face got redder, his scowl deeper.

The Chief frowned. "What the hell's wrong with you, Mayor?"

When he got no answer, Hunter responded. "I found his wife a few days ago in the middle of an intersection. It bothered me. I asked for a meeting with social services, who told me everybody takes care of Matty, which didn't make any sense. I'm here to see if the counselor followed through on her recommendation to find the woman a safe place. It didn't happen. So, I decided to talk with you or an investigator in the station to figure out why this woman isn't getting the care she needs."

"The Mayor takes care of her," Chief Watters blustered. "Everyone knows." He turned his gaze on Dink. "How'd she slip away from you?"

When he tried to speak, Hunter interrupted. "She wandered into an intersection, Chief. If I hadn't happened along, she could've been injured."

Hunter tucked his hands into his pockets and allowed a slight grin. This had turned out even better than he'd hoped. Dink's face now bordered on purple. Sweat had popped out on his forehead. Maybe he hadn't had his daily dose of stimulants today, which is what he figured constituted the contents of the "packages" Matty collected.

"Chief," Hunter continued, handing him a business card. "When your party's over, would you get in touch? Call it professional courtesy."

He pocketed the card. "Sure. Good to meet you."

"Tell Matty I said goodbye," Hunter told Dink, and returned to his car, feeling the scorch of Dink's glare on his back as he walked away.

An hour later, his phone buzzed with a Virginia area code. Hunter pressed the icon on the Jeep's steering wheel. "Faraday."

"Sergeant Faraday, this is Chief Watters. You asked me to call."

Hunter took a few minutes to explain his concerns. The Chief murmured the usual responses, but didn't seem concerned. Hunter anticipated a hit to his stress level, which meant his stomach lining would soon complain. He continued listening to the Chief as he dug out the antacids he kept in the glovebox.

When the conversation lagged, Hunter knew he'd lost the first round, and decided to regroup. "Maybe my concerns were unwarranted." He told the Chief. *Like hell, but it's looking like I won't get any support from you.*

Hunter smacked the steering wheel. "What is going on in Locust Grove?"

Sixty minutes later, he stalked into his condo, mumbling about how he couldn't save everybody. He couldn't dig any deeper into Matty's mess, but he knew someone who could.

"Hey!" Olivia answered on the first ring. "You made it home yet? What'd you find out about your latest 'rescue'?"

"It's complicated, and I'm enjoying nice, cold brew to help me relax." With a smile, he took another sip.

"Let me get this straight. You require a week in rehab for me, but you continue to drink. How's that going to work?"

He thought about the question. "I don't know."

She laughed. "I'm *not* an alcoholic. I had a bad run with Hannah and Beth. It took too much out of me. The wine helped. End of story."

He thought about all the people he knew who'd said the same thing and found themselves at the bottom of a bottle every night. "Not why I called. I shouldn't have said anything about the beer, sorry." He put the frosty bottle on the counter in his kitchen.

"Forgiven."

"I still want you to do at least a week in a rehab."

"I plan to. I know I need help to slow down. Or quit. Whatever. I'll do it for you. Do you have a place in mind?"

"Woodlawn Acres. Forty-five minutes from you, and an hour from me. I'll send you the link."

"Wait. Isn't Matty there?"

He texted her the link to Woodlawn and the workforce program he'd read about in the brochure he'd slipped into his pocket earlier.

"If you run across Larissa, maybe have a chat. Since she works in a rehab, I imagine she's had struggles of her own. You'd have lots of talking points. All I'm looking for are details about the facility or her personal history. Anything that doesn't feel right to you."

"How's this intel supposed to get transferred? I won't have access to a laptop or a phone."

"The priority is to get tools to help you stop depending on the wine, babe. If snooping around gets in the way, drop it."

"Understood."

Hunter could hear the lilt in her voice. He just hoped she'd focus on sobriety first, investigating a distant second. Or third. He scowled. Maybe this was a bad idea.

"I figured a rehab facility would have much more appeal with an interrogation attached."

She laughed. "You're such a dork."

"I'm *your* dork, though."

"I'll figure out our workload, and see when they can get me in. I'm looking at the website. I still think I can get drinking under control myself, though."

"I know too many people who think they can do it themselves, and it never ended well. Put me on the ROI form without the 'Sergeant' attached, but don't talk about me. I'm not the most popular person there, right now."

Chapter Fifteen

Sherry

Sherry watched Jason toss his backpack on his desk and head for the break room. "Good morning to you, too," she called across the room from her desk.

"Oh. Sorry. I'm so hell-bent on coffee, I forget courtesy." He walked back into the lobby with a steaming mug. "You're here early. Good morning."

She frowned at her screen. Her laptop revealed at least twenty new emails from current and prospective clients. "I'm not much good before coffee, either," she said, distracted.

Ruffling his still-wet-from-morning-shower hair, he walked to his desk and unloaded his backpack. "What can I help you with today?"

Her fingers flew across the keyboard, answering the easy ones, putting the others on hold until she could figure out priorities. "Olivia's going to be gone at least a week, starting tomorrow," she said. "I'm trying to figure out who does what in her absence."

"Where's she going?"

Her gaze lifted from the keyboard for a moment. "It's confidential. So, let's tell anyone who calls we'll take a message and have her get back to them. I'll take her business emails."

He nodded. "Okay."

"Did you invoice Collins?"

"Yeah. It seemed strange, though. What's he going to do, drop this woman?

He didn't get any answers other than he thinks she's some recruiter for an escort service, and he's going to leave it there?"

"If he wants us to stop, we stop." She put her fingers back on the keyboard and squinted at her screen. "Why? Did he act weird when he got the invoice?"

"He emailed back a 'received' response. Then he wrote, 'he'd take it from here.'"

She blinked. Collins's connection to Barnes Imports had put her on edge. "Did you get a sense of what he meant?"

Opening his laptop, he said, "When a guy says 'he'll take it from here,' it means he's going to take action. I'm assuming he'll confront her."

"You didn't give him any indication about what we discovered, did you?"

He laughed. "Sure. 'Dude. You've been dating an undercover cop. Run.'" He gave her a look. "Of course I didn't."

"Do you think he could've guessed?"

"One thing I know," Jason said as he perused his screen. "We gave him a road map to dig deeper. He can go straight to her profiles on those sites now, and have his own conversations. I hope he's a good guy."

She frowned. "He used to be."

"How long ago did you date him?"

"Fifteen years."

"Long time. People change."

"Guess so," she said, with a resigned lift of her shoulders.

"Go ahead with the Instagram plan. Put your fake Insta guy in DC, which is close enough to get his blood going. A guy like Alex is always sniffing out new business connections. Or, he has someone on payroll who does."

"Which might be Collins," Jason added.

Sherry stopped staring at her screen and looked at him. "I never even thought of that."

"When you have history with someone, it messes with your objectivity."

She nodded. "Try to get him to talk, and let me know what he says."

"You got it."

Her cell buzzed. With a frown at her screen, she rose. "I'm taking this in Olivia's office."

She closed the office door and plopped into one of the armchairs. "Hey, Callie."

"You got a minute?"

"Sure."

"First, I want to tell you I'm sorry I lost it with Olivia. I'm sure she told you about it."

"I understand, Cal. Her drinking problem's been hard on everyone. Did you know she's getting help?"

A two-second pause ensued as she digested this information. "She *admitted* she needs help?"

Sherry smiled. "People surprise us, sometimes."

"I couldn't take it anymore, you know?" she whispered. "I didn't know what else to do but try to avoid her."

"You're a sweet, cute cupcake, Cal. Olivia and I have gotten used to tough situations through this job. We're beef jerky, and you're still a cupcake. I'm sure she understands. Who'd you find to help you with Graham?"

She let out a sound somewhere between a groan and a cry of frustration. "I don't like any of the other investigation firms I've talked to! To hire someone else feels like...like betrayal. You guys are my friends, and I trust you. Is there any way you can fit me in? Graham's been released, and he's sleeping on someone's couch in Eldersburg. He's already bugging me to see Amy. I've been avoiding his calls, but I can't put him off forever. No telling what he's become after a year in prison. I'm nervous. Not for me, but for Amy."

She tapped her fingers on the end table, thinking. All her instincts told her to point Callie in another direction, but loyalty for a friend prevailed. *Jason lives in Eldersburg. Where Graham's staying. It'd be easy to hand surveilling him off to Jason.* She smiled. "I think I might have an idea, Cal."

Sherry finished her conversation with Callie as Marlowe dashed in. Sherry ruffled his ears and gave him a hug. Olivia followed a few seconds later and plunked her purse and backpack on her desk. "Good morning." She smiled. "What are you doing in here?"

"I had a call I wanted to take in private."

"Who was it?"

Sherry's mind raced. Should she tell her about Callie?

No. They needed to repair the relationship first. "New client."

"Yeah? Don't we have enough to take care of?"

"I'm thinking of putting Jason on more assignments."

Olivia nodded. "We knew he'd be able to hit the ground running as ex-military and former cop. Do you think it's time?"

"I do."

"Make sure his license is on the way," Olivia told her. She rubbed her eyes and put her fingers to her temples. "Bad headache this morning."

I wonder why, Sherry thought, darkly, questioning whether she'd done the right thing by hiding the identity of the "new client." Once she's in rehab, she'll need all her focus to confront her demons, and stressing over the strained relationship with Callie would distract her.

Walking out of Olivia's office, she dropped into her chair and scrutinized the contents of the case folder. Alex had been right. The police report was curiously devoid of specific details or diagrams. A typical police report included details related to the accident, diagrams, statements from parties involved, witness statements, and any other important findings. The report is the single most important element for an insurance company to make a determination. *This* report didn't even contain road conditions or a single diagram. She noted the name of the police officer who'd taken down the information and called the station to request a meeting.

Olivia left her office and walked into the lobby. "How's it going today, guys?"

"Check it out," Jason said. He turned his laptop around and displayed the fresh Instagram account. "For the Barnes Imports case."

She approached Jason's desk and studied the account, clicking through the profile, the assortment of photos. "Impressive work," she told him.

"Since you're going to be out, as we discussed, it's a good time to turn Jason loose, right?" Sherry took in Olivia's red eyes, pale complexion, and undereye shadows. A final fling with the bottle on the night before checking in, she figured.

"I'll keep you in the loop every step of the way," Jason said. "So. Let's brainstorm. What should my gig be?"

"Maybe he's bringing in a group of investors? From overseas?" Sherry threw out.

"Spoiled brat rich kids?" Jason added. "Someone who knows his family?"

"Don't these kinds of businesses have an inspection or regulators or something?" Sherry asked.

"Yep. They do. FTC Trade Commissions CARS Rule." He recited: 'The agency dedicates itself to exposing unscrupulous car transactions and assuring fair trade practices with transparency.'"

"It'd get his attention, for sure. He'd have to respond. Wouldn't he?" Sherry rose from her desk and walked to Jason's to stand beside Olivia.

"I'm sure you two will crack the code." Olivia looked at her phone. "I've got to get going. I have to check in by eleven."

Jason looked puzzled, but didn't say anything.

Olivia glanced at Sherry. "Haven't you told him?"

"I didn't think you'd want me to."

"Oh, for heaven's sake, I'm not keeping it a secret. Jason, I'm checking into a rehab. I'll be unavailable for a week or so, and I can't believe I forgot about this, but would one of you be willing to take care of Marlowe and Riot while I'm gone?"

Sherry walked over and hugged her. "I will. I'm glad you're going. Don't worry, we'll be fine."

Olivia forced a smile, and left.

Chapter Sixteen

Olivia

My grip on the steering wheel tightened. My vision narrowed. How had it come to this? When had the drinking become my favorite channel of escape from life? I had a pretty good life. Didn't I?

My mind flew back to the mad dash through the Florida wetlands; gunshots flying, an abused friend on the run. Yes, that had been a nightmare, but the final straw in a long line of straws had been her lies and betrayal. I didn't need a therapist to understand I had all the symptoms of PTSD.

I should've talked to a counselor. Instead, my workaround had been wine. "Admit it. You could've avoided the seizure, and losing Callie as a friend," I whispered into the safe space my beloved Land Rover. "And, what about Hunter? Does he still think our relationship works?"

My mind rotated to Beth, the perfect neighbor who turned out to be oh-so-*not*-perfect. I wiped tears off my face, and focused on the road. Ten minutes until eleven o'clock in the morning. Ten minutes until I'd not have *any* chance of liquid consolation, and the spiral down a very deep rathole had already dug its claws into me. The past year had been a series of ratholes, strung together by two, maybe three glasses of wine after work. I never drank during the day, and figured that was as good a boundary as any. I had to admit, though…the pull had gotten stronger. I *did* need help, or it might spill over.

Most nights, I couldn't sleep.

Wine helped.

It *still* helped, even so many months later. I knew the drinking had gotten out of hand, but the point is…does the desire for a life free of alcohol dependency outweigh the lovely, delusional warmth it brings? The gratifying option to forget everything except another glass of wine out on my porch, staring at the galaxies and moon and beautiful trees? An hour or two of blessed peace?

Of course it does.

But, still. I'd miss it.

* * *

Two hours later, I'd checked in, given over all valuables and electronic devices, and endured a humiliating search through my belongings. A gaunt, polite young man escorted me down a linoleum hallway to a small bedroom which held two twin beds, a small desk, and a single window framing a depressing view of a parking lot. The smells of disinfectant and musty bedding curled into my nose. A can of air freshener sat on the desk. I wrapped my fingers around it and sprayed until I had to shake the can to get any more out. "Hunter, you better appreciate this," I muttered. The window wouldn't open, it had been painted shut. The duffle bag I'd packed had been shoved underneath my bed. The gaunt man popped in. "Dinner's at four-thirty. Your group meets at six. You'll be with Larissa tonight." He left.

I sat on the bed, stretched, yawned, and reached for optimism. Yes, I'd have to sit in and share my story, yada yada…but for *Larissa* to facilitate my first gathering? The primary person Hunter wanted me to seek out? A miracle. With a sigh, I wandered through the facility on a self-tour until time for dinner.

* * *

The folding metal chairs in the room had been arranged in a circle. I was the first to arrive, and my nerves had gotten the best of me. Studying the chairs, I wondered where I should sit. Larissa introduced herself, extended an arm toward the chair beside her, and, taking a deep breath, I sat. We engaged in small talk as others drifted inside. She called the meeting to order when each cold chair held a warm body. Once I settled into the flow of the meeting, listening, pondering, and applying their stories to my own, I started to relax. Just knowing others had experienced similar experiences encouraged me to share a few pieces of my own story. I learned the tag "social drinker" is code for what could become a dangerous journey for the people who don't have a "stop" button. I left my first support group wondering if I had a "stop" button. I wanted to believe that once upon a time, I had.

After the meeting, Larissa approached me in the corridor. "How did you like your first session?"

I stared at the floor, trying to string my words together, wanting to atone for my actions; to justify my existence, somehow. Make her believe I was a good person, not this terrible version of myself. "I've never had this issue before. My life had gotten so hard and out of control..."

"We all get support from somewhere. Alcohol seems to be the main escape for so many people."

My brows jerked together. My fists clenched. "I don't want it to be *mine*."

She smiled. "No one does, not really."

My body felt like a coiled spring, straining and primed to explode. I longed for a glass of good Cabernet.

She put her hand on my shoulder. "You've made a choice to be here. It's the first step to evaluating your priorities."

After our chat, I speed-walked back to my bedroom and closed the door behind me, grateful I didn't have a roommate. Larissa brought me some meds to "help me sleep." I took them, and slept like the dead.

Chatting with women over breakfast the next morning, I made a promise to myself—no matter how much life threw at me; no matter how much the world around me was shaking—I wouldn't *drink* to avoid facing it. Listening to their tragic stories had triggered emotions I'd tamped down for years, and I'd felt them begin to trickle out like rusty water from an old pipe. It felt uncomfortable and cleansing at the same time. It felt like *hope.*

After breakfast, we filed back into the room and sat on the metal chairs. In Larissa's place sat a middle-aged guy with black, darting eyes and a habit of licking his lips every few seconds. He reminded me of a snake. He introduced himself as Leland, and we dove right into a recitation of the Serenity Prayer. After the group prayer, he asked who wanted to go first. My arm shot into the air.

He pointed at me.

The next eight minutes passed in a blur of self-revelation. When I finished unloading a few of my unsavory experiences, everyone thanked me for sharing and applauded. The rest of the meeting faded into the background as I thought about the sensations moving through me. My doubts about this "deal" I'd made with Hunter evaporated. He'd recognized a drowning woman and pulled her out of deep water with both hands. After the meeting, I walked into the carpeted corridor and leaned against the wall to think.

Larissa walked by. We chatted until the receptionist's frantically waving fingers interrupted us. "My appointment is here," she said. "I can reschedule if—"

"No, no," I reassured her, registering Matty and her husband standing in the lobby. "You go on. I'm good. I'll journal, okay?"

She offered a baby clap of celebration. To Larissa, the habit of journaling ranked right up there with chocolate and kittens. "Excellent. I'll check in with you later, okay?"

"I'd like that."

With a final pat on my arm, she left. I watched her greet Matty and Dink with her characteristic warmth and lead them down an alternate corridor.

One twin bed sat against the far wall, underneath the window, and the other sat against the near wall, which held the door. In between the twin beds, sat a desk and a small, ladderback chair on a patterned area rug. Pulling out the chair, I sat and opened the journal I'd received upon sign-in to record my feelings as suggested by Larissa. As I finished writing, a knock sounded on the door. I closed the journal and turned around.

"New roomie alert!" a young woman announced as she entered, dropping her backpack on the bed underneath the window and extending a tatted arm. "Delia."

I put my hand in hers, marveling at the intricate, colorful tattoo spanning wrist to shoulder. "Olivia. Nice sleeve."

"Thanks." She sat on the bed and leaned back on her arms.

Delia had hair the color of a ripe tomato, a nose ring, a lip stud, and piercings rimming her outer ear. She looked roughly the age of my daughters. A vine tat climbed her neck. Her backpack, the color and consistency of brittle, late-fall leaves, looked like it could fall apart any second. "My third time. You?"

I blinked. People did this more than once? "First."

She laughed. "Welcome to the party."

"I guess."

She studied me. "Yeah. You won't be a regular."

"There are regulars?"

"Sure. Sometimes it's not about getting a handle on the habit. We need a bed and hot meals for a few days. Where you from?"

I gave her a vague answer.

"I live on the street," she said, her voice matter-of-fact.

I took in the rough ridges on her elbows, the soles of her shoes worn to mere millimeters, the stark, raw red of her cheeks. All testaments to living outdoors. My heart twisted painfully in my chest. "I'm sorry."

Chipped front teeth appeared with her smile. "I'm used to it."

Ten minutes later, Larissa knocked on the door. "I'm done with my appointment. Would you like to chat?"

I rose from my chair. "Sure."

A niggling guilt prodded my conscience, but I swept it away. I only needed to ask her a few leading questions, not interrogate her to death. Our sneaker-steps whispered down the corridor.

"How'd your meeting go?" I asked as we walked.

"Oh, it's always something with those two. I shouldn't talk about it," she said, opening a door and ushering me inside her office. "Have a seat anywhere." She closed the door and sat beside me. "The wife has Alzheimer's, and it's getting worse, which creates a lot of friction in a marriage." Leaning toward me, she whispered, "Her husband's the mayor." She pushed a lock of blond hair off her face. "I need to keep him happy." She chuckled.

The info-dump surprised me. I must look like someone who can keep a secret. My gaze fell on the coffee table in front of the couch we shared. I stared at the big bowl full of Barnes Chocko Bars sitting right in the middle of it. Alex Barnes's face zipped into my brain. Larissa noticed me staring.

"Oh, take one, dear." She fiddled with her skirt, then clasped her hands in her lap. "Often, ongoing trauma will build and build until it *has* to come out. This can look like rage, obsessions, drug use, or drinking. I'm glad you're here. It's a big first step."

My eyebrows rose. "First step?"

"To your breakthrough."

"To…"

"Sobriety, of course." She laughed. "It's obvious this is unfamiliar territory for you. Have you ever had counseling?"

"I used to have an excellent therapist, but she retired and moved to Florida. I tried to get my ex-husband into marriage counseling at one point, but he'd already become involved with the bimbo."

She nodded. "The bimbo with no name. You're still distancing yourself."

"I am?"

"Do you know her name?"

I sucked on my lower lip. Did I? "Maybe once I did. I can't remember, now."

We spent the next fifteen minutes talking about my awful marriage. I couldn't stand talking about him, and pivoted to the assault which had upended my life, which led to additional experiences which made her eyes widen and a red flush climb her neck. As I watched various versions of disbelief cross her face, I laughed. She told me even the strongest, most emotionally stable person would reach for a bottle after all I'd been through.

"I have to congratulate you on your tenacity. You've endured…and survived…more than most." She remained quiet a few seconds, her eyes on the floor, her hands cradled together. I waited, wondering about her past, if my story was in any way similar to her own.

As if coming out of a trance, she straightened her shoulders. "After your stay, you'll need support to stay on track. AA is a good place to start. For the duration, we'll do all we can." She glanced at her office door. "Be right back."

She left. I looked around her office. No husband picture in a frame. No kid pictures. No framed degrees or awards. I catalogued this information in my brain to tell Hunter about later. She returned with two bottles of water, and handed me one of them. I smiled at her, and we looked at each other; two fake-bonded souls, each seeking clarity and significance in our own ways. I steered the conversation back to Matty. "The people who had an appointment looked familiar."

"Mayor Stricklin's picture is all over the place. He's running for another term."

"His picture must've popped on my feeds when I researched this facility."

She laughed. "I'm sure. He's the spokesman for all the tourism ads, plus running for another term. Anytime you search 'Locust Grove,' his picture is the first thing you see."

"Sad about his wife. Alzheimer's is a tough diagnosis."

During the next few minutes, I realized Larissa needed space to talk about her life problems, too. I made sure to keep my mouth shut and listen. As she spilled all the beans and started to open more cans, I felt a desperate need to preserve the information, which would give Hunter a deeper look into her perspective and help him figure out why Matty and Dink were permanent fixtures at Woodlawn. A stack of notepads sat on her desk.

When she took a breath, I broke in. "Do you mind if I jot down a few notes while we talk?"

Her face shimmered with the rhapsodic enthusiasm of perpetual note-takers. I almost felt guilty, for I was the furthest thing from a perpetual note-taker, and only doing it for Hunter. She scurried over to her desk, grabbed the small notepad, and found a pen. "Here you go."

I scribbled on the pad, striving to remember every detail she'd told me. Should I be ashamed of myself? Maybe. Suddenly, my hands started shaking so hard it caused the notepad and pen to drop to the floor. I clutched the armrests and closed my eyes. Hot flashes soaked me with sweat, followed by chills freezing me to death. I felt dizzy. The floor seemed to sway and rock, my eyelids fluttered, and I was gone.

* * *

After the worst night in the history of my erratic memory, I opened one eye and looked at the clock. Eleven in the morning. The headache and dry mouth felt like I'd dragged myself through the Sahara. On the nightstand beside my bed, someone had placed bottles of water, Saltines, and a few pieces of hard candy. I tore the packets open and stuffed the crackers in my mouth, and drank the whole bottle in three long swallows. I propped myself on one arm. Delia's bed had been made. I wondered if she'd already checked out. A pill bottle sat on the nightstand, too. I read the label. Librium. They must've given me some before they put me to bed.

I heard a chorus of voices outside my door. I'd missed the morning group. Larissa knocked, then swept into my room like a guardian angel. She glanced at me, then the water.

' "Good morning, sunshine! Welcome to your third day without alcohol. You had a hard time last night. Are you feeling better? You'd be wanting a shower about now, I'd think."

I grunted. Rubbed my eyes. "At least I slept through the worst of it. Whatever you gave me worked."

She nodded. "It's a tiny dose. You're very small, which plays a part in how difficult the detox process is. Your blood sugar dipped, and you had some terrible nightmares last night. Do you remember?"

"I must've been out of it. I don't remember anything but stomach cramps, vomiting, and a monster headache. What kind of nightmares?"

"I sat with you until the evening crew came on." She cocked her head. "*Violent* nightmares. I had to hold you down to keep you on the bed. Who is

Niles?"

Falling back on my pillow, I stared at the ceiling, my mind spinning. Had I been blocking the trauma caused by the assault so many years ago? I frowned. Had the drinking taken my thoughts to dark places, with the result that I relived the assault I'd suffered seven years ago in my dreams, now? "Ohmigod," I whispered.

"Don't worry. It'll take a few days, and after you've experienced life without alcohol again…you'll be right as rain." Her smile lit the dingy room.

I hoped she was right.

Chapter Seventeen

Hunter

"So much for discretion," Shiloh fumed. "What were you doing checking out dating sites, anyway? You're engaged."

"Olivia had a health issue, so I'm helping until she gets back on her feet. Their client is the same guy you're tracking." Hunter laughed. "I have to admit, you have some great disguises."

She snorted. "Not that good if you saw right through them."

"Nobody would've suspected if I hadn't been there. I noticed right away."

"How?"

"Your profile. The way you hold yourself. The curve of your jaw."

Hunter waited through her silence, listening to the agitated breathing.

"Couldn't you have kept my aliases to yourself?"

"They needed to know. They won't tell Browning."

Her frustration sizzled through the airwaves like grease in a hot skillet. He decided to change the subject. "Last I heard, you were going to quit the force. How's the leg?"

"I'm not a candidate for a marathon, but I can walk."

"I'm glad to hear it."

"When are you getting married? Maybe you're already married. I've lost track."

"Not yet. She has to sort out business issues. It's complicated."

She made a rude noise with her lips. "If I remember right, she's had 'complications' for years. Are you sure you know what you're doing, Faraday?"

Hunter frowned. "Why is there an investigation into Collins?"

"You know I can't tell you."

"Okay. I'll talk, and you say yes or no."

She didn't respond.

"Collins is a regular customer of Barnes Imports, a company owned by a distant relative of the Barnes Candy Bars empire. According to one of his friends, he wouldn't have the money to buy three Maseratis over a period of a few years, and it seems suspicious. My guess is you're working an investigation requested by the regulatory commission of Barnes Imports' business practices."

Shiloh huffed under her breath.

"That would be a yes. So. You've taken early retirement, or riding a desk due to your injuries. Maybe a *forced* retirement. In which case, you'd be looking for opportunities to stay in the game. Like consulting. With aliases."

"How the crap do you do that?"

"It's a gift," Hunter said. "What I'm worried about is how delicate an operation this is, and whether I need to tell Olivia and her associate to make sure they're armed."

"Yes."

Hunter gripped the handset a little tighter. "Anything else?"

"On a generic note, you know these exotics come at a premium, and involve some of the most powerful people in the world."

"My Jeep is about as exotic as I get."

She laughed. "Millions and millions of dollars. It's like the casino business. Lotta bad guys."

"Which leads me to ask again…" Hunter began.

"Tell those women to make sure they have their weapons on them. And, not to step on this investigation!" She ended the call.

His phone screen lit with a call. His buddy, Nick Ramsey. He rose to close his office door and returned to his desk. "Hey, stranger."

"Dude! Where have you been? Are you married yet?"

"Almost." The word had become his pat answer for the question, an irritating thorn in his side.

"Don't you guys go and get married without me. I'm the best man, right?"

Hunter laughed. "I'm not even sure how big a wedding she wants, yet. She's so busy with that damn firm."

"Has she agreed to move? I remember she's been conflicted."

He started to make excuses for her, but snapped his mouth shut. No more excuses. Ride or die.

"How many years has it been? You've put a ring on her finger, and she's still dragging her feet? I couldn't take it."

"I gave her an ultimatum last week. One way or the other, it'll work out. How's the Assistant District Attorney gig these days?"

"Evolving. My boss retired, and I'm planning a run as his replacement."

Hunter winced. A political campaign would rank high on his list of the worst things a person could take on. "How's *that* going?"

"A Richmond PD endorsement would go a long way. Can you find out which way the Chief is leaning? I want to schedule a lunch."

Hunter laughed. "You know good and damn well who to call."

"The vicious guard dog outside his door?"

"That would be Detective Abigail Fabrizio."

"Please. Tell me there's someone else."

"She handles his calendar and would be the only person who knows which way he's leaning. If you can't get past her, I don't know what to tell you."

"Understood. Thanks, bro. Let's get a drink soon. Best of luck with your reluctant bride." He clicked off.

Hunter put the handset back in its cradle. Nick's remark had aggravated him. He reached for his stash of antacids and signed out of his laptop in preparation to leave for the day.

When he got home, he walked through his condo tossing his gun and belt in its drawer, removed his blue oxford shirt and khakis, tossed them in the laundry basket, and changed into a T-shirt and athletic pants. After a microwaved dinner, he grabbed a beer, plopped on the couch, and clicked through the sports channels. "She should be here," he whispered, taking a swig of his beer. "Watching TV with me, like a normal couple with normal lives."

The cell phone beside him buzzed.

With a sigh, he answered. "Larissa?"

"No," Olivia hissed. "It's me. I snatched her phone. I have five minutes."

He put his beer bottle down, hard. Beer splattered on across his T-shirt. "You're going to get yourself in trouble."

"No, no. She's gone to manage some hysterical client. She'll be a minute. Listen. Matty and Dink were here today. I hung out by her office and tried to hear. Raised voices and a lot of crying. When they left, Larissa was very upset."

"Huh. Maybe because I crashed the Chief of Police's birthday party after I left your place?"

"What?"

"I needed to talk to someone at the local level, and I learned half their force had taken off the street to go to their police chief's retirement party. I dropped in. My surprise visit didn't go over very well. I'm on her husband's hate list now, and the PC didn't see any reason for concern. It's almost gaslighting at this point. It's obvious to me she's being manipulated for whatever reason, and needs a secure, safe Alzheimer's unit."

"I have, like, one minute. Larissa's not licensed, by the way."

"Makes sense. She changed the subject when I asked about credentials."

"She let her guard down with me today and dumped all kinds of information. I asked her how long she'd been a social worker, and she laughed, like we had a mutual secret. She's a former drug addict who got clean and became a rehab counselor to give back. My take is she's a good, kind person, but not a professional."

Hunter heard voices, the scuffle of footsteps in the background of the call. "Gotta go," she whispered.

The line went dead. Staring at the phone, he wished he'd gotten a chance to ask her how she liked the program. He hoped his request hadn't jump-started the PI part of her brain to overtake the getting-sober part. "I should've known she wouldn't stop at asking a few questions," he muttered with a sigh.

He pointed the remote at the TV and unmuted it.

Chapter Eighteen

Sherry

Sherry smiled at the sounds of Riot and Marlowe chomping the food she'd put in their bowls. Each morning and afternoon, she performed a quick walk-through of Olivia's house, then fed them. On a whim, she went upstairs, dropped the pull-down, climbed the stairs into the attic, and poked around. "All is well," she whispered, retracing her steps. Jogging down the stairs, she took a few minutes to pet Riot, after which she and Marlowe walked outside. The sun had topped the trees, and the porch looked *so* inviting. She let Marlowe roam the front yard for a few minutes as she sat in the porch swing, watching the birds and thinking about how much she'd miss Olivia after she moved.

"C'mon, boy," she called. "We need to get to the office." She opened her car's back door, and Marlowe jumped in. After parking, she lingered in her car a few seconds, checking her phone calendar, mumbling to herself. "Check in with Alex Barnes, get specifics from Callie, and tell her our consultation is still on at nine, find out if Jason's gotten a response from Alex on his messages..." Marlowe whined. She dropped her cell into her purse. "Okay, buddy, let's go."

As they walked toward the office building, Marlowe began growling. He dropped into a crouch, as if waiting for a command.

The hair on the back of her neck prickled. She blinked. Groped her waist. Had she remembered her gun belt? No. She'd been leaving her weapon in the office safe. The dog took off, barking. "Marlowe! Come!" she yelled. After a minute or two, he returned.

Sherry let out the breath she'd been holding and snapped the leash onto his collar, thinking it must've been a deer. She stroked his back, the fur on his shoulders still ruffled with tension. Biting down on her lip, she unlocked Watchdog's front door and eased it open. Marlowe struggled against the leash. She released him. He ran inside.

She searched the lobby, her desk area, and checked drawers and windows. Marlowe scoured each room before he dashed back to the lobby, barked at her, and ran through the break room to the back of the building again.

He wants me to follow.

Pausing at the safe in the breakroom to get her weapon, she watched Marlowe snuffle and whine at the guest bedroom door. "I have a gun!" she shouted, jerking open the door. A rush of air blew in from an open window. Marlowe dashed to the other side of the bed. A soft groan startled her. A hand appeared, then another, as someone attempted to hang onto the comforter and rise from the floor. "Keep your hands where I can see them!" she shouted, aiming her weapon.

"Don't shoot!"

She watched, horrified, as Callie's ex-husband, Graham, rose from the floor. Blood streaked the side of his face. "Graham! What. The. HELL are you doing in this office?" She let her arms drop and stuck the gun in her waistband.

"I'm sorry, I…" he dipped his head. "Callie's trying to limit my visitation with Amy."

Callie's supposed to be here in an hour. "Doesn't tell me why you're here, Graham."

"She'd hire you guys, of course." He shrugged. "I wanted to figure out her game plan. It was stupid. I shouldn't have come."

Her temper spiked. "Our information is confidential, and you know it. Do you want to go back to prison? What are you thinking?" She flung out her arms. "Breaking and entering is a crime! Not to mention taking a file is considered burglary."

"Someone left the window open. Technically not breaking and entering. The minute I started climbing through the window, I cracked my noggin on the corner of the frame." He scowled. "Thanks for that."

Sherry inspected the bump on his head. "You need to get it looked at."

"Please don't tell Callie." After casting her a pleading glance, he left.

She had no time for a police report; Callie was due any minute.

Confused, she stood in the middle of the lobby biting a fingernail.

Jason walked inside. "Good morning." He frowned. "You look tanked. Already."

Rubbing her eyes, she agreed. "I need coffee."

As they stood side by side preparing their coffees, she told him about Graham, whom he'd never met, but heard his name mentioned in connection to Callie's.

"Aren't you about to sign Callie as a client? Like, today?"

She nodded. "Any minute. And, I need to find out what Graham did." She frowned. "It looked to me like he didn't make it any further than the bedroom before I got here, but you never know."

"Are you going to tell Callie?"

"Do you think I should?"

He sighed. "Your call. But, why wouldn't you? Are you filing a report?"

"Not yet. We've had so many issues here they'd just toss the report in the trash can." She shrugged. "I want us to discuss her concerns before I think about reporting him. To be honest, I don't want him to get busted back to prison so soon. For their daughter's sake."

On cue, the door opened. "Am I early?" Callie's professionally whitened teeth sparkled with her smile.

"We open at eight-thirty. You're fine. Let's use Olivia's office. It's more comfortable, and she's out today," Sherry said.

They settled into armchairs while Marlowe plumped his dog bed into submission with his paws.

Jason walked in with a cup of coffee with cream and sugar on the side. "Thanks," she said, watching him leave. Callie's eyebrows raised. "Cute guy," she said.

Sherry didn't want to talk about Jason, she wanted to get down to business. She grabbed her notebook and a pen. "Shall we get into specifics of what you're wanting?"

"I don't even know." Picking up the spoon, she dumped two packets of sugar and one creamer into her coffee and stirred. "To see if he's changed, I guess? If prison has taught him anything? Amy is crazy about her father, but I've kept his dark side from her." She stared at the floor a few seconds. "It's her father, y'know? She doesn't need to know those things about him, but...I don't want her in danger, either."

"So. What would make you feel better? Surveillance? What kind of result would help you?"

"What do you suggest? Two or three days of following him? Maybe..." She snapped her fingers. "I know! Put a camera in the place he's staying, in his bedroom or living room or whatever."

Sherry focused on taking notes. "Surveillance is easy. Trespassing and putting up a camera? Not so easy."

"But you can do it, right?"

"Callie—"

She rubbed the back of her neck. "I don't *know* what it'll take to give me some peace, but you're familiar with the situation. I can trust you guys to find out if he's trying to become a decent person, or if he's going to continue being manipulative and self-destructive. One way or the other, I have to know. It would be awful to have to tell Amy, but if something happens or have to go to court to keep him away from us, I'll have your report to fall back on."

Sherry remained quiet, wondering when—or if— to tell Sherry he'd broken in this morning.

Callie glanced at Olivia's desk. "I would rather Olivia not be involved."

"I'm not sure we can accommodate this request." After a pause, she continued, her voice soft. "She's getting help, Cal."

She grunted. "I'll believe it when I see it."

Sherry sighed. Folded her hands in her lap. "Cal. I need to tell you something."

Callie's calm gaze fastened on Sherry's face.

"I found Graham trying to break into our office this morning."

She blinked. Frowned. "What?"

Sherry repeated what she'd said.

"But…why?"

"He told me you guys are still hashing out custody issues, and he wanted to see if you hired us."

She shook her head and closed her eyes briefly. "And, of course, I *have.*" She chuckled. "He knows me too well." She cursed. "He's the father of my child, but I-I…" She looked away, tears leaking down her cheeks. Turning back to Sherry, she continued. "So. He's going back to prison? Will they jerk his parole?"

"I haven't reported it." An idea prodded her brain, and she went with it. "I thought I'd ask you first."

Callie sat quiet, her shoulders slumped, her fingers cupping her chin.

Minutes passed as Callie continued to stare out the window, thinking.

"Hard one, huh, Cal?"

She shook herself from her reverie. "He used to be such a good man. We had some great times together. Before and after Amy became a part of our lives."

"I know, honey. It's why I've been conflicted about the police report. I want him to have changed, too. But…" The unspoken thought fluttered in the air like a tattered rag on a clothesline.

The softness in Callie's eyes vanished. "Yeah. What are we supposed to do now? He broke in, which is criminal behavior. Doesn't appear as if he's changed at all." She put her head back and stared at the ceiling a few beats. "I don't want him to go back to prison so soon, either," she whispered.

"How about this," Sherry said, leaning toward her. "Let's do the job and get you more information. Meanwhile, I still need to look around the office and see if anything's missing. Maybe he only *attempted*, and wasn't able to carry on before I caught him."

Callie sniffled. "We can hope, huh?"

After Callie left, Sherry dropped into her desk chair, lay her head back, and groaned, putting her hands across her face.

"Rough one?" Jason asked.

"Remind me never, *ever* to do business with personal friends."

Jason stopped typing and draped an arm over the back of his chair. "What happened?"

"Callie wants to hire us to surveil her husband, Graham, and do it without telling Olivia."

"Did you tell her about Graham breaking in this morning?"

"I sort of…" She straightened in the chair, folded her hands on her desk. "Left it to her to decide."

"Ah." His eyes flicked across her face. "I've been thinking about it, too. What are the odds of Graham trespassing right before his ex-wife has an appointment? I mean, what a coincidence, and I don't even believe in them."

Shaking her head, she strode to the break room and returned with a fresh mug of coffee and plopped into her chair. "Did you get my email?"

"Yep. Planning on the first phase of surveilling him tonight. I have the address in Eldersburg where he's been staying. I'll get the report to you asap. Have you heard from Olivia? How's her 'recovery' going?"

"She's not supposed to communicate with the outside world. I'm not sure when she'll be back. At first, it was a week, but she's also helping Hunter with his rescue project."

He laughed. "You two are so predictable. You guys needed me."

Sipping her coffee, she cast curious eyes at him. "We did?"

He stood, raked his arms down either side of his outfit, a colorful, tropical-themed shirt he might have scored from Goodwill; his perpetual Birkenstocks, the latest tattoo added to the remaining un-inked skin on his arms. "Yes. For one thing, comic relief. For another, someone needed to pull both of you off the ceiling once in a while. A case is a job, not a chance to make the world a better place. There's too much estrogen. You definitely needed a male employee."

Scraping Callie and Graham off her brain, she let out a long exhale. "I get your point. We do let our emotions get in the way, sometimes, don't we? You're right. We needed you, Jason." With a smile, she continued. "How's it going with the fake Insta account? Is Alex responding?"

Jason unplugged his laptop and walked to her desk. "Here," he said, logging into the account he'd made and turning the screen to face her. She spent a few minutes studying the page, scrolling through the photos.

"Boy," she said. "You outdid yourself with background. Where'd you get this photo?"

"Pixabay. Free image. I made it as generic as possible with some great car posts. I tried to be subtle, but brilliant."

"You should be proud. Has he messaged you? Commented?"

"Lots of people have commented, and yeah, he messaged me this morning." He scratched his head. "It feels like he's digging around for personal stuff. He wants to meet."

Opening the messaging, she began to scroll. "This is a lot of communicating for a new connection. Do you think he's in sales mode? That could be why he wants a personal meet-up."

He nodded. "I wonder."

"What's your feeling about the connection between Collins and Alex? If there is one, I mean. As Hunter says, we shouldn't assume without evidence, but Olivia and I want to make sure we're not taking on a case involving something illegal, or even the *whiff* of something illegal. Keep going." She tapped her chin. "He could be interested to see if *you* are interested in the escort business. What if sex trafficking is their common ground?"

"Yeah. But...disgusting."

"Keep in mind, we don't want to interfere with Shiloh's investigation. At the first hint of anything weird, please let me know. Even if we end up jerking the contract, we can use the messaging to help Shiloh."

Jason's forehead wrinkled. "But he's hired us to look into the accident report so he doesn't get sued, right?"

"Yes, but it feels contrived. *I* think he and Collins are working together, and Collins hired us to look into the woman online as an exploratory exercise. I'm sure when we told him about all the aliases of his so-called 'love match,' he connected the dots and realized she was hunting for something. I mean, maybe he doesn't realize she's hunting for human traffickers, but he knows she's hunting for something. It's a miracle we haven't blown Shiloh's case, and worst-case scenario, what we gave Collins may have put him on high alert, so we may have already blown it. Seriously, though, I doubt Alex realizes we are looking into him, but we need to proceed with caution. You should've seen the security guards posted around Barnes Imports. And the dogs. *Rottweilers.* Very big heads." She shivered.

"Intense."

"Like I said. Be careful."

Chapter Nineteen

Olivia

My five days had stretched to eight, and I almost wanted to stay longer. The support groups had become a lifeline, and I'd learned more about myself in the past eight days than in the past eight years. For the first time this year, I felt better about facing life without wine as a crutch. I got out of bed, grabbed my towel, bodywash, and shampoo, and walked to the women's showers down the hall.

As water cascaded down my body, I thought about returning to the real world. Here, I'd been insulated. The freedom from my phone or laptop had provided a much-needed sabbatical. It disheartened me to realize Larissa might discover our relationship had been based on a subtle mining of intel, but Matty's well-being took priority. Rubbing my hair with a towel as I walked back to my bedroom, I reminded myself to remember my first priority: find a way to enjoy sobriety more than non-sobriety.

The cafeteria bustled with energy. I took my tray of food and sat beside Anita, one of the women in my group. She greeted me with a gentle hug.

I stared at the limp bacon and fruit past its prime.

"Pretty terrible, huh?" Anita said.

Laughing, I said, "I'm looking forward to real food. I should be in my own house for dinner tonight."

"How's that feel? The thought of going home?" She pushed her tray away, and looked at me.

"Good."

"I've been here three weeks. It almost feels like home."

"After what you've survived, I'd imagine so. When are you checking out?"

"Whenever Larissa decides I'm ready."

Her comment gave me pause. "I was told we can leave whenever we want."

She considered my words with a tight smile. "She's the lead facilitator here. As far as I know, she always makes the call."

After I swallowed what had to be the worst bacon on the planet, I asked if she was sure about that.

"Has she brought you your release documents?"

"When I signed in, I suggested a time frame. They agreed."

Instead of answering, she focused on her food tray.

My heart skipped a beat. "They don't keep us here against our will, it's one of their foundational principles."

"Ask her for your release papers. See what she says." Anita picked up her tray, and left.

A sense of doom inched its way into my brain. Larissa had been so sweet and understanding…she wouldn't keep me here against my will. Would she? I thought about our conversations. How kind she'd been. Sensing a presence behind me, I looked over my shoulder.

"Good morning. Are you enjoying breakfast?" The scent of Larissa's light, floral perfume reached my nose.

Did she have the room bugged?

"I wouldn't use the word 'enjoyed.' Are you leading the group, today?"

She smiled. "I thought we'd walk together."

I dropped off my tray and followed her, feeling our fragile bond beginning to fray.

"Have you benefited from your time here?" Walking slowly, hands clasped behind her back, she glanced at me.

This didn't sound like a question someone would ask if they were trying to force me to stay. Maybe Anita had been wrong. Why should I even worry about someone trying to keep me here? I'd just leave, period. Hunter would show up, I'd get in his car, and go. The halcyon thoughts of staying longer had slipped away. After what Anita told me, I wanted to get the heck out of here. I glanced at the light pink lipstick, the claw clip holding her blond hair. The mid-calf skirt swishing as she walked.

A few women with vacant eyes and slumped shoulders passed, not even registering our presence. A man sat in a chair in the hall, murmuring nonsensical phrases over and over. Anita's remark had set me on edge, and I questioned the legitimacy of whatever meds the staff doled out on a daily basis. The patients lined up like sheep to receive them, right after breakfast. Larissa had assigned me the same protocol, but I'd not taken anything other than the first or second round to get me through detox. After that, I pocketed the pills and flushed them down the toilet. I refocused on Larissa's question.

"Your support groups have been the best part of my experience, and helped me process my choices. I feel I've made progress." I laughed. "I *hope* I've made progress."

She smiled. "You have, and support will be important. Learning what works for us is a lifelong journey, don't you think?"

"I do, now."

We were the first to arrive. I picked up a program from the stack beside the door before we sat on the metal chairs.

"It's wonderful to hear that you feel validated and heard," she said, folding her hands in her lap and adjusting her skirt. "Now, it's time for the next step."

My forehead creased. "What next step?"

"Commitment to the truth." She glanced at her watch. Her eyes grew steely. "You have five minutes to tell me the real reason you're here."

My mouth dropped open. "What?"

"You've been refusing the medication. Sneaking around and listening at doors. Watching my interactions. Am I under investigation?"

The knot in my stomach loosened. She thinks she might be in trouble because of her lack of credentials. I shook my head. "I'm here because my fiancée thinks I have a drinking problem."

"I'm listening."

"As to all those meds." My mind raced to find some kind of rationale she'd believe. "I'm sensitive to certain medications, and I didn't want to take the chance."

A scowl contorted her pretty face. "You left this information off the forms."

"What is up with all those meds, Larissa? It seems like a lot to give people."

She let her shoulders relax. "I agree. I've had several talks with the Board, who think it's necessary to keep patients calm. However, on the bright side, we do have a benefactor in that regard."

A big, fat "ping" sounded in my head. "Benefactor?"

She smiled. "The mayor. I know Dink's a lot to handle, but he funnels thousands and thousands of dollars to our little community. He's even funding a nonprofit start-up for those who can't afford the medications they need. If we get people on the right medications, it won't be necessary to sedate our patients as often."

My PI radar started quivering. I had a hard time keeping still. "Necessary" to sedate them? What? "Who's on the Board, here, Larissa?"

"No one you'd recognize." She started rattling off names, and when she got to Collins Browning, my heart thrashed like a wild animal in a cage. I prayed a pink flush wouldn't climb my neck...the curse of being a redhead.

"That's a healthy amount of board members." *Keep her talking. Have no reaction to the mention of Collins. None.*

Two women walked in and sat across from us.

Larissa patted my arm. "We'll talk later," she whispered.

"One more thing," I insisted, tingling with anticipation. I was *so close* to something big. "What else does the Board do? They sound like generous people."

She clapped her hands in that way she had, like a happy child. "It's amazing to me, too. They also find our graduates employment options."

"What kind?" I glanced at the additional women filing inside.

Larissa busied herself pulling notes together. "You'd have to ask the mayor, but Collins Browning is his placement coordinator."

After a shocked few seconds to digest the implications, I tried to peel the onion further. "Do you think he'd have a job for me?"

"Why?" She placed reading glasses on her nose and looked at me above the rims. "You already have one. You own a private investigation firm."

She couldn't have surprised me more if she tried. I didn't know what to say.

Lifting a shoulder, she smiled. "We realize people lie on the forms, thinking it'll help protect privacy. We always perform routine background checks. All of you have your reasons. We aren't here to judge."

"Welcome, everyone," she began, officially starting the group.

I fanned myself with my program.

Later, as the meeting concluded, Larissa stayed behind to chat with some of the patients. She'd left her phone in her chair. I grabbed it before it timed out and dashed into the hallway for a quick conversation.

"Hey! Are you coming back today?" Sherry's bubbly voice sparkled through the airwaves like actual bubbles.

"Maybe. Listen. Collins is on the Board here. He gets people *jobs.*"

After two blips of stunned silence, she asked, "What kind of jobs?"

"I'm not sure. Either way, I think the weird mayor and Collins and the mysterious 'doctor' I keep hearing about are using the rehab as a front for that escort service Collins mentioned. If he's pulling people out of rehab when they're fresh and vulnerable, with few options to make money, they're the perfect candidates for some sleazebag to come along and suggest an opportunity."

I waited for her response, but none came. The disclosure must've shocked her into silence.

"Now, I need to prove it," I continued.

"No, you don't!" Her voice wobbled with alarm. "You need to get back here before you get 'disappeared' as they say in bad gangster movies."

She had a point. "I've got to get this phone back. Tell Hunter, okay? And to come break me out of here."

"Why? Are they trying to keep you?"

"Not sure yet, but it's in the air." I powered off, slid back into the meeting room, and returned the phone to her chair, my eyes darting. I had to get out of here. My pulse racing, I ran down the hall, skidded around the corner into my room, slamming the door behind me. I could sure use a phone, I thought, dropping onto the bed, out of breath. And, sorry to say, a nice glass of wine sounded good, too. I reminded myself to focus on why I was here.

Chapter Twenty

Hunter

"Wait. Slow down." Hunter told Sherry, glancing at his admin, who held documents which needed signing. "Give me a minute, Becker." The young man left. He put the phone back up to his ear.

"All right, Sherry. Go."

"You've got to go get her! She thinks there some kind of sex ring happening. Her counselor told her Collins Browning and Alex Barnes are on the board of directors, the crazy mayor is a rich benefactor, and they dispense meds like candy. She thinks they're trying to stall her release, too."

Asking Olivia to check on Matty while in rehab had been a bad idea. A *terrible* idea. She couldn't help herself; she kept digging. He hadn't meant to put pressure on her at all. He'd just needed a little direction, and now he had it.

Hunter ran his fingers along his chin. "I always wondered about Dink …but I had no idea about Collins's involvement, or Barnes Imports."

She groaned. "And, to complicate things, Collins is a long-time friend of mine, remember? I can't believe it, but three Maseratis in five years? Where did he get the cash? It fits, though. Kickbacks from an escort business could buy him *thirty* Maseratis."

"Any interesting chatter from the account Jason set up?"

"I'll check on it and circle back. Please. Get Olivia out of there."

They ended the call. Detective Becker walked in and got his documents signed, then left. Hunter tented his fingertips and thought about what he'd learned. Becker knocked on the door three minutes later.

"Lieutenant Nicholson to see you."

Nicholson strode into the office and dropped into one of Hunter's guest chairs. "How's your day going, Sergeant?"

Hunter's lips tightened. An unannounced visit meant he had to put out a fire, somewhere. "Good."

"I got a call. An FBI Task Force has been put together on a sex trafficking and drug ring up and down the East Coast. Detective Shiloh McPherson is on the task force and requested you. Since you know how McPherson works..." Lt. Nicholson smirked before he continued. "Rather intimately, I might add...and have ties to Baltimore PD because of the Callahan assault case a few years ago, they feel you're a good fit." He stared at the wall, tapped his fingers on the armrest. "Do you have any problems working with her? Things good between you two?"

"Absolutely. It's not an issue."

The lieutenant gazed at him a few seconds, then gave a curt nod. "They suspect an exotics car dealer located in downtown Baltimore is using their transport vehicles for trafficking, and the two principals running the operation are on the Board of Directors of some kind of rehab. Ever heard of Locust Grove, Virginia?"

Hunter struggled to keep a straight face. Had he heard of it? It's all he'd been thinking about. "I have."

"Detective McPherson's benched, as you know, due to her injuries after bringing down 'Stick,' but he wasn't the only mob boss in this organization. McPherson's been gathering digital evidence, and we need to know what's going on in Woodlawn. McPherson's run across incriminating coded conversations online that track back to Woodlawn's board members and the only exotic car dealership we could find in Baltimore. It's down in the Inner Harbor area."

Hunter nodded, stunned. How could his lieutenant have known he'd recently stumbled across Shiloh by accident on those dating websites? *Did* he know? Was this some kind of test? *Stay neutral. You don't know where this is going.*

Shaking his head, he continued. "Million-dollar, money-suckers. Never saw the point. A car's a car." He grunted. "We have a source who tells us the mayor of Locust Grove and as-yet-undetermined staff on his payroll might be involved. Locust Grove is a speck on the map. If you blink, you'll miss it."

His mind raced. Should he tell the lieutenant he had his own set of eyes down there, right this second? Would it do any good to tell his boss he'd randomly rescued Matty, inadvertently placed his fiancée in danger, and planned to get her out of there...*tonight?* He tapped his fingers on his desk. Nope.

"Whatever you need, Lieutenant," he said, his voice solemn. "I'll appoint an interim to bridge the gap in the meantime."

The older man lifted his towering frame out of the chair. "Good. Call Baltimore PD for specifics on their end. Get to Locust Grove as soon as you can, blend in, and check things out. The FBI has presented a warrant affidavit to the magistrates. Shouldn't be a problem, and it's high priority. They should have it soon."

"This thing must be huge," Hunter muttered to himself as he drove home to throw some clothes together. Trying to keep from exceeding the speed limit, he called Sherry at Watchdog Investigations to let her know what was going on. His mind raced. What had he done? A simple snoop assignment to see if Matty needed more intervention had turned into an all-out FBI task force investigation. He needed to get Olivia out of there.

An hour later, he strode inside the lobby of Woodlawn Acres in Locust Grove. "I'm here to pick up Olivia Callahan."

"Let me check," she murmured, her fingers racing across her keyboard. "Hm. I found the ROI form, but not her release from Larissa. Wait a sec." She got up and walked down the hallway. He peeked around the corner. Larissa and the receptionist stood together, their mouths working overtime, obviously not happy. He returned to his chair. Larissa walked into the reception area, folded her arms. "She has to complete some exit testing and fill out a survey before we can release her."

"I'll wait here." He crossed his legs at the ankles and settled in for a comfortable surveillance opportunity. The unexpected setup pleased him. He'd stay here all day if necessary, and perhaps, as a bonus, Matty and her asshole husband would cross his path. Sliding down in his chair and staring at the ceiling, he tried to make sense of the inner workings of this place. Larissa's position of influence had become a slippery slope. He couldn't find any information on her in their databases, and no qualifications. She was a ghost. The situation with Dink made no sense. A rehab center wouldn't have the tools to counsel a struggling marriage plagued by a dementia diagnosis. Maybe Olivia could fill in some of the blanks. Glancing at the corner security cam near the ceiling, he turned, subtly put his phone on video record, and put it into his shirt pocket.

A woman's voice interrupted the trickle of canned music dribbling through the speakers. "All female patients scheduled for release, please go to the cafeteria. Repeat. All female patients expecting release this week gather in the cafeteria."

His eyebrows rose so high he thought they might fly off his forehead. He cursed under his breath. What did *that* mean? The receptionist's eyes were glued to her cell phone. His gaze darted toward the cafeteria, then back to the receptionist. Rising from his chair, he slipped away.

He stole into the cafeteria, grabbed a few handy brochures, and sat in a chair at one of the tables as an interested potential client, gambling on the fact that most people here had no idea he was a cop. Pretending to study the content of the brochures, he watched women enter the large cafeteria and take seats at the circular tables scattered around the room. He counted thirty-two women. The mood was electric. Excited. Larissa walked in and started passing out brochures, pens, and notepads. "Remember, the positions fill up quick. No guarantees. But Mr. Browning will do his best to place you. If not this round, maybe the next." She wove her way through the tight spaces between each table. A few minutes passed before Olivia arrived. She looked good, he thought. Better than eight days ago. She'd recovered the bounce in her step, but the narrowed eyes and wrinkled brow revealed some important facts. One, she was stone-cold sober. Two, she'd burrowed deep into her PI-head, and this might be the first she'd known about this "cattle call" situation. When her eyes landed on him, he gave her a warning look. *Don't act like you know me!*

After a minuscule nod, she took a seat on the fringe. She folded her arms, winked, and settled in for the show.

Hunter hoped the receptionist didn't crash the party, screaming her head off because he'd wandered away.

Deliberate, measured steps strode down the hall. Collins Browning entered. He paused just inside the door, holding a leather binder above his head with one hand, like a trophy. "Welcome, everyone. Are you ready for this?" he shouted. Cheers erupted. Shrieks of "Choose me!" bounced off the ceiling. Strolling into the room to enthusiastic applause, he continued his spiel. "Who needs a paycheck?' He wiggled his eyebrows. "I've got very good news for some of you."

Hunter glanced at Olivia, who rolled her eyes.

What happened next struck Hunter as multiple rounds of speed dating. He couldn't quite hear what Collins discussed with the people at each table over the buzz of conversation, but when the older women started leaving, he felt sick. The culling of the herd had begun. To what end? He needed to get this intel to Shiloh forthwith.

Soon, tinkling bells sounded, as if the chosen ones had been sprinkled with fairy dust. His brow clamped down in confusion. He tried to identify the prize at the end of the rainbow. A job? A test? A graduation certificate? This racket had to end with some sort of big bang for all this commotion. One of the women shrieked with joy. "I've been selected! Thank you, thank you!" Hunter squirmed. He glanced at Olivia. Her cheeks flamed red with anger and frustration. The fairy-dust tinkling sounded over and over. One by one, the older women returned to their rooms, and the younger, cute ones got the tinkle. Larissa cooed over each "winner" and congratulated them with release documents. The others got a sympathetic pat on the shoulders and consoling words.

Had they been *competing* for the privilege of *release?* He watched Olivia drop her head in her hands. He needed to get her out of here. He cocked his head toward the door when she looked at him. She nodded.

Larissa pivoted and walked over to Olivia. They chatted. Larissa pointed at Collins, who caught her eye and smiled. "Be right there," he called.

Hunter frowned. What had they been talking about?

The receptionist burst into the room, located him, and trotted to his chair. "You can't be in here!" she stage-whispered. "I need you to return to the lobby."

Two super-sized, muscle-bound thugs approached.

Wincing at their firm grip on his biceps, he allowed himself to be taken out of the room. He glanced over his shoulder. *Olivia didn't get a tinkle sprinkle. What is going on, here?* He watched Collins take a seat at her table.

The men deposited him in the lobby. The receptionist re-seated herself at the desk and glared. "Those meetings are by invitation only, and Olivia isn't scheduled for release yet, so I suggest you call Larissa for an update. It would be best if you leave, now." The men had camped out by the entrance, their gazes lingering, cold and unblinking. With a sigh, he decided to comply. The timing didn't fit yet. Matty and Dink pulled into the parking lot. Matty smiled and pounded on the window.

Hunter chuckled. He could only imagine what Dink was thinking. She hopped out and ran toward him, but Dink tugged her back, pointed to the entrance, and shot an icy stare in his direction. He leaned against his Jeep, thinking if looks could kill, someone should be digging his grave about now. As they walked up the steps, he called out. "Another couples therapy session, Mr. Mayor?"

Dink ignored him. Matty gave him a sorrowful look as her husband urged her inside.

He hoped a federal search warrant would be executed shortly, but first, he needed to alert the task force of his findings and talk about next steps, carefully deleting his plan to break into Woodlawn tonight and get Olivia out of there before anyone realized the whole place might go up in flames when the Feds served the warrant.

Chapter Twenty-One

Olivia

Collins Browning barreled toward me. I couldn't tear my eyes away from the doorway which, courtesy of two thugs, had swallowed Hunter whole. My pulse pounded in my ears. Had Collins recognized Hunter from the office? More importantly, what if he realized Hunter was a cop? I tried to remember. When he'd shown up unannounced a week ago, we'd hustled Collins right into my office. He and Hunter had barely spoken. *Thank goodness.* I straightened my shoulders and watched Collins's jaw flex and his hands fist by his sides as he walked. Moisture sprouted on my forehead. What had I gotten myself into?

I don't think Larissa looked in Hunter's direction at all. He'd hidden himself at a table well away from the rest of the group. I let out a small exhale of relief. Maybe I hadn't been compromised, after all. Taking a deep breath, I shook off some of my tension. Hunter knew enough about the weirdness here that he would stay close. I trusted him. He'd insert himself when necessary.

Collins was five paces away from my table, now.

He shot me a questioning look before pulling out a chair. Searching my face, he said, "I didn't realize you were investigating Woodlawn Acres. How can I help?"

He thinks I'm on the job. Good. When I tell him the real reason, he won't suspect I'm trying to figure out what's going on here, and as a bonus, he'll be relieved I'm not investigating Woodlawn. Struggling to keep my composure, I lowered my eyes. "I checked myself in. I… uh…developed a drinking problem."

After a few beats of surprised silence, he apologized. "I had no idea."

I smiled. "People with addictions are good at keeping secrets." By now, I knew the script, the demeanor, the ubiquitous path to "denial" which each group facilitator impressed upon us. Yes, I had a problem. Yes, the support group had taught me a lot. And, yes, I'd scale back the wine if not stop altogether. But I still didn't believe I had the genetic predisposition for a full-blown addiction. I'd developed a dependency, and there was a difference. I could play the part of full-blown addict, though, and if it helped me dig intel out of Collins, I'd become whatever it took.

"You're the last person I'd expect to see in rehab," I told him. "Are you operating some kind of halfway house?" I asked, rounding my eyes like an innocent wood nymph.

"It's a way to give back." A wariness lay behind his smile.

"What do they win? It's a competition, right?"

He squinted. "Do you realize Alex Barnes and I do business together?"

I acted surprised. "I knew you bought cars from his import dealership, but didn't know you two *worked* together. He's hired us, you know."

"I just found out," he said, stroking his chin and watching me under hooded eyes.

You suspect nothing. Give nothing away by a tone, or an expression. Stay in the zone. Light. Humble. "We love Alex." I laughed. "He might even sell me a car."

When he brightened, I patted myself on the back. I'd assuaged any fears he had about my firm's business becoming intertwined with whatever nefarious plot they had going on. I kept going.

"So. Do you guys team up on these opportunities for Woodlawn's graduates?"

"We do," he said, distracted. "Alex and I funnel quite a bit of money to…" He bit his lip, watching Larissa glance at us. "I think I need to get back to it."

"It's wonderful what you're doing," I cooed. "Please keep my, uh…stay here, between us."

He gave me a curt nod. "Of course. Nice chatting with you. I wish you all the best with your recovery."

When he returned, Larissa gave me a troubled glance, then seated herself. I counted five people waiting for Collins to continue doling out his fairy sprinkles. One woman sat apart and alone at a table. She couldn't keep still, bit her fingernails, and played with her hair. I guesstimated her age between thirty and forty-five. The yellowish tinge to her complexion told me her liver might be giving out. I couldn't believe she'd been invited to Collins's little party. She didn't look in the least ready or able to leave the facility.

As quiet, one-on-one conversations resumed, I slid past two tables undetected, and sat at hers. She almost jumped out of her skin.

I chuckled. "Sorry. Didn't mean to scare you."

This close, her appearance concerned me even more. "Are you okay?"

She shrugged.

I stuck out my hand. "I'm Olivia."

She offered a tiny uplift of her mouth. "Elizabeth."

"Pretty exciting, huh?"

"I guess."

"How often does this guy do a "job fair"?

"Once a month," she said. "I'm not sure what kinds of jobs, though."

A jolt of adrenaline shot through me. "What do you mean?"

"A friend of mine accepted one of Mr. Browning's opportunities. She didn't mind moving, she said, since the position included paid travel. I went to see her off." Staring at the top of the table, she continued. "The van had people wedged in there so tight, I don't know how they could breathe. But she didn't care; she was happy about a fresh start." Elizabeth lifted her gaze to mine, her lower lip trembling. "I haven't heard from her since. I've tried and tried to call, and her phone is dead. No one can tell me where she is."

I had trouble keeping calm. The table occupants had thinned to three, now. All young, attractive, and—from what Elizabeth just told me—in for a big shock. My heart ached for them. "I don't think you should accept an offer."

She focused her quivery lips and watery eyes on me. "I don't have any other prospects. I have a daughter to support and—"

"Elizabeth." My firm voice shook her. "Do *not* accept an opportunity. Hear me? Don't. After we're out of here, I'll help you. When are you being released?"

"Depends on if I accept an offer."

I shoved my weight against the back of my chair, so angry I wanted to hit someone. Did an inpatient's release depend on accepting one of Collins's mysterious jobs? And if so, how could Larissa think his offers of employment were valid? I wondered if Alex and Collins had blackmailed her, or lied to her about her role. I fished my notebook out of a pocket and scribbled my number on a piece of paper. "Here. Do not accept. You hear me? I'm serious."

She took the slip of paper. Her shoulders relaxed. Already, she seemed more peaceful. "Thank you. I was sitting here praying about what to do. And God sent you."

I swiped a sudden tear off my cheek. "Call me when you feel strong enough to leave."

"It sounds like you're getting ready to get out of here. How are you leaving if you aren't taking one of these jobs?"

"I have a job already. I'm trying to figure out what's going on with Collins and his little circus," I whispered.

Footsteps approached our table. Hard fingers gripped my shoulder, and I looked up into the angry face of the jerk who had facilitated our support group the night Larissa couldn't be there. Leland.

"No talking. Mr. Browning is using this time to help our patients." He glared. "It would be better if you return to your room."

I adopted the expected "sheep" mentality. "I wanted to watch how these opportunities work. I'm getting released today, and..."

He got down in my face. His breath smelled of nicotine. "You are *not* getting released today. Or tomorrow. Go back to your room."

Elizabeth gave me an apologetic glance. "Nice talking to you."

"Same," I said, thinking what a fantastic day it would be when Hunter and I got to wipe the floor with this asshole. They couldn't hold me unless they used force. I'd signed a document which stated, "Full payment is owed in the event client leaves before agreed duration." Which meant there *was* an agreed duration. If they tried to hang onto me, I'd sue so fast their bank accounts wouldn't know what happened.

As I walked back to my room, I didn't worry about my own safety so much, because I knew Hunter would come for me. My concern focused on Matty and Elizabeth. Delia, too. However, I needed to focus on the priority—sobriety—but all I wanted to do was find the source of the rot infecting this place. I sank onto the bed and groaned. My roommate walked in.

"What's wrong, Chestnut? Delia gave everyone nicknames. She'd started calling me chestnut because of the color of my hair.

I pulled a second pillow into place, put my hands behind my head, and considered the question. "Do you know about Mr. Browning and his 'opportunity' speeches?"

"Phhht," she said, flapping her hand. "Those things are bogus." She frowned. "Why? Are you considering?"

"No, I have a job when I leave. What is he offering?"

"These people have no idea…good God…I lived on the street six years, and I've known guys like Collins Browning all my life. Scammers. Pimps. Always with their hands out to give you something, but at a price."

"What's the price?"

She sat on her bed and gave me a knowing look. "What do you think, Chestnut?"

My heart dropped. I so hoped we were wrong about this, but Shiloh's investigation couldn't be ignored. "You tell me."

"Since I've been here, he collects more women than men, so I came to the conclusion he's farming them out to pimps or traffickers. It's an old story." She straightened her nose ring, leaned back on her arms. "You going to group tonight?"

"I'm supposed to get released today."

She grinned. "Yeah, right. You're exactly what those sickos want. Better lay low."

Fear crystallized in my chest. "I am not! I'm forty-six!"

"They don't care. Pretty is what counts. You don't look forty-six. I'd sleep somewhere else tonight."

"WHAT?"

"Take my bed. I'll switch with you. They're not into the tats and piercings and skinny girls, so they leave me alone. When they snatch girls, they have to be quick, they won't take the time to check the other bed. They'll think I'm a mistake."

My mind spun. Delia talked about this transaction as if sharing a recipe to make a cake. "But, why would everyone act so excited to be picked?"

"Some aren't so excited, but they have nowhere else to go."

I took a minute to examine her little truth-bomb. *These people prey on the vulnerable who have been so beaten down they don't fight back. Collins must be the front man for something far more sinister than we thought.* "Have you warned the others?"

"The ones who still have a chance, yeah. Some don't care. This is a privately funded facility, and many residents pay for their stay here, but twenty-five percent or so are funded by contributions. These residents see a hot meal and place to lay their head, and a job offer is a huge bonus. If Browning is offering what I think he is, it's a terrible life. Worse than the street, in my opinion."

I rose from the bed and walked to the desk between us. Grabbed my notebook and started writing.

"You're pretty serious about journaling, aren't you?" Delia said.

"It helps," I told her, masking my quest to write down every piece of intel so I wouldn't forget. This place would get torn apart in short order, and I wanted to preserve all the information I could while in residence. "This is your third time here, right?" I asked, adjusting the chair so I could look at her.

She nodded. "Larissa likes me, so I always have a bed, here."

"Have you noticed how often the mayor and his wife are here?"

She frowned. "Yeah. Makes me mad, how he treats her. Such a creep."

"I agree. What do you think is happening?"

Delia put her arms across her chest. "I try not to get involved. It's safer."

"I won't tell. Promise."

Two beats of silence.

She let out a breathy sigh. "Something's wrong."

"I've noticed it, too."

"He's using her. I've known enough abused women to recognize the signs. She's like a whipped dog most of the time." She chewed on her lower lip. "Sometimes not, though. She can be right on her game, too. Must be something wrong with her brain."

"How often do Matty and Dink come talk to Larissa?"

"Once a week, like clockwork." She glanced at the door. "Swear you won't say anything," she said.

"I won't. But, she's not any use to Browning's placements, right? What do you think is going on between this facility and her husband and the Board?"

"Drugs if you ask me. It's always drugs. It's like…a river of money. I really don't know anything about the Board, except they're a bunch of suits."

I thought about the patients, so over-medicated they couldn't even communicate. "Don't you think the guests here are getting too many medications?"

She smiled. "I can see you're new to this world. Most rehabs, in particular the ones with private funding, like to keep the general population soft and easy. I've learned how to fake it. But, sometimes, I don't mind the zoning out."

My mind ran to my first two days. I'd needed the help. "I don't do drugs, but whatever they gave me worked."

"Benzos. Your problem is booze, right?"

"Wine."

She grinned. "Lightweight."

"Hope so."

"What do you do when you're not in rehab?"

Should I be honest? What would be the harm? In Delia, I sensed an ally, and I knew she'd keep her mouth shut. "I'm a private investigator."

Her eyes lit with interest. "Where?"

CHAPTER TWENTY-ONE

I chuckled. "A town you've never heard of. Glyndon, Maryland."

"Who do you work for?"

"I own a small firm called Watchdog Investigations. Please don't share, okay? Private investigation isn't the most celebrated profession." I smiled.

"You got it, Chestnut. No problem."

We sat in comfortable silence. The door to our room opened after a quick knock. "You two coming to group?" Larissa asked.

Delia hopped from her bed, and left the room. I remained in my chair, head tilted, watching Larissa's mind tick through all the reasons I hadn't followed suit. "You're not coming?" she asked, her eyes blinking fast.

"I'm waiting on release papers and an exit interview."

She fanned herself with a file folder. Larissa always seemed to carry a folder. "I guess it is day eight, isn't it?"

I waited.

She cleared her throat. "Mr. Browning has concerns."

My forehead creased. "Why would Collins Browning's concerns have anything to do with my release?"

"He's…I'm…" She swallowed, hard. "This facility is in great debt to Mr. Browning, and he *is* on the Board. He feels you might not be ready."

My temper roared to life. "Excuse me, but he's not a licensed counselor, or a doctor, is he? Why would he have *any input into this at all?*"

With an apology in her eyes, she pressed the ever-present panic button she wore on a chain around her neck. Within seconds, steps pounded down the corridor.

My mouth dropped open. "You *cannot* keep me here!" I ducked under the bed to grab my duffle, but it had been removed. "Where are my things?" I screeched.

"We filed a Petition with the Court." Larissa backed out of the bedroom into the hall. "We were granted a hold." The same army-green-uniformed employees who had removed Hunter stormed into the room, one with a syringe. I formed my hands into fists and pounded their chests and struggled against their grip, but they were too much for me. I fell onto my bed and kicked with all my might, trying to land a shoe right in the crotch. They restrained me easily, one guy at my head and the other holding onto my bicycling legs. The one at my head plunged the syringe into my neck. I searched frantically for my friend. My counselor. My confidant. "Larissa!" I screamed. My vision blurred around the edges. "Don't do this—" I began, and the last thing I would remember were strong arms holding me still as a drug-induced, foggy nothingness claimed me.

Chapter Twenty-Two

Hunter

Twilight crept into the dingy room he'd found on the outskirts of Locust Grove. He sat in the chair, listening to the low hum of the TV he'd turned on for background noise. What would be the best move? Collins approaching Olivia's table at the job fair rankled him. What had they discussed? He'd communicated status to everyone but Sherry. He reached for his cell to try calling again.

"Hey," she answered on the first ring. "What's up?"

He filled her in on Collins's strange placement meetings.

"This sounds creepy. Olivia's out now, right? At least she's safe."

After a brief hesitation, he responded. "She's not out yet. I'm headed back later tonight."

"Oh, no."

"I'll get her. I have a plan."

"What if their plan doesn't coincide with yours?"

"It's not complicated. I'm going to break in."

"They'll have alarms."

"I know. I've got it, Sherry."

She sighed. "Do you need me or Jason? You remember I know how to pick locks, right? We can be there in an hour."

"The fewer people involved, the better. I want to get in and get out."

He stared at the threadbare carpet in the grungy hotel bedroom and tried not to think about whether the sheets had been sanitized. "I never should have suggested she enter a program, there." Hunter ran one of his hands through his hair. "I guess I should've thought it through. But I don't think she would've checked herself in if Matty hadn't needed a savior."

"Do you think eight days helped?"

"I do. She's probably gotten more involved in tracking down intel than I'd hoped, but she's attended the groups and done the work. She'll need support, but I'm sure she understands that."

"I hope you're right. Are you sure you don't need us?"

"I can't wait on you two to get here. I need to get her out of there tonight."

"Great. Now we might have *two* of you stuck in the stupid rehab, or whatever it is—clearing house for young and nubile escorts." She let out a long sigh. "I won't be able to sleep until I know you guys are out of there."

"I'm the one with a badge and gun. It'll be fine. How's everything on your end?"

"Good. I guess the most recent news is Jason's surveillance of Graham."

His forehead furrowed. "I still have trouble believing Graham hitched his star to Monty, even if they've been friends for years. How long does it take someone to realize a relationship with a psychopath cannot end well?"

"We don't know yet if Graham is doing anything other than trying to retain a relationship with his daughter. For Callie's sake, I'm hoping he's changed."

Hunter didn't believe Graham had changed for one second, but she hadn't asked for his opinion, so he kept his mouth shut. "I'll give Olivia your regards and tell her the firm is running like clockwork."

"Please get her out of there. *Tonight.*"

* * *

He rolled quietly into Locust Grove, passing two-story, brick buildings, small town storefronts, a library, a post office. A 7-Eleven gas station and convenience store. 7-Eleven seemed like the only business open in Locust Grove at two a.m. in the morning. A few minutes later, Hunter doused his lights and parked in a vacant lot next to Woodlawn Acres. The hoots of owls and nocturnal chorus of crickets and katydids faded to a whisper. His plan was a big risk. The right thing to do would be to report the facility and let the police handle getting Olivia out of there, but he didn't trust the local cops, and suspected all of them were in Dink's back pocket. Olivia would be targeted, and these small-town knuckleheads would find a way to ban him from the facility. He had no choice but to break in and get her.

He squinted, ran his hands across the steering wheel, retracing the plan in his head. Night shift security teams weren't typically the jacked thugs he'd experienced earlier in the day. He hoped for a few lucky breaks in his mission tonight...no tasers, no bullets, and a way to find Olivia's room. With a deep exhale, he exited the Jeep, his eyes scanning for cameras. He pulled on nitrile gloves, covered the hundred feet to the Woodlawn building, searching for electrical wires powering the alarm system. A small utility room had been left unlocked. Stealing inside, he located the main electrical panel, and shut off the master switch. A heartbeat later, darkness blanketed the building. He heard shouting, footsteps pounding the floor. Babbling voices. Mass confusion had hit. Exactly what he intended.

He got busy with a packet of small tools. When he heard the pins click into place in the housing of the lock, he opened the door. "Haven't lost your touch," he whispered into the cool, night air. He could tie a mean clove hitch, too. A man of many talents. Once inside, he paused to listen. The hysteria had cooled, and he had mere minutes to locate Olivia and get her out of there.

His flashlight beam illuminated piles of laundry and commercial-sized washers and dryers. Leaving the laundry room, he stole through the corridors with the aid of the cop-issue flashlight held low against his hip. As he walked, he wondered how deep the corruption went in this place. Who started this dumpster fire, anyway? He hadn't suspected a thing, and wondered if it had been no accident he'd been tapped for the task force. The Feds had already been surveilling, and probably saw him arrive with Matty, and perhaps his interactions with Dink. He'd dropped off Olivia, so they (hopefully) would understand his frantic need to get her out of here. They wouldn't want to jeopardize the bigger picture, though, so if they knew of his presence at this moment, they'd lie low. Maybe.

He cursed.

He couldn't think about that right now.

Hunter frowned as he walked along the dark hallway. Dink dragging his poor wife in here every week made no sense at all. And why the opposition to long-term care for her?

The sound of heavy footsteps and irritated voices reached his ears. He looked around for a handy place to hide. His gaze fell on the door handle of a closet.

Locked. Glancing over his shoulder, he used the tiny tools on the less challenging lock, squatting behind shelving, listening to the footsteps and voices of two men pass the door and continue down the hall. Rising from his hiding place, he blinked at the size of this enormous closet.

Various sizes of refrigerators, many with glass doors. The refrigerators held small glass bottles of product. He scratched his head in confusion. What was this? Fragile compounds in a lab or pharmacy-grade unit often needed refrigerating, but this wasn't a lab; it was a huge storage closet. The bottles had no name, just batch numbers. Beside the door, a "Primary Treatment Coordinator" log reflected various check-in times and quantities. Scrawled notes. A column entitled "Side Effects." Bins filled with syringes, nitrile gloves, and containers of pills, and various medical supplies sat upon miles of shelving, but refrigerators dominated the space. He took photos of everything.

His gut gurgled at him in premonition. He doused the flashlight.

The door opened.

A beam of light strafed the room. He dropped to the floor.

The sounds of male voices and slight burble of a TV in another room reached him. Lighting flared outside in the corridor. The master switch had been flipped on. He slid across the floor on his stomach until he lay underneath the shelves. A flashlight beam slanted across the ceiling, through the shelves of product bins, and across the floor. "The batch room is fine," a male told his counterpart before he closed the door. Steps receded down the hallway. "Someone forgot to lock the door again." They walked away.

Hunter stared at his watch. Two-twenty a.m. He needed to find Olivia's room. He let fifteen more minutes pass before he left the closet. LED sensor lights flipped at ankle-level as he walked. Laughter and light-hearted conversation resumed. High-fives all around as they congratulated each other. Random blackout—solved. When he crept past the door to the rec room, he counted five people sitting in chairs, focusing on a large flatscreen. He smelled popcorn. *Probably the whole night crew, right there in one place. I've got time.* He lengthened his steps, silently thanking the facility for labeling each door with occupant names and diagram of who slept where. Olivia Callahan and Delia Griggs. Quick as a wink, he stole inside. No locks on these doors.

The room had one window. A shaft of moonlight fell across the floor between twin beds. According to the diagram, Olivia's bed sat against the wall closest to the door, and Delia's on the wall, underneath the window. He nudged her leg. "Olivia. Wake up." Nothing. He moved to the head of the bed and patted her shoulder. "Wake up," he whispered. She yawned. Her eyes flew open. "What are you *doing?*" she asked, her voice low, like a growl.

He jumped back. *Not* Olivia.

She reached underneath her pillow and pulled out a knife. Fisted it and jabbed at him with a nasty-looking blade. "Move away."

Across the room, a soft cry. "Hunter! Is that you?"

He held both arms straight out in front of his chest and backed away from the bed. "Put the knife down." The last thing he'd expected was getting shanked in a rehab.

"You know this guy?" Delia asked.

"It's safe. He's a cop," Olivia whispered.

She stuck the knife back under her pillow and laughed. "Since when do we trust cops?"

"You can trust this one." Olivia slid her feet into the waiting shoes she'd put beside the bed. "We need to find my duffel. They took it."

Delia plumped her pillow. "What do you want me to tell them?"

"You didn't hear anything. You woke up; I was gone."

She nodded.

"Are you sure you want to take the time to find the duffel?" Hunter whispered.

"It has my journal in it. So, yeah. It has my Woodlawn notes and stuff about Matty. I don't think it would end well if Larissa or one of the board members read my notes."

"Your bag and your phone are in the closet behind reception," Delia said, yawning.

Hunter considered a few seconds. "How often do they do rounds at night?"

Delia snorted. "The night crew spends their time watching TV, drinking booze, and cramming popcorn down their throats. They're useless, and they performed a bed check forty minutes ago. I think you're good."

With a sigh, Delia padded over to Olivia and threw her arms around her. "Best of luck, Chestnut."

"Come with us." Olivia searched her face.

She shook her head. "Girl. I got a bed and all the drugs I could possibly need. Three meals a day. I don't care what their side hustle is."

Olivia tucked herself underneath Hunter's arm. "If they're doin' what I think they're doin'...Hunter said. "They'll come for you, too."

"What do you think is going on?"

"Sex trafficking, for starters. And maybe medication or vaccine experiments," Hunter said. "Using clients as guinea pigs."

Delia laughed. "I'm not worried about vaccines. I've actually volunteered as a guinea pig myself, to make a little cash." She scratched her cheek. "Look. I don't have anywhere to go. I'll take my chances. I'm not a fan of the way people walk around all zombied out, but I'll be outta here in a week or two."

Hunter dug a card from his pocket. "Call us. Stay safe."

"You're the ones who need to stay safe." Delia returned to bed.

Hunter took Olivia's hand. "They're still watching TV. We have a window."

They crept into the hall. Sensors flared along the baseboards like accusing eyes. The sounds of laughter, ice cubes tinkling in glasses, and crunch of snacks floated through the corridor. The reception desk with its half-circle surround lay ten feet away, the storage closet behind it holding Olivia's phone and belongings probably locked.

"Drop!" Hunter hissed, as steps proceeded from the rec room. They made a mad dash for the desk, and dove to the floor. The steps jogged past, toward the patient rooms. Hunter yanked out his lock-pick set. "Here. Hold this." He put the flashlight in her hand. "Point it so I can see."

"Thanks for coming," she said.

"You *have* to marry me, now." He grinned. The lock popped open. "Turn off the flashlight. Want to bet the minute I open this door, an automatic light comes on?"

"It does. I remember."

Hunter closed his eyes. "Listen. Hear anything?"

"I don't," she whispered.

"Let's do it, then. When I open this door, follow me as quick as possible, okay?"

She nodded.

"One, two…" He turned the knob. "Three!"

They scuttled inside and closed the door.

He flung his arm across her chest as darkness fell. "Be still. Wait."

The sudden darkness after the flare of light rocked his sense of balance. Rainbows bent his vision. He blinked. "Can you see?"

"Yes." She peered underneath the door. "I don't see any lights or hear footsteps."

"Do you know where your stuff is?"

She groaned. "The phones are in baskets. I think they have the first letter of our last names on them. The duffels and suitcases are packed tight in here."

"Okay. He rose, patting the wall until he found the switch. "When I say go, get the phone first, then look around for the bag."

"Got it."

"Now!" The light blazed.

Olivia went straight to the baskets and found her phone in record time. The bags were another matter; every inch of shelving was stacked two to two-to-three bags high. Hunter doused the light.

"I didn't see it."

"Let me make sure we're clear, then I'll flip the switch again."

Minutes passed. The voices and tinkle of ice cubes had stalled. "Uh oh," Hunter said. "Too quiet."

The door flew open. The closet light snapped on. Hunter studied the slender, lightweight young man holding open the closet door. His assumption had been correct. *The wimpy guys work the night shift.* He stepped out, his hand flapping behind his back in mute hope Olivia would understand: stay down.

"Step out, please," Wimpy Guy said when he'd regained his composure. He took a deep, shuddering breath, then exhaled. "Do you need help returning to your room?"

Hunter tried to look sheepish and sincere, as if he were a patient there. Though the counselors and receptionist might remember his status as a cop...the night crew had no idea. When Wimpy Guy took his arm to return him to dreamland, he clocked him with a hard right to the jaw, followed by a left jab to the midsection. His mouth a small, shocked "o," he staggered back a few steps, but didn't go down. Huh, Hunter thought. Thin, but tough. Before Wimpy Guy could regroup, Hunter shot another right to his head. He crumpled to the ground like a sack of dry sticks, all bony arms and legs. He had too much booze in him to fight back, and was out cold, dead to the world. Hunter found a firearm on his belt, emptied the chamber, and placed it out of reach. He dragged Wimpy Guy toward the back of the closet and waited. The sound of chatter and clinking of ice in glasses had resumed. The TV noise, as well. They must've taken a potty break, visited the kitchen, and returned. Another boring night shift at Woodlawn. What a job. Watch TV and eat. Can't beat it anywhere.

When Olivia emerged, she held up her bag and his phone, stepping across the guard's inert form. "Look what I found! Ready?"

They ran.

Chapter Twenty-Three

Sherry

She picked up her phone for the third time in an hour. No texts, no calls. Jason hadn't checked in, either, and she wondered how his surveillance of Graham was going. Rubbing her eyes, she let out a long, tired sigh. "Maybe I'm not meant to do this for a living." Her cat, a one-eyed, three-legged rescue she'd gotten from the Humane Society, yawned and rolled over onto his back. Sherry smiled, reaching to the foot of her bed to pet his fluffy tummy. When her phone buzzed, adrenaline hit, hard. She almost dropped the phone. "Sherry."

Jason laughed. "Why have you been blowing up my phone? You knew I was on the job tonight. I didn't want to check in until I had something."

Lazarus watched her with his one good eye, a brilliant shade of blue. He stretched, and hopped across the bed to her lap. "Where are you? Can you talk?"

"I'm on the way home. It's four a.m. Should I have stayed longer?" He chuckled.

"You get an 'E' for effort. Find out anything?"

"He and a buddy bowled for three hours. I went inside, found a chair in a dark corner, and became invisible. They bowled and drank beer. He won. Typical guy stuff. I took photos."

"And after?"

Jason recited an address in Eldersburg.

She nodded. "Must be the place he's staying while he sorts out getting a job."

"I sat there from eleven until two a.m. and almost went home, but…"

Sherry rubbed her forehead. "But, what?"

"A car pulled into the driveway." He shrugged. "Some woman he knew. Still there when I left."

"Did you get decent photos of her?"

"I got side shots. Graham answered the door, and seemed happy to see her. They hugged and went inside. The light in the family room stayed on the whole time. Medium height, medium build. From the way she moved and dressed, I'd put her around forty. Ponytail."

Her heart sank. "Blonde?"

"Yeah. How'd you know?"

"Do you think it could've been Callie?"

A pause hovered. "But, why would it be Callie? She's the one who's having him followed."

"We can discuss tomorrow. I'm fine if you want to take extra time to get caught up on sleep." She clicked off.

What the heck was going on? She moved Lazarus off her lap, set her alarm, plumped her pillow, and crashed. She'd think about it tomorrow.

* * *

Her alarm buzzed. Sherry's eyes flew open. She looked at her alarm clock. Wait, she'd set her alarm for ten, and it was only nine. The *phone,* not her alarm. Rubbing her eyes, she grabbed it and tried to focus. "I waited all night for this call. Have you got her?"

"You're on speaker," he said.

"I'm here! He busted me out." Olivia laughed.

She closed her eyes, laying a hand over her heart. "You have no idea how happy I am right now."

"Makes three of us," Hunter said.

She got out of bed and padded down the hall to feed Lazarus. "So. What's next? Did you get any closer to finding out what's going on?" The cat watched as she opened the small can of Fancy Feast and emptied the contents into a bowl on the floor.

"Let's talk when I get to the office," Olivia said.

An hour later, Sherry walked inside, listening for suspicious sounds in the too-quiet office. Sounds of the fridge humming, wall clock ticking, and heat rushing through the vents. Nothing else. "You need to stop being paranoid." In spite of her bravado, she walked the length of the building, checking windows and doors. Satisfied, she returned to the lobby and switched on all the lamps before taking a seat at her desk and opening her laptop. The incident with Graham had spooked her. Now, she'd make sure all the windows and doors had been checked before leaving for the night.

Jason walked in. "Good morning." He walked to his desk and plopped into his chair, opening his laptop and scanning emails before grabbing coffee. "You're quiet," he called from the break room. "Do you want coffee?"

"I've had a ton already." She studied her monitor. "I see you've already turned in the report for last night's surveillance. Thanks."

He returned to the lobby with a steaming mug in his hand. He pursed his lips and blew on it. "I couldn't sleep, so I thought I might as well pack it into an email for you to open this morning. Any thoughts?"

"I'm looking at the photos." She leaned back in her chair, closed her eyes, and threw out her arms as if welcoming a firing squad. "Shoot me now. It *was Callie.* I thought this would be a simple assignment. What's going on with her?"

"Don't ask me," he quipped. "I've never been able to figure out women."

"It's whiteboard time." She hopped from her chair and strode toward Olivia's office, looking at him over her shoulder. "You coming?"

Jason blinked. "Oh. Sure."

Rolling the stand holding a four-by-three whiteboard over to the area rug, she gave Jason a dry-erase marker. Olivia would be here any minute to talk about Woodlawn, so this needed to be quick.

She scrawled "Callie's Case" across the top and scrawled bullet points, leaving space for Jason to add his hypotheticals. When the assignment parameters and results of last night's surveillance had been written on the board, along with annotation of Graham's file theft, they looked at each other in confusion. "It doesn't make sense," Jason said.

Capping her marker, Sherry tapped it against her chin. "If I squint hard enough, sometimes I can almost see lines connecting the dots." After a few seconds of squinting, she grunted. "Not happening. We need Olivia."

"Here I am!" Olivia sang, waltzing into her office. Marlowe trotted in after her, shoved his snout into his bed, flattening it out as he liked it, then dropped.

Sherry walked over and hugged the dog. "I was nervous without Marlowe this morning."

Olivia laughed. "He *is* a true watchdog, isn't he?"

"Here," she said. "You can sit here."

Jason rose. "She can have my chair."

Olivia shot them a confused glance. "You guys! Don't treat me like I might break or something. Show me what you're working on."

"You sound good. You *look* good." Sherry smiled.

"Thanks. I haven't had a drink in nine whole days." Her eyes twinkled. "And counting. I feel great."

"Where's Hunter?"

"I left him at my house. Told him to get some more sleep."

The front door opened. "Anybody home?" Hunter's voice boomed.

Olivia rolled her eyes. "Do men *ever* listen to women? Just wondering."

He walked straight to Oliva, put his arms around her, and kissed her. "Good morning."

Blushing, she extricated herself. "Thank you *so much* for the inappropriate PDA," she said, with an embarrassed glance at Jason and Sherry.

He dropped into one of the armchairs. "It's appropriate behavior after a man saves his damsel in distress. Right, Jason?"

"Absolutely." He laughed. "Good job, bro."

Olivia patted his arm. "Yeah. Good job. Can we get down to business, please? We have news. Hunter has been *assigned* to check out Woodlawn now, and he needs to get back to the investigation after we process, here."

She took a minute to digest the whiteboard's information. Her eyes widened. "Callie visited Graham?"

Jason nodded. "I imagine she did more than that."

The slow crawl of heat climbed her neck and stamped her cheeks. "What is wrong with her? I've told her a million times to stay away from him. We can't trust *Graham.*"

Sherry fidgeted with her marker, staring at the floor. "I have a confession to make."

Olivia waited, quiet. Hunter looked uncomfortable. "Do I need to leave?"

"No, stay. It's okay. I found him in the back bedroom after you went into rehab, bleeding from a head wound. He hit his head on the window frame." She offered a thin smile. "He said he wanted to find the case notes because of a custody battle." She waved her arm at the points on the whiteboard. "We're trying to make sense of what's going on."

Olivia frowned. "Who did Callie hire? Wasn't she going to get someone else? Did you get the cops out here and write him up?"

Sherry reddened. "No. I left it up to Callie. And…" She cleared her throat. "Cal couldn't find anyone else; she wanted us. Uh. *Me,* I guess. I took the investigation and put Jason on it."

After a few seconds, she nodded. "Okay. Makes sense. Have you checked to see if anything's missing from our files?"

"I haven't had time to check, but it didn't look like he got very far. He'd just come through the window."

Olivia gave her a look. "Or he was *leaving* through the window."

The large filing cabinet against the wall in the lobby held hard-copy backups of every document since the inception of Watchdog Investigations. Jason and Sherry watched her finger through the files. "Here it is." Opening the file, Olivia thumbed through a stack of standard-sized pieces of paper. All blank, except for the first page, which she extracted and displayed. Graham had drawn a happy face on it.

Chapter Twenty-Four

Olivia

I tossed the useless file on Sherry's desk and leaned against the file cabinet. "He must've gotten the file before you arrived." I rubbed my forehead where a headache had begun to build. "Who would've left that window open?"

Sherry shrugged and stared at the whiteboard bullet points.

"Okay. Let's explore Graham. He's fresh off an eighteen-month sentence for withholding evidence, or accessory after the fact. He got off light with eighteen months. He's on probation now, so I don't understand why he'd take this risk."

I pointed at bullet point number three on the whiteboard. "There's something going on here." I muttered a soft profanity. "It's never simple with Graham, and I have no idea why Callie went to see him. Who surveilled, again? Jason?" I turned toward him, folding my arms. "What did you observe?"

He gave her the short version of the bowling alley activity and repeated what he'd told Sherry about their friendly, affectionate greeting.

I rubbed the back of my neck. "Has she learned nothing?"

"Maybe she decided to take things into her own hands." Jason shrugged.

"If you have a theory, I'd love to hear it," I said, my gaze washing across both of them.

"We underestimate Cal," Sherry offered. "She presents this ex-cheerleader, ponytail, rah-rah vibe, but I've seen her in action, especially where Amy is concerned. If she thinks her daughter could be in danger of being kidnapped, she'd do whatever needed to be done. Is she faking, maybe?"

"Sounds plausible," Hunter said.

I agreed. "Let's give her a call. Put her on speaker."

Sherry frowned. "Are you sure?"

"Why not?"

We indulged in a few minutes of exploring possibilities. In the end, we couldn't find a reason not to let her know we'd seen her race into her ex-husband's arms. We all agreed Callie would *not* plan something awful with Graham or Monty.

I pressed in her number. We waited in a semi-circle, staring at the phone as if it would sprout wings and take flight. "Hey. Good morning." Callie's voice was bright and shiny and unencumbered by dark thoughts. Unlike the four of us.

"You're on speaker, and Sherry, Jason, and Hunter are here, too. We wanted you to know—"

"Before you start, I have a confession."

I glanced around our little circle. "Okay."

"I know you won't like this, but I went to Graham's on my own discovery mission. When he left the room to fix me a drink, I looked around, and ran across my file. Why did he have my file?"

Three sets of rounded eyes stared at me. Sherry stepped closer to the phone. "I was stupid to think he hadn't done anything. Remember when I told you he'd broken in? He took your file."

"Wow," she breathed. "I'm certain he didn't see me put it in my purse, so I'll get it back to you. The downside to my visit is he thinks I'm serious about reconciling, now. It's the only way I could engage him."

I frowned. "Why did you stay until four a.m.?"

A pause hovered. Jason grimaced, mouthing, "Does she need to know about my surveillance?"

I shrugged. Maybe. Maybe not.

"How did you know?" Callie asked.

"You gave us a surveillance assignment. We were on the job. We have photos of you hugging him, going inside…" I let the assumption hang. Would she have slept with him? I hoped not.

"Olivia," she chastised, her voice full of indignation. "I know what you're getting at, and I would never! Give me some credit. I should've figured you guys might've been there. Sorry I didn't give you any notice, but I knew you wouldn't approve, and I wanted to see for myself if he's changed. We fell asleep on the couch, watching a movie. I would've left sooner, but it felt…comfortable."

"You would be correct about us not approving."

Sherry and I exchanged looks and smiled. We should've known Callie would try something like this. She had all the patience of a flea.

"Oh! I forgot. You're back, aren't you? How was it?"

"Good. I'm nine days dry."

After a pause, Callie said, "I only want the best for you."

I smiled. "I know. Give us a quick rundown of the file's contents to make sure he hasn't removed anything.

We listened to the rustle of pages. Music in the background. "Reports. Notes. Um. Police reports. A copy of the custody agreement. A copy of the restraining order."

"I looked at Jason, jerking my head toward the door. "Do you mind if we come get it? I want to put it under lock and key."

"Sure, but…"

"I'm on it," Jason said and left.

"Please, girl. Stay away from Graham. He stole the file from our office. He knows you hired us, now. And why."

"Another thing…" she began, her voice soft. "He has a firearm."

I looked at Hunter sitting in one of the guest chairs, one arm slung over the back, legs stretched out straight, watching me with a solemn, concerned expression. I squeezed his shoulder. "I'm okay," I whispered. The furrowed brow smoothed.

"Does Graham even know how to shoot?" Hunter asked.

"I'm not sure if it belongs to him, but I thought you should be aware. And, no. We were married a long time, and I never knew him to want or need a gun." She took a deep breath. "He's a very different guy, now. I found out something else, too. He and your ex had a falling out."

My lips parted in surprise. Graham and Monty had been best buds since the beginning of time. Nothing had separated them, not even when Monty had gotten convicted and sentenced. What happened?

Prison happened.

Graham had been *so* supportive of every little thing Monty did. When he'd gotten slapped with an accessory charge, he realized the truth about his "friend." I understood. It was a horrible feeling. Monty used people like puppets, then discarded them. I doubted he had any friends left.

"What do you mean, 'he's a different guy, now'?"

"He's angry. About everything."

Hunter frowned. "Maybe that's what the gun is for."

I could almost feel Callie wince through our phone connection. "God. I hope not."

"He's already violated parole." With a glance at Sherry, I continued. "My suggestion is we file a police report about the break-in. Are you okay with this?"

After a slight hesitation, she agreed.

"He's proven he's volatile. Please, for your own safety and Amy's…stay away from him. And, keep all windows and doors locked. You can borrow Marlowe if you want. Anytime."

We ended the call. I wrapped my arms around my chest, fending off a sudden chill.

"What now?" Sherry asked.

Hunter slapped the armrests of his chair, stood to his feet. "Send Callie an invoice for services to date, and be done with it. She's gotten all the intel she needs, I'd think." He grinned at me. "Right now, we need to celebrate Olivia's nine alcohol-free days. How about Harriman House for a steak? My treat. I'm getting an early start and driving back to Woodlawn Acres in the morning. As far as Callie is concerned, my suggestion is she talk to Amy. I mean, Amy is eighteen. A legal adult. She should know what's going on with her dad."

"Agree," I said, walking to the whiteboard and erasing the whole thing. "Done and done."

After dinner, Hunter and I sat on my porch, enjoying the silvery moonlight and hot tea. The soft murmur of night sounds chirped around us. Marlowe lay at our feet. "I remember this," he said, putting his arm around me.

"Feels good to drink tea instead of wine. When did I start drinking every night, anyway?"

"See how much you need me? If we'd been married, I'd have held you accountable."

I lifted a shoulder. "Maybe."

He laughed. "I would've tried."

I finished the tea and set it aside. "I called a real estate agent today."

He blinked in surprise. "You did?"

"We're getting together next week to talk. My house is worth more than I thought."

He tightened his arm around my shoulder. "You're *doing* it."

"I am," I whispered. "I'm sorry I've made life so difficult for you."

He stared at me a second, took my face into his hands, and kissed me. "Anything worth having never comes easy."

I leaned into Hunter, enjoying the sturdy feel of his body, the light scent of his cologne. The way our fingers interlaced when we held hands. "So. You're back to Woodlawn tomorrow."

He nodded. "Me and my trusty warrant to search the place." He grinned. "Shock and awe. I can't decide whether to shock the receptionist with the warrant, or awe Larissa with my overwhelming cop powers."

"I wonder if they know I'm gone, yet. Are you going to get in trouble for knocking out the security guard?"

"My word against his. I felt threatened, and they weren't letting you leave." He stood, stretched. "I need to get some sleep. You coming?"

"I'll be up in a few."

He yawned. "Okay."

His steps receded up the stairs. I reached down to pet Marlowe. Alone in the stillness of the night, questions bombarded my mind. Will I miss my house? Had I made the wrong decision? Would my pets adjust? And, since I'd discovered the market value of my house…could Sherry afford it? I rubbed my forehead. Also…*packing.* It made me tired even to think about.

The overwhelming need for a glass of wine hit me, hard. I ran my palms across the cushions on the loveseat. It had been a habit to sit on this porch and work through issues with a glass of wine as my companion. Like a good friend, it had soothed my anxiety and made problems seem less difficult. However, my short stint of sobriety had already taught me the importance of clarity. If I wanted to maximize life to its fullest potential, my mind had to be sharp, not blurry. I missed wine, but its allure faded by the day. More than ever, I wanted to move forward. It would take time, but the few days of forced sobriety convinced me I could kick it. My hands curled into fists. And, I *would.*

Marlowe accompanied me down the steps into my yard. I stared at the bushes Monty and I had planted before our marriage fell apart. The trees we'd planted as babies, now mature and huge. My gaze fell on the monstrous light pole down the lane close to the office. The previous owner had put it in. I'd hated the damn thing, but I'd left it as a reminder. *Watch your back.*

I shuddered. The past few years had been hard. If I were honest, I had more bad memories than good ones, here. Would moving to Richmond be a good thing? A fresh start? Maybe. It didn't matter. My life lay with Hunter, now, and I had to grab my future, not stay trapped in the past. I gathered the remnants of our tea and began to walk inside.

Marlowe growled. The hackles on his back lifted.

I put the teacups and saucers down. I grabbed his collar and stared into the shadows. What had he seen?

He broke free from my grip. "Marlowe! Come!"

Hunter lifted the second-story bedroom window. "What's happening?"

"Marlowe took off toward the office. He saw something."

"Be right down." Two minutes later, he walked outside, car keys jangling. "Hop in the Jeep. Let's go check it out."

When we pulled into the lot, I heard Marlowe barking. "Not again," I muttered under my breath, thinking about how many times this building had been broken into. "Marlowe! Come." He stopped barking and slid down the trunk of the tree he'd cornered. With a backward glance into the upper branches, he slunk to my side and sat. Hunter shone a flashlight into the branches and started laughing. I let out the breath I'd been holding. "What is it?"

He pointed. "Look."

Two terrified bear cubs clung to the branches.

"We better get out of here. Mama is probably on her way."

"Thank God," I breathed, pushing away visions of shots fired and bloody assaults. *Bear cubs. I'll take it.* We hustled Marlowe into the Jeep and took off.

Chapter Twenty-Five

Hunter

The sunrise cast gentle pink and gold rays across Woodlawn Acres, overlaying the property with a false sense of peace. Hunter sat in his Jeep, contemplating the developing shit show about to happen. He'd gotten up at dawn, texted Lieutenant Nicholson with an update (deleting the story of whacking one of the staff and removing Olivia without a release). His lieutenant had sent reinforcements, the FBI had procured their federal warrant, and would arrive any minute. If the mountain of circumstantial evidence collected proved viable, Woodlawn would cease to exist. What they didn't have, though…was direct proof.

A car drove into the lot. A young man with a swollen jaw and a sullen attitude trudged to the door. Hunter chuckled. His heavy bag workouts had done their job.

Five minutes later, Larissa pulled in. Her brow wrinkled at the sight of his Jeep. Hunter grinned. *This is going to be fun.* He powered his window down as she stalked toward his vehicle.

"What are you doing! Did we not make it clear enough yesterday? Have you made an appointment?" She fisted her hands on her hips. The tight knot of hair wrapped into a bun and round wire-rimmed glasses put him in mind of an angry librarian—one who was about to have a very, very bad day.

Hunter opened the driver side door and exited the Jeep as two patrol vehicles rolled in. Her eyes widened at the slam of doors and slap of heavy-soled shoes as four uniforms strode toward them. Then, the Feds arrived in a monster, black SUV, wearing body armor emblazoned with FBI. Hunter thought he might have to grab her before she fainted, but she held on. He gave a curt nod to all. The cops waited outside to secure the crime scene as the Fed stormed inside and served the warrant. Larissa made a primal sound. Somewhere between a growl and a wail. "What is this about?" she demanded, her petite form shaking like a leaf in the wind.

"They're serving a federal warrant. You could save us all a lot of trouble if you'd just tell me what you know. If you're not involved, you have nothing to worry about. If you *are* involved, this would be a good time to worry."

Wiping moisture from her forehead, she tugged at his sports coat sleeve in a futile attempt to keep him from entering the premises. "Please!"

Removing her hand from his sleeve, he explained the uniforms would maintain order and secure the scene while a thorough search was conducted inside, and she needed to keep her head down and cooperate. "It'll go better for you if you start talking."

"Come into my office," she hissed. "The Board is in the conference room for their monthly meeting."

Hunter grinned. "Perfect timing."

Once they were seated and behind a closed door, Larissa leaned across her desk, studying him. "Tell me something. Are you and Olivia investigating this facility together? Did I miss that little nugget when she 'forgot' to fill in 'private investigator' on our registration forms? With her own firm, no less!"

Hunter winced at the sounds of ransacked drawers and closets, the voices telling everyone to stay calm, wait in their rooms. Heavy boots stomping through the halls, accompanied by the scurrying of staff moving out of the way, or cluster in guarded rooms. "Is that really what you want to talk about right now?"

"The minute I found out she had her own investigation firm, I suspected."

"She attended to stop drinking. Period." Hunter shook his head. "It doesn't matter. I'm sure you have opinions about what's going on here. If you give us something, it'll be worth your while." With a long sigh, Hunter waited, elbows on armrests, fingertips steepled.

She slumped, dropped her head. "I came here with such hope and optimism. I wanted to help people."

"You *have* helped. Don't go there. This isn't your fault." *But, did he know for sure?*

"When Alex Barnes started packing the Board with his contacts, I had initial concerns, but all those heavy hitters meant a lot of money pouring in. I had dreams of expansion, and hiring better qualified counselors than myself." She chuckled. "All I have is one little certificate of attending a six-week drug counseling seminar."

Hunter thought about her lack of credentials. Her history as a recovered druggie. Her inherent gentleness. The lack of online information, the result of sealed records, perhaps. Had the higher-ups seen a presentable, malleable person who would believe whatever they told her without the complication of questions or government agency checkpoints? "A dream come true, then."

She ran her palms across the files on her desk. "People started disappearing." She let out a long exhale. "I tried not to worry, but I talked to the patients and realized the job fair was dishonest at best. They stuff people into vans and cart them off to who knows where." Tears leaked from her eyes. "I didn't want to believe it. I approached Collins. He reassured me. Even showed me pictures."

"How did he reassure you?" If Collins was such a great guy, Shiloh wouldn't have been assigned to cyber-investigate him.

"He had a connection who would give them jobs and a place to stay. Like a halfway house, he told me. They'd be given a minimum wage position and free room and board."

"What were the jobs?"

"Entry-level. Restaurants, loading docks, moving companies. That sort of thing."

Hunter left his chair and started for the door, urging her to follow. "I want to show you something."

They walked out of her office, down a corridor, past the laundry room, and stood in front of a locked closet. "Do you have keys to this closet?"

She frowned and shook her head. "No one's allowed in it except qualified personnel."

"Huh. And what are the qualifications of the 'qualified personnel'?

"I-I'm not sure. Everyone just accepted it, I guess."

"Watch this." Hunter extracted his handy lock pick kit and went to work. The door popped open. "Go inside," he told her, checking the hall before he closed the door behind them and turned on the light. She stared at the rows of shelving populated with tidy labels, numbers, and bins full of small glass vials with metal tops.

Larissa gawked. "What is this?"

"Didn't you wonder about the sign-in sheet on the door?"

"This room is reserved for our clients' medications and our visiting physicians or nurses. That's what I was told, and under no circumstances should I allow myself or anyone else to use it."

He pointed. "See these bins?"

She adjusted her glasses and inspected the shelves. "Batches of liquid labeled with a series of numbers. As I said, I've never been in here, before."

Hunter cracked the door and pulled the clipboard inside. "Read the top."

"'For Pharmaceutical Coordinator,'" she recited.

Hunter waited for her to connect dots, but she didn't. "We feel Collins's job fairs involve pharmaceutical experimentation on human subjects."

Larissa closed her eyes and held her hands to her chest. "No...no..."

"When the intake patients are detoxed, Collins offers them a fresh start. Desperate people without options jump at it. They're still vulnerable, and most of them need a job. At this very moment, the FBI is tracking previous clients who were 'selected' in his job fairs."

Larissa trembled with anger. Her voice shook. "You're wrong!"

"We'll know soon enough."

"Matty," she whispered, almost to herself.

He shook his head. "Yeah. I have Matty to thank for blowing the lid off this place. Other than realizing Dink has never had Matty's best interests in mind, what else have you observed?" Leaving the closet, Hunter left the door open. He knew samples would be part of the warrant.

She tapped her chin in concentration. "I *did* wonder why he came to see me so often, and each time, she was different. Sometimes slurring her words and forgetful, and other times, coherent and energetic. Dink said her doctor had adjusted her medications. He's always been so convincing."

Hunter snorted. "I'd use another word." He scratched his cheek. "Whatever this is, I doubt it's an approved clinical trial, and I'm almost positive Matty's a victim. So. The next question is, what is Dink's role? Other than poisoning his wife, I mean?"

Hunter returned to the parking lot and watched the uniforms do their job, enjoying Dink's shocked expression as he parked his car. Jerking his door open and striding across the lot, he said, "You're like the flu. No matter how hard you try, you can't get rid of it." He blinked at the vast array of cops and police vehicles and crime scene tape.

Hunter shrugged. "Guess maybe you should've taken your annual flu shot."

Dink's face turned an interesting shade of red. "Watch that blood pressure, Mayor," Hunter called after him as he stalked inside the facility.

How did monsters like Dink Stricklin live with themselves? He strolled to the lobby, making his availability known and watching for conspiratorial conversations, or a runner. Patients huddled in dazed groups. Investigators and crime scene techs were in charge, now. Cops had been stationed outside certain rooms or offices to protect evidence. Olivia's former roommate, Delia, walked through the lobby and down the hall, giving him a wink and a nod as she passed. The pretty, young receptionist sat at her desk behind the semi-circle surround and eyed him. "I knew you were trouble."

"If I were you, I'd look for another job," he said.

* * *

The closed conference room door held a small, square window at eye level. He peeked inside at the board members. Sure enough, Collins, Alex, Dink, and five other men in suits with pale, stricken faces and blank eyes sat around a table noshing on doughnuts. His cell buzzed. He stepped away, found an alcove, and took the call. "Faraday, the task force located five of the patients from Woodlawn. Pretty easy trail, and the transporters gave it up with no problem. Woodlawn's patients got dropped at a couple of labs in Virginia. One outside DC, the other in Richmond. Feebies busted in, and the staff nearly crapped their pants. The lead virologist slipped through, but we'll get her. Her lab assistants were cogs in a well-oiled machine, and I don't think any of them were complicit in this. We have them in interrogation rooms. How's it goin' up there?"

"The bomb has been dropped. It looks like the apocalypse in here."

"Good. These people are evil." He slammed the handset down.

Hunter let the surge of vindication thrum in his chest a few seconds before striding to the conference room. He pounded the door three times. "Richmond PD! Comin' in!" When he jerked the door open, eight sets of dropped jaws and beady eyes regarded him with suspicion. Alex Barnes sat at the head of the table. Collins Browning looked as if he'd toss his cookies any second.

Hunter pulled aside his sports coat to display his badge. "Sergeant Hunter Faraday, Richmond PD. "Just sit tight, gentlemen, I hear you guys are so special, you get to stay for interviews. Do you need anything? Just say the word." He smiled.

Chapter Twenty-Six

Olivia

We dug into our existing caseload, trying to put Woodlawn out of our minds. For me, I just hoped Hunter had made it out alive. I tried to focus on the latest report.

"We've still got the fraud case for Barnes Imports on tap. Jason? How's it coming along?" I asked.

He gave Sherry and I a look of disgust. "The report was crap. The officer who wrote is under investigation. The adjusters can't use it, so I'm not sure how to proceed. Anyway, it may be a moot point. Alex and Collins are a little busy with the Woodlawn investigation right now, correct?"

I stared at my phone. No word from Hunter, yet. My gaze flicked to Jason. "I don't know if we should close Barnes Imports' fraud case yet. Did you ever surveil the other party?"

He nodded. "You have the report in your email, but in summary, two days of surveillance as requested, and no evidence of physical labor or faking the injuries. The guy left his house once, and his wife had to help him into the car. I tracked them; they went to a doctor's office. I annotated my conclusions in the file and the email you *haven't read,*" he prodded, with a slight grin. "He's legit got injuries. And therefore, has a case."

Sherry came around from behind her desk, and leaned against Jason's. "Tell her what you told me about Alex and the Instagram account."

His fingers flew across the keyboard. He turned his monitor screen toward us. I scanned the messages.

"He's not very talkative, lately."

"I wouldn't have any idea how to engage with someone who navigates the world of multi-million-dollar vehicles. Maybe he couldn't relate, and ghosted you," I said.

Jason nodded. "Pretty sure he did. I learned a few things, though." He scrolled through his messages. "He mentioned a 'shipment.' I never could figure out what kind of shipment he meant. I don't think we'd been talking about cars." He scrolled, his eyes tracking. "I threw out a softball at one point, and asked him what he did for a hobby..." Scroll, scroll. "He responded with a wink emoji and said he had a 'shipment of deluxe, age-appropriate exotics' on the way." Jason frowned. "I sent the entire thread to you guys in an email." He returned the monitor to its proper spot. "Don't you guys ever look at my emails?"

My blood ran cold. I felt dizzy. I leaned against his desk for balance. "Does anyone know how exotic vehicles are transported?" I whispered.

"Sure," Jason said. "Enclosed car carriers." His fingers moved again. "Here."

I looked at images of huge, enclosed transport vehicles. More than enough space to transport exotic cars...*and sedated victims.* My voice cracking, I continued. "Did you find out where Alex gets his vehicles?"

"Europe. Asia. Why?" His forehead knotted.

"Oh, Collins," Sherry whispered, covering her face with her hands.

"Escorts is a nice way of referring to sex trafficking. Hence, Shiloh's investigation." I chewed on my lower lip. "Collins used our firm to research his supposed 'girlfriend,' and we confirmed his suspicions about an investigation. Gave him all the intel he needed. *That's* why he was smiling when he left the office."

Sherry shook her head." I'm so mad at myself right now. I should've vetted him like any other client."

Jason shrugged. "You two had history. I repeat, there's a reason cops don't mix personal and professional on a case."

I started pacing back and forth, trying to lay facts out in nice, neat rows, but these cases had become so intertwined I didn't know where to start.

I frowned, spun around, and kept pacing. If Collins had us busy with his "online girlfriend" assignment, a cover to find out if he and Alex were being investigated, then what was Alex's fraud case about? A diversion? Keep us busy so we'd look the other way? I jerked to a stop and held my index finger in the air with an "aha" moment. "Didn't Hunter discover Matty around the same time we accepted Collins's case?"

She nodded. "Why?"

"Think about it. Hunter poking his nose into Matty's business…Collins hiring us to investigate his fictional girlfriend…and Alex trying to delete the transport truck, which we now suspect carried a fresh cargo of trafficking victims." I raked my hands through my hair in frustration. "And, it all happened within a few days. We upset a delicate balance."

"I can see it. Wow," she whispered.

"We weren't supposed to know about the 'age-appropriate imports.'" Jason's chest puffed out. "I found a piece of good intel, didn't I?"

"I haven't studied the police report," I said. "What was in it?"

"The report was sketchy," Sherry said. "You know, we should tell Hunter to track Alex's bank records the week after the incident. He'd have made a big payout to someone."

I tapped my chin. "I'm sure they already have his financials."

She nodded. "Okay. But do they have the video we finagled from the private residences across the street? I mean, you went to rehab, and I didn't think you'd want me meeting with Alex by myself, so I held onto the footage. It proves a transport vehicle was parked there right before the collision, and interfered with line-of-sight roadway issues. Also, I figured the Baltimore Crime Unit would do a sweep, but maybe Jason's right. Some of the cops are on Barnes' payroll." She paused, her eyes growing wider by the second. "Exotic, age-appropriate imports," she whispered, her palms covering her mouth as the pieces fell into place. "Alex made sure we looked the other way. If we spent time surveilling the other driver…"

"We'd ignore what really happened, and our report would be used to erase any liability on the part of Barnes Imports," I said. "The *transport truck* blocked the road and caused the other driver to swerve into their vehicle, and if the accident report revealed the transport truck sitting there, questions would arise, which Alex did not want to answer."

"The accident report did *not* indicate a big transport vehicle."

Jason leaned back in his chair, crossed his arms. "Sometimes, when a new high roller moves in, it's the first thing they do. Sniff out crooked local cops. They whitewashed the report. I guarantee it." He opened the residential video on his laptop and flipped it toward them. They huddled at the front of his desk, watching. "Look at the time stamp."

"It blocked his view," I said, in disbelief. "Someone definitely left the presence of the transporter out of the police report.

We stood there in collective shock.

My cell buzzed, and we all jumped. I blew out a long breath, and answered the phone.

"Hey," Hunter said.

"Hey, babe."

"We got quite a bit accomplished today, I'm glad to say."

"We are all dying to hear the status of Woodlawn. Can I put you on speaker?"

"Sure. Is the whole gang there?"

"We're all here," Jason said, jerking a thumb at my office. "Let's get comfortable. This is going to be good."

We filed into my office and sat in the armchairs. Jason plopped into his seat and put his feet on the coffee table. Sherry perched in her chair at full attention, legs together, hands in lap. I put my phone in the middle of the coffee table, and sat. Trying to keep the nerves out of my voice, I told him we were ready. It had started to sink in. I'd been a hair's breadth away from a fake clinical trial experience, or being hustled into an overcrowded van to be trafficked. Hunter's persistence and determination to find the underlying cause of this mess had not only saved me, but countless future victims.

"I would put it in the 'epic takedown' category. While the FBI served the warrant and tore the place apart, another team put together a surprise party for the labs."

My forehead wrinkled. "Labs?"

"DC and Richmond. They're still working on connecting Woodlawn's clients to Collins Browning's 'job fairs.' We now have solid evidence and first-hand accounts of fraudulent clinical trials."

"I think I'm going to be sick," Sherry said.

"Me, too," I said. "What about Elizabeth and Delia?"

"I'm getting there," Hunter said, laughing. "The Board is being interrogated. I'm not aware of any arrests yet, but arraignment hearings are the next step." He snickered. "I know this judge. I bet their bail will be set at a million bucks or more."

"Which they'll post," I muttered.

"Maybe Alex. Not Browning. I can tell by lookin' at him he lets his cash run through his fingers like water. All show. No responsibility. He'll be in a cell."

"What a waste," Sherry said, downcast. "He could've made a good future for himself. I bet he has no one to bail him out."

I sighed. "Please tell me you found former Woodlawn patients who are still breathing."

"At last count, thirty-seven still living. Twenty-five with serious side effects, in the hospital, or dead."

I felt the blood leave my fingertips, my face. "How many in all?"

"We put together a list, but some of the people never left a forwarding address or phone number. We may never find them. But of those we were able to trace, one hundred or so. I don't know the final number of deaths and survivals, yet."

Sherry closed her eyes. "My God."

It felt as if all the air had been sucked from the room. We stared at each other blankly.

"What about Larissa?" I asked.

"I'm told she's cooperating with authorities. She convinced me she didn't know. When I showed her the batches, she had no idea what they were."

"You should get a medal."

He laughed. "I'm still tryin' to figure out why I start things like this."

"Thank God you did. Where are you, now?"

"In my Jeep, going home."

My abs clenched. The word "home" felt like a punch to my stomach. I wanted to hug him long and hard. I wanted his home to be mine, too. I wanted to watch him come in the front door, put his badge and car keys in a cute receptacle on the foyer table, unholster his weapon and put it in the safe, and walk into the kitchen where we'd share takeout for dinner and talk about work. Then, we'd forget the awful things we'd seen and the horrible things people do to each other by making wild, passionate love. The visual rocked me to my core, but all I could manage was, "I wish you were here."

"Same," he said.

I smiled.

"Aw." Sherry fluttered her lashes.

Refocusing on Woodlawn, I continued. "You never told us about Delia and Elizabeth."

"As it all went down, people started coming out of their rooms. Delia found me, and became my shadow. The place was a madhouse. The occupants huddled together like confused sheep. They didn't understand what was going on, but Delia did, because we'd offered her a way out after discovering what was in the closet, remember? I'd seen Elizabeth with you in the cafeteria, but I couldn't remember what she looked like. She had the good sense to approach with the piece of paper you wrote your number on, and told me you'd offered to help."

"I *will* help her."

"The interviews are ongoing. Larissa told me she'd relocate the residents as best she could. Delia and Elizabeth offered their assistance." He paused. I held my breath and waited for him to proceed.

"We've only scratched the surface. This is turning out to be more convoluted than anyone thought, and it'll take a while to figure out. I'll know more as the investigation continues."

"What happened with Shiloh?" Jason asked.

Hunter chuckled. "Even tied to a desk, she continues to excel at her job. Baltimore PD and her home office in Savannah are calling her a hero. Ten bucks says she gets a promotion."

CHAPTER TWENTY-SIX

"She's single, right?" Jason asked.

"You don't want to go there, bud," Hunter said.

I frowned. "Sure, he does. Go for it, Jason."

"But she'll chew him up and spit—"

"Ignore him," I interrupted. "If you want to meet her, do it."

Later, I'd fixed myself a cup of tea and settled on the loveseat on my front porch when my phone buzzed with Hunter's number. I scooped the phone into my hand. "Hi."

"Man," he breathed. "What a freaking day."

"I bet."

I stared at the inky sky and its countless. brilliant points of light. A star arced across, a bright tail streaming behind. I blinked. "I just saw a falling star!"

Hunter laughed. "A sign from the heavens?"

"Tonight, it means I am one lucky girl to have escaped before I ended up in an enclosed vehicle carrier."

"Uhh…you're going to have to explain."

I took a few minutes and told him about the video at Barnes Imports which had been edited to delete the transporter, how their fraud case had been primarily to create a distraction from their sex trafficking operation, and how Jason's Instagram surveillance had resulted in the comment "age-appropriate exotics" delivery. "But the poor guy who rammed into their car! I doubt he gets a payout if the company's filing bankruptcy, but without him, we never would have known a thing."

Hunter shook his head. "Anything involving exorbitant amounts of cash and overseas transports reeks of criminal activity. The minute the words, 'high-end exotics' came out of your mouth, I would've told you not to take the case."

I smiled. "Of course you would have, silly. Why do you think I didn't tell you?"

"Sounds about right. I *am* starting to figure you out, you know."

"Impressive, since I haven't even figured myself out."

He laughed. "I think you're further along than you know. Speaking of forward progress, you've got a winner in Jason."

I nodded. "He's catching on fast. I think he'll make a great PI."

"Are you seriously going to let him loose on Shiloh?"

"Why not? No offense, but they're about the same age, and I think he'd be a breath of fresh air after all she's been through. She's on limited assignment, right?"

"Yeah, but—"

I felt the hair on the back of my neck prickle. "But what? She could use a good, sensible, go-getter. Besides, he looks like a young Brad Pitt."

Hunter remained quiet.

"I think they'd be cute together."

"She's one tough woman. He—"

"Who needs a guy like Jason to soften her rough edges. He's got this 'steady strength' vibe. I can see them together."

"Okay. But when she rips him to shreds, don't come crawling back to me."

I laughed. "I think they're old enough to make their own choices."

After a brief pause, he switched course. "I've been meaning to ask…how are you doing?"

"You mean the seizure?"

"Well, that too."

I traced patterns on the loveseat cushions with my fingers. "I'm being careful. I drink like, a thousand ounces of water a day, I make sure I eat enough. But, the most important thing is not drinking."

"Not even a little?"

I could hear the apprehension in his voice. "No. Promise. To be honest, I think it's the main reason I'm feeling so much better. I can't believe it took me this long to realize."

"I've had my fair share of toilet-hugging. I'm glad those days are behind me."

"Yeah? How did you quit?"

"I made a choice. I have the after-work beer now and then, but if you need me not to drink, it's fine. I mean it."

A cozy warmth wrapped itself around my heart. "Thank you. Very thoughtful, but I don't think that's necessary. So, you said Matty had been admitted to a facility?"

"Dink's out on bond, like the rest of the Board. Arraignment hearings are being scheduled. He'd used his wife like a human voodoo doll. Larissa has a spot for her at an appropriate facility close to Richmond, and told me she'd called their grown children, who are coming in tomorrow. I wouldn't want to be Dink facing those kids. The FBI is trying to figure out if Dink is also involved in the trafficking side. From what I hear, it's a mess. Each Board member had been recruited by someone with a great resume and an impressive scientific background. Too bad they looked the other way when Collins and Alex decided to use Woodlawn's patients for their drug experiments." He shrugged. "Maybe some of them didn't know. We'll find out."

I thought about how Alex had seemed edgy as he'd shown us around his showroom. How he'd avoided looking at me. "To think I was nervous around Alex. I wanted him to *like* me so he'd hire us." I laughed. "Sherry saw him as a big funnel of money for the firm.

"All his money won't do him any good behind bars."

"What's going to happen to his business? Did he have someone in place in case of—"

"The buck stopped with him. Another red flag. He should've had checks and balances. Now, his customers have backed off, the press is annihilating him, and he'll be looking at selling those amazing vehicles for pennies on the dollar. I doubt the business will survive." He shrugged. "Another power broker bites the dust."

"Yeah, but…now he's exposed. The evil stops."

"Evil never stops. It's an eternal fight."

After a few seconds of silence to ponder the human condition, I said, "I'm *so proud* of you."

He hated compliments. As usual, he changed the subject. "Will you have time for a break? Or are you still working the Collins insurance fraud case?"

"I've alerted Baltimore PD and given them the footage and all our case notes. Watchdog is out of it. I'm hoping to enjoy some peace for a while."

"You deserve it. Are the bears behaving themselves?"

I laughed. "We haven't seen a single bear since the night Marlowe chased those cubs up a tree."

After the call, I'd turned out the final light in the kitchen and put my tea cup and saucer in the sink when someone pounded my back door so hard I thought it might fall off its hinges.

My heart fluttered. My throat constricted. Marlowe loped into the kitchen, his barks deep and sonorous. I gripped his thick, leather collar like a security blanket.

"It's Callie! Let me in! Hurry!"

Chapter Twenty-Seven

Olivia

I calmed Callie down with a glass of water and a brownie. "Breathe," I told her. "We'll figure it out. Let's go sit in the den." Her hands trembled holding the glass of water. I took the plate and glass from her. "I'll take these. You just go sit."

After a few minutes, the color returned to her cheeks, and the slightest sound didn't make her jump. I put my hand on her shoulder. "You're fine, and Marlowe is on the job."

"Good boy, Marlowe," she whispered. His tail slow-wagged, and he stood at the sound of her voice, his bright, brown eyes taking in every detail.

I rubbed her back. "If someone tried to hurt you, he'd be on them in seconds."

She wiped tears off her cheeks. "I should've known better," she said, cradling herself with her arms.

I returned to my seat and settled in to wait. I had learned over the years that Callie's brain processed events like an assembly line. It took her forever to get to a point, but if I rushed her process, or became impatient, the assembling would shut down.

I smiled.

With no alcohol in my system, I kept learning new ways to handle situations. For instance, how to keep my mouth shut and wait. I'd been *so* upset when she'd approached Sherry instead of me to surveil Graham. Not anymore. The reason for not contacting me had been simple: the booze released my inner bitch.

She cocked her head and smiled. "You're not going to tell me to hurry and get to the point? What's wrong with you?"

"I'm learning patience."

She took a breath, held it in, then exhaled. "Me, too, girl. Me, too."

I leaned back against the couch cushions. "What happened?"

She shuddered. "On my weekly trip to the store today I felt someone following me." Glancing at my windows, she asked me if the doors and windows were locked.

"If anyone's outside, Marlowe will let us know."

"I got through checkout, then rolled the cart out as fast as I could. After I unloaded the groceries and shut the hatch, I jumped in my car and got the heck outta there." She pinched the bridge of her nose. "Then I saw the note. Someone had put it underneath one of my wipers."

"*Graham*," I concluded.

She nodded. It said: "Why haven't you returned my calls? We're meant to be together. You know it and I know it."

I rubbed my forehead.

She chuckled at my reaction. "I know. It sounds just like something your ex would say, doesn't it?"

"It does. We're their 'property'. You'd think he'd be more careful. Have I told you we filed the police report about him breaking in? They know he took the file, too." He may have been investigated by now. And, if he's stalking you, also…the parole board will have a cow." I shrugged. "He's going to have to explain to his parole officer one way or the other.

She frowned. "It's my fault. He's grown this weird set of principles, and he even got tattoos in prison. He acts like this big badass now, and I played into it." She bonked her head lightly with a fist. "I should've talked to you before I went over there."

I smiled. "You couldn't trust me."

Callie grabbed my hand. "Wine, Whine, and Win' girls forever, right?"

I laughed. "I think I'll focus on the 'Whine and Win' part for now."

Callie flapped her hands. "We won't mind not drinking if it helps you. Bottom line is I saw someone looking in my window, and got scared."

Marlowe rose to his feet with a low growl.

I turned off the table lamp, jumped from the couch, closed the curtains, and ran into the kitchen for the firearm I kept at home. After slapping a fresh cartridge into my weapon, I returned. "Did you walk over here?"

"I drove."

I nodded. "Remind me to check your car for a tracking device."

She groaned.

Marlowe's agitated barking bounced through the foyer.

I looked at Callie. "They know there's a big, mean dog inside. They'd be stupid to try to break in." I stole to the window and peeked outside. "I don't see anything," I whispered.

"I know he's out there."

"Someone is," I agreed.

Marlowe sat on his haunches, staring at the door, head cocked. After a few seconds, he stood. The fur along his back crested to an imposing height. His low growl sent shivers down my arms.

Callie's chin quivered. "What's happening?"

"Shh." I locked into a shooter's stance—arms rigid, weapon braced in both hands, barrel leveled at the unseen chest waiting beyond the door. My pulse thundered, but I clung to the muscle memory of yesterday's rushed trip to the range, silently praying it would be enough.

Soft steps climbed the stairs. The squeal of the taut spring attached to my red screen door told me they'd opened it. Moisture sprouted on my chest. My hands grew clammy. I tightened my grip and widened my stance.

We listened to the press of fingers slide across the front door. My shoulder muscles flexed. Callie's peeping tom stood a mere five inches from the business end of my weapon.

Marlowe went crazy. Snarling. Barking. Scratching at the door.

As predicted, the reaction to a big, barking dog happened fast. The screen door banged shut. Footsteps lumbered across the porch and down the steps. Into the lawn. My heart slowed. I lowered my weapon and thumbed the safety back on, feeling my pulse and mind slacken. With my free hand, I slid the curtain aside. A dark form sprinted through the yard, hopped the picket fence, and ran into the shadows.

"They're gone." I leashed Marlowe and urged her to come outside with me for a closer look.

We walked onto the front porch, down the stairs, and into the yard. A spring breeze tossed our hair. The typical nightsong of crickets and tree frogs wrapped around us, a fragile calm at odds with what had just happened. An owl whooshed across. The moon, radiant in a clear, night sky, cast its comforting glow across the yard. "Do you think he's gone?" Callie whispered.

Marlowe had seated himself beside me. "All clear."

We walked back to the porch. Callie gasped.

"What?" Marlowe tugged at the leash, anxious to go back inside.

She pointed. An envelope taped to my front door. With a sigh, I peeled it off.

Safely behind a locked door, I pulled my supply of nitrile gloves out of a kitchen drawer and put on a pair, handing some to her as well. "Someone doesn't want us to trace it to an IP address," I told her. Extracting the contents, I scanned the letter. With a sympathetic look at my friend, I laid it on the table in front of her.

Her lips moved as she read the note. She raised her head and stared at me. "He did it. He took her."

With fumbling fingers, she pulled her phone from her pocket and tried her daughter's number. Straight to voicemail. A chilling thought raced through me. Amy and Lilly roomed together. They hung out with the same people. "Try Lilly." Had he been crazy enough to take my daughter, too? Callie pressed in the number. It rang and rang before going to voicemail. I clutched Cal's hand. "I think he's got both of them."

My cell buzzed. I grabbed it, my fingers ice.

"Mom, I'm using Amy's dad's phone. He offered to take us to dinner with one condition: leave our phones at home." She laughed. "He didn't want us glued to our phones. He wanted you to know where we were in case you called."

I stared at Callie. "So, you guys are all right?"

"Of course. He took us to a great place in downtown Richmond. The food here is awesome."

"What's the name of the restaurant?"

Instead of responding, I heard her irritated cry. The call disappeared. I stared at the phone. Had he used a burner? No. The ID on the digital readout hadn't changed. We could trace the location from the tower signal. I'd had this number in my phone for years. *If he hadn't thought far enough ahead to realize we could locate the girls, maybe he just wanted to see Amy. Not kidnap her!*

My eyes darted to Callie as I pressed in Hunter's number. "He's got them both," I explained. "They think he wanted to surprise them." I pressed my knuckles to my eyes as I waited for him to answer. "Come on, come on!" When he answered, I blurted out, "Where are you?"

"Almost home."

"No! Specifically. Where are you? Graham's got our girls in a restaurant in downtown Richmond. He made them leave their phones at the dorm, but had Lilly call me on his phone. He wouldn't let her tell me where they were." I took a breath, forcing myself to stay calm for Callie, who looked as pale as a ghost. "I think including my daughter was unintended."

"You know Richmond PD isn't going to follow up on a father taking his daughter and her friend out to dinner."

I put the phone on speaker. Callie sat on one of the barstools. "He's not supposed to be out of state. He's a parolee! Callie's been worried he'll do something desperate, and here we are."

Callie moved closer to the phone. "Someone's been following me. It can't be Graham, because I have a protection order. He must've paid someone."

Hunter let out a long exhale. "There goes my peaceful night. First order of business: call his PO. Do either of you have his information? Did he use a burner?"

I took the phone back. "It's his old number. I doubt he'd even think about buying a burner. I'll send you his contact info."

"I'll get it over to our guys and see if they can ping the tower the latest call came from. Don't worry."

Callie grunted her response to the last two words.

I rolled my eyes. "Lost cause, we're already worried," I told him. "Call us with any updates, okay? I'm not sure of his mental state."

"I'll be in touch." He clicked off.

My sweet friend had hunched herself into a ball of misery, chewing on one of her meticulously maintained fingernails.

"I'll get the guest room ready for you."

She gave me a speculative look. "He wouldn't hurt them," she whispered, searching my face

"Of course he wouldn't. What did the note say, again?" I furrowed my brow, trying to remember the exact words.

She recited: "I just want to tell my side of the story."

Chapter Twenty-Eight

Sherry

"I'm getting up." Sherry rolled over to plant a kiss on Duncan's cheek.

"Wait," he said, tugging the waist of her pajama pants. "It'll only take a few minutes." He grinned.

She slapped his hand away. "It's never a few minutes. I've got to get to work."

Padding into the bathroom, she slapped on minimal makeup and got dressed. The smell of eggs and coffee tickled her nose as she walked out of the bathroom and into the kitchen. "You're too good to me," she murmured, wrapping her arms around Duncan's waist from behind as he flipped the eggs onto a plate and set it on the table.

"Remember those words the next time you turn down my offer of an exclusive relationship." He grabbed two mugs from the cabinet. "Fix your own coffee, wench."

"Hey. I didn't say no, did I?"

"Implied."

She frowned. "We've been dating, what. Four months?"

"So?" He sipped his coffee.

"I'm fine with you in your house and me in mine. Speaking of, when are you going to invite me over for dinner?"

"As I said, remodeling takes time, and my house is a wreck. I want to wait until the whole project is finished." He took the plate he'd fixed for himself and sat at the kitchen table.

She stuffed the rest of her eggs in her mouth. Wiping her face with her napkin. "Gotta go." Her head swiveled. "Where'd I put my gun?" she mumbled to herself.

Duncan laughed. "Not something you hear from your girlfriend every day."

"Lock up when you leave," she said, blowing him a kiss as she left.

* * *

Marlowe greeted her at the door, stuffing his muzzle underneath her hand. She gave him a hug and petted him for a minute before looking at Jason. "What's going on with this needy dog? He doesn't do this."

"Olivia booted him from her office, so he's looking for some love."

"Huh," she said, walking to her desk. "New clients?"

"Well, let's see," he said, ticking off points on his hands. "One, the Instagram relationship with Collins is over. I archived the account." Next finger. "Two, the Feebies have control of Woodlawn and its various criminal activities, so that's on hold…and maybe closed as far as the firm is concerned." Next finger. "Three, Barnes Imports is officially done. I saw on their socials where they're closing until further notice with 'regrets to their customers.' He put his hands down. "The good thing is the fire sale."

Sherry furrowed her brow. "Fire sale?"

"They're selling off their inventory. I still can't afford one of them, but Olivia could."

She laughed. "That Rover has around a hundred-fifty-thousand miles on it. She should've traded it in years ago."

"I told her I'd help her pick one out."

"Well, then. I have hope, now."

"Are you being sarcastic?"

She lifted her shoulders. "I'm going to see what she's been working on in there."

Olivia smiled as Sherry walked into her office. "Good morning."

"How's it going?"

"Trying to catch my breath. It's been a stressful few weeks."

"Right. How can I help?"

Olivia ran her fingers through her wavy hair. Sherry noticed her boss looked extra nice today, and wondered why. She cocked an eyebrow, taking in her outfit. Pale yellow, silk blouse, gold hoops at her ears, Yurman bracelets, her Rolex watch; reserved for special occasions. The necklace Hunter had given her for one of her birthdays. Her gorgeous emerald engagement ring flashed and sparkled with the morning sunshine streaming through the window. Marlowe's faint whines oozed from the other side of the door.

"Um." She frowned, eyes darting across her desktop. "I'm good for now."

Sherry's crossed leg started swinging gently. "You're being cagey this morning."

Olivia blinked. "Am I?"

Sherry tilted her head. "See?"

Olivia blushed. Sherry folded her arms and waited.

"Would you let Marlowe in?"

Such a dodge. "Sure."

Marlowe galloped across the room and landed in his doggie bed. With a series of satisfied grunts, he circled twice and dropped with a thump.

"He's such a wuss. He can't live without me for an hour and a half?"

Her eyebrows rose. "You've been here that long? It's eight-fifteen."

She chewed on her lower lip. "I can't keep anything from you."

"Nope."

"I was served with a request to complete interrogatories regarding Woodlawn, and I needed to focus." She patted a pile of pages on her desk. "After I answered the document, I printed it out and read my answers from a different perspective. I had to be sure I wasn't, you know…perjuring myself or whatever."

"Understandable."

Olivia wiggled her fingers at her outfit. "Our firm was given an award by the International Association of Chiefs of Police for excellence in criminal investigations. So I had to dress up."

Sherry yelped in surprise. "What? Wow! Awesome. Congratulations to us." She paused at Olivia's hesitation to join in. "Right?"

"Well, yes, of course. But there'll be press, they'll take photos of me fraternizing with the area Chiefs." She groaned. "I don't need the notoriety. I tried to turn them down, but they wouldn't hear of it. No telling what it'll shake loose. I mean…" Taking a breath, she continued. "Monty has eyes everywhere, and I'm not exactly popular since becoming a PI. I don't want to put you or Jason at risk, either."

"I'll come with you if you want. Would that take off the pressure?"

Olivia smiled. "No, but sweet of you to offer. Maybe I'm being paranoid." She switched modes. "I have to leave pretty soon, and I noticed we haven't been keeping up with new business. I emailed you some of them. Do you think it's time to cut Jason loose? We're at a quiet point, at least until something breaks in the Woodlawn case. I keep thinking more corruption will come out, and I hope it doesn't…implode or whatever. Our firm could face charges or Hunter might be implicated. I don't know, the whole business model was corrupt. The over-medicating, Larissa's lack of credentialing, the orderlies muscling Hunter outside one day…I don't think we've heard the last of Woodlawn. I hope we aren't an unintended casualty."

"Did you know eighty percent of what we worry about doesn't even happen? I'm just glad you made it out of there alive."

"You're right. Thanks. I'm overthinking."

Olivia slapped her palms on her desk and lifted from her chair. "Okay. The ceremony's at nine. Send help if I'm not back by lunch." She rolled her eyes. "Meanwhile, take a look at those cases."

Sherry stooped to pet Marlowe. "If you're back by lunchtime, let's go out somewhere."

As Olivia's vehicle left the parking lot, Sherry cast a celebratory look at Jason. "She's serious about not drinking. I think we have her back. All the way *back!*"

Jason smiled and kept pecking at his keyboard.

"What are you working on?" She approached his desk.

CHAPTER TWENTY-EIGHT

He shook his head, kept the smile. "You wouldn't believe it."

"Tell me!"

"I'm talking to Detective Shiloh McPherson. I'm taking her out this weekend."

Sherry's eyes grew round. "No kidding?"

"I'm not giving you guys ANY details. You'd stalk us"

"Oh. My. God. I can't wait."

He closed his laptop and put his elbows on his desk. "You're not getting me to talk."

"Yes, I am. Count on it." She went to her desk, sat, and opened her email, arranging them in order of priority. "Process server needed. Locate missing teenager. Locate missing brother," she mumbled under her breath as she waded through the emails. "I should've been a bounty hunter."

"More came in this morning," Jason said. "Assign me some."

She nodded, keeping her eyes on her screen. "I am. Trying to figure that out now." Leaning back in her chair, she put her hands behind her head. "Where do you think your talents work best?"

He grinned. "Women like me."

"They like your six-pack and Brad Pitt vibe."

"Nothing wrong with that, is there?"

"You're right, though," she murmured, thinking. "We need to put your 'California surfer vibe' to good use." Making a quick decision, her fingers flew across the keys. "I sent you three. Since you're a computer genius, flesh out their backgrounds before meeting with anyone."

"Will do."

She returned to the fresh job requests. As she googled, she gaped at photos of a potential new client linking arms with a man who looked very much like Duncan. Her lips pressed into a terse line, she kept scrolling. The request for information about a missing sibling had come from Marjorie Linda Matthews, age 43, mother of two. Partner, D. L. Carson, age 45. Cold sweat popped out on her forehead. D. L. Carson. A twin of the man she loved, who likely sat at her kitchen table this very moment. She googled work history and discovered Marjorie Matthews, aka the apparent partner of D.

L. Carson, had taught elementary students in Maryland Public Schools for twenty years. She patted her chest, willing her racing heart to slow down, wiping sweat off her forehead. Jason gave her a puzzled look from across the room. Ignoring him, she clicked 'Images' in the search bar for D. L. Carson. It populated with a screen full of shots of Duncan and Marjorie and their *two kids*. The full background check under "Duncan Malone" had been spotless. Who was this D. L. Carson? Frowning, she zoomed in on the photos, one after the other. One photo erased all doubt. D. L. Carson was *her* Duncan, right down to the birthmark on his left forearm.

She pressed the client's number with a deliberate calm which belied the storm simmering in her chest. "Ms. Matthews? This is Sherry Lattimore, Watchdog Investigations. You inquired about our services, and I'm calling to set up a meeting to discuss. When are you available?"

Chapter Twenty-Nine

Olivia

The short drive through rolling hills and acres of farm country provided a peaceful space to pick through the messy jambalaya my brain had become. The awards ceremony couldn't have come at a worse time, and the possible abduction scenario had taken over the prime spot in my head. I decided Hunter and I would manage Callie's escalating terror, and we'd try to keep Sherry out of it. Someone had to manage the crescendo of new business proliferating in our email inboxes.

My grip on the steering wheel tightened. I stopped at a stop sign.

Personally, I thought since Callie hadn't budged on Graham's supervised visitation, he'd taken matters into his own hands. I moved through the stop. My destination lay just five minutes away, in the heart of Westminster's historic district.

I could be wrong about Graham, though.

As I pulled into Westminster PD's parking lot, I groaned. A small army of cameras and mics and urgent reporters swarmed my car, shouting questions. When I parked, they started knocking on my window. I sat there in silence, begging God for patience. I'd hoped the fuss about my past as "Mercy's Miracle" had slowed to the occasional trickle instead of an onslaught like this. I closed my eyes and remembered the bristle of microphones poked into my face as I walked out of the hospital after a difficult, five-week rehabilitation seven years ago. Why they'd chosen me as the feel-good story of the year, I had no idea, but it had created a deranged fan club known as the "Foofoos" (Friends of Olivia), and a litany of issues which would've never happened without the damn press. And now, the spotlight had found me again. Resigning myself to my fate, I tried to form a genuine smile while slipping my purse strap on my shoulder and cursing the tight skirt which made it impossible to exit my vehicle with any grace at all.

"Olivia, how's your health? Did you have a setback? We heard you were in rehab."

"Are you excited about the award today? Why do you think they chose your firm?"

"How's the drinking problem, Olivia? Do you think your TBI caused the problem? Do you think you should still be working?"

As I tugged my skirt down after the awkward disembarking, I gritted my teeth in frustration. Who had ratted me out? The rehab situation had been confidential except for my team. Had they leaked it? I walked to the entrance, climbed the concrete stairs, and pushed my way to the gleaming double doors, signaling the waiting press liaison inside to wait while I dealt with the frenzy. Her face, drawn and anguished, her arms spread wide; made it clear she'd fought a losing battle against the tidal wave of statewide press and social media. I turned toward the group from my position on the landing abutting the glass doors. The press and photographers arranged themselves on the lower stairs, camera crew behind, reporters in front.

"Olivia! When are you getting married? Are you moving?"

"How's your health? Are memories still returning? When will you write another book?"

"Is it true your first book is being made into a mini-series?"

My press-ready smile faltered. My agent needed to do a better job of keeping the lid on things. I patted the air with my hands. They quieted. "Five minutes, okay? "My health is fine. I had a small setback, but our excellent local hospital has a great staff, and thanks to them, I'm good. I've made some lifestyle changes—"

The group surged forward. "What kind of changes? Are you an alcoholic?"

"No," I declared. "I'm not an alcoholic."

"Then why did you check yourself into a rehab?"

I stared at the sea of reporters holding their microphones in my direction, and tightened my resolve. "I can't comment. The Woodlawn investigation is ongoing, and I don't want my comments to be misconstrued or put anyone at risk. As to getting married..." I held up my engagement ring in hopes of refocusing the conversation. "We're planning the wedding." I held the smile, my hand in the air, an irresistible photo op. Cameras clicked. The relentless flicker of flashbulbs strobed my eyes.

"Will Detective Faraday move to Maryland?"

I smiled. "It's *Sergeant* Faraday now, and we are discussing."

After a few more questions, I thanked them for their interest and went inside.

"I'm so sorry, Ms. Callahan. We, uh...I had a lot of calls and tried to mitigate the interest, but..." Her owlish eyes behind the glasses pleaded for absolution as she wrung her small, white hands.

"It's okay," I said, taking a deep breath. Checking for spittle stains on my silk blouse from over-zealous mouths, I straightened. "Where's the ceremony?"

"Follow me."

* * *

After the awards ceremony, I fought through the throng once more, trying to be gracious before slamming my car door and shutting them out. I sat there a few seconds, embracing the tingle of pride at the framed certificate and trophy signed by every police chief in the state. I hadn't wanted to make a big deal of it, but it *was* a big deal. I started backing out of my parking slot. The cameras and mics had been put away and the reporters had begun to trickle back to their waiting company cars and vans. I put the Rover in drive, my little reservoir of happiness spilling over for the first time in a while.

A gentle knock sounded on the driver's side window. An anxious face bent down and peered inside. *Callie.* "What are you doing here?" I asked, shocked.

If the press found out about my bestie's daughter's possible abduction, they'd go crazy trying to get a headline. "Get in," I commanded, taking stock of her tear-streaked face. "Slide down in the seat."

Once I got on the highway, I relaxed. "What the hell, Cal? I'm trying to avoid press coverage, not attract more."

With a glance over her shoulder, she unhunched her back and sat properly in the seat. "I heard about the ceremony on the news. I'm going crazy. I couldn't get Hunter to answer his phone, and Graham's blocked my number. Or, ditched his phone."

"So you thought you'd track me down in the middle of a presser? Cal, Amy is over eighteen. Don't you think you're overreacting? I'm not sure we should panic, yet."

Her lips parted in surprise. "Aren't you worried about Lilly?"

"You heard her. Did she sound scared? Besides, no news from Hunter is good news."

Callie jammed her arms across her chest.

"The restaurant he took them to is in downtown Richmond. By now, Hunter has pinpointed the location. Don't worry." I pressed the button on my steering wheel and told it to contact Hunter's phone.

He answered after the first ring. "We found the restaurant."

Callie absolutely wilted with relief. "Thank God."

"How are the girls?"

A two-heartbeat pause passed. Callie stared at the dashboard, waiting; her lips fashioned into a hard, straight line. With a nervous glance at her, I asked him if he heard the question.

"He dropped Lilly off."

"Good. And...?"

"We have his license plate. The only problem, it's a rental. He flew to Richmond and rented a car. After he dropped Lilly, he took Amy for ice cream. Your daughter begged off because she had to study. The car hasn't been turned in, and I'm driving to the rental company now." He cleared his throat. "They haven't been able to reach him."

Callie's face reddened. She fanned herself furiously, an inch away from hyperventilating. I patted her leg.

"So…what are you thinking?"

"I'm thinking if she doesn't get back to the dorm before he turns the car in, we might have a problem. I'm going to look at the rental company's CCTV."

"He'd be insane to steal a rental car and disappear with Amy. It's unsustainable. He'd be violating parole, not to mention possible kidnapping charges."

"Unless he leaves the country." Callie fumbled with her purse to find a Kleenex.

"What did she say?" Hunter asked.

"Cal. Has he talked about leaving the country?"

"When I went over there…"

"She went over where?" Hunter asked.

"She dropped in on Graham. They talked. I'll fill you in later. *Cal.* What did he say?"

She looked into the distance. "I didn't think he'd take the risk…I mean…" Callie fixed me with a terrified stare. "He must've heard from the Parole Board, and figured 'screw it'." She bit her fingernail. "It would be his last chance to spend time with his daughter, and he told me even if he left the state, his PO would only tack on a few months."

"Did you hear that, babe?" I asked.

Hunter exhaled into the phone. I imagined him putting his hand across his eyes in frustration. So much for trying to exclude him from Callie's drama. "So, you went ahead and filed a police report on the break-in?"

"We did."

"I wouldn't be surprised if he's running, then. I don't think he's stupid enough to add 'kidnapping' to the parole violation, though."

Callie sobbed, trying to catch her breath.

Hunter's reassuring voice drifted through my car speakers. "We'll get her, Cal. Tell me your impressions when you were with him."

She mopped her face with Kleenex, sniffling. "He'd had a few beers and seemed happy to see me. He kept mentioning reconciliation, so I encouraged it to keep him talking. He mentioned a fresh start in Canada or Europe. We laughed about it."

My eyes widened. "How could you not tell me?"

"I thought he was joking!"

"Let's get back to Amy," Hunter said. "Maybe he'll drop her off all safe and sound. Maybe a judge won't be too hard on him for leaving the state to see his daughter. We don't need to panic unless the rental isn't returned. He's got until ten o'clock tomorrow morning."

"So, we wait," I said, stating the obvious. I pulled in beside Callie's car and parked. "In the meantime, I'll call Lilly and get her perspective."

Hunter told us he'd keep us updated.

Callie and I said our goodbyes, and I tried to reassure her as best I could. She trudged to her car disconsolate and numb. I sat there a minute, wavering between joy at Lilly's return and sorrow at Amy's uncertain fate. A liquor store marquis across the street caught my eye. My heart beat double-time in anticipation with a Pavlovian urgency. Disgusted, I gritted my teeth, started the Rover, and left.

I arrived at the office ten minutes later, scooped the framed certificate and trophy into my arms, and marched into the office to present them to my team.

Sherry slipped from behind her desk. "Let me see."

I put the items in her hands. After admiring, she showed them to Jason, who made appropriate sounds and returned to his tasks.

She pointed at a spot on the wall. "These should go right there."

I smiled. "Whatever you think. We still on for lunch?"

"Yep. Meet you in twenty minutes at Eddie's."

* * *

The hostess led me to "our" table, the one featuring a picture window overlooking Westminster's busy main street. I draped my purse on the back of the chair and watched life outside the window while waiting for my colleague. A used furniture store sat across the street, accompanied by an art gallery, a Salvation Army retail outlet, a boutique clothing store, and a local coffee shop. I counted three Bradford Pears per block, showing off their spring blooms. Busy Marylanders strode up and down the sidewalk. Diners populated every table in Eddie's, and the two remaining chairs sat at our table, conveniently pulled out and waiting.

Sherry rushed in a few minutes later. Distracted. Not her bubbly, vivacious self. The server approached. After ordering the quiche and a glass of orange juice, her eyes glistened.

Uh oh. I frowned. Didn't we have enough balls dropping all over the place? I put my hands on the table and interlaced my fingers. "Go ahead. I can take it," I said, with an exaggerated grimace.

Her smile lacked substance. "It's not about you, it's..." She groaned. "I thought Duncan was one of the good ones, you know?"

My heart sank. No one deserved a good guy more than the woman sitting in front of me. "What happened?"

"It started with a new client request." She released a dramatic sigh and arranged her purse on the windowsill. "I have a meeting tomorrow. Ms. Marjorie Matthews. Do you know her, by chance?"

"I think Lilly or Serena had her as a teacher?"

Sherry nodded. "That's her. The job is locating a missing brother."

"And...?"

"A routine background check revealed images of her spouse." Folding her hands, she put her elbows on the table, and shellacked me into my chair with sad eyes. "It's Duncan. Right down to the birthmark on his forearm. They have two kids."

I spent a few seconds engaging in fruitless finger-tapping.

"As I told you, when we first met, I researched the crap out of him. I mean, after your experience with Monty? And Hannah's horrible abuse situation with the man of her dreams?" She grunted. "No way I want to end up like Hannah. Believe me, I did my due diligence."

"I'm sure you did."

"Based on the new info, I changed the search parameters, and he's all over the web as 'D. L. Carson.'" As I look back, the information on Duncan *did* look thin as in *whitewashed.* How could I be attracted to an asshole who paints a whole new identity to pursue a side piece? Which is what I am. A side piece!" A light pound of her fist on the table caused the salt and pepper shakers to bounce.

"Maybe you don't have the whole story. And, you are not a side piece."

Tears slid down her cheeks. "He's been with her seventeen years. They have kids!"

"You're not a side piece because you didn't *know* you were a side piece."

She frowned. "That doesn't even make sense."

I flapped my hands in dismissal. "Whatever. You know what I mean. Besides, you may not have all the facts. Are you sure they're together?"

"The residence address under 'D. L. Carson' and the residence address under 'Duncan' are different. One's in Hunt Valley, the other is in Westminster. All the images I found of them together are in Westminster. The one in Hunt Valley might be his business location? I feel like I'm sinking into quicksand. This is ridiculous, he's an asshole, and I don't want to put in the effort to tail him to figure out the truth. Maybe I should vet everyone I date through our dark web expert, Cosmo. He would've matched images. Why didn't my search pull up similar images, anyway?"

Lapsing into a sad silence, she studied the historic restaurant's original wood flooring, fashionably worn and imprinted by centuries of restless steps. "You know as well as I do two people can't have the same odd birthmark." Her eyes hardened into blue steel. "The deeper I got into his 'D. L.' persona it looked like he uses one for socials and networking, and the other for driver's license, LLC, website, and bank accounts."

The server arrived with great pomp, setting our plates before us as if serving royalty. "For my two favorite regulars. This is on the house, ladies."

We made appropriate remarks. He flushed with pleasure, and slid away.

"I'll give him a big tip and put it on Watchdog's tab."

"You always do that."

"Well. A *huge* tip, then."

She laughed. "I guess there are worse problems than a lying sleazebag. Look at poor Callie."

A tingle of guilt percolated through my gut. "I need to tell you something."

CHAPTER TWENTY-NINE

"Oh, sure. Add to my growing weight of despair."

"Okay. I won't tell you." I dug into my Cobb salad and took a sip of my Diet Coke.

A few minutes of brisk chewing ticked by before she raised her head and pointed her fork at me. "Okay. Go."

"I didn't want to pile on something personal while you had a full roster of new client calls on your plate."

She cocked her head and squinted, swallowing a bite of quiche. "You are *not* telling; you are providing rationale for why you *haven't* told me. Therefore, it must be significant."

"I'm trying to shrink it."

"In your head, you mean."

"Yeah."

We chewed in silence.

"Graham?" she concluded.

I nodded. Her eyes narrowed. "He's got Amy?"

I gave her a pained look. "He does."

"Oh. My. God. Cal was right to be concerned. Why are you so calm?"

"Hunter's on it. Graham got a flight to Richmond and rented a car to surprise her and take her to dinner. Since they were both in their dorm room when he arrived, he asked Lilly, too," I said, as if it was just another nice thing a dad did for his daughter. Except this dad's a felon and in violation of parole. And now, a flight risk.

"He has LILLY?"

"Had. She's back in her room now." I frowned. "Quit. I'm getting stressed. I don't want to stress about this. Or anything." My pulse raced. My head throbbed. I couldn't risk another seizure. I'd be no good to anyone.

Sherry made a heroic effort to contain the dramatic expressions wafting across her face like thunderclouds on a windy day. "Okay. Sorry." She forked another bite of quiche. "If Hunter's on it, I won't worry, either."

We continued chewing in silence.

Chapter Thirty

Hunter

Lieutenant Nicholson burst into Hunter's office, a scowl on his face. Hunter jerked his gaze from his laptop screen.

"I got a status update on Woodlawn a few minutes ago. "

Hunter closed his laptop.

"So far, we've got Alex Barnes for human trafficking, and enough evidence to make a judge very happy. No worries there, and his import hustle is selling off inventory and shutting the doors."

Hunter smiled. "In exchange for a lighter sentence?"

Nicholson shook his head. "He didn't put up much of a fight before he confessed, and his empire is crumbling. I heard the family disowned him, too." He scowled. "Seems the whole damn town is complicit. I mean, we can't arrest an entire town, but the Chief of Police you met out there, the one who retired? He's looking at ten years."

"Doesn't surprise me. Did they get the mayor? Dink something?"

He nodded. "Stricklin. He wouldn't talk. We gave him incentives, but he didn't budge. He's sitting in holding until he decides he might want to change the judge's mind about house arrest until trial. Nicholson ran his palm across his balding head. "What a mess. The labs had been funded by some non-profit in DC, and a group of clueless pathologists looking for the next big tax write-off. All that aside, I'm gettin' off track here…what can you tell me about Larissa Ivanov?"

Hunter blinked. Why would he ask about Larissa? "I left her doing clean-up after the place got investigated. She was supposed to get Matty Stricklin into a proper facility and redirect their current clients. By all accounts, Larissa had been hired as a layperson counselor and had no idea what was going on. I asked about her credentials, and she didn't have any other than a six-week certificate and experience as a recovered addict. Knowing the basics about rehabs, I believed her. They don't always have someone with a certificate, much less a degree, on-site."

Nicholson chewed his lower lip. "Huh. Wonder why she cleaned out her office, her residence, and flew the coop."

"Damn, "Hunter whispered, shaking his head. "We never considered her a suspect since she seemed eager to help us."

"We tracked the funding and discovered the mayor sold out his wife for a few bucks, so his lawyer can add domestic violence felony charges to the list. Poor woman had broken veins and bruises from all the needle sticks she'd been given. There's a word for a man who could do this to his wife, but I can't think of one bad enough. As you suspected, the doctor's house pick-ups included different iterations of a breakthrough drug for Alzheimer's. But who oversaw the technological implementation? The research? Those lab techs weren't doing it without direction."

Hunter rubbed his forehead. "What did the techs say?"

"Zoom calls on a dedicated, secure server, and they used voice changer software. He dropped into a guest chair in front of the desk and steepled his hands. "We've got twelve confirmed dead, so far. My bet is the autopsies will show markers related to the inventory we found in the Woodlawn facility. Of course, no one wants to take responsibility and we can't get Collins Browning or his buddy Alex Barnes to talk, either. They have bigger problems, and the whole board seemed unwilling or unable to identify a lead pathologist. Dink Stricklin handled the day-to-day. He conscripted community leaders to stay quiet…the Chief of Police, certain judges, power brokers. The FBI interviewed some of the Virginia senators, who all think Dink Stricklin is the best thing since the invention of the wheel, so it appears the drug experimentation had an implied seal of approval. They liked him. Believed him." He frowned, making his jowls more pronounced. "Dumbasses. The whole lot of those political types disgust me." He sighed. "We need to find and interview Ms. Larissa Ivanov."

Hunter stared at his desktop, deep in thought. "I couldn't get a lot of background intel on her from NCIC, and at the time, I figured she must live a boring life but now I wonder if it was legit. It did seem odd I didn't turn up anything pointing to an individual with a drug or alcohol problem."

"If this woman led a research effort, she'd have degrees out the wazoo. And, not to be puttin' her in a box, but her last name *is* Russian. Lots of scientists from around there."

"Maybe it's not her real name."

Nicholson touched the folds of his neck. "Could be."

"Have you checked with the US Marshals? What about WITSEC?"

He smiled. "Now we're talkin'. I'll put in a query. I have a friend or two working with the DOJ." He put his hands on the armrest and rose from his chair. "Appreciate the help." He left the room.

"Keep me in the loop," Hunter called after him.

As soon as Nicholson left, he called Lilly. She answered on the first ring. "Hey!"

"You busy?"

"This is perfect. My next class isn't for an hour. How are you?"

Lilly sounded normal, thank God. Perhaps she hadn't picked up on anything scary when she went to dinner with Graham and Amy. "Fine. Mind if I ask a few questions?"

Slight pause. "About what?"

"Amy's dad. He…" How should he position this so it didn't come off as terrifying? He cleared his throat and started over. "Did everything seem okay at dinner?"

"Yeahhh," she said, drawing out the word. "Why?"

"Since his release from prison is fresh, he's supposed to stay in Maryland to report to his parole officer, and Amy's mother is concerned he'll get in trouble."

"Huh. Well, Amy must not have known. We had a nice dinner, and Amy loved seeing him. They're very close. They went for ice cream after." After a couple of seconds, she added, "Amy didn't want to go, but he insisted."

"Where did they go after they had ice cream?"

The pause became worrisome. "Lilly?" he nudged.

"She didn't come back to the dorm last night, which I thought was weird because she needed to study for a test, but she could've been with her boyfriend and gone straight to class from there."

"Did her dad seem angry or irritated when she said she didn't want to go with him?"

"He did. But he's always like that."

Hunter's shoulders tensed. "Do you know where Amy's phone is?"

"Sure, it's on her dresser by her bed."

"Do you know her security code?"

"We shared our codes with each other in case of an emergency."

"Good thinking. I need you to unlock her phone and check her texts with her dad."

He heard the scraping of chair legs, light steps, the slight whoosh of a mattress.

"Okay. Here it is." She rattled off a boring text thread before hitting some messages which elicited a gasp. "This had to be why she acted weird all night…"

Hunter's forehead crunched. "She acted weird? At dinner? In what way?"

"Like she and her dad had a secret. I wonder if this is what it's about." She began reading.

'Can't wait to see you, honey. I know your mom means well, but she's hell-bent on keeping you from me.'

'She only wants to make sure you've adjusted to life outside prison.'

'I have. Promise. And, ten days of missing school isn't bad. It'll be easy to make up the work.'

'Dad! I told you I can't! I have graduation.'

'Let's talk about it at dinner.'

Lily gasped.

"Do you think they—"

"Let's not go there yet," Hunter said. "Not a word to Amy's mom for now, okay? Let me call the rental place and see what I can find out. Let me know if you hear from Amy, and if she calls, tell her she should not, under any circumstances, take a road trip with her dad."

"I will. You don't think her dad...*forced* her to go, do you?"

"I hope not."

After he ended the call, he spoke to the rental outlet again, and got the same person he'd talked to before. He inquired about the vehicle's return.

"Looks like he's late," the counter person said. "Also, he's outside our boundary zone. The alert would've gone off...but wait...the car's parked."

"Can you give me a location?"

"Sure." The man gave him an address about six hours north. Hunter winced. Sounded like a trip to Canada. Or...board a flight from Canada to Europe? His pulse thundered in his ears.

"Do me a favor. We may have a kidnapping in progress, and I need you to keep an eye on your vehicle and let me know if it starts moving. In all likelihood, he's going to dump the car and find an alternate form of transportation, but I need to know if he's still driving the car."

"You got it. Damn weirdos. This is the third time this year someone tried to steal one of my cars." He slammed down the receiver.

Hunter's landline started blinking. He grabbed it and listened to the voice on the other end. They needed his collaboration on the unfolding Woodlawn investigation, ASAP. Muttering under his breath, he called Olivia and pelted her with quick bits of information.

"Graham's headed north with Amy. Tell Callie to file a Missing Persons report with Richmond PD immediately. I'm assigning one of my detectives, who will contact Graham's parole officer and get things moving from that direction. I will keep you in the loop."

Olivia's stunned silence spoke volumes.

"Look, I don't have time to flesh out the details. I have to go into a meeting. Get the ball rolling with Callie. Love you. I'll call later."

Chapter Thirty-One

Olivia

I stared at the phone in my hand, thoughts pumping through my brain, terror spurting through my veins. Had Graham become infected with Monty's nefarious, sinister approach to ex-wives? Was this my fault? I shook my head fiercely. God. No. I cannot take on one more thing and call it "my fault." I'd already taken on too much, and it had almost broken me, which had been the reason I started relying on wine in the first place. I couldn't fix everyone's problems, and many of them were not even mine to fix.

I pressed in Callie's number.

"Any word?"

"Cal, I…"

"Oh, no. What happened?"

"Graham's headed north with Amy."

The shriek pierced my eardrum. I held the cell away from my ear, putting the phone on speaker, my own tears mixing with hers. Could Graham be trusted not to harm Amy?

"You have to file a Missing Persons, Cal."

I could feel the immediate shift as she struggled to overcome a terrified paralysis. "H-How do I do it?"

"I think the quickest way is to go to the station, and if they give it to an investigator, you can talk to them on the spot. Also, Hunter told me once there's a Missing Persons, they will contact Graham's PO and from there, things will happen fast."

"He wouldn't hurt Amy."

"Of course he wouldn't," I said, though I didn't know for sure. Prison can twist a person.

"I thought this might happen." A paper-thin terror skimmed the words.

"Be strong, Cal. Hunter needs the report. It's a first step."

"I'll drive to the station right now. Thank Hunter for me."

My chest felt like it had caved in. I put my palms across my face. My own daughter had been a breath away from the same fate. By the grace of God, I'd gotten a reprieve. Now, I needed to pray for my friend to get her daughter back. I forced myself to re-orient and get back to work. "Jason?"

He appeared at my office door. "Hi."

The microwave beeped. He held up an index finger. "Be right back." He returned with a steaming hot Marie Callender's chicken pot pie and a fork, and leaned against the door.

"Have you heard what's going on with Callie?"

"Her crazy ex has her daughter."

I nodded, appreciating Jason's unique talent for discretion while simultaneously internalizing every detail of our cases. "Your thoughts?"

He walked in, sat in one of the guest chairs in front of my desk. The smell of the Marie Callender's pot pie had roused Marlowe to a seated position in his dog bed. Over the edge of my desk, I could see his black nose held high in the air, sniffing.

Jason swallowed a mouthful of pot pie. "Isn't Hunter handling it from his end?"

I nodded.

"She's filing a Missing Persons, right?"

I nodded again.

"Has anyone checked the daughter's socials?"

"She doesn't have her phone."

I could almost see ideas slotting into place in his younger, more pliable brain.

"They have to stop for potty breaks and food. She's a smart kid. What if she grabbed his phone and messaged someone? He can't keep eyes on her twenty-four, seven. What about a burner? If she had some of her own cash, maybe when her dad went to the bathroom, she had the good sense to buy a burner?"

"Long shot."

"Is there a BOLO?"

"In the works. Graham may dump his rental, though. But with the Missing Persons, pictures will show up all over the country, as you know. That's in the works, too."

"How's Callie?"

"She's gone to the police station to file the report."

"Let's go to my desk. I think better at my laptop."

I followed him to the reception space and pulled a chair beside his. As he typed, he asked random questions about Amy, if she had our office number, who she hung out with at school other than my Lilly, how close the dad-daughter relationship had been in the past. I had to smile. "You'd make a great private investigator," I joked.

He didn't even crack a smile. "Okay. I did a random search of all her socials. Her last posts were a couple of days ago. Now. Let's look at Graham's."

"Callie's tried. He's made his accounts private."

"Ah. Easy. I'll figure it out. Give me an hour."

I gave him Cosmo's number, and a budget. "If you need help, Cosmo's the guy. Thanks, Jason."

I walked out to my Rover and stood there a second, taking in my office building, the baby-blue sky, the marshmallow clouds. The trees around the building had leafed out into a jubilant spring green. Down the twisty lane ending at my farmhouse, the hickory, maple, oak, and white ash trees appeared to touch fingers high overhead. Like a benediction. Driving down the lane to my house in the evening had become such a treat, with the natural canopy making it feel insulated and secure.

I laughed outright. After all the misadventures occurring on my property over the last seven years, only a fool would consider the half-mile drive from my office to my house "insulated and secure."

However, even after so much tragedy…arson, assaults, stalking, trespassing…it hurt to think of leaving my home and starting over in Richmond. I'd just gotten in my car to go get lunch and bring it back to the office when Sherry squealed into Watchdog's lot on two tires.

What now?

I turned off the ignition.

She got out of her Toyota, slamming the door so hard I thought she might have strained her arm.

"Should I ask?"

She flung out her hands in frustration. "Why not? Everyone else has."

"Who is everyone else?"

"Oh, I don't know…the cops, Duncan's wife, his kids."

I put a cautious arm around her. "I'm so sorry."

"It's hideous! He *is* married. Separated, but married. I went to Marjorie's house to talk to her about her brother's case, and guess who knocked on the door to see his kids?" She wiped away tears. "An out-of-body experience, for sure." She gulped in a deep draught of air.

"What'd you do?"

"You mean after he hyperventilated?" She laughed. "Then, he had the nerve to ask me *what I was doing there.*"

"Wow."

"Marjorie didn't know how to react. I had to tell her we had a conflict of interest and wouldn't be able to take her case. I texted her some referrals." She swallowed, hard. "I mean…how often does the truth just fall out of the sky like that? He didn't handle it well, and tried to explain, but I cut him off."

I frowned. "Explain, how?"

"Blathering. He's a blatherer," she muttered.

"I repeat, how did he explain?"

"Something about being married for the wrong reasons… Marjorie never took his last name, and the kids didn't either, which makes no sense to me. His name has to be on the birth certificate, doesn't it?"

I nodded. "Unless they had a home birth. Maybe it's just her name on the certificate. Are you sure they're his kids?"

She groaned. "It doesn't matter, now. I'm done."

"It is puzzling why he wouldn't tell you. You guys have been together a while."

She lifted a shoulder. "I've never even been to his house because of constant 'remodeling'." Drawing air quotes around the phrase with her fingers, she huffed out a sigh and continued. "I'm questioning every single thing he told me, now."

"People are complicated."

"Something else," she said, her fire breathing its last, leaving a sad husk.

I felt so bad for her. She'd fallen hard for Duncan.

"He told me this wild story about working for a security firm, and he'd been given a sensitive assignment. He couldn't tell me more." She squinted. "Would it be a waste of time to check out what he said? It might be a lie, but..."

I smiled. "Of course. I'll get Hunter to track him down. Do you think Duncan Malone is his real name?"

"I doubt it. He also told me he hasn't told his wife what he does."

We remained silent a few beats.

"How did you leave it?"

"I was mad. I had to get the heck outta there. He went back inside."

"So, his wife didn't listen?"

She shook her head. "We went outside. He didn't want the kids to hear."

Out of the corner of my eye, I watched a tall male wearing professional casual attire thread his way through the tables toward us. He had dark hair, startling blue eyes which matched Sherry's, and caramel-colored skin. Worry lines framed his mouth and crinkled his forehead. I pointed.

She turned. "Dammit."

I smiled. "This should be epic."

"Ladies." His nod was curt. "May I join?"

"No." She scowled.

"Please," I said, smiling and extending my palm toward one of the chairs.

Sherry pouted in my direction.

He pulled out the chair and sat, his eyes locked on Sherry. "I'm telling the truth."

She didn't respond, so I decided to facilitate. "I hear you guys experienced a significant stumbling block."

Duncan studied his tented fingers, then lifted his head and looked first at Sherry, then me. "I need this to stay between us. People could get killed."

Well. *That* got my attention. I straightened in my chair.

He reached for her hand. She pulled away. "Please listen," he told her, his voice gentle. She focused on the table and pressed her lips together. The hurt seeped from her like a fragile cloud.

"I left the Army last year. A private vendor recruited me for a security firm and assigned me to an exotics dealer in downtown Baltimore."

He waited for our reactions.

Sherry's mouth dropped, along with my own. "Are you talking about Barnes Imports?" she whispered.

He nodded. "I was given a short leash and an alias."

"How…what…?"

"The situation has become untenable." He took a deep breath. "The job required a relationship with someone who worked at Watchdog Investigations." He flinched at her expression. "I'm so sorry. When you guys accepted the Barnes Imports job, my handlers saw a way in. They've been tracking illegal drugs, sex trafficking, and homicides originating from that location."

Completely gobsmacked, we sat there with our mouths hanging open. Hunter's words came back to me: "the Woodlawn situation has grown more legs." My heart began to pound. One of the legs sat right here, in the chair beside me. My mind got to work stitching bits and pieces together. Shiloh had been working the case when Sherry and Duncan met and started dating. The investigation must've led them to the intel that she and Collins Browning knew each years ago. They had to have been watching Collins, and realized Sherry would provide the perfect pipeline to him. Duncan's handlers may have even thought our firm *supported* the tangled mass of crime going on with Barnes Imports. The thought made me shudder. I looked from Sherry's anguished face to Duncan's weary one. I believed him.

"I want to be clear. Yeah, it started out that way, but …Sherry, you have to believe me. They wanted me to ask you to wear a wire, but I told them I couldn't do that. I fell in *love* with you."

She shook her head in frustration. "I don't know what to believe," she said. "I've been dating a man who's been married for seventeen years. How do you expect me to react?"

"Someone got it wrong! Our families were friends. I've *known* her for seventeen years. She had a bad marriage, a nasty divorce. Her kids call me "Uncle D." We leaned on each other through some tough times. I needed a deep cover identity for the sensitive assignments. It's common and easy for the Feds to create a temporary identity, so D.L. Carson was born. You met Duncan Malone, though, because I knew you'd do a deep dive on me, and we wanted it to appear as authentic as possible. I had to keep up the alias until the agreed-upon date of termination of contract. Marjorie had agreed to assist, and pose as my wife. All those images of us online helped solidify the alias. In exchange, I moved in and helped out with the kids, and she got a good portion of my paycheck. When you and I started dating, it became so complicated I insisted we end the charade, and when we could, we did." He chuckled. "I couldn't believe it when I walked in to visit the kids and…there you were. I thought I was seeing things. After you left, I told her about you."

Sherry yanked several napkins out of the holder and dabbed her face. Since she couldn't seem to find her words right now, I stated the obvious. "So. The kids aren't yours."

He shook his head. "Don't get me wrong, I love those kids. Their father left them when they were babies. I've tried to help her over the years. But no, they're not mine."

She sniffled and pulled out more napkins. I smiled. Maybe hope had decided to grace this relationship after all.

"Is Duncan even your real name?" She asked, struggling to keep her emotions in check.

"Yes. I'm sorry I couldn't tell you about the alias." He drew in a breath, and let it out, slow. "For me to work security on these situations where they were looking for information, the FBI had to scrub my military background, which is why you didn't run across it. I've put in a request to restore my full background, but I don't know what they consider appropriate for someone who has opted out of a security detail with a lot at stake. Due to the circumstances, I've asked to be released from their employ altogether. They agreed. D. L. Carson will disappear, and I'm hoping to get my life back."

"Are you sure you don't have any other aliases hanging around?" I grinned.

"No more aliases. Promise."

Sherry crumpled the wad of napkins into her fist and became very still.

I watched and waited. "Still" for Sherry typically preceded some sort of explosive response.

With a happy squeal, she leaped from her chair into his lap. He wrapped his arms around her.

Two tables over, a man smiled at us. "Somebody getting a ring?"

I laughed. "Maybe."

Chapter Thirty-Two

Hunter

He left the round table discussion with his superiors, wondering why Richmond PD had to be so damn pivotal in the Woodlawn debacle. Striding back to his office, he realized the meeting had taken up most of the afternoon, and now, his sinking energy level demanded caffeine. Detective Becker held out a Starbucks to-go cup. "Thought you might need it."

Hunter snatched the cup and drank. "You read my mind. Thanks."

He extended a file. "This came for you."

Taking it in his free hand, he cocked his head and scrutinized the label. No label. "What is it?"

"I was told to keep it confidential, so I didn't look."

"Okay." He walked into his office, rounded his desk, and sat in his chair with a thump. "Why did I have to cross paths with Matty Stricklin, anyway?" He opened the file, feeling his nerve synapses waking up with each swallow of coffee. He took a deep breath before reading the confidential dossier on Larissa Ivanov, aka Katerina Petrov, an inch's worth of documents which would take hours to digest.

* * *

"I'm tellin' you, dude, I'm in a quandary here," Hunter told his friend Nick

Ramsey, Richmond Assistant DA. "I need your legal perspective."

"I see no implication of complicity. Your role as Olivia's fiancée pre-supposes the priority, right? Yes, you stumbled across the batches of experimental drugs, but you had no idea what they were, and as far as anyone knows, you wanted to get your fiancée out of there. Period. No judge would doubt it. I think you're covered."

Hunter tapped his fingers on his desk, staring at the spread-eagled file. "How could I have missed this? The woman is a genius. Three degrees. Microbiology, vaccinology, biochemistry. Undergrad work in Russia, then she managed to get accepted into an American program. No wonder she didn't have any credentials on the walls in her office."

"She must've missed the boat on common sense, though. How'd she rate WITSEC, again?"

"Expert witness in fraudulent drug trials." Hunter chuckled. "Oh, the irony."

"I remember. About ten years ago? Lots of threats in the air back then. Mafia, right?"

"Yeah. The Mafia had their fingers in the cookie jar and got mad when the cookies disappeared. She took a bullet and ended up in Mercy Hospital. That's when the US Attorney General got involved." He blew out a long, measured breath. "She's lived as Larissa, the mild-mannered, recovering addict and rehab counselor for years while growing her research team and virology department. The grants alone astounded me. How could they dole out money without vetting the labs? The staff? She played the con of all cons. My lieutenant's getting chewed out by all the higher-ups, and I get the leftovers. It's not been fun."

Nick laughed. "If you hadn't been such a choir boy, none of this would've happened. I can see it all now…the press potential is limitless: 'Hero rescues mayor's wife and exposes criminal enterprise'. It's big. Get ready for the publicity. How's Olivia?"

"She's good. Working through some things, but I think she's realizing her future is in Richmond."

"About time."

"Yeah." The men remained silent a few beats. "Hey. How's the DA race shaping up?"

"So far, so good. I resigned as ADA, and as of next week, I'm interim DA."

"Congrats, Nick. You deserve this. You've worked hard."

He laughed. "I think the hard work is just beginning. You ever think about sitting in the Chief's chair?"

"Not once. Seriously. I'm good where I am."

"I wouldn't worry about this investigation. You're a detail. Plus, they have no idea about your suggestion that Olivia dig around in Woodlawn. This thing is like a gift falling in the Fed's lap. They're not going to look at you for anything. Besides, it'll take years to unravel in the court system."

"Okay," he said, feeling weight lift from his shoulders. They ended the call with promises of lunch soon.

An all-out international search for Larissa had been called, but Hunter figured she'd booked a flight the minute the Feds stormed Woodlawn Acres with their search warrant. She could be anywhere. He'd bought her to act like a kid being offered a puppy. "Get over it," he whispered, rising from his desk, restless. His cell buzzed in his pocket. He yanked it out. "Faraday."

"Hi, babe."

The mere sound of her voice calmed him. "Hi, yourself. How's your day?"

"I miss you."

"Same."

"Let's get married."

He laughed. "Trying."

"Are you okay?"

The cell pinned to his ear, he strode down the corridor, past the receptionist in the lobby, and out the double doors into the bright Richmond sunshine. He sat on his usual bench just off the pavement and underneath a sprawling oak tree. The scent of jasmine blooming permeated the air. "I'm good. I have a reprieve on the Woodlawn investigation, at least for a while."

"I wondered how things were going. Has Larissa been found?"

He frowned. The fresh intel on Larissa/Katarina threatened to bubble out. Should he tell her? *You can't.* "She's still in the wind. They'll find her."

"Maybe she needed a break. I figured she'd had enough, and got the heck out before they interviewed her."

"She answered questions to everyone's satisfaction. But when they tried to contact her later, she was gone. How's Callie? Any news?"

"She's a mess, as anyone would be. He did let Amy call her mom, proving he still has a heart. It was a burner, though. They couldn't track location."

"How'd Amy sound?"

"Fine. She thinks she's on a vacation with her dad."

"Well, I hope she enjoys it, because we *will* catch him."

"Callie told me he doesn't care. He's focused on spending time with his daughter."

"The longer they're out there, the more dangerous it gets."

"I know," she said, her voice soft. "I'm trying not to freak out. I thought they'd get him when he turned in the rental car."

Hunter's eyebrows rose. "When did that happen?"

"Yesterday."

He cursed. "The guy at the rental place didn't call me."

"Callie also discovered he'd taken cash from her purse, which tells me he doesn't have much money. I bet they're on a bus."

"I hope it's a bus back to her dormitory."

"I feel so helpless."

"The worst feeling in the world is waiting on something like this to break, but you have to let the cops do their job." He couldn't tell her his true feelings, or what his experience had been, but he knew the longer Graham evaded the authorities, the more desperate he would become. He'd drag his daughter into hiding, and from there, it's anyone's guess. He struggled to picture Graham capable of homicide-suicide, but he'd been surprised before. Eighteen months in prison can turn a person into a ticking time bomb.

He would share none of these thoughts. He must remain hopeful, for Callie's sake. For Olivia's sake. Feeling an urge to put his arms around her and never let go, he blurted, "Put your house on the market."

She chuckled. "How did you get from *abduction* to me selling my house?

CHAPTER THIRTY-TWO

Funny you should bring it up, though. I talked to an agent this morning."

A wave of relief washed over him. "What's the market like up there?"

"Good. She told me my house would sell fast. I still have to get it ready, though, so Lilly and Serena are coming in to help me. Lilly's last class before break is next week, and Serena's taking vacation days from her job in DC."

He smiled. "All that's missing is your mom."

"Oh, she's coming, too." Olivia laughed. After a pause, she continued. "Amy *has* to be home by then."

After the call, he opened his laptop, completed reports, and sent them to his lieutenant to review, and Becker, to archive. He checked in with his team in the field. Everyone seemed on track and in no need of his assistance. He frowned at the unexpected lull. In his experience, the calm wouldn't last long. His cell buzzed. Hunter rolled his eyes. "Like clockwork," he whispered, answering. "Faraday."

"*Shots fired.* She needs your help!"

Panic flickered in his chest at the tense, insistent male voice slicing through the airwaves. His hand tightened on the phone. Who is this?"

"Jason. From Watchdog. *It's Shiloh.*"

He jumped from his desk chair and began pacing back and forth behind his desk. "What do you mean 'it's Shiloh'?"

"We…we've been getting to know each other. We were on the phone when I heard a male voice, then shots. I think she might've gotten hurt. I thought you'd be faster than nine-one-one."

Hunter grabbed his weapon and stuck it in his belt holster. "You made the right call. Where is she?"

"She's there. In Richmond." He gave him the name of her hotel. "Some meeting she had to attend."

"Headed there now. Stay close. I'll let you know."

* * *

He felt his oversize tires catch serious rubber as he screamed into the parking lot of the Marriott on East Belt Boulevard in Richmond. Someone had already alerted the authorities. He gauged the status of the scene. Three cruisers sat in the lot, and two cops had been stationed on the ground, the others inside. He exited the car, flashed his badge, and raced into the lobby. The wide-eyed young woman at the front desk pointed and told him the room number. Third floor. Faster to take the stairs. His legs pumped hard until he reached the third floor, panting and cursing his lack of time for proper PT. Taking a breath, he strode down the carpeted hallway and into a room bustling with activity. Downstairs, he heard the faint whoop-whoop of an ambo on the way. The intact door told him she'd known the perp, or maybe someone pretended to be hotel staff. He showed his badge and scooted past the cops at the door. "Where is she?"

A female uniform pointed at the bathroom. "Changing her shirt. She got clipped in the shoulder."

He sagged in relief. "Shi!" he yelled.

She poked her head out of the bathroom. "Faraday. What a surprise."

He covered the three paces to the bathroom and took her face in his hands. Blood streaked her cheeks. Her discarded shirt had been deposited into an evidence bag. He could feel her trembling underneath his palms. Her cheeks were cold to the touch. He glanced at the makeshift bandage on her left shoulder. "How's the pain?"

"I'm okay, Faraday," she murmured, putting her hand over his. "A flesh wound. They'll fix me up and I'll live to become a target another day." Her smile faltered. He dropped his hands and glanced around the bed. "Forensics on the way?"

She nodded, turned to the sink, and soaped up a washcloth. He watched her in the mirror as she drew the washcloth across her face. "So much for riding a desk, huh?"

Hunter sat on the toilet lid. "What happened?"

"Collins Browning happened."

"How did he find you?"

"What I'd like to know." She discarded the washcloth into an evidence bag, and wiggled into a loose top one of the cops had gotten from her suitcase. "I'm thinking maybe I should avoid Richmond." She gave him a wry smile.

"He walked right into the room, shouting my alias: *Belia.* From the online investigation, remember? When you recognized my fabulous disguises on the dating profile. I guess your "Watchdog girls" did a good job on his case. It gave him enough intel to find me on the other sites and put it together." Hunter moved aside to allow space for her to exit the bathroom. "Let's get out of the room. Forensics will be here any second." On cue, a white-garbed army of ghosts invaded the premises. Hunter and Shiloh walked out of the room, down the hall, and leaned against the wall. "What I'd give for a cigarette," she muttered.

"I bet," Hunter said. "So. You and Jason?"

Her eyes narrowed. "What about him?"

"He's the one who called. He heard the shots."

"Oh. Yeah. He called you?" Smiling, she pressed her fingers on her shoulder bandage and winced. "It only grazed me. Collins didn't mean it. He's just scared. I can be quite…"

"Infuriating," Hunter finished.

"He was out on bail, letting off steam. He wanted to confront me, as if confrontation *ever* makes anyone feel better." She rolled her eyes. "I shouldn't have opened the door."

"Why did you?"

"Distracted. We were having a serious conversation."

"So. You went to answer the door…"

She nodded. "A rookie mistake. I didn't even hesitate. I thought room service had arrived. I left my cell on the bed, on speaker, that's why Jason heard everything. Collins burst in, wanting to talk, and I couldn't get rid of him. When he pulled out a handgun, it didn't register at first. I just stood there in shock, watching blood drip from my shoulder."

"Jason must be more distracting than I thought."

"Oh, he is." She grinned.

"Well, call him. He's freaking out." He bent and kissed her on the cheek. "Glad you're okay."

He walked to the elevator. When the elevator doors opened, paramedics moved into the hall with their collapsible gurney, clicked it open, and wheeled it toward the room. As he walked inside the elevator, he heard her irritated voice telling them under no circumstances would she need a gurney, for God's sake. She'd walk. He laughed, shaking his head. "Jason, buddy, I sure hope you know what you're getting yourself into."

Chapter Thirty-Three

Sherry

The days had gotten longer. Warmer. The sun dipped behind the trees, and shadows stretched across the pavement of the parking lot. Orioles and wrens chirped and fussed as she walked to her car, a perpetual smile lingering as she thought about Duncan. Yes, his revelations had been hard to hear, but she'd been thrilled to discover the truth. She'd never forget the confused look on his face when he walked in and found her with Marjorie in the living room.

Doubt crept through her mind.

She wanted to believe him. Needed to believe him.

Olivia had believed him when he'd shown up at Eddie's and disclosed his story. Shouldn't this be enough? His Special Ops training made perfect sense, as she'd loved watching the graceful physicality of his movements and enjoyed rubbing her palm along the chiseled muscles of his legs. His back. His chest. She giggled. As she pulled away from the office onto the highway, she answered his call.

"Hey. Wondered if you'd gotten cold feet."

"Why? Have you?" Sherry smiled, feeling a cozy warmth bloom in her chest.

"Just the opposite."

"I'm sorry I didn't trust you."

"I'm sorry I couldn't loop you in."

"I can't believe you've given up your job."

"I'll figure it out. I got a nice little nest egg from the Army, so I'm good. It's too easy to get sucked into something terrible with the kind of job I was doing."

"What are you going to do with all the free time?" Making a right turn, Sherry drove down a hilly street and made another right into her driveway. Her two-bedroom cottage sat on an oversize lot on the outskirts of Westminster, twenty minutes from Watchdog Investigations. She gathered her purse and tote bag and walked to her front door.

"For starters, I'm going to fix you dinner."

She laughed. "Wow. Is it time to unveil your house?"

"Yes, indeed, young lady. How about tonight? You bring the wine, and I'll fix you the best Maryland crabcakes you've ever put in your mouth."

"Deal. What time?"

They arranged a time, and he gave her an address in the sedate, small community of Sparks, Maryland. The address tracked with what she'd found online.

An hour and a half later, she sat parked in her car with her mouth hanging open. Had she walked into a trap? What was this? She half-expected security guards to trot out the elaborate front door and shove her into a waiting abduction van. Jabbing her Bluetooth to life, she called Olivia. "Hey. I'm in front of Duncan's house, and it's like something out of a movie set. I'm not sure I trust this…this whatever it is. I've been so relieved he's been honest with me, and now I'm not so sure."

"Has he?" Olivia asked.

Sherry scowled. "You *believed* what he said."

"I did, of course. Yes. But any further verification, in light of what he told us, might be useless. At this point, I think you either believe the man or you don't. Has he shown you proof of military service?"

"Not yet. But here I am, refusing to drown in a sea of magical thinking again, sitting in his ridiculously elaborate driveway. Are you at your desk?"

"Sherry. It's seven-thirty."

"Oops. Sorry."

"It's fine. Plus, I do have my office laptop in my uh…lap."

"Quick. Find what you can, maybe I missed something on our databases. I don't think he knows I'm here, yet."

She waited through long minutes, listening to Olivia's pecking on her keyboard, the subtle 'ahhhs' and 'hmms' every so often. Maddening. Agonizing. She glanced at the clock on the dashboard. Seven-thirty-eight.

"I have a snapshot, I think," Olivia said. "Duncan or D.L. Malone, age forty-two, Special Forces. He had fifteen years in and left. Not sure what's up with that. I see no prior marriages or children. No sheet, not even a speeding ticket or DUI."

"It doesn't take a genius to figure out an Army enlisted guy's salary wouldn't pay for a multi-million-dollar property in a neighborhood like this." Sherry kept her eyes trained on the front door.

"I ran across his parents' bios. Both deceased. Maybe he inherited?"

Sherry's blood ran cold. "How'd they die?"

"You know how obits are. They never say." More pecking. "Let's see if I can find news headlines in the weeks before. Sherry almost fainted at Olivia's sharp intake of breath.

"Car wreck. Brakes failed. His parents were like…social icons or whatever."

They shared a moment of contemplation. Sherry spoke first. "You don't think…?"

Olivia cleared her throat. "I'd take your firearm inside."

"Darn it," she whispered, pulling it from her console. "I was so looking forward to a nice evening."

"We don't know anything. It's a precaution."

"Did anyone open an investigation about the failed brakes?"

"Inconclusive."

Sherry bit her lip.

The front door opened. Duncan stepped out and waved, then motioned for her to come inside.

"I have to go. Pray for me."

Olivia laughed. "Enjoy yourself. Let's not jump to conclusions."

She made sure her firearm rested in its holster, tugged her jacket tighter around her, and walked to the front door. If he asked, she figured it would make sense she'd still be wearing it from work. At the very least, she could remove it and drop it into her purse, thereby accomplishing a preemptive strike. He wouldn't try anything outlandish if he knew her firearm lay within arm's reach.

"Hey," she said, stepping into his open arms. He smelled of Maryland crab and Old Bay spice. She laughed. "I can smell dinner on you."

He brightened. "It's in the oven. Come on in." He swept his arm toward the foyer and followed her inside.

"Wow," she said, making a show of removing her weapon from her belt and slipping it inside her purse. "Sorry. I'm sure you're the same way, forgetting you even have it on."

"You won't need it here. You're safe." He grinned.

Am I? "So." She spread her arms and spun in a slow circle, staring at the mile-high ceiling featuring a fabulous chandelier. "When do I get the tour?"

"Whenever you want it."

"Can I help with dinner?" She extended the bottle of wine she'd brought.

"Thanks, but everything's done." He glanced at his watch. "We have ten minutes. I'll pour us some of this, then show you around. Where do you want to start?" He walked into the kitchen. Sherry followed, and sat at a chic, minimalist kitchen table.

"What a fantastic kitchen."

He pulled down the rabbit ears on the wine opener, releasing the cork with a soft pop. "Great wine selection, by the way." Two wine glasses had been set out on the counter, which he filled halfway, handing one of them to her. With a smile, he lifted his glass. "To us."

"To us," she echoed, her voice a whisper. She'd watched intently as he'd poured, to make sure he hadn't slipped anything into her glass. *Stop. You're being paranoid, now.*

"Let's start down here. The master's on the first floor, along with kitchen, TV room, dining room, laundry. He walked into a large, comfortable den. The flatscreen on the wall was the size of a small dance floor. Four large, leather recliners sat in front of the TV; coordinated seating areas on each side of the room.

As Sherry strolled through the house, her mind spun with questions. "I have to say, it's rare to meet a guy who invests in a home like this. I need to meet your real estate agent."

He chuckled. "I didn't pick it out, I inherited it."

Okay. Check one question off my list.

"Rich aunt?"

"Rich parents." Anger tinged his expression, then vanished. "They loved their money."

"The house is beautiful."

"They had good taste, for sure. I never cared much about money."

"Because you always had it," Sherry replied, quickly.

His eyebrows arched.

"My folks struggled for every penny. It taught me the value of a dollar. I'm grateful."

He sipped his wine. "Just the opposite for me. My parents treated their cars and furniture with much more care and appreciation than their own son." His laughter held a dark note. "I wouldn't have taken a penny from them, but they both died at the same time, and here I am, thinking about selling."

"I'm sorry about your parents," she said. "What happened? I mean, if it's not too personal…"

"No, of course. Car wreck. They died instantly."

"How awful."

"I couldn't get home right away. An assignment had me taking out bad guys overseas. After that one, I decided I'd had enough of military life."

She winced. The words held the same tone as if he were talking about the weather. But if she could prove he was out of the country when their brakes failed, it would help.

Duncan grinned at her stricken expression. "Sorry. I forget civvies don't get our toughened sensibilities."

She drank more wine, moved closer, and put her hand on his arm. "I'm sure it was hard. I hope you've gotten counseling, and I hope you start sleeping better. Your nightmares are pretty intense."

He leaned down and kissed her. "Sweet. Sounds like you have your own 'vet' experience."

She absolutely did not, but she decided to go with it. "Yes. My brother."

He cocked his head. "Gulf War?"

"How'd you know?"

"If he's around your age, it would follow."

"Shouldn't you check on the crab?"

His head whipped around to the kitchen. "Oh, no!" He dashed away.

While he tended the crab cakes, she returned to the foyer and found her purse. As she cocked an ear toward the kitchen, she scrutinized hiding spots where she could grab her firearm within seconds. Ever since the shootings on Watchdog's property, she'd learned to keep a gun close. Her gaze fell to a small end table with two drawers sitting beside one of the armchairs in the den. It abutted the foyer, making acquisition of her weapon a straight shot from the den, the kitchen, or the foyer. "Perfect," she whispered, bending over and stashing her purse inside, leaving it open at the top.

Chapter Thirty-Four

Olivia

I wandered out onto my front porch holding a cup of tea instead of a glass of red wine. The habit of drinking wine still tugged, and drinking tea instead of wine felt strange at this hour. My brain had hard-wired wine at a certain time, in a certain place. However, the freedom of a light heart instead of chronic headaches and exhaustion more than made up for the loss. Replacing wine with tea seemed a small price to pay for getting my friends, fiancée…and my *life*…back.

I set the teacup and saucer on the end table, and sat on my floral cushioned, wicker loveseat. Marlowe whined inside the door. I let him out, and patted the loveseat. He hopped onto it with a contented sigh. Rubbing his head, I whispered to him of his greatness and wondered for the thousandth time who would surrender such an exceptional animal. My phone buzzed in my pocket. *Callie.* My pulse immediately rocketed into the stratosphere. "Hi, there."

She answered with a high-pitched wail followed by long, drawn-out sobs. My heart sank. "Dear God, Cal. What's happened now?"

"They found them!" More sobbing. "Olivia, she's on the way home. I can't even describe what I'm feeling."

My heartbeat re-entered Earth's atmosphere. My body melted into the loveseat. "Great news, girl. Tell me all about it."

"The border guards stopped the bus at the Canadian border. Graham even had sunglasses and a hat on. Amy had the presence of mind to give one of those signs like…the ones when a young girl has been taken against her will? Four upright fingers, then folded with thumb underneath? Someone on the bus notified the driver, who called the authorities. They've put her on a plane with an escort back to Richmond. Hunter called your mom to pick her up." She broke down. "Sorry, I'm… I can't even describe my joy."

I smiled. "My mom is the best possible sounding board. I bet she'll have Amy sleep at her house tonight, maybe even call Lilly to come over. You need company? I know you're going to head up there."

"Do you have time? I'd appreciate it."

"I'll make time. Can Marlowe come?"

"I insist!"

"I'll grab my stuff. We can be there before sunrise."

I threw jeans and tops into a duffel, gave Riot a ton of dry cat food, filled his water bowl, and high-tailed it out to my Rover in the garage. Marlowe blinked sleepily, but seemed to smile at the unexpected road trip with Mom. I stopped by the office to put a note on Sherry's desk, since it had gotten very late and I didn't want to wake her with a call or text. I also wanted to get my firearm out of the safe and take it with us. Drawing closer, I noticed a light on. I frowned. Maybe Jason left on a light? Not like him, though, as we had a strict policy of "last person out turns off all lights." A ball of dread forming in my stomach, I turned into the parking lot and sat underneath the halogen lights blazing as bright as day, ferreting out the best options. The building looked empty. Marlowe seemed unconcerned as I leashed him to take in with me. Since he hadn't growled, maybe the light had been left on by accident. However, I didn't want to risk it. Holding tight to Marlowe's leash, I walked to the front door, unlocked it, and waited on the stoop, holding my breath.

My cell buzzed. Callie had texted: *Where are you?*

Be there in a second. I stopped by the office, I texted back.

The stealthy sound of footsteps inside made my heart stop. Marlowe whined and pawed the door, but didn't growl. On the other side, a soft voice whispered, "Who's there?"

I nearly dropped the leash while yanking the door open. A young woman let out a cry and fell to her knees as Marlowe tried to bark her to death. I flicked on the overheads. "Who are you?" I demanded.

Her tangled, dark hair reached her shoulders. She looked tired, young, and hungry. Her backpack hung from one shoulder—a backpack the color and consistency of dried leaves in the fall. My mouth fell open. "Delia!?" I told Marlowe to back off and put my hand on her shoulder to show him she was not a threat. Not quite convinced, he held an alert stance.

With a wry smile, she wiped tears off her face. "Hi, roomie."

She'd found an unlocked window, she explained, and taken advantage of the guest room for two nights. With apologies, she begged me not to report her to the cops, and said she'd needed a shower and a clean place to sleep and remembered me talking about my office. "You had a different vibe. When I left Woodlawn for the last time, I thought what the hell? I don't have to stay in Virginia. Time for a fresh start, y'know?" She gave me a guilty look. "I just wanted to drop in, ask for a little help, but it had gotten so late. I found an open window." She grinned. "Opportunity knocking."

I frowned. Who kept leaving a window open? I needed to make a poster or something.

Her chipped-tooth smile broke my heart, but I needed to think about the liability of letting a recovering addict stay in our guest room. "And, before you ask," she continued, "I'm clean. Thirty-three days." She lifted her chin in a valiant attempt at courage, reminding me of my daughters. After telling Callie I'd be late, I dropped her at a hotel, pre-paid for three nights, and pressed a hundred-dollar bill into her hand.

It had taken forty minutes to sort her situation, and when I made it to Callie's, she ran out, dragging a small roller behind her. "We can take my car."

I thought about her pristine vehicle versus my Rover's extensive WeatherTech mats and dog-hair-embedded back seat. "Marlowe's going to be rough on a Cadillac, buddy."

"Oh." She put an index finger on her chin. "I guess you're right. Okay. The Rover it is." After stowing her suitcase in the back, she hopped into the passenger seat. "Let's go," she whispered, smiles wreathing her face; the perpetual pony-tail bouncing. The old Callie was back.

* * *

We arrived at Mom's place in Richmond at five a.m. Mom's hero-husband, Dr. Grayson Sturgis, or Gray for short, let us in. I wrapped my arms gently around his thin shoulders. His body trembled with the effects of an advancing Parkinson's diagnosis. He patted my shoulder. "Sure glad you got Amy back." He shook his head. "What an awful thing."

Callie dragged in her roller. "Hi, Dr. Sturgis. Where should I put this?" Thank you so much for letting us stay."

"Wouldn't have it any other way," he said, waving his arm toward the hallway. Second and third doors on the right. We have air mattresses as well, so let me know."

Callie disappeared down the hall. I dragged Gray to the couch in the den and sat beside him. "It's so good to see you. How are you feeling?"

He lifted a bony shoulder. "Good days and bad. Grateful for every one of 'em. Staring mortality in the eye has a way of changing a person's perspective." He grinned. "You should know."

I squeezed his shoulder affectionately. "Boy. Do I ever." I could laugh about it now, but seven years ago, the firm grip of death had been very real. As my former neurologist, Gray's efforts had been pivotal to my survival. "Has Mom been in touch?"

He nodded. "She's an hour out. Amy's real upset."

"I imagine she would be."

"Sophie told me her father got downright nasty. Got to be hard on his daughter."

Tears sprang to my eyes. "I don't know what drove him. His early release means nothing, now. All he needed to do was prove he could stay out of trouble."

"Funny thing about a man." Gray rubbed his chin. "All of us have a problem with being told what to do."

CHAPTER THIRTY-FOUR

"He had more on the line, though. You'd think he would behave."

"When a woman won't let a dad see his child…if he's a good dad…it does something to them. He snapped, I imagine."

Callie walked into the den of Mom and Gray's condo. The spacious den flowed into the kitchen, separated by a long, quartz-topped island with an overhang under which sat four stools. She pulled one out and sat. "Amy said they'll be here in forty minutes." Her hand dropped to her stomach. "I'm so excited, I can't eat. I can't even remember how long it's been since *that* happened," she said, patting her fluffy tummy.

"I'm happy for you, gal," Gray told her. "Sophie and I have prayed non-stop since we found out about it. There's a lot of power in prayer."

"Yes, there is," she said, her eyes slicking with tears.

Gray started to rise from the couch. I offered help. He refused. "If it's okay with you two, I'm going back to bed. Make yourself at home. Olivia, hon', you know where everything is. Help yourself. When Sophie gets here, tell her I love her."

I hopped off the stool and gave him a long hug. "I will. Good night. We'll try to be quiet."

He shuffled down the hall. Callie cocked her head at me. "How bad is it?" she whispered.

"He's very weak. It's made him susceptible to airborne diseases, or broken bones. He can still swallow, though. He can walk, and he's hard-headed as a mule. Parkinson's should go ahead and back off now, before he kicks it in the behind."

She smiled. "I remember when you spent five weeks in the hospital here, and he visited you you every day. Such a special guy."

"Yeah. He wouldn't let me spiral, either. I went through some dark times, but when Gray walked in, the darkness lifted." I laughed. "I remember the first time Mom laid eyes on him. I think it took about an hour for those two to fall for each other."

Callie rested her elbow on the counter, a wistful look on her face. I left the couch and sat beside her. "I know it's hard being a single parent, Cal, and I'm sorry Graham hasn't become a better man. Someone will come along."

"I appreciate you," she whispered. "I'm so proud of you for making the decision to cut back the drinking. It's not easy to admit you have a problem."

I grunted. "I didn't admit it soon *enough*. I'm amazed at how good I've been feeling."

"I'm not drinking as much either. You inspired me."

We went into the den to watch for Mom's car from the window. Callie paced the room like a caged tiger. Half an hour turned into an hour. Then, two hours. Finally, we heard the scrunch of tires.

Callie rocketed out the door. I followed.

"Mom!" Amy shrieked, leaving the car and throwing herself into her mother's arms. They hung onto each other for long minutes.

I gave my own mom a huge hug. "How was the drive?"

She swept strands of hair away from her face. "Good. And what a miracle they hadn't crossed into Canada, yet."

We watched mother and daughter laugh and cry and hug until we wondered if they'd find a way to crawl inside each other's skin.

"How is it we don't appreciate what we have until it's gone?" Mom said, squeezing me a final time before taking her arm from around my shoulders. "I'm going to go check on Gray."

"He's fine, Mom. He took care of us, and went back to bed. He said to tell you he loved you."

She smiled. "I'll just check. You all come on in when you're done."

I got pulled into a group hug just as Lilly's car appeared in the driveway. She hopped out and raced toward us. "Amy! I'm so glad you're okay!" Callie and I backed out of the hug. The girls, best friends since elementary school, cried and sobbed into each other's shoulders. I reached for Callie's hand, and we stood watching our daughters with a quiet gratitude.

A scream pierced the veil of our celebration.

My chin jerked. I let go of Callie's hand. "What on earth," Callie whispered, eyes wide.

I scanned the yard, Mom's house, across the street. My eyes gritty and bleary from staying up all night with Callie, I barely noticed the pinks and golds streaking the sky as the sun rose. An anguished wail ripped through the calm morning. "That's from inside the house!" I hissed at Callie. My heart pounded as a staggering thought slammed into me with all the force of a meteor strike. *Oh, no. Gray.*

I ran inside as fast as my legs would carry me.

Chapter Thirty-Five

Hunter

He'd expected an update on the Woodlawn investigation, or the happy news of Amy's return, or *anything* else. He rubbed his eyes, letting the water spill over him, upturning his face into the shower spray. Great waves of sadness threatened to consume him. He stepped out of the shower and grabbed a towel, roughly drawing it across his body. The suffocating reality closed his throat. He threw the towel back on the rack, and wandered into his closet in a fog of grief. How does one dress for a morgue visit? And how does one prepare to say good-bye to a man who had become like a father to him?

His cell buzzed. "Where are you?" Olivia asked.

"I'm having a hard time getting it together."

"We'll be leaving in about ten minutes. If you can't make it, don't worry about it."

The lump in his throat hardened into stone. "I wanted to…I have to…be there for Gray. For you. For Sophie and your girls."

"We're okay. But I know you two had a special relationship. We'll tell them to hold on until you get there, okay? Join us at Mom's condo when you're ready." A pause lingered. "I love you," whispered Olivia.

"Same," he said, his voice cracking.

He dropped onto his bed and allowed a few tears before raking them off his cheeks and stalking into the closet for khakis and a shirt. "Man up, dude," he told himself. "People need you to be strong."

Two hours later, Sophie, Olivia, Hunter, Lilly, and Serena sat in the den, feeling the sharp sting of Gray's absence. No one felt like saying much. Sophie glanced around at each person. Setting her jaw, she rose from the couch.

"I need you all to know something. I'm sad, of course, but not without hope or joy. I know where Gray is. We'd talked about this. He didn't want to linger while his body deteriorated. He must've told me a hundred times he didn't want to be a burden I'd have to take care of. He's in Heaven, now, cracking bad jokes with God, and telling him how glad he is to be taken before muddling through the worst of it." She swiped at tears. "I'll see him again. Until then, I'm grateful for all of you. Your support and strength mean the world. Gray would've been proud of you."

Hunter found himself squeezed into another family hug. Everyone agreed to scheduling a Celebration of Life in Richmond. Later in the evening, he draped his arm across his fiancée's shoulders. "Are you ready to go?"

She glanced at her mother. "I need to stay here tonight."

"I'll catch up with you tomorrow, then. Get some sleep." He kissed her, then walked to his Jeep and drove off into the night, his hand soft upon the gearshift.

* * *

After the morning debriefing, he returned to his office where Detective Becker began droning his morning task list. Hunter sighed. "Becker. Give it a rest. You don't have to do that the minute I walk into the office."

He put the list down, his cheeks red.

"Sorry. It's been a lot. I'm just tired."

"No problem, Sarge."

"You're doing a great job. Carry on."

Becker beamed. "Good to hear."

"Anything going on I need to know about? I've been gone a while."

Becker's eyes shifted left, right. His Adam's apple bobbed when he swallowed nervously.

Hunter's eyes narrowed. "What is it?"

"Woodlawn."

He snorted. "Of course it is. Let's have it."

"The lieutenant is hopping mad that no one can locate Larissa…I mean Katarina."

"I'll get on it."

Becker looked uncomfortable. "It's been reassigned."

Hunter frowned. "How can they reassign it? My team's done all the background."

"Well…"

A shimmer of foreboding hovered. The emotional upheaval of the last few days had drained him, and he'd much rather be catching up on sleep than sitting here, watching Becker squirm. "I thought you might want a heads-up. The word is you're being suspended."

Suspended? Why?

A sudden snapshot of his lieutenant's mouth flashed into his brain…*if you miss any more work because of Olivia Callahan, I'll have to do something about it.* Hunter sat tight-lipped and still a few seconds. "Thank you, Becker. That'll be all."

He shot to his feet and left.

His landline lit up. "Faraday."

"Welcome back. Sorry for your loss. You got a second? We need to talk. In my office," said Lieutenant Nicholson.

"Sure." Hunter rose from his chair, wondering what else life could throw at him. He plodded to the elevator as if slogging through mud. "There goes my perfect record," he murmured as the doors opened. When the elevator dinged for the second floor, he got out and walked straight ahead to Lt. Nicholson's admin's desk. She smiled and told him good morning. Hunter cocked his head, puzzled. "Why are you being nice to me today?"

She flipped her hand as if brushing the question away. "I don't know why you think I don't like you, Sergeant."

He grinned. "I didn't get an invitation to your Fourth of July bash last year, for one thing."

"Be glad. It turned into a drunken brawl, and I had to kick everyone out." She laughed. "I suppose you're here for the lieutenant."

"I got summoned. Any hints?"

"Nope." She rose, walked to the door, and poked her head in. "Sergeant Faraday for you, Lieutenant." She held the door for Faraday and closed it behind him.

Nicholson leaned back in his desk chair, his gaze steady. Focused. "Take a seat, Faraday."

Hunter sat. His stomach fizzed, and he wished he'd popped an antacid or two before getting punched in the gut with a suspension. It would be okay, he reassured himself. He could use the time off to catch up on sleep. Clean his house. Something. He straightened his shoulders, waiting.

"The Chief has cancer."

Hunter took a second to register the words. Not what he expected.

"Sorry to hear it."

"It's bad. End-stage. Caught too late, sad to say."

"I'll have to check in with him."

Nicholson shook his head. "Don't. He's adamant about it not getting out. He wants business as usual. He says he feels okay, and will work until the treatments make it too difficult to manage." He leaned forward, placed his elbows on the desk, and interlaced his fingers. "The mayor's been in touch. He's impressed with your record. How do you feel about stepping into the office of Chief of Police?"

Chapter Thirty-Six

Sherry

Her phone buzzed with a text. She flopped her phone over. Duncan, again. She swore under her breath.

She glanced at Jason across the room. He must've felt her eyes on him, because he lifted his head from his laptop and looked at her. "How's your day?"

"It's stupid."

He returned to his typing. "Does it have something to do with your phone going off every five minutes?"

She groaned. "Sometimes I wish you weren't so...so..."

"Intuitive? Brilliant?"

She laughed. "I'm having second thoughts about Duncan."

"Ah. The Duncan dilemma. Do you want to know what I think?"

She frowned. "No."

He shrugged. The only sounds in the room were the muted click of his keystrokes. Seconds passed.

Sherry jammed her arms across her chest. "Why do relationships get so complicated?"

He kept typing as he responded. "First off, the guy's a beast. As former Special Ops, he's seen things that'll haunt him for life. The potential for PTSD and erratic behavior is huge. Has something happened? Last I heard, you were excited and happy about his separation from government contract work." Lifting his hands from the keyboard, he turned his chair toward her desk.

"He *quit his job* so we could continue dating. How can I not believe he's telling the truth?"

"And yet. You don't. What's bugging you?"

"I went to his house for the first time. We've been dating six months and he's kept saying he's been doing all this remodeling..."

"Okay."

"So, when I saw it, I couldn't believe it. He lives in a freaking mansion! No way a retired cop can afford a place like that. He said he *inherited* the house. Okay, so I find out it's true. However, his parents both died in a car wreck due to faulty brakes. The reason for the brakes failing is inconclusive. Oh, and the life insurance went straight to him. Two million bucks."

His eyes rounded.

"I know," she said, sliding down in her chair. "I'm so depressed."

"Let's go back to the date. Did he fix you dinner?"

"Yeah. And after dinner, he took me on a tour of this enormous house and..."

She studied her fingernails.

"And?" he prodded.

"Maybe I'm paranoid."

"You're not paranoid. You have every right to be cautious."

"Where's Olivia?" She looked out the window behind her desk.

Jason frowned. "Don't change the subject."

"He showed me every bedroom suite but one, and didn't explain why."

"Everyone has a private space. Don't you?"

"But I heard something in there."

"Maybe he had a house guest."

"He would've said something, wouldn't he? Instead, he acted like he didn't hear it, and hauled me back downstairs."

Jason stroked the beginnings of a sparse goatee. "I'm trying to think of all the reasons he'd not want you to look in one of the bedrooms. Maybe he has a big, mean dog."

"A dog would bark or whine. Besides, I've talked about Marlowe. He knows I like dogs."

The door opened, and Olivia breezed inside. "Hey, team. What's going on?" Marlowe rushed in behind her and raced to her office.

"We were talking about big, mean dogs," Jason offered.

Sherry popped from behind her desk and gave her boss a hug. "How are you? How's your mom doing? I am so, so sorry for your loss."

"Thanks. It's been awful." Olivia blinked fresh tears away. "Mom's doing surprisingly well, though. She and Gray had prepared. She knew what his final wishes were, and he'd made it easy on everyone. To his final breath, he'd been thinking about everyone but himself. I'll need to return for his Celebration of Life in a couple of weeks."

"Is Amy okay?"

She nodded. "She didn't get scared until she realized her dad had no intention of returning her. We talked her off the ledge all the way home. Graham's facing a parole board hearing, new charges, and up to six months in prison. What an idiot."

"Wow," Sherry whispered. "Poor Graham."

Olivia shook her head in disgust. "I have no sympathy for him at all. At least Callie can sleep, now. It'll take a while for her to let Amy out of her sight, though."

"Is Amy going to take some time?"

"The university gave Amy three weeks and her instructors have been notified. She'll be here with Callie. Olivia exhaled, smiled, and put her hands on her hips. "It's been an intense ten days." She plopped into a visitor's chair in front of Jason's desk and swiveled so she could see both of them at once.

"Duncan is a question mark," Sherry said.

Olivia squinted in confusion. "Still? I thought you guys worked it out."

"How about we grab a coffee and talk in your office?"

They filed into the break room, then settled in their usual spots.

"How's the greatest ginger tomcat of all time these days?"

Olivia laughed. "Riot's getting older and crankier. If Marlowe's not careful, he'll get a scratch on the nose." She sipped her coffee, looking at Sherry thoughtfully. "So. What are we talking about?"

"Don't you think Duncan's involvement with Woodlawn is a little too coincidental?"

"I've always thought so."

"You never said anything."

Olivia smiled. "Would you have listened?"

She stuck out her lower lip. "Maybe."

"I would've discussed it with you further, but between Callie's crisis and Mom losing Gray…I lost track of anything else."

"Of course," Sherry said, going on to explain the dinner date, the tour, the strange noise in the forbidden room.

"Why didn't you ask him?"

"Should've, I guess. But I could tell he didn't want to talk about it, and now, I'm ghosting him. I'm a terrible person."

Olivia laughed. "I don't know if it's the best policy to ghost former Special Ops military."

"What if he's still using me to get intel?" asked Sherry, cracking a smile.

"About what? Woodlawn's been reassigned and broken into separate cases and handed over to the Feds. We don't have anything to do with it anymore."

"Aren't you nervous about retaliation?"

Olivia put her mug to her lips. "Hmm. Haven't had time to think about it."

"Is your firearm in the safe?"

"Thanks for reminding me." She grabbed her purse, retrieved her weapon, and put it in the break room safe.

"I'm wearing mine," Sherry told her when she returned.

Olivia's eyes twinkled. "My. You *are* nervous."

The front door opened. Voices exchanged greetings. Jason buzzed Olivia's landline. She walked to her desk and pressed the speaker button. "Yes?"

"Duncan Malone's here. He'd like to talk."

Sherry groaned.

"Send him into my office." With a wink at her colleague, Olivia walked back to her chair and sat. "Let's get to the bottom of this."

A knock sounded. "Come on in and take a seat," said Olivia. "We've been chatting about you."

"That doesn't sound good." Glancing at Sherry, he folded his tall frame into a chair. "I need to explain."

Sherry lifted her chin, a glint in her eye. "I can't even keep up with what you've *already* explained."

Olivia laced her fingers in her lap and settled in to watch the fireworks.

"I realized later the way I acted on the house tour…it might look bad."

Her eyebrows drew together. "I know you heard it, too."

He nodded. "Yeah. But I had to get those crab cakes out of the oven."

"Yum," Olivia said.

She furrowed her brow at me. "Whatever. I don't care if you have some room you keep private, but I could almost see you jumping out of your skin when something crashed or whatever happened in there. You made a point of ignoring it, and dragged me downstairs. From a PI's viewpoint, you *have* to realize I'd go straight to criminal activity."

"One of the pitfalls of the job," Olivia added.

Sherry jerked her head sharply. "You don't have to lighten the mood. Stop."

"Give the poor man a chance."

Duncan leaned forward, elbows on knees, hands clasped. "I know it sounds impossible, but everything I've told you is true. I've gotten clearance to back away from the case, but they had a witness they needed to protect. A whistleblower. His life's at risk." He glanced around the space. "You don't have CCTV in here, do you?"

"We do, but…" Olivia yanked out her phone, adjusted an app setting, and put her cell back into her pocket. "Okay. You're not being recorded. Whatever you tell us in this office stays here."

He visibly relaxed. "Since my house is somewhat 'off grid' and I have like, a hundred bedrooms…I offered to let him stay with me. He knew I had company coming, and promised to keep a low profile. His dinner plate fell and broke on the floor."

Sherry's eyes widened. "Who is it?"

He winced.

Sherry stood to her feet, her small hands curling into fists. *"Who is it?"*

"Your old buddy, Collins Browning."

Sherry sank into her chair, shocked. Olivia exhaled a long breath and closed her eyes. A thick curtain of silence fell.

"Wait. This is a good thing, right? I mean, I always thought he was a decent guy." Sherry searched Duncan's face. "I couldn't believe he'd gotten himself in so deep with Alex Barnes' network."

"He's trying to make things right, isn't he?"

"If you say so. From my perspective, he's trying to get a reduced sentence. They always try to get the bad guys to rat each other out." He studied her a few seconds. "You still care, don't you?"

She frowned. "Of course I care. Like I'd care about *any* of my good friends from back in the day."

He smiled. "Oh, come on. He had to be more than a friend."

"Whatever," she said. "I don't like to see people's lives implode. He made some bad decisions, and I hope he turns it around."

"I agree." He rose from his chair, spread his arms. "That's it. I couldn't leave you hanging like that, Sherry." He turned his attention to Olivia. "I appreciate your time and patience."

"We appreciate your honesty," Olivia said, glancing at Sherry, who scrambled from her chair to walk him out.

They stood uncertainly beside his vehicle. Finally, Sherry gave him a brief hug. "Thanks. I'll call."

"I hope so," he said, bending to plant a kiss on her lips. She returned inside, more confused than ever. After so much deception, should she trust him?

Chapter Thirty-Seven

Olivia

I felt a little poke of empathy for Sherry. If it had been me, I'd have hightailed it from this guy as fast as possible. But she hadn't initially asked what I thought, so I hadn't said anything. The emotional blender cutting me into tiny pieces over the last two weeks had finally begun to slow down, and I didn't have the energy to dive into Sherry's blender. Selfishness…or self-preservation? How, I wondered, do I remain a good friend, maintain a professional relationship, and keep my opinions to myself? Is it even *possible* to be both friends and business colleagues and remain honest with each other? Biting my lower lip, I thought about my habitual bluntness. Before the brain injury, my personality had been very different, but now, I blurted out whatever came to mind.

Closing my eyes, I lay my head back, listening to the opening and closing of my office door. Steps padding to the armchair hub. The slight wheeze of a seat cushion depressing.

"Don't worry. I'm not going to drag you into this." Sherry said.

I raised my head and stared in amazement at this tiny woman who continued to read my thoughts like a seer. "Okay."

"You have enough going on." She chuckled. "As usual."

I frowned. "What does that mean?"

"Nothing," she said. "We both do. Jason seems to be the one who sails along without baggage."

"Everyone has baggage. He keeps his to himself."

Sherry's eyebrows arched. "Whatever happened to making him an honorary member of Wine & Whine? Maybe if we get him drunk, he'll dump all his secrets."

I laughed. "Shoot out a time and let's coordinate. I have to catch up on work, so not tonight."

She nodded, bounced from her chair, and left.

My landline lit. "Real estate agent on line one."

I answered. "Hi, Pam."

"Are you ready for this? Your listing hit yesterday, and you already have four families interested!"

My heart dropped. I hadn't expected to sort out showings the minute I got back. Plus, the recent discoveries about Duncan might preclude he and Sherry moving forward as a couple, so my dream of a close friend owning my house—gone. A quiet breath of frustration slipped from my lips. "Okay. I need time to make it presentable and get Riot out of there. After five is best for me."

"Tomorrow? I'll see if I can set some back-to-back so it won't be so hectic."

"I'd appreciate it." We ended the call. My agent may be excited, but I couldn't get there. I hoped I would. My cell buzzed. Hunter.

"You got a few minutes?"

I stared at the pile of file folders, the junk mail, a summons. I frowned. A summons? I tore my eyes away and focused on his voice. "Sure."

"There's a rumor I may receive an appointment as Chief of Police."

I gasped. "You're kidding."

"I'm not."

A deep joy radiated through me for this wonderful guy. No one deserved it more. "What an honor!"

"Wanted to talk to you first," he said, his voice somber. "It's a big decision. A police chief's wife is going to be very different from a sergeant's wife. The politics can get nasty. This is your decision, too. I haven't received official word yet, but I won't do it without your support."

I smiled. In a flash of insight, I realized I couldn't wait to move; to live with

Hunter Faraday twenty-four, seven…to share meals…to do life together as his *wife.* I assured him I'd support him and, furthermore, I'd traversed enough political landscapes as "Mercy's Miracle" to understand how media coverage works. At least I had experience with the consequences and could support Hunter through them.

"My personal notoriety may become a problem," I said.

"Why? The book?"

"The Foofoos continue to haunt me, and yes, my book gathered its share of haters."

"Not an issue. Your notoriety has more positives than negatives. What else?"

"If I open a second location…"

"*When* you open your second location," he corrected.

"Fine. When I open Watchdog Two, will it be a conflict? Will I be able to do it?"

"Of course you will! I…well, I'll talk to my lieutenant about it."

I felt a flicker of disappointment. If I couldn't open a second location, what then? Would I still be as excited to move to Richmond? Not being able to remain a PI would…what? I didn't know.

"I think it'll be fine. We'd have to keep business and personal separate, though. The only issue I see is if you accept a case related to what we're trying to keep out of the news," Hunter said.

"Watchdog operates with confidentiality. Tries to, anyway."

He laughed. "You may not have noticed, but you have a way of making headlines."

"Maybe not so much in Richmond."

"True," he said, his voice thoughtful. "And, there you go. I can make the argument if the mayor makes it a condition."

"Makes what a condition?"

"He won't. Don't worry."

But I would. I *would* worry, and I definitely needed to think about this.

"I am one-hundred-and-fifty percent behind you running for Chief of Police."

CHAPTER THIRTY-SEVEN

"What I needed to hear. I love you, babe. Talk later." He clicked off.

I groaned. My mind spiraled all over the place. Taking a deep breath, I attacked the pile on my desk.

* * *

Three hours passed in a glorious tribute to isolation and focus. I'd rerouted my worry into a tornadic flurry of desk clearing. I reclined my chair. Just a twenty-minute nap, then I'd be good to go. Marlowe started whining at my office door fifteen minutes in. I opened one eye, listening to angry voices and shouting.

Shouting?

Sherry screamed. A door slammed. Shots fired. One. Two. Three.

What the hell?

I scrambled from my chair and rushed into the lobby. Marlowe followed, barking his head off. "What's going on?" I demanded, taking in the room. In slow motion, I registered Sherry kneeling behind her desk, and immediately thereafter, the surrealistic visual of Jason on the floor, clutching center mass, his hand and torso weeping blood, and the barrel of a revolver trembling in his direction. I cursed my stupidity for not stopping to get my weapon from the safe. My mind spun. Marlowe became the hound from hell.

"Call off the dog!"

My stunned brain stumbled to make sense of the small, fair-skinned woman holding the gun in a shaky hand. I squinted. Blonde hair, thin, skirt and sneakers. Oh, no. *Larissa.* What was she doing here? "Marlowe, come!" He walked toward me, his head lowered, his fur ruffled and threatening along his spine "Sit." Teeth bared and a low growl rumbling in the back of his throat, he sat. Our dog would not hesitate to attack on command. But first, I needed to calm the shooter. "It's been a while, Larrisa."

She wiped sweat out of her eyes and kept her weapon trained on Jason and Sherry. "Put the dog in another room."

I grabbed my dog's collar.

Her chin trembled. "Do you have any idea what you've done? When you checked in to Woodlawn, you needed help, and got it. Even when I discovered what you did for a living, I treated you like one of ours, and look what that got me." Angry tears glistened on her cheeks. "I was weeks from a breakthrough! The trials had been *so* promising. We were doing some *good* in this godforsaken world! And here you come, you and your cop friend. All my research, down the drain, never to see the light of day." She groaned. "When I think about wasted hours of agonizing over results…the sleepless nights." Refreshing her grip on the firearm, she glared at me. "The next generation wouldn't even have to worry about ever losing a loved one to dementia again!" She wobbled the gun at me, her mouth pulled down at the corners. "The investigation caused all my grants to be pulled, and *you* are the reason millions of suffering people are going die." Her voice dropped to a whisper. Sherry peeked from behind her desk.

But at what cost? I screamed behind clamped lips, my eyes darting toward my office, back to Jason. I took a breath.

"Get rid of the dog!" she shouted. Gripping Marlowe's collar before he ripped himself from my grasp and sank his fangs into her, I walked him toward my office. As I deposited him there, I put my phone on silent and dialed nine-one-one before returning to the lobby. With a calm voice, I reassured her I hadn't checked into Woodlawn to expose her, I'd checked in to stop drinking too much. Using all my powers of concentration, I kept repeating this in different version, hoping she'd believe me, and added the suggestion of an ambulance for Jason.

Her eyes grew softer, but she didn't lower her firearm. "It can't be a coincidence you're engaged to a cop."

"I'm telling the truth, Larissa. The investigation came as a shock. My fiancée didn't even know about it until later. Matty Stricklin's situation had him worried, and he found out about her by accident. But when you put a legal hold on me, how could you think that would not become a problem?"

Her jaw clenched. "Stay where I can see you." She jerked the gun in Sherry's direction. "You, too. Get off the floor and sit in your chair. Put your hands on the desk."

"It's not too late to turn yourself in." Jason had lost a lot of blood. He needed help, fast.

Her laugh sounded like a sob. "I've been down this road for the last time. The damn "protocols" and roadblocks to real and lasting medical breakthroughs are unbelievable." Letting her arm drop, she rubbed it, as if trying to ease a cramp. I glanced at the firearm, now held loosely in her hand. Was I fast enough to grab it? Would it go off if I knocked it away? "I'm sorry about this one," she mumbled, gesturing toward Jason. "He ran at me. I panicked."

"I don't believe you're a bad person, Larissa," I told her, striving to remain calm. "Whatever is going on, maybe we can help."

"My name isn't Larissa," she whispered. "You didn't know, did you? You never suspected."

A shape hurtled by the window behind her. I glanced at Sherry, who offered a curt nod of reassurance. The person outside was ours.

My heart a wrecking ball in my chest, I waited for her next move. I could get her to talk if this played out the right way. At Woodlawn, her rush to share had surprised me. Maybe the same would happen here. "I'm a good listener, and *I want to help you*. There's a solution. Let's talk."

As I hoped, the floodgates came crashing down. She hadn't planned this, she insisted, referring to crashing into our offices and holding us at gunpoint. A sad desolation flitted across her face as she told me the first person she'd thought of after clearing out her office and house had been me.

Lucky me.

"You have to understand!" she cried. "I had it all. The degrees, the published research papers, the awards. Credibility in my field. Respect. I was so close...*so close to a discovery for these precious people*." Pacing in tight circles, waving her firearm, it became obvious she was unraveling. "So many stupid details, all the forms, the subterfuge, the regulations..." She completed another loop before jerking to a stop, narrowing her eyes. "Did you know Matty was my most valuable test subject? I had to let her husband take her to a lockdown unit, and it was the hardest thing I've ever done. The improvements in her memory and behaviors had been remarkable." She inhaled sharply. "They ruined me, you know. Years before you and I met, I was dumped into witness protection. They expected me to fade away." She snorted, using the gun as a baton of disdain. I was pretty sure she'd left the safety off, and a quick tug of the trigger could kill someone. Sherry watched, still and silent, from her desk. My quick nod told her to stay there. From the floor, Jason groaned. I closed my eyes. *Thank God. He's still breathing.*

Larissa seemed lost in her own small, sad world. "I fooled them all. I found investors and used every resource I had to continue my research and perform the testing unnoticed." She scowled, walked closer, and stuck the barrel of her firearm two inches from my nose. "Until you showed up."

"I believe you," I said, desperately searching my brain for how to handle imploding perpetrators. I'm sure Private Investigation 101 had taught me something about this, but I couldn't remember right now. Sherry, Jason, and I could become her final act of defiance, and a guaranteed way to grab national headlines. My heart pounded. What better message to the medical research community than dying for the cause, and taking us along for the ride? Perspiration slicked my face. My hands had become wet and clammy. She wanted *her story out there*…was I supposed to be her mouthpiece? Then what good would it do to kill us?

Tilting my head at Sherry, she nodded; subtly hiding the cell she kept on her desk beside her laptop underneath her palm. I focused all my attention on keeping Larissa occupied so she wouldn't discover Sherry's covert texting.

"I am very sad about your research," I said.

She looked at me with angry, red-veined eyes.

"When COVID happened, my world fell apart. No more funding for my little niche, no one cared about dementia-related research anymore, with everything focused on what basically amounted to a strange iteration of influenza. All my work, all the effort. I felt helpless." After a slight pause, she said, "I'm not proud of what I did."

The gun dangled from her hand. My ears picked up more vehicles rolling into the lot. *If I can just get closer...*

"Whatever you did, we can work it out." I forced my feet to move inch by inch without alarming her.

"The FDA gave me a deal. One of the pathologists I worked with had taken shortcuts on verification. He falsified the test results, and didn't report test subject deaths, or list all the side effects. I testified to this in court."

I masked my shock. Did this woman not understand how many people had died because of her *own* fraudulent clinical trials?

The crunch of footsteps. Murmuring voices. I didn't have much time.

She cursed. "I was forced into WITSEC. Everything gone. My credibility, my name, my reputation. Better a new identity than dead, they told me." She shrugged. "Turns out, for all his posturing and degrees on the wall in his office, the man I testified against was a thug on the Mafia's payroll." She smiled, an odd gleam in her eye. "Then Alex Barnes came along. He and I understood each other. I shared my vision, and he immediately wanted to invest. After a single conversation, he gave me a hundred thousand dollars to start over. My new name became an asset, a clean slate. When he discovered my clinical psychology experience, he asked if I'd be interested in counseling for Woodlawn as well. Such a happy day." She smiled. "He told me I could use the facility as a shield for my work. He believed in me." She gave me a stern look. "He believed in *the work*. Do you realize how much this meant to me? My purpose in life had been restored. I'd saved all my research on a hard drive, so I didn't have to start over; I could continue without all the red tape. Alex recruited other investors, which also sat on the board at Woodlawn. And this time, instead of fighting regulations I could do as I bloody well pleased."

I struggled to keep my expression neutral, but my thoughts ran wild. *Yes, you did what you bloody well pleased...without any vetting at all, and using vulnerable subjects under fraudulent circumstances and Alex's import operation as a cover. You were just one of his horrific, cash-producing venues, and in fact, a golden ticket if you succeeded at producing a successful treatment for dementia.*

I had seconds before vehicle doors slammed, a small army of uniforms ran inside holding firearms, and shouts and commands blotted out any rational thought. Larissa clung to her weapon, confused and staring. My hatred for Alex Barnes grew. She'd been his victim as well. Alex Barnes was a predator and Collins had been his predator-in-training. My lips curled in disgust.

No wonder Shiloh, Duncan, and Hunter had been tapped from different jurisdictions to investigate Woodlawn. The FBI hadn't known which head of the Hydra to cut off first.

I inched toward Larissa, who stood in the center of the lobby, exhausted. Reeling. My eyes slid to her loose grip. The weapon could *not* remain in her hand.

I shook my head at Sherry. *Don't engage.* By this time, I'd almost reached her. She fixed weary, sad eyes on me. "I have nothing to live for, anymore." I held her gaze and reassured her everything would be fine, adding every palliative phrase I could muster. A flurry of heavy steps clambered onto the front stoop, but Larissa didn't react, hypnotized by my calm and calculated words.

The door flew open. "FBI!" one of them shouted. In an instant, her fury erupted like a thunderclap; her lips twisting in a vicious snarl. Steadying her stance, she gripped her weapon with both hands and took aim. With all my strength, I lunged, forcing my arms underneath and up between hers, and digging my thumbs deep into her eyes. We fell to the floor, my weight crushing her beneath me. She let out a piercing scream and squeezed off two erratic shots before the gun slipped from her hand as she flailed against the torturous pressure on her eyes. One of the uniforms saw an opening and slammed his heavy tactical boot down on her shoulder. She shrieked in agony. I pinned her to the ground while he retrieved the gun and carefully placed it out of reach. Sitting astride her body, I locked onto her watering, angry eyes and mouthed, "I am truly sorry."

And I was.

In short order, the cuffs clicked, her rights were read, and her future dreams lay lifeless beside her in the back seat of a cruiser. I shook my head as I watched them take her away. Such a waste of genius. Heaving a great breath, and ratcheting myself back to the crime scene activities in my reception area; I head rhythmic thumping. *Marlowe.* He'd been hurling his weight against the door of my office for some time. Unwisely, I opened the door. He took one look at all the strangers in his space, snarled and leaped two feet off the ground with the intent of sinking his teeth into anyone within range. I froze. There were *ten police officers* in the room. "Down!" I yelled. Marlowe unclamped his teeth from an arm, and dropped to the floor. My fingers curled around his collar. I apologized to the young patrol officer nursing his arm, and put Marlowe back in the office. Sherry ran to find our emergency first-aid kit.

The door burst open. Paramedics wheeled a gurney inside. They loaded Jason carefully onto the bodyboard and lifted him to the gurney and wheeled him out. We walked outside with the paramedics. Jason's eyes fluttered open. "Exciting day, huh?"

"We'll see you later at the hospital," I told him, patting his arm. "Trust me. You missed most of the exciting stuff."

He smiled. The ambulance sped away.

As the forensics team arrived, relief crept into my chest. Maybe Sherry and I could go home, now. The patrol officers had rolled tape, the investigators huddled together chatting, and it looked like news had leaked to the press since a van with a familiar logo had arrived. I'd had enough of the damn press. I looked at Sherry.

"Let's get out of here.

Covering a yawn, she agreed. We started walking toward our vehicles. A man wearing a Baltimore PD badge and a stern expression approached us. "We need you both to come down to the station and start at the beginning."

Chapter Thirty-Eight

Olivia

Two weeks later

The perfect, hushed, rose-gold sunrise whispered of gentle breezes and calm sailing. It was about time. I'd opened all the windows in my house to let it breathe. The absolute insanity of the past few months had begun to taper off, and my adrenaline levels had settled into their new, non-crisis, normal. I called Mom more often. I couldn't bear to think about how lonely she must feel without Gray. Soon, Hunter and I would live close by. Maybe, I mused, we would even invite her to live with us.

Riot sensed change in the wind. I gave him a big hug before Marlowe and I left for the office, and told him everything would be fine. He settled in his favorite spot on the couch pillows. Marlowe sat at the door, excited to see his leash in my hands, which meant we were going for a walk. Before I could leash him, he ran ahead.

Hitching my backpack high on my shoulder, I set out after him. The sweet smell of a fresh, Maryland morning permeated my senses. I loved to walk to work once in a while as it had a way of clearing my mind, but this particular morning, I noticed how overgrown my five acres had become. Marlowe zig-zagged through the dense undergrowth, his nose to the ground.

"Hunter's right," I whispered, the solitude of my walk inspiring personal introspection. "There might be more bad memories than good ones, here. Remember..." I reminded myself, smiling. "Fresh starts are a good thing." Marlowe jumped over a bush to chase a rabbit. The rabbit got away.

Staring at the bright blue of the sky through the leafy bower that entangled itself across the road each spring and summer, I wondered how much I'd miss this.

I had three offers on my house, now, including Sherry's.

The Duncan fiasco had given me pause, so I'd told her if she wanted the house, it would have to be without his name on the contract. A guy like Duncan had enemies. My house could get shot to pieces, or worse, *Sherry* could get shot to pieces. My shoes slapped softly on the road, and as I rounded another curve, my office building came into view. Birdcalls rang out in raucous symphony, louder than usual. Shifting the weight of the backpack on my shoulder, I called for Marlowe.

No response.

"Marlowe, come!"

His distant bark sounded urgent. "Great. You've probably got a raccoon up a tree." With a sigh, I carefully picked my way through weeds, around overgrown bushes, and tangled vines. The barking grew louder, more insistent. A branch popped me across the face, and I shoved it away, taking a minute to catch my breath. When I spotted him, he slow-wagged his tail and whined. I covered the remaining fifty yards between us. "What are you—"

My heart stopped. "Oh, no," I whispered, staring at the ground. "Delia!" I dropped and checked for a pulse.

Her eyelids slowly rose. She moaned. "Hey, Chestnut. I couldn't pay for any more nights, so..."

I squeaked out a cry of anguish. With everything going on, I'd forgotten all about *Delia.* "I am so sorry! Why didn't you call me?"

"I lost my phone. It's all right, I just camped out here for a few."

I helped her to her feet. "Can you stand? I'm calling an ambulance." I yanked out my phone.

"I'm fine," Delia insisted, flapping one of her hands. "I need food and a shower. A toothbrush." She gave me a guilty look. "I didn't know where else to go."

"Grab your stuff."

She frowned. "Where are we going?"

"My office," I said, a deep stab of regret piercing my chest. "My office" wouldn't be mine for much longer. She hoisted her backpack, which promptly fell apart. "Oohh," she whispered.

"I'll buy you a new one," I told her as we gathered her few belongings—a water bottle, a framed photo, two sweatshirts, two pairs of athletic pants, a pair of tattered athletic shoes and underwear which had seen better days. A tin of tuna. A packet of crackers. A stuffed lamb. The lamb hit me hard. Not for the first time, I wondered how she'd ended up homeless. "Who's this?" I asked, pointing to the framed photo, before I put it in my backpack along with the rest of her things.

She slid her fingers across it. "My mom. She died when I was eighteen." With a shrug, she continued. "My dad left us a long time ago."

"No siblings?"

Her expression clouded. "A half-brother. He's all about sticking a needle in his arm. I don't know him very well."

"Where is he?"

"Portland."

So. She had no one.

No one but me.

"Put your arm around me." She wrapped her left arm around my neck, and I supported her with my right arm around her waist. I could feel her ribs underneath my fingertips. We started walking.

She lifted her chin. "I don't need your handouts. I can take care of myself."

I shook my head, smiling at the naiveté of youth. "How old are you?"

"Twenty-two."

"Can you type?" We navigated the vines and stepped over exposed roots and dodged low-hanging branches on our way to the road. Marlowe trotted ahead of us.

She scowled. "Of course I can type."

We stumbled forward. Delia had become weak from hunger and dehydration. I bit my lower lip, thanking God I'd found her before she landed in an emergency room. Or the morgue.

"Let's get some coffee and food into you. I remember you loved coffee, right?"

The silent plea in her pale blue eyes spoke louder than words. "Thank you."

We arrived at the office just as Sherry's car pulled into the parking lot. Her eyes saucers, she parked and burst from her vehicle. "What happened?"

"It's okay," I told her. "This is Delia. She and I met at Woodlawn."

Exhaling the breath she'd been holding, she said, "Nice to meet you."

"Let's give her the guest room for a few days." I unwrapped myself from her body, keeping a hand out in case she wobbled.

"Of course," she said, immediately energized. "I'll grab her some fresh towels and soap and stuff."

"Great," I said, experiencing another stab of regret. I'd miss Sherry's enthusiasm and optimism. Her generous heart. She'd become my wingman.

Wing person.

Whatever.

We walked inside as Jason pulled into the lot.

Popping out of his car, he arched his eyebrows at me.

"Delia, meet Jason. He's one of our private investigators."

His chest puffed out a bit.

In retrospect, I realized I'd referred to him as a PI instead of an admin for the first time. I smiled.

* * *

Three hours after a quick shopping spree and bite of lunch, we returned to the office. I loaded her down with shopping bags filled with the clothes and toiletries we'd purchased, and sent her off to settle in the guest room. She emerged an hour later, attired in new jeans, top, and Nikes; smelling of soap and shampoo and youth.

"I feel reborn," she said. "Thanks for the clothes. And the food. And…and everything."

"You're welcome. And, as it happens, you need a job and we need someone at the reception desk."

Jason's chin jerked in surprise. "We do?"

I nodded. "Sherry's taking my office. Guess you'll be right over there." I pointed at her desk across the room, tucked into the corner.

He grinned. "Did I know this?"

"Olivia's getting married and moving to Richmond any day, now," Sherry said.

"Yeah, but I thought…" He swiveled his chair nervously. "I thought we had more time."

"I have three offers for my house on the table," I told him. "It's getting real. My agent is supposed to get with me this afternoon to discuss the offers. Would you mind giving Delia an overview of what you do?"

With a glance at her, he smiled. "Sure."

"If it doesn't work out here, we'll find you something else," I assured her.

Smothering me in a quick hug, and embarrassed by the display of affection, Delia backed away. "Sorry. I…I'm not used to people being nice to me."

Jason pulled a chair around for her. "We'll be fine," he told me, winking.

"Wow," Sherry said, following me into my office, taking a seat in an armchair, and turning on the end table lamp. "What a way to start your morning."

"I must've forgotten to tell you about the first time I found her. Pointing to the guest bedroom, I explained. "Somehow, she spent a night or two back there without anyone finding out."

Sherry snickered. "What is it about that bedroom? I never heard of a bedroom with a checkered past, but it appears we have one."

I laughed. "There's no reason to go back there if no one's in there, right? So, maybe she only slept there, and snuck out early. I didn't mind. She's been homeless awhile. Anyway, I gave her some money and put her in a hotel."

"And then, you went to Richmond to support Callie. I remember. And

Gray died. You couldn't think of everything."

"Yeah," I said with a sigh. "Forgot all about her. She couldn't pay for the room anymore, lost her phone, and probably used the money I gave her on food."

"Where did you find her?" Sherry asked. "I did check the back bedroom, by the way. The locking mechanism was damaged. I called a handyman."

"Which explains why she couldn't get in. Marlowe found her on my acreage. He disappeared into the brush when we walked to work this morning, and wouldn't come when I called. I thought he might've gotten tangled in a sticker bush or something…and he'd *found her*. "I almost called an ambulance, but she seemed okay."

Sherry smiled. "Hunter's not the only one who rescues people, huh?"

I rolled my eyes. "I feel awful. I should've told you guys to extend her stay. She's not some random person; she's smart and street-savvy. I think she's perfect for us."

"Maybe. We have to make sure she can, um…read, first."

"Jason will fill us in on her skill level. She's special. I can feel it."

"Yeah, we both have such great track records at predicting human behavior."

This statement struck both of us as hilarious. Our laughter turned into a full-on gigglefest with laugh-tears and inappropriate comments. Finally, I wheezed to a stop, wiping my cheeks. "Man. We've had some experiences, haven't we?"

"Understatement of the decade."

I whooshed out a long exhale. "How're you feeling about Duncan?"

"He's been calling every night. He's relentless." She frowned and pushed herself off the chair. "I'm getting coffee. Want some?"

I'd touched a nerve. "Nope. Had too much at home already. I'm fine."

When she left, my cell buzzed. I smiled. *Hunter.* "Good morning."

"Good morning, future wife. What's on your agenda today?"

"Not sure, yet." I told him about my Delia adventure.

He laughed. "Perfect. You cannot accuse me of being the ultimate rescuer any longer."

"You met her, remember? When we haunted the corridors of Woodlawn?"

"I do. I liked her."

"Good. Confirmation."

"For what?"

"I'm giving her a job."

After two heartbeats of silence, he continued. "Make it a trial run."

"I will. She knows. But I'll find work for her somewhere. She doesn't belong on the street. Poor thing is only twenty-two, the same age as my firstborn."

"Huh. I thought she was around thirty. Life outside is hard on a person."

I shuddered. "I don't know what would've happened to her if I hadn't found her. Thank God for Marlowe."

"And to think in a few short weeks I get to live with him. I don't know what I'm more excited about…you or the dog."

Very funny. I made several insulting retaliatory comments.

"How is the counteroffer process going?"

I tapped my chin. "Do you think I should accept Sherry's offer? Even though it's much lower than the others?"

"If you want to."

Sherry walked back in.

"I need to run, babe. Call me later," I told him. "Love you." We ended the call. I looked at her. "You were saying?"

With a deep breath, she set aside her mug and crossed her arms. "You know when a guy has such a pull on you it destroys objectivity and common sense?"

"Didn't we just have a maniacal fit of laughter about our selection process?"

She smiled. "Duncan is a hard man to ignore." She tapped her fingers on the end table. "Graham had a similar pull on Callie. Look how that turned out."

"I agree it's hard to trust after something awful happens, but Duncan is not Graham."

"No, he's *much* more complicated," Sherry snapped. "I have no idea what to do."

I remained quiet.

"Bottom line? I'm not holding my breath."

"You do have a big transition coming. Your social calendar may be limited," I said, with a slight grin. "Watchdog will need your full attention."

"True. I'll need to focus," she said.

"Men can be such a *huge* distraction."

She nodded somberly. "No doubt about it."

"Such a nice distraction, though."

She groaned.

Chapter Thirty-Nine

Hunter

Lieutenant Nicholson sat in a guest chair, his large hands rubbing the armrests, deep in thought. Hunter swiveled his chair behind his desk, waiting for Nicholson to get to his point.

When he could no longer stand the silence, he blurted, "Aren't we done with Woodlawn? Seems like the Feds should have a handle on things by now. Collins Browning bared his soul, right?"

Nicholson folded his arms. "Alex Barnes has been in a holding cell on sex and drug trafficking charges, and thanks to Collins, formally charged on those counts. But Collins Browning is scared, and as we both know, when a whistleblower is scared, they tell you whatever you want to hear, and it takes time to validate the intel. Their attorneys are fighting over next steps."

Hunter spread his hands. "I'm supposed to make an offer on our new house at three p.m. Do I need to reschedule?"

Nicholson smiled broadly. "She's finally moving, huh? I'm happy for you, Faraday."

"I'm happy for me, too. Sick and tired of driving to Maryland every few weeks."

"You and me both," the lieutenant said.

"Before we get back to whatever the heck is on your mind, I need to ask a question," Hunter said.

The slate-gray eyes, which missed nothing, locked in.

"She wants to open a second location for her investigation firm here in Richmond. Will this be a conflict if I get tapped for Chief of Police?"

Nicholson's pause hung heavy. Hunter felt his gut go sideways. He reached for an antacid and popped one in his mouth.

The lieutenant cleared his throat. "It's a "gotcha" waiting to happen. Access to sensitive information, which she could benefit from, perceived favoritism, erosion of public trust. There's a huge potential for ethical violations. Once a defense attorney gets wind of what your wife does for a living, they'll try their damnedest to figure out a way to use it."

His hand drifted absently to the back of his neck. "Oh. I didn't realize…"

"I'll take it to the mayor and explain the situation. I know you're as straight an arrow as they come. I'll see what I can do." He chewed his lip, making his jowls wobble. "I wouldn't bring it up to the press, though."

"Thanks. I won't highlight it. She hasn't even put out feelers for new office space yet, so it may be a while." He squinted. "Where were we?"

"Katarina Petrov. The recording Olivia made when this woman held her staff at gunpoint is being thrown out." He shook his head in frustration. "It's not fatal, since we have plenty of other first-person accounts, but as you know, Maryland is a two-party consent state. The judge is sympathetic to Katarina, and refers to her as 'a misunderstood genius', which is absolute nonsense, but there you go. It'll be an interesting trial."

Hunter stroked his cheek, thoughtfully. "She's slippery. Like Jekyll and Hyde. So, no deals? Her case is going to trial?"

He nodded.

"Yeah, she'd want to sell her side of the story," Hunter mused. "What about the WITSEC angle? Has her real identity been released to the public?"

"Yes, which gets us to the bigger issue. Someone talked, the press went crazy, and now we have the problem of trying to protect the prisoner. Since she violated the terms of her bail and went all commando on your wife's firm, her bail has been revoked and she's in a holding cell, here in Virginia. She'll be sentenced concurrently, but for now, she's our problem. My guess is she'll be put in max security, and won't be safe there, either. She was in WITSEC for outing a scientist with strong mafia ties."

"Yeah, I heard. Big, long, mafia *ropes*, as I remember."

Nicholson sighed.

"What do you need me to do?"

"Would you organize a protection detail?"

How do you expect me to do that?

"Sure, Lieutenant. No problem."

Later, over lunch with his buddy, Nick Ramsey, Hunter shared his concerns. "You're still acting assistant DA, right?'

Nick swallowed the final bite of his hamburger, wiped his fingers on a cocktail napkin, and slurped the dregs of his Diet Coke noisily. "One more week. Then I pull out the big guns, bro."

"You'll be a shoo-in for DA, man. I have no doubt. But I need you to take something to the current DA. I mean, I know he's going through chemo, but he's still on the job, right?"

Nick nodded, pushing his plate aside. "Yep. The old warhorse keeps on fighting. What do you need? I'll do what I can."

He told him about his lieutenant's request to put guardrails around Larissa, aka Katarina Petrov.

Nick stared at him a few beats. "Tricky. I'll have to think about it. Yeah, I'll take it to him, but…she's incarcerated."

"In a minimum-security for now. The problem will be when she gets moved to max after sentencing."

Nick gave him a speculative look. "You ever think about the situation takin' care of itself?" He hooked an arm around the back of his chair.

Hunter frowned. "You can't be serious."

"I read about her, she's a real wacko and a threat to civilization. I say let nature take its course."

Hunter chuckled. "And as a potential Chief of Police, I'm becoming more tight-assed by the minute. *I* say adhere to the law."

"You're going to be much less fun, you know. When you're Chief."

"As are you, Mr. District Attorney."

The men sat in comfortable silence for a few seconds. "I assume we need to fold a few correction officers into our budget temporarily?"

CHAPTER THIRTY-NINE

"Your assumption is correct."

His nod was curt. "I'll see what I can do." He rose. "Good talk, buddy." Hunter watched him walk away, thinking about how long they'd known each other, how much they'd partied together, and how excited they'd been about each other's promotions. And now, here they were, carrying the weight of a potential Mayor's appointment to the office of Chief of Police and an almost guaranteed political race for District Attorney. For him, the sense of responsibility became heavier with each passing day. He wondered if all men felt crushed and conflicted before stepping into a momentous decision about their future.

The afternoon passed in a flurry of meetings, and by the time he got home, it had gotten dark. He threw his keys and backpack on the kitchen table, popped a beer, and sat on his tiny patio watching the stars as he called Olivia.

"Hi, there," she said.

"Guess what I did today?"

"Cop stuff?"

"Remember the listing I showed you last week? The one you loved so much?"

"I do."

"I put in an offer."

He felt her smile through the airwaves. "Excellent. Well, then…you'll be glad to know what I did today."

"Okay."

"I accepted Sherry's offer. She's ecstatic."

He laughed. "We should celebrate."

"Not until we know we've got the house."

"I think we will. I offered full price. I've already heard from my agent, and she said to start packing. It's not a done deal yet, but it will be after the inspection's done."

"Is this really happening?"

"Not fast enough." He took a sip of his beer. "I miss you."

After a pause, she continued. "It's hard letting go of my house."

"I know it's hard, sweetie. Remember the first time we met? I couldn't take my eyes off you—this thin, little thing with sad eyes; so confused and somehow incredibly sexy at the same time."

"Huh. I never knew you felt that way."

"I had to use my poker face every time I talked to you."

Olivia laughed. "What I remember is my friends kidding me about how cute you were and calling you 'my detective'. I got so irritated with them, and now it's come true. After seven years, you *are* my detective."

"Hopefully, your Chief of Police."

"Yes! Did you find out about the conflict of interest if I open another location?"

"My lieutenant and I talked today, and he made some good points, but he's going to run it up the food chain and vouch for us. I'm sure it'll be fine."

The pause lingered. He imagined the fidgeting of her hands, or the faraway look on her face as she thought about what he said.

"I know my place is with you, and if I can't open a second location, so be it. I'll work with the home office remotely. The priority is you and me."

He smiled. "You continue to surprise me. How was your day?"

"Jason told me Delia is personable, smart, and intuitive online. She also has ideas to market the firm on social media, which is a big plus."

"I'm glad she's working out. They're going to miss you."

With an unladylike snort, she responded. "They'll be too busy to miss me. What's our new timetable? I need to call the movers. Sherry's already started packing up her house, and is on the way over to help me finish mine."

"Okay. I'm thinking two weeks?"

Olivia groaned. "I'll do my best."

"Wait," Hunter said. He scanned the fresh email from his agent and smiled broadly. "We got it! We have a house, pending inspection issues. The sellers asked for thirty days. We have a month to pack."

"Congratulations to us," Olivia said quietly, feeling as if she'd launched a canoe from the bank of a very big lake, without a paddle.

Chapter Forty

Olivia

I folded a blanket and put it in a box. Sherry puttered around, emptying cabinets and drawers and moving so fast I couldn't keep up. I sat cross-legged on the floor. "This would be a perfect time to break out a bottle of good red." I laughed. "Oh, wait. You already have."

She paused, holding her wine glass in mid-air. "I don't have to drink. I'll put this away."

"I'm kidding. It's okay. I'm feeling so good, I'm almost afraid to drink at all. One of these days, I may tiptoe back, but for now, I don't want to jinx my sobriety. Oh, and a side benefit? I've lost five pounds without even trying."

Sherry rolled her eyes. "As if you needed to." She put her fists on her hips, all business. "This is great progress for one night. Thanks so much."

"Now I have to start packing up my own stuff." I stretched, yawned.

"Why don't you put it off until I can get over there to help?"

I sipped my energy drink. "Have I told you Hunter bought us a house today?"

"He what?" She threw out her arms. "I'm so happy for you guys!" She ran over and squished me in a hug, pulled away, a question mark in her eyes. "You *did* vet it first, right? He didn't pick something out all by himself, did he?"

"Of course not. We looked at the listings together, and it's the one we both liked the best. Nice, quiet community out of the mainstream, bike paths, and big lots. It won't have the character and history of my, I mean *your,* house; but it's big, with plenty of bedrooms for company and a fenced yard for Marlowe."

She shook her head. "It's happening fast. Can you believe it?"

I smiled. "My family's in Richmond now, which helps."

"You have family here, too," she said, her voice soft.

"Don't. I'm trying not to cry."

"Too late." She wiped tears off her cheeks and lifted her wine glass. "To the Wine & Whine girls."

I lifted my energy drink and clicked her glass. "May it rest in peace."

She frowned. "You think we should dismantle it?"

"I guess I just assumed."

"I have Delia, if she works out, which I think she will. I'll make her a mandatory member. And, you'll be back every so often, right? Jason is our honorary male…I don't want to let the group die. I may recruit one more worthy sister, closer to my age. *You* have a lifetime membership, of course."

"Okay. I formally bequeath the Wine & Whine to you. Should I knight you or something? I don't have a sword."

She jumped off the floor, raced into another room, and returned holding a plastic kid's sword. "A neighbor's child left it. Perfect!"

Laughing, I rose from the floor. She handed me the twenty-four-inch plastic sword. I held it high. "Kneel," I commanded.

She put her hand over her heart, bowed her head, and dropped to one knee.

I touched one shoulder, then the other, and the crown of her head in my best recollection of movies that included knights. "I, Olivia Rosemary Callahan … bequeath to Sherry Lattimore, the Wine & Whine group which originated in Glyndon, Maryland in…"

"Seven years ago," she whispered, keeping her head bowed.

"…seven years ago, and relinquish all rights, claims or privileges to said group. Amen."

"Amen!" she said, her voice jubilant. "I won't let you down."

I put the sword on the couch. "I know you won't. The Wine & Whine group and Watchdog Investigations are both in good hands."

"Did I mention I've been looking at dogs?"

My eyes widened. "Seriously?"

"What would Watchdog be without a dog? I mean, I won't find one near as good as Marlowe, but we *have* to carry on the mascot theme. I'm looking at the same breed."

"Such a great idea," I said, deeply touched. Whatever problems we'd had, no matter how many setbacks had occurred, we'd built something significant, here. Together. With hard work, sweat, and determination. And she wanted to continue what I'd begun. A swell of pride stirred in my chest. "You're going to be a great boss."

"Thanks. Means a lot coming from you."

"Don't keep looking at me with those big, blue eyes," I said. "I really don't want to cry."

She laughed.

Letting the emotional moment pass, we studied the packing we'd done. "A new day dawns," she said.

My phone buzzed with a text. "That's not all that's dawning," I muttered. "Our whistleblower disappeared."

Sherry frowned. "You mean Collins?"

"Yeah." I slid my palms across my cheeks. "Now what?"

* * *

I frowned. A text at two a.m.? I rubbed my eyes, and read it again. It sounded plausible, but I fervently hoped I hadn't gotten it right the first time.

Collins Browning's body found inside Barnes Imports' shuttered location. Dogs tore it apart. Suspect gang-related as he took a kill shot to the back of the head. Baltimore PD onsite. Thought you should be aware.

I put the phone down, rolled onto my back, and stared into the darkness. He thought I should know? Why? Did he think I was in danger? I knew better than to call, he'd be up to his eyebrows in tactical discussions, and no one wanted to see a private investigator hanging around their crime scene. The big question on my mind glowed like a marquis in Times Square: Who's next? I threw off the comforter. Marlowe yawned, stretched, and accompanied me to the kitchen. I grabbed the boxes I'd bought, and started taping them together. By the time the sun rose, I'd packed my attic and another bedroom. Afterward, I fixed coffee and sat in my recliner, thinking. Riot jumped into my lap and curled himself into a furry, orange doughnut, sensing his owner needed comforting.

I smiled. Between Marlowe sleeping beside my chair and Riot in my lap, I felt pretty darn comforted.

When I walked into the office at eight a.m., I had bags under my eyes and needed a nap. Jason tore his gaze from what he'd been working on and studied my face. "Rough night?"

"Couldn't sleep," I replied, deciding I didn't want to tackle telling him about Collins. "Where's Delia?"

"Still in bed, I guess."

I nodded. "So. You feel good about her?"

"She surprised me. The girl has skills." He sipped his coffee. "I sent you and Sherry the latest batch of new client requests. Let me know which ones you want, and I'll take the rest. In other news, I have a sit-down with a woman who lost her sixteen-year-old daughter."

My forehead furrowed. "How awful."

Jason grunted. "Sixteen? She might have spent the night with her boyfriend. I told her to wait on a Missing Persons until I got there and sniffed around a little."

I smiled. "Your cop skills sure come in handy."

He slung his backpack over his shoulder. "I'm out. I'll check in."

"Okay. Be safe out there."

"Always." He breezed out the door as Sherry walked in.

"Bye," she called. "Um. Who's going to answer the phone?"

"Guess we are."

"Where's Delia?"

"I'll check on her." I walked through the break room, past my office, and knocked on the guest room door. "Hey, sleepyhead. You in there?"

"I'm up," she called. "Be out in a few."

I walked back into the lobby. Sherry shot me a relieved look. "Whew. I hoped she hadn't disappeared, too."

"Told you, I have a feeling about her."

"Yeah, I know. We'll see. I hope you're right." She sat behind her desk.

Delia walked in fifteen minutes later and sat at Jason's desk like she'd already taken ownership.

With Delia's help, two hours later, we had our cases sorted, assigned, and cherry-picked. Jason returned with the happy news the sixteen-year-old had come home, and he'd gotten to witness the reunion. We immediately handed him three new cases, and after some phone calls to set up meetings, he disappeared again.

"I feel horrible about Collins," Sherry said, as we sat chatting, later in the afternoon.

"I knew you would. I'm so sorry."

"He stayed in contact with his parents. They knew he'd gotten in touch with me, and reached out to find out what happened. I didn't know what to tell them. They don't understand the difference between a PI and a cop. They thought I'd know more about it than I did, and I couldn't..." Her eyes grew shiny. She rose and began to pace the floor. "I didn't have the heart to tell them the truth."

"I know. No parent wants to think of their child in that way. Devastating." I watched her stalk back and forth across the room, her hands clenched.

"I felt helpless. They said they'd let me know about funeral proceedings. I almost lost it."

I nodded in understanding. "It's hard to balance empathy and the job in this business."

"I have no idea how to separate the two." The pacing grew more frenetic.

"Would you sit down?" I said, waving at the two chairs in front of my desk. "You're making me seasick."

She flopped into a chair and hung her arms dejectedly over each side. "I've started on the new cases. Waiting on them to get back to me."

"Want to work with Delia, then? Get your mind off Collins?"

"She's already up to speed, answering the phone and reorganizing." Sherry offered a slight smile. "She's so grateful she squeaks when she walks."

I laughed. "I need to go out there and see how she's doing. Let her know she can take a break whenever. I don't think she ever takes a break."

"Okay. Do you need packing help tonight?"

I looked at her sad expression, her slumped shoulders. If anyone needed company tonight, she did. "Yes. Come on over."

She brightened. "I'll be there around six."

* * *

After three hours of packing and pizza, we called it a night. I waved goodbye from my front porch and watched her taillights disappear down the lane. After Sherry left, I walked through the upstairs bedrooms, gawking at all we'd accomplished. Apparently, her antidote to sadness included extreme physical effort. I was thrilled by the help, but my home looked less and less like home, and I'd officially gone into mourning. How would I get through the next twenty-eight days? Marlowe wandered around, a little lost. I stooped to hug him, then went into the kitchen to fix a cup of tea. Since we'd already packed much of the kitchen, locating my tea ball became a treasure hunt. After five minutes, I found it. As the tea steeped, I called Hunter.

"Hey, gorgeous. I was just about to call before I went to bed."

"Guess what I'm doing?" I smiled.

"Tea. On the front porch. It's a perfect night for it."

"How did you know?"

"Glyndon is on my weather app. I look at your weather every day."

The words settled deep in my soul, like an embrace. I didn't tell him, but I looked at his weather in Richmond every day, too. "By the way, I got a call from Mom about Gray's Celebration of Life. She's asking about our availability to attend in three weeks. Do you think we'll be in the house by then?"

"Maybe."

"What do you think about christening our house and our new life together by celebrating Gray's life there?"

"I don't know if we can get in so quickly. Three weeks? And get everything ready for a group?"

"We could do it in the backyard. It's so nice, with all the trees and landscaping. The patio is huge. We could rent some tall pub tables and cater the food and—"

Hunter laughed. "You've thought about this, I see Hey, if you're set on it, you'll find a way. I'm fine either way, babe."

It felt right. One beautiful season of life ending, and ours just beginning. "I think Mom would love it, too."

Decision made. Unless the previous owners dragged their feet on vacating the premises, I'd make it happen.

Chapter Forty-One

Sherry

Duncan had become a problem. Glancing at her phone, she noted three new texts between four and five a.m. She groaned. The OCD texting had begun yesterday, with a plea to reconsider the break she'd suggested. "He's going to make the break permanent if he doesn't get a clue," she said through gritted teeth.

An hour later, another one. "This is becoming ridiculous," said Sherry, firing off a mandate.

Give me a week with no contact, okay? I'll have an answer by then.

He responded with a thumbs-up emoji, a bouquet emoji, and a kiss emoji

His relentless texts weren't just intrusive—they were harassment, a chokehold of digits and words which constituted cyberstalking. How would it feel to be married to this behavior?

Not good.

She fluffed her hair, checked her makeup, and walked out to her car, eyes darting around the yard. For all she knew, each overgrown bush might conceal an angry and determined Duncan. He'd made it impossible to get him out of her head, and now, she saw him around every corner, every tree, through every window. The more she thought about him, the worse her mood became. Jabbing the start button with her index finger, she selected the most upbeat music she could find, set it to ear-splitting, and drove to the office.

"Hi," Delia called, when Sherry walked in. "Isn't it a beautiful day?"

She wondered if she would *ever* be able to endure the girl's perpetual, wondrous gratitude. Maybe it would ease away in time. Or, perhaps Duncan had put her in a bad mood, and every little thing irritated her. She dropped her backpack on her desk.

"Coffee?" Delia jumped from her chair and raced to the break room. "You take it with cream, right?"

"I'll get it myself, no need to—" But the Keurig had already started gurgling.

Delia exited the break room with a mug in her hands. "Here you go."

She reached for the mug. Okay. Maybe she could try to get used to this. "Thanks."

"No problem," Delia said, zipping back to her desk. "Jason said he'll be out until noon. Something about Cosmo?"

"Did he tell you about our Cosmo?" asked Sherry, laughing.

"No. What about him?"

"He's our dark web secret."

Her brow furrowed.

"An expert hacker and webmaster. We use him sometimes to get elusive information for clients when we have trouble finding it."

Delia grinned. "I know a couple of those."

Sherry's eyebrows arched in surprise. "You do? We can always use back-ups."

"You'd be surprised how many *very* smart people live on the street. It isn't just high school dropouts and druggies. I can hook you up if you want. I know two people right now who would kill for the money."

Hoping Delia didn't mean that literally, she said, "We'd have to have some sort of background check before we worked with someone."

"Might be difficult, especially since Woodlawn's closed. Plenty of them were frequent flyers there."

Sherry leaned back in her chair. "Huh. So did Woodlawn take advantage of their talents?"

"Sure did. Larissa, especially."

"In what way?"

"I never knew details."

"Have you talked to the police about the Woodlawn investigation?"

She chuckled. "Heck, no. I tried to help Larissa place patients for a while, then got outta there as fast as I could. I knew they were into some gnarly stuff, but when the search and seizure rolled in, I had to go."

Sherry thought a minute. "Where did she place Matty?"

"I'm not sure."

"Did you know Collins Browning?"

"Everybody knew him. He was the "job" guy. The ticket out." She slid her fingers across her desk, thinking. "I never trusted him, though."

"He's dead."

Her lips parted in surprise. "What?"

"Can you think of anyone who'd want to hurt him?"

Jason burst inside. "Another case on the books," he announced, pumping a fist and walking over to his desk. "Looks like a hefty payday for us as well. Can I have my desk back? For a minute?"

Delia popped out of her chair. "Larissa did it," she said, her voice matter-of-fact. "I can see her putting out a hit on him."

Sherry regarded her under half-closed eyelids, stroking her chin. "And you know this because…?"

"I study people. Larissa was nice on the outside, but scary on the inside. The most dangerous people are the ones who are really good at pretending they care, but when you get right down to it, they don't care at all. People trusted her, but I overheard her talking with Collins a few times. Both of them referred to the Woodlawn inpatients as "human subjects." She's…what do they call those people who have no regret when they hurt someone?"

"Sociopaths."

"Yeah. I figure she wouldn't want Collins to rat her out." She raised her hands, and added, "If he knew the truth about everything."

Sherry nodded. "A viable theory, but Larissa's been in a cell for a month."

"Convicts hire a hit on people outside all the time." She shrugged. "It's easy."

Sherry stared sadly at her young charge. How horrible to have awareness of such a horrific reality at twenty-two. Still. Even if what Delia had told her was true, how could they prove it?

They couldn't.

She sighed.

Jason rose from his desk. "Okay, I'm done," he announced. "Do you need help with anything? Did you get the new clients in their own folders on the desktop?"

"I did," said Delia, returning to the desk. "Teach me some other stuff."

He laughed. "It's a pretty basic job. Be polite and welcoming on the phone, send them to the right person, go through emails, and organize."

She frowned. "You make it sound easy."

"It is easy. And you're smart."

She flashed him a giant grin. Her reaction made Sherry wonder how long it had been since this disenfranchised young woman had been complimented. From the glow on her face, too long. The front door opened, Marlowe trotted to each person with his slurpy greeting, then disappeared into Olivia's office. "Good morning," Olivia said, beckoning her to join.

They closed themselves in her office. Sherry settled in the armchair and switched on the lamp. "What's on your mind this morning?"

Olivia laughed. "What isn't?" She grabbed a file folder from her desk and sat in the armchair closest to her colleague. "Thanks again for your help last night. My house is looking so bare, I don't know how I'll manage for another three weeks."

"It's got to be hard for you."

Olivia pursed her lips. "I've been thinking about it. I can't remember many of the brighter moments of early years as a mom because of the TBI, and don't know if those memories will ever return. Mostly, I remember trauma and Monty, or I should say 'trauma caused by Monty'. Except for bits and pieces, there's a fifteen-year blank. Maybe that's where the good stuff is." She chuckled. "And, think about it. If Facebook made a highlight reel of my life over the past seven years, I'd see arson, assault, kidnapping, gambling debts, mysterious thugs pounding on the door, and more. I *try* to shut it off, but it's not so easy. When everything gets quiet at night and the world stops spinning, I can finally see myself in Richmond with Hunter and my family around me. I have this *joy*, about moving, now. It feels like a shot at real peace for the first time in my life. Apparently, before my injury I kind of lived in this naïve bubble. Why else would I have tolerated the way Monty treated me? Maybe I *never* experienced this kind of, I don't know…hope? It feels like one book's finished and a new one is beginning."

Sherry felt envy trickle into her heart, and quickly pushed it away. Olivia had earned the right to experience real joy, but her words sparked deep regret for her own failed marriage, and a desperate wish for the same kind of peace. She reached out and squeezed Olivia's arm. "I am *so* happy for you. It's a dream come true, and you deserve it."

"Thanks, girl." They locked eyes for a few seconds.

"Wine & Whine girls, forever, right?" Sherry whispered.

"Forever."

A pause lingered.

Sherry broke the spell by changing the subject. "Delia had some interesting observations about Larissa."

Olivia chuckled. "I bet she did."

"I think you're right about Delia, she's smart and intuitive."

"What'd she say?"

"She thinks Larissa is a killer. And a sociopath."

"We realized, right?"

"Not exactly…but, yeah, if you're talking about the test subjects. However, she said Larissa and Collins were linked together like ham and cheese. Delia thinks she hired a hit from her cell."

Olivia put a hand on her chin. "Interesting. So. Maybe she discovered Collins was working on a reduced sentence. He probably knew too much."

"Makes sense, don't you think? But how would we prove it?"

I made rude noise with my lips. "We are *out* of this. Tell the Feds what she said and let them figure it out."

"Sounds like a great idea."

Sherry put her hands on her hips. "Okay. Enough about work. When can I start moving into my new house?"

Chapter Forty-Two

Olivia

Three weeks later

I watched my movers load the last piece of furniture on the truck, check their list, then stride toward me with a clipboard.

"Wait!" I called, fresh panic churning through my chest. Had I forgotten anything? It didn't matter, because I'd be back every four or five months to check in with Sherry, but it felt urgent. My gaze washed across the front yard, the porch, then back to the yard. *The bird feeders!* I motioned at the approaching mover and his clipboard. "Hold on a sec, I'll be right back." I rushed through the gate, into the grass, past my carefully tended Rose of Sharon and daisy bushes and the bramble roses blooming on the fence. It took quite an effort to yank my four pole feeders out of the ground and carry them on my shoulders to the movers.

"Anything else?" He shoved the poles into the truck.

"I think this is it. So, three days, right?"

The lead guy nodded, switched his cigarette to the other side of his mouth, and scribbled on the clipboard. I initialed a release document for him, and they took off down my lane, the top of the truck scraping the leafy arch above. I wiped tears away. "This is so hard," I whispered into the sky. With a final glance, I turned and studied the historic farmhouse I'd called home for decades. The porch looked strangely bare without my white wicker furniture and porch swing. I walked onto the porch and slid my fingers along the banister as memories floated through my mind. I'd taught Hunter about Maryland's tea traditions and various tea rooms on this porch. I chuckled, thinking about the time I'd taken him to The Kate Pearl Tea Room. Talk about a fish out of water. He hadn't been able to leave fast enough. Riot sat inside the door, looking at me. He'd been nervous and fidgety all week.

I'd had the paint refreshed for Sherry and hired a deep cleaning crew. The fresh smells lingered in the air. I walked down the foyer and looked into the den, where Sherry's boxes and some of her furniture had been placed. Like the passing of a torch, I felt the sense of ownership slipping away. Feeling an urge for one, last look in the attic in case I'd missed something, I walked upstairs, tugged the pulldown into place, and climbed the stairs. The scent of acrid smoke drifted into my senses, conjuring vivid images of flames devouring the rooftop. I walked the perimeter and peered into dark corners, remembering the day I'd been allowed into the attic for the first time after the fire had been contained. An entire section of the roof had caved in, and the attic had been a sloppy mess. I walked over to the letters I'd left on the wall and traced them with my fingers. I hadn't wanted to cover them, I'd wanted to remember—an attempt to learn from past mistakes—but *Sherry* didn't need this memory. The house belonged to her, now. Glancing around the space, I found an old rag with the paint cans and used it to rub off the letters as best I could. When I was done, I stared at it in satisfaction. You'd hardly know that once upon a time, someone had left a cryptic, threatening message there. In a darkened corner underneath the lowest point of the slant of the roof, I saw a small box. I got down on hands and knees, and finally my stomach; to grab it. After a quick walkthrough of the rest of the space, I climbed down and put the folding stairs back into the ceiling.

Tomorrow my new life begins.

I went into the kitchen to open the box.

A musty smell escaped, hinting at years gone by. To my delight, it held a photo album, a small diary, and a young girl's jewelry. I flipped through the pictures of a past I didn't remember. My sweet girls, Lilly and Serena, at approximately age six and eight. My eyes watered. How I longed to remember their childhoods! Both wore swimsuits, and I must've been taking the pictures of them playing in the sprinkler. Monty lurked in the background, watching them play. Monty waving his arms. Monty walking toward me, hand outstretched, an angry look on his face. In a few of the photos, tension radiated from their young faces. In one, Monty must've taken the camera from me, because I was in it. Off to one side in the background, arms rigid by my sides, head down. Picking up the small bracelets, I realized the names "Lillian" and "Serena" had been engraved in tiny script. Baby bracelets? I hugged them to my chest before returning them to the box. The locket held a photo of me and the girls. I put it on immediately. The diary had heart stickers all over the cover, and Serena had tediously printed her name on the inside. I flipped through the pages, smiling. "School was good. Lilly won't leave me alone. She wants me to play with her all the time, and Mom says I have to."

Each page had been meticulously dated with month, day, and year. Serena had been eight and Lilly six when this diary had been in use. I turned to the next page, and gasped at the drawings.

Stick-figures of an angry daddy and a cowering mommy. Big letters spelled out "Daddy's being mean to mommy again. Lilly and me are hiding in my room. I locked the door."

My stomach constricted. What had my daughters been through? I flipped through the rest of the diary. The mean stick-figure daddy dominated about one-third of the pages. "I'm so sorry, girls," I whispered, holding the little book to my chest, thinking if I'd been a stronger woman, I would've left him. "So sorry."

A knock sounded on the door. "Anybody home?"

"In here."

Sherry's steps pattered down the hall and into the kitchen. "How's it going?"

"It's hard saying goodbye to a house." I tapped the box. "Found it in the attic. Lilly and Serena's things."

"Aw. How sweet. I wanted to let you know my mover's coming in the morning. I just got confirmation."

"Perfect timing. Mine just left."

"Are you spending one final night in uh, my house?"

I laughed. "Yeah, on an air mattress. How's your day going?"

"Jason's out on a case, Delia's started buying plants, and I'm still moving stuff into your office. Do you feel like an orphan?"

"Kind of," I admitted. "But I'm enjoying the break. If you need anything, call. Day or night, okay?"

She bent and rubbed a spot on the floor, then rose, folding her arms. "I gave the Feds the information we talked about."

"Delia's information?"

She nodded.

"Good. We can leave it there, don't you think?"

"I do. We have so much new business coming in, we don't have time to think about it, anyway. I'm not going to tell people you're gone until I have to. Business will drop off when word gets out."

My brows pulled together. "I stopped being a news item five years ago. You guys will be fine. It's the 'Watchdog Investigations' branding that's bringing in business. Cosmo has been so helpful with SEO optimization and setting up the website and social media accounts. His marketing genius is bringing in clients, not me, so don't even go there."

"Okay." She scooped me into her arms with a bear hug. "I'll have an early morning meeting tomorrow, and won't be in the office until late. Have a good night, and a safe drive. Let us know when you get to Richmond."

"I will. And, I know you're coming, but what about Jason and Delia? Gray's Celebration is Saturday."

"We're all piling into Callie's Cadillac SUV. It's big enough for everyone. We're planning to get there early afternoon."

We stood uncertain and awkward, unwilling to part.

"It's not good-bye," I finally said.

"I know, but it's still hard."

I hugged her. "I love you, girl."

She hugged me back. "Same here." With a final squeeze of my shoulder, she left.

Chapter Forty-Three

Olivia

I walked through my new home in Richmond, surveying my domain with satisfaction. I'd only been here a few days, but thanks to help from Mom and my daughters, the bedrooms and kitchen had been organized. The sound of laundry swishing in the washer and another load whirling in the dryer gave me a huge sense of accomplishment. I ran my hand across Riot's back. Poor thing was still freaked out and uncomfortable and sticking to me like glue. On the other hand, Marlowe kept going in and out through the doggie door. He couldn't believe he could go outside whenever he wanted. The growl of Hunter's Jeep made me run outside and wait for him. "Come look," I called.

He walked down the sidewalk and up three stairs to the covered front porch. He picked me up and swung me around until I got dizzy. "Don't you love that you still have a front porch?"

"I *do* love it. Come see all we've gotten done."

He followed me inside, his jaw dropping. "You guys have been busy."

"We've gotten so much accomplished! I haven't even had time for a shower, yet."

"Do I hear an invitation?"

I ran, laughing, into the first-floor bedroom, Hunter close behind.

After the impromptu couples' shower, I wrapped my hair in a towel and made us hot tea to take out onto the front porch.

"I think you should sit here." He patted his legs. I put the tea on the wicker side table and sat in his lap. The porch swing sat at the far end of the porch, waiting for Hunter to hang it. My white wicker patio furniture had been arranged in the same setup as I'd had on my porch in Maryland. I put my lips to his ear.

"We're getting married tomorrow," I whispered.

He kissed me. "How do you think your mom will react to your surprise?

I wriggled off his lap and sat beside him on the loveseat. "She may kill me. She still thinks she's helping me plan the wedding next week."

He waved one of his hands in dismissal. "She's going to love it."

"I've gone over it in my head a hundred times. Gray's Celebration will conclude around four, then the string trio we hired will start playing a Bach fugue, which will signal us to get into place. Mom will be so confused." I laughed.

"Nod at me or something to let me know when to get into place. I have no idea what a fugue is."

"You're adorable," I said. Then I kissed him.

* * *

I rose with the sun, rubbing my face and squinting against the light coming in through the windows. The previous owners had planted many flowering shrubs along the backyard fence, and even carved out a patch of tilled soil for growing a few veggies if we wanted. Our house rested on a slight incline, which provided a nice view since our property backed to a protected state park. Since my new home had been built within the last three years, it didn't hold the historic charm my farmhouse had, but it didn't matter, I knew I'd be happy here. With a smile, I entered the ensuite bath, showered, and yanked on a T-shirt and shorts, determined to make it a day to remember—a day to hold in my heart like a fragile treasure. I inhaled a quick breakfast and walked out the back door onto the large patio, upon which sat twenty pub tables, a podium and speakers with a microphone, thick electrical cords snaking across, and a white arch set a distance behind the podium. As Mom and I decorated for the celebration, I'd have to hide my secret wedding. It made me giggle like a little kid when I thought about it.

An impromptu wedding ceremony after Gray's Celebration of Life sounded perfect and redemptive to me. I hoped she'd think so, too.

A knock sounded on the door. I could barely see Mom's head for all the bags and boxes she carried. "I brought everything I could think of."

I relieved her of some of her bags. "I can see that. Come on in. The tables arrived yesterday." We walked outside into the fresh air. Marlowe raced around the perimeter while we discussed our décor plan for Gray's celebration.

"This looks great," she said, squinting behind the podium. We dropped her bundles on the patio. "What's the arch for?"

I flapped my hands as if swatting away a detail. "Oh, they threw that in. I thought I might as well take it."

Tilting her head, she said, "I have a faux vine we can use to make it look festive."

I curtailed the bubble of joy threatening to pop out of my mouth. She had no way of knowing she'd be decorating the arch under which Hunter and I would promise to 'love, honor, and cherish'.

By late morning, the patio and half the yard had been transformed into a giant, celebratory tribute to Dr. Grayson Sturgis. Mom scanned the yard as we finished, her eyes wet. "What do you think?"

"Gray would love it so much, Mom." I hugged her.

She gripped my shoulders and looked into my face. "For you to live here with Hunter is a dream come true, and I don't want you to worry about me. Gray and I had seven lovely years together when I thought I'd never find love again. I'm grateful."

She fisted her hands on her hips and studied what we'd done. Across the space, we'd hung LED rope lights to hold enlarged photos of activities or causes that Gray had loved. On the sign-in/remembrance table, we'd arranged his surgical scrubs, an aging stethoscope, and various personal medical artifacts. Music drifted through the yard, all Gray's favorites, from vintage jazz to classic country and Josh Groban. "I think we're good," she announced, checking the time. "Let's grab lunch and get ready. I brought my clothes." I pointed out a bathroom she could use, and disappeared into my bedroom to check in with the caravan from Maryland.

Callie answered on the first ring. "Hey, girl! We'll be there in less than an hour. How's it going?"

"We're getting there, I said. "Did everyone come?"

"Yes, and we have a last-minute addition."

I smiled. "Good. Who?"

"Shiloh. Hope you don't mind."

I blinked. Shiloh? Oh. *Jason.* "Of course not, "I said, although I wondered how it would feel to meet her in person. I grinned. She didn't know she'd be watching *my wedding*, either. Only a few people knew. How perfect. The best woman won, and all that. Feeling both vindicated and petty at the same time, I continued. "We have the decorations done, and the caterers should arrive any minute. We also have a full bar and bartender, compliments of Mom." The doorbell rang. "See you in a bit, the caterers are here." Clicking off, I ran to the door. We'd ordered all of Gray's favorite foods. Spaghetti with meatballs. An antipasto tray. Chicken Cacciatore. I leaned against the doorframe, watching the staff arrange the food.

A member of the catering staff patiently sliced the Ciabatta, a type of Italian bread which Gray favored. When finished, he placed the knife into his pocket. I wondered if he had his own personal knife for slicing Italian bread. When he saw me watching, he smiled. I smiled back.

I rushed to get my makeup on and slither into the pale blue stretchy two-piece suit I'd selected for both Gray's Celebration of Life and my wedding. Sitting on the bed, I took out the ring case holding Hunter's wedding band. I'd chosen one in silver, the exact opposite of Monty's, which had been black. Like his heart.

I studied myself in the full-length mirror. The blue suit (something blue) with a pencil skirt complemented my fair complexion. I'd arranged my hair in a French twist, a style Hunter loved. I wore a pair of my favorite earrings, a vintage set handed down to me from my grandmother, (something old), I'd carry the small Bible Callie had let me borrow for the occasion, (something borrowed), and the locket which I'd discovered a few days ago in the attic of my former house (something new). Satisfied, I walked into the kitchen. Mom positively beamed. "You look fantastic."

"Thanks. I thought I'd put a little effort into it." I smiled. "You do, too."

Dabbing her cheeks with a napkin, she groaned. "I shouldn't have worn mascara."

After we ate a quick lunch, the doorbell started ringing and didn't stop. Guests poured in from Mercy Hospital, Richmond PD, and, of course, my home state of Maryland. By the time we had everyone signed in, I counted over seventy guests, with more coming. Mom was beside herself. "Gray was so loved, wasn't he, honey?"

"He was," I agreed, my troubled gaze on the reporters and photographers amassing on the road in front of our house.

Mom frowned. "What?"

I pointed.

"Why would they be here?"

"No idea. They'll have to stay out front, don't worry."

I walked over to Sherry, who seemed glued to her phone and distracted. I jabbed her lightly with my elbow. "Hey. How was the drive?"

She startled. "Oh. Hi! It was fine. How are you?" Her eyes slid down my outfit. "You're glowing, girl. You look beautiful."

"Thanks. You seem intent on the phone. Is something going on with work?"

She shook her head, rolled her eyes. "Duncan! He's in the front yard, and I told him *not* to come. Now he's texting me a zillion times, begging."

"He can come if you—"

"No! That's the thing. He won't respect the word 'no,' and it's driving me crazy. I do not *want* him back here." She sighed. "I broke up with him last night."

I frowned. "And he still came?"

"Yeah, see what I mean?"

"It'll be okay." I gave her a quick hug. "I'm going to find Hunter."

She grinned. "Has he seen you yet?"

I laughed. "I don't think so. We slept and got ready in different places last night, and now I can't find him."

I hadn't seen Hunter all morning. We'd agreed to part on our final "unmarried" night. He slept at his house, and I slept in our new one. I found him looking dapper and fresh in a navy suit, white shirt, and pale-blue tie to match my suit. As I approached, he whistled. "Look at you. What a babe." He crushed me in a hug.

"Don't wrinkle my outfit! And watch the lipstick." He stepped away, holding up his hands. "Couldn't help myself."

"You look great, too," I told him. "Would you flash your badge or something and tell the press to back off? Duncan Malone is out there, too, texting Sherry to death. If you can find him, would you tell him this is not the time?"

"Sure. And, why is the press here?"

"Who knows? I don't want anything to ruin Gray's Celebration."

"I'll take care of it."

The next few hours sped by in a combination of hilarious stories and heartfelt tributes. The crowd had swelled to one hundred or more, and people stood around the edges of the yard, listening, laughing. Remembering. Crying. Hugging. Honoring him well, which had been Mom's objective. I prayed my plan wouldn't steal the limelight or diminish Gray's send-off in any way. Biting my lip as the Celebration concluded, I signaled the string trio to begin playing the Bach fugue. Sherry caught my eye, dashed away for a second, returned with a bouquet, and thrust it into my hands. Callie and Jason removed the podium and moved the arch front and center. Hunter and his friend, Nick Ramsey, took their places beside the arch. Heads began turning, puzzled expressions all around. I glanced at Mom, deep in conversation with friends. Her head wobbled in surprise upon realizing the music had changed. She murmured an excuse and peeled away from the group, eyes scanning. A soft, breathless laugh escaped me—nerves bubbling like champagne in my chest. When she spotted me, she moved in for a hug, then stopped short at the sight of the bouquet in my hands. Her lips parted in surprise. A gasp. Her gaze jumped from Hunter to Nick, then slid to

Callie and my daughters beneath the arch, piecing it together in stunned silence. Her radiant smile instantly silenced my doubts. How could I have ever imagined she'd resent this?

The wedding march began.

I smiled at her. "Mom, I'd be honored if you'd stand in for Gray and walk me down the aisle."

Arm in arm, we walked through the grass. The crowd parted to make room. Some lifted their glasses, others smiled, still others cried. I couldn't help glancing at Jason and Shiloh. Her frozen expression and covert glances at Hunter told me all I needed to know. I couldn't resist a big grin in her direction. She blinked in surprise. From her expression, you'd think I'd smacked her in the face.

The haunting strains of the wedding march faded away. A hush fell as Hunter's lieutenant stepped into place in front of us, holding an open Bible. Callie took my bouquet and gave me Hunter's ring. Nick took Hunter's wedding band from his pocket and slipped it to Hunter, who considered his lieutenant in surprise, then looked at me. "What did you do?" he whispered.

"I asked if he'd get a JP license and marry us," I whispered back.

Lieutenant Nicholson beamed. "Gotcha," he told him.

Nicholson switched on his handheld mic.

"We're gathered here today not only to celebrate the life of a wonderful doctor, husband, and stepfather, but also the uniting of two people he loved. His stepdaughter and a man who'd become like a son to him, Sergeant Hunter Faraday."

* * *

After the ceremony, the revelers, quite tipsy by now, offered hugs and congratulations. The celebration lasted well into the evening, and my bouquet toss sailed right into Delia's arms, making her blush. Later in the evening, as people said their good-byes and began to drift away, we heard shouting and the sounds of a struggle. "I'll go see what's going on," Hunter said, rushing away.

Mom shot me a worried look. I brushed it off. "It's the press fighting over who gets to the bride and groom first." I laughed. "But, the joke's on them. We're not going anywhere. We're staying right here in our new house."

Two sharp blasts tore through the night, leaving a trail of smoke and a distant echo. Mom and I ducked. Our guests cried out, screamed, ran in every direction; hiding behind tables or underneath chairs. Hunter exploded into the backyard. "Down! Everyone down!" Mom and I dropped. From my prone position on the grass beside Mom, I watched Shiloh and others jerk out their weapons and leap into action. Whoever fired those shots must not have known how many cops had been invited, some in an official capacity. I belly crawled closer to Mom. "You okay?"

She groped for my hand.

The cops shouted at someone to stand down and drop their weapon. The shouts became frantic, loud, insistent. A savage burst of gunfire rooted everyone in place. Stunned and paralyzed, we could almost smell our own fear.

Silence fell. Minutes passed. Smoke drifted around us.

We waited on the ground. The murmur of quiet conversations floated from the front to the backyard. People began rising from the lawn.

Hunter walked into the backyard. "All clear, folks. The shooter isn't a threat anymore." Mom and I stood on shaky legs as he approached us. His arms felt strong and reassuring as I melted into them.

"What happened?" I whispered.

"Duncan. He got tired of waiting and waved his weapon around, demanding to see Sherry." Hunter shook his head. "They tried to diffuse the situation, but..."

I gasped.

"Unfortunately, he refused to back down or release his weapon. When he took aim, we had no choice but to return fire. He didn't make it."

I felt like the breath had been knocked out of me. "Does Sherry know?"

"I'm not sure, but I figured it'd be better coming from you." He squeezed my shoulder. "I love you, Mrs. Faraday. I'll be back." He jogged to the front yard.

Two hours later, I numbly walked through the yard staring at debris, crushed decorations, overturned pub tables. The bedraggled arch. Toppled speakers beside the podium. I looked down at my beautiful suit, now ripped and covered in grass-stains.

Mom wagged her hands toward the mess. "Don't start on all this, I'll be over to help tomorrow."

I started to cry. "I ruined it…my wedding ruined your beautiful Celebration of Life," I wailed. "I'm so sorry, Mom."

She reached for my hands. "You did no such thing. Thank goodness it didn't happen in the middle of Gray's ceremony, or *your wedding.*" She smiled.

I palmed my cheeks, swiping off hot tears. "We gave that lunatic every chance to redeem himself. I don't know what was going on in his head that he thought a gun would solve."

"Such a horrible waste of a life," said Mom. "How did Sherry react when you told her?"

"She feels responsible. She ended the relationship last night. It must've set him off." I tilted my head back and stared at the inky black of the sky, the bright stars. "Poor thing. She'll never go out on a date again."

She gave me a quick hug. "I have to go. And *you* have a brand-new husband waiting inside. I'm splitting the Maryland crew between his place and mine. I need to make sure they have everything they need. Make it a night to remember." She hugged me, hard. "Congratulations, honey."

I held out my hand to look at my wedding ring, accompanied by a slim, white-gold band set with alternating diamonds and emeralds, thinking I didn't necessarily need to make it a night to remember…it would be seared in my consciousness for all time. I gave her a tired smile. "Thanks, Mom."

Glancing over my shoulder, I thought about the randomness and futility of life…how even the most well-intentioned plans are stalked by evil.

Tomorrow, I told myself, would be better. The fog would lift, and we'd have more clarity. I turned a chair right-side-up and sat in it, staring at the sky. After a few lovely minutes of enjoying an almost physical embrace from the velvety night breezes and tapestry of stars, I walked inside.

Later, wrapped in Hunter's arms, it hit me. We were *married.* Until death do us part.

I traced circles on his chest with my fingers. "Why do you think people crack? What tips them over the edge into doing something so desperate?"

He pressed me tighter against his body and entwined his legs with mine. "No telling what Duncan had to do. He may have been forced to engage in horrible torture methods. One of his best friends could've been blown up by a land mine. We'll never know. The consequences of special ops duty are brutal, and like many of them, he became a mercenary, which, in essence, kept him on the battlefield. Sherry should've cut him loose a long time ago. Some PTSD issues are unfixable."

"I suggested, but as she put it, 'he was a hard man to ignore'. I wonder if he meant one of those bullets for Sherry?"

"Don't go there," he said. Putting an arm behind his head, he smiled. The moonlight shimmering through the window fell across his face. "Did you see the wedding gift I brought inside?"

"I saw something in the kitchen. Where'd you get it?"

"It was on the porch. I brought it in after everything settled down. I'm hungry. Do you want to order pizza?"

I laughed. "Why not? Let's eat pizza and stay up all night. It's our honeymoon!" I tossed off the comforter. We walked down the hall into the kitchen. I ran my fingers along the quartz countertops and the Shaker-style cabinetry. "I haven't ever lived in a house this new. It's amazing."

"I love the huge garage. My Jeep never had it so good."

I chuckled. "Your Jeep and my Land Rover fit perfectly."

He frowned. "We are selling the Rover asap."

"I know, I know. It's time. I'll miss it though."

"It's about to fall apart."

"I'm opening the present," I told him.

He pressed in the number to the pizza place and held his cell against his ear. "Okay."

I sat at the kitchen table and inspected the gift. A huge, sparkly, gold ribbon tied in an elaborate bow accented gold-and-white-patterned wrapping paper. I gently tugged the bow loose, and set it aside. As I relieved the box of the wrapping paper, a small envelope fell onto the table. With a smile, I opened it and read the words: "It is the shaking of your world which sparks the greatest transformation."

"Wow. Intense," I said, showing it to him. "Too bad it isn't signed."

He finished the call. "It's not?" He studied the gift. "Let me," he said, lifting the box and shaking it. "Pretty heavy."

I waited as Hunter broke through the seals, pushed back the flaps of the box, and unwound the twist tie around the opening of a plastic bag. When the twist tie gave way, he looked inside. He scowled and blinked, like he'd smelled something terrible and needed to cut it off as soon as possible. With a glance at me, he put the twist tie back around the bag, and slapped the box flaps down. "This isn't something we want, sweetheart."

My heart hammered in my chest. "What is it?" I whispered, pulling the box toward me.

He put his large, strong hand on mine. His eyes were soft. Gentle. "Please. It would be better not to."

As if drawn by a force I could not resist, I opened the box and untwisted the twist tie. A lump formed in my throat. I peeked inside.

At first, it looked like a toy, a stuffed animal, perhaps a sentimental gift from someone.

Then, I saw the blood.

I opened the mouth of the plastic bag wider and stared.

Familiar, golden eyes stuck open, as if searching for me…the tiny tongue protruding from one side of his mouth…

My heart dropped like a stone.

"Riot?" I whispered, searching Hunter's face, his eyes mirroring my pain. My voice cracking, I shrieked. "Riot! No, no, no…!" I reached into the box with the quick fury of desperation to hold him, but Hunter jumped from his chair, grabbed the box, and put it on the counter. "You don't want to remember him like this."

I dropped my head into my arms on the table and cried great, wracking sobs. Clutching my stomach, I raced into the half bath off the kitchen and threw up. Watching the remnants of wedding cake flush down the toilet, I rinsed out my mouth, then stared at my pale, grief-stricken face in the mirror. Who could do such a thing?

As I walked out of the bathroom, Hunter pulled me into his arms. "I'm so sorry," he whispered into my ear.

The tears would not stop. Hunter grabbed some napkins, placed me in a chair, and sat beside me at the table. I gasped out "Why?" between sobs. "Who would do this?"

"Someone who knows you well enough to understand how much Riot means to you. Someone cruel and unstable." He frowned. "We both know who did this."

My forehead knotted. My ex? He'd promised to leave me alone. If he didn't, he'd get more years tacked onto his sentence.

"Do you know where your nitrile gloves are?"

I scrounged through my kitchen drawers until I found the box, and tossed it to him. "Grab some baggies, too. For the note."

I located my Ziplocs and brought them to the table. I felt my heart breaking into a thousand pieces. Life without the ginger kitty who instinctively curled himself into my lap at the slightest hint of emotional distress was unthinkable. Riot could never be replaced. I grabbed more napkins and pressed them to my face.

He pulled out another envelope. "A second one. Here we go."

Neatly typed on a small square of paper were the words: *Now both of us have lost something precious. Much love.*

A chill crawled up my spine. I remembered Larissa's words: *I was so close to a discovery for these precious people.* Larissa had been fond of the word "precious." As I watched Hunter bag the items and stow the box and baggies in the refrigerator, I started shivering. Hunter reached for my hands and held them in his. "We will get to the bottom of this."

My eyes rounded. "Oh. My. God. The caterers."

"What about them?"

"This guy…"

My shoulders sagged. "I saw one of the employees put a knife in his pocket.

I didn't really give it much thought, but he…he smiled at me while he was cramming it into his pocket. He smiled because he *knew.* He had to have tracked down Riot while everybody else was outside." Fresh tears spurted down my cheeks.

"We'll get a list of staff. Maybe you can remember his face."

We sat silent, our hunger forgotten. After a few minutes, Hunter said, "Look, it's been a long day, and we're both exhausted. I'm going to call this in, and we'll give a detailed report in the morning. Let's go to bed."

My eyes slid to the fridge, where Hunter had put the box. "I can't leave him in there."

Hunter's expression softened. "I'm sorry, but if we want an investigation, Riot's body will be needed for a vet exam and DNA tests. They'll keep him in refrigeration, and we can bury him after the exam."

I burst into tears again.

After I'd taken a long, hot bath and had a cup of chamomile tea, I forced my thoughts in another direction. I'd go mad if I kept thinking about Riot's last moments, looking for me. I padded out of the bathroom, my robe pulled tight, a terry cloth shield against the pain. Hunter lay in bed, his eyes soft with concern. He wanted to comfort me, but didn't know what to do.

Marlowe walked in and licked my face. I hugged him fiercely. After I put his dog bed beside ours, I walked to the gun safe and got my weapon, making sure it held a fresh cartridge. I put it on the nightstand. With a glance outside into the darkness that lay beyond the bedroom window, I lifted it from the nightstand and put it beneath my pillow instead.

At three a.m. I gave up on sleep.

Clipping my hair into a knot on top of my head, I walked into the kitchen and stood in front of the fridge. "I can't leave you in there," I whispered, pulling out the box and putting it on the table. With trembling fingers, I reached inside. His fur felt cold and stiff to the touch, but his body was still pliable. His head dropped to one side as I took him in my arms. I gasped at his cut throat, the dried blood, the tiny tip of tongue hanging out of his mouth. Holding him carefully in my arms, I rocked him, whispering a prayer and telling him how much I loved him. I rocked him harder, pressing him to my chest, as if I the intensity of my feelings might transfer and bring him back to life. After a few more minutes, I whispered goodbye.

I felt as if I'd been run through a wood chipper. My hands were shaking. My stomach had shriveled into such a tight knot, I wondered if I'd ever have an appetite again. I closed my eyes. *This,* I told myself…is what pure evil feels like.

Footsteps approached.

"What are you doing?" Hunter asked.

"Help me," I said, gently replacing my sweet Riot in the box. "I want to bury him. Now."

He didn't argue.

I searched for one of my nicer table coverings, and wrapped him in it. Hunter brought a shovel to the backyard from the garage. We selected a spot. He dug a grave, and we laid him in his final resting place. As I watched Hunter shovel the dirt over his form, my eyes were dry. Cold. Determined.

He put the last remants of dirt on the grave, patting the small hump firmly with the back of the shovel. "Want to say a prayer?"

"Already did," I said. The cool night breeze whispered through the trees, cooling my sweaty neck, calming my heart. "This is the end of it," I stated flatly.

Hunter's eyebrows stitched together. "The end of what?"

"I'm taking a break. I'll help Sherry and Jason with the firm, but I'm putting a hold on a second location. My…my perspective needs adjusting." I locked eyes with his. "I need to spend time breathing. Enjoying family. Making this a home, instead of immersing myself in the horrible things people do to each other." I studied the small mound of earth, then glanced at the sunrise beginning to peek above the horizon. It made me happy to discover that Riot's grave faced the sunrise. "I need to take an inventory of my life. Maybe get a mentor who will help me find some balance. Join an AA group to make sure I'm done drowning myself in a bottle. Learn how to find contentment, if such a thing exists." I shrugged.

Hunter put his arm around me. "I realize what a sacrifice this has been for you."

CHAPTER FORTY-THREE

I squinted at him. "Do you?"

"You had a comfortable life. A house and business you loved. Friends." He stroked my cheek. "I want you to know I appreciate your choice to move here. It wasn't easy."

Folding my arms, I thought about what he said. "That's the point, isn't it? Weren't you the one who said, 'nothing worthwhile ever comes easy'? I stared at the radiant sunrise streaking the sky. "I look at it this way. God has allowed everything to be shaken that could possibly be shaken, and I'm still *standing*. It hasn't destroyed me, and I won't let what's happened over the past seven years turn me into a terrified jellyfish, always looking over my shoulder." I shook my head in disgust. "I was used to reacting, not *acting*. Even though Woodlawn Acres was a big scam, the support groups were real. The women's stories were real. I learned a lot about myself. Those conversations began a process. I am determined to replace bad choices and terrible consequences with better choices and better outcomes. Before I launch a new business which takes all my attention and energy, I'm going to make sure I'm grounded." I took a breath. Hunter looked confused. I laughed.

"Okay. In conclusion… here I am, in Richmond, trying to make the right choices. It's messy, it's uncomfortable, but I'm *standing firm.* I pointed at Riot's grave. "In spite of tragedy. In spite of evil." I pulled the clip out of my hair and shook it out, letting the breeze whip it around. "At this moment, *we* are the priority, not my firm. I'm going to learn how to do life without crisis after crisis, even if it kills me."

Hunter nodded. "I'm with you, babe."

I kissed him, hard.

After a shower and fresh pajamas, my new husband lay in bed exhausted and snoring, while I looked out the bedroom window, heart aching, staring at Riot's grave and the rising sun cloaking it in gold. After getting some sleep, I'd buy some flowers and plant them there; perhaps find an appropriate memorial marker. Drawing the curtains, I fell in bed beside Hunter, too numb and overwhelmed to think clearly. As my head touched the pillow, I remembered my loaded weapon underneath. Tugging it out, I held it in my hands and stared at it for long minutes.

Then, I pushed aside the comforter, walked into the closet, and locked it away in the safe.

A Note from the Author

This story was very personal. After probably thirty years of "happy hour" drinking, and a love of fine wine (as you, dear reader, suspected from the "Wine, Whine & Win group," I determined my love affair with the great reds of the world had affected my health. The decision to stop took a bit of convincing. I'd become dependent on that important, relaxing glass of wine as five o'clock rolled around, but my body decided to start waving red flags. My sleep, health, and overall stamina began suffering. It's been a year since I surrendered that holy glass of wine (or two), and I've never felt or slept better! I will always miss the art and ceremony of wine, though. (Insert sneaky tear here.)

I started thinking about all the stressful, horrific situations my character, Olivia, has endured since the inception of my series in 2021. A long, troubling recovery from a TBI in the early stages…the snake-in-the-grass, determined ex who continues to haunt her…betrayal by close friends… attacks on her reputation. Constant threats to her life. It made perfect sense to me that she, of all people, had earned the right to be forgiven a slow-creeping wine dependency. It would also be completely understandable why she had developed a PTSD disorder and used wine as her therapy pet. And how intense and disturbing, I thought, smiling as my imagination worked itself into a frenzy; to fold her struggle into a mysterious conspiracy she couldn't resist untangling.

So.

I plopped her into a shady rehab facility with shadowy secrets hiding behind locked doors. Sitting in my chair, staring at what I'd written, I leaned back and considered the resultant juxtaposition—her earnest decision to control the drinking had led up a steep, narrow path to the edge of a cliff.

Which started me pondering.

Isn't it true that the pivot to a better, more enriching life choice often leads to a confusing and dangerous intersection? Suddenly, the slings and arrows start flying and we race for cover, discouraged; only to slide back into the habit we tried to overcome. To move forward we must choose: please the naysayers who mock and insist change is impossible or too extreme; or jump off the cliff into the unknown, trusting our decision and rejecting disapproval. It takes a lot of faith to change. It's uncomfortable and loss is involved, but there's so much life on the other side. I've ended this series on a high note, excited for Olivia as she starts a new life. I've shed a few tears, too. It's tough saying good-bye to characters I love.

Acknowledgments

As always, I want to thank my publisher, Level Best Books; my editors Verena Rose and Shawn Reilly Simmons; and the entire team for making the publishing dream a reality. I'm grateful for the steady support of authors around me, including Brian Thiem and Susan Crawford, both stalwart encouragers. The fabulous wit of J.R. Sanders and Greg Stout kept me laughing, and their generous willingness to read and blurb my books always makes me smile. Thank you to authors Tina de Bellegarde and Mally Becker for setting up the Level Best Zoom calls which keep us all connected, and many thanks to the lovely managers or booksellers who have invited me to share my writing story and my books. A big shout-out to Miranda Bretz and Barb Palmieri, manager and assistant manager at my local B&N, who have exceeded all expectations with their unwavering support. Thank you so much! And finally, to my readers: Thanks for the reviews, the kind words, the deep dive into the complexities I wind around my characters like tight, snarled cords. I feel privileged you've stolen some of your precious time to savor my stories. You are what the writing journey is all about.

About the Author

Kerry Peresta is a former advertising account executive and copywriter turned thriller whisperer, whose sharp wit and Southern roots fuel gripping tales of suspense. After decades of crafting punchy headlines and captivating campaigns, she traded the corporate world for full time writing and the salty air of Hilton Head Island, South Carolina. Kerry is the author of the Olivia Callahan Suspense series, a nail-biting thrill ride where secrets simmer beneath the surface of polite society. With the fifth installment in this series hitting the shelves in August, 2025, she continues to prove that danger can be as close as the neighbor next door. Once a humor columnist for a daily newspaper, her articles, stories, and interviews have appeared in *Local Life Magazine, Island Events Magazine, Lowcountry Woman, Pink Magazine,* and various anthologies. Kerry is a longtime member of Sisters in Crime, International Thriller Writers, Mystery Writers of America, South Carolina Writers Association, and Island Writers Network. When she's not figuring out spine-tingling plots, you'll find her strolling along the Atlantic coast with her husband, spoiling grandchildren, or planning the next road trip. Discover more at kerryperesta.com.

AUTHOR WEBSITE:

https://www.kerryperesta.com

SOCIAL MEDIA HANDLES:

Instagram: https://www.instagram.com/kerryperesta
Facebook Personal: https://www.instagram.com/kerryperesta
Twitter/X: https://www.twitter.com/kerryperesta
Bookbub: https://www.bookbub.com/profile/kerry-peresta
Goodreads: https://www.goodreads.com/kerryperesta

Also by Kerry Peresta

Olivia Callahan Suspense

The Crushing, Book 4, Olivia Callahan Suspense, 2024

The Torching, Book 3, Olivia Callahan Suspense, 2023

The Rising, Book 2, Olivia Callahan Suspense, 2022

The Deadening, Book 1, Olivia Callahan Suspense, 2021

Back Before Dawn, standalone domestic thriller, 2023

"The Lighter Side," weekly newspaper humor column, *The Capital Journal*, 2009-2011

Short Stories:

"The Day the Migraine Died," Anthology, *Rock, Roll, and Ruin*, 2022, Triangle Sisters In Crime

"The Toad Lady," Carroll County Chapter MWA Anthology, *That One Left Shoe*, 2012

"Princess," Carroll County Chapter MWA Anthology, *That One Left Shoe*, 2012

9 798898 200312